MEMORIES OF SILVER BAY

Written by

Ruth Lafevor

Dear Billie,
Thanks for taking the
time to pick out a nice
gift. I hope you have picked
out other nice gifts.
Thanks also to Walt for his
contribution to our kids lives.

Ruth Lafevor

MEMORIES OF SILVER BAY

Chapter 1

I should have been asleep long ago, but I couldn't put my book down. Maybe I was a mystery book addict; only an addict would stay up till 2:00 in the morning to read when she knew she had to be up at 8:00. Of course, as exciting as the book was, I knew that I would have put it down if I thought sleep would come quickly, without my having to toss and turn and remember. Before last Christmas I used to drift off to a peaceful sleep just by picturing my upcoming wedding and my future as Mrs. Paul Morris. Now instead of dreams, I had drear memories that kept me awake. "At least I've lost those twenty pounds I wanted off before the wedding," I thought bitterly; I hadn't been able to eat much since last Christmas either.

The lovely heroine in my book was alone in the proverbial eerie, ancient mansion when she was startled by a knock on her bedroom wall. I was so involved with the plot, at first I didn't hear the noise. When I did hear the soft pounding, I couldn't believe my own senses. I thought someone was adding sound effects to my mystery novel.

Finally, when I realized the noise was real, I put down my book and listened more closely. Along with the pounding noise, I heard a keening wail that I at first mistook for the wind. Evidently, someone was at the front door of my cottage in great distress. Now I could barely distinguish the pounding of my heart from the pounding on the door. All the dire warnings my worried mother had given me about women living alone in desolated places came tumbling down on me.

"Never open the door after dark to anyone," she had said. It was not only after dark; it was 2:00 a.m. But what if the person really needed help, I wondered. Wouldn't a thief sneak in rather than pound on the door? Taking a job as a lighthouse keeper obligated me to help travelers, didn't it?

Eventually, my curiosity overcame my fears, and I threw on my robe and walked cautiously to the window in my bedroom overlooking the parking lot and driveway. The only car there was my little red Taurus. I couldn't see the front door where the noises were still persisting.

Mustering all the courage I could manage, I walked to the hall that led to the staircase and flipped on the light switch, giving me momentary relief against the intimidating darkness. Again I listened, but the noises were still there, now maybe a little more desperate than before. I knew what I had to do, but my trembling hands and feet would not respond. Finally determined to get control of myself, I virtually pushed myself down the wooden staircase just beyond my room. The noises were louder as my fingers made a clumsy effort at unbolting the two heavy bolts my mother had insisted I install on the front door. When the heaviest one reluctantly tore open, I fearfully turned the handle. In the split second after the door swung open, I saw no one, but then to my great astonishment, I felt little arms clutch my legs and then fall limp as a diminutive bundle collapsed in a heap at my feet.

The bundle turned out to be a small, feather-light girl whom I lifted up and carried over to the Early American horsehair couch on the other side of the room, and I turned on the antique, global lamp on the marble-topped end table next to the couch. Blessing my recent first-aid course, I checked the child's vital signs. She was breathing normally, but her pulse was racing. There were a few scratches on her legs and arms, but no bruises on the rest of her body, and my meager first aid knowledge gave me no clue to the cause of her unconsciousness.

I knew I had to have some help. Since I didn't know anyone in the area, had never been to a doctor here, and had never encountered an emergency, I was deeply grateful for the instigation of the 911 network that could be contacted virtually everywhere in the country. As I dialed the three numbers, I thought of the absurd joke I had read of someone asking, "What is the number for 911?"

The phone rang only once, and a calm, collected female voice said, "Emergency, Randolph City, may I help you?"

"Hello," I stammered, "m-my name is Amanda Stevens. I'm the caretaker of the museum and lighthouse at Silver Bay, taking the Sanders' place."

"Yes, what can I do for you, Miss Stevens?"

"I have a little girl in the cottage, here on the couch. She was pounding on my door a few minutes ago, and when I opened it, she fainted and hasn't come to, yet."

"Is she all alone? How old is she?"

"She looks to be about five or six, and yes, she's all alone. She has Raggedy Ann pajamas on, and there's no identification on her."

The calm voice continued, "Are there any signs she's been hurt in any way?"

"No, she has some scratches on her legs and arms, but they look like they were made by briars in the woods. She has little pink slippers on, and they're dirty and torn."

"We'll send an ambulance soon, but it will take at least 20 minutes for them to get there. Do you think she'll be all right until then?"

"I don't know; what if she comes to?"

"I guess you'll have to deal with that when it happens. But if she stays unconscious, I think she'll be all right, if she's breathing okay. Also, I don't think you should open the door until you see our ambulance and our EMT's identify themselves."

A cold chill gripped my heart. Up to that moment I had not thought that someone might have been chasing the little girl, and that he might figure she was here. She might have escaped from a kidnapper or even an abusive parent.

"Okay, whatever you say," I promised. "Please send someone as soon as you can."

Immediately after I hung up, I rebolted the door and pulled the heavy, damask draperies over the picture window that overlooked the mouth of Silver Bay Harbor. As I was pulling the draperies, I thought I could see a tiny light bobbing a few feet above the lake, but I couldn't see anything else, not even the lake, through the dense fog that was typical for this area. When I again checked the child's breathing, I felt her arms and legs and discovered that she was cold. After scolding myself for not thinking of it sooner, I walked upstairs to my bedroom to get her a cover. In a cedar chest at the end of my bed were several beautiful, homemade quilts like my grandmother used to make. I took one out that I believed had been made in what was called a wedding- ring pattern, and I tiptoed downstairs and tucked it gently around my little patient. Then I pulled up a kitchen chair next to the couch where I could sit and watch her.

I was afraid, but excited, too. At least, for a few minutes, I had something else to think about besides my broken engagement with Paul. It might delay the onset of that ulcer my best friend said I was going to get because of "harboring resentment against Paul." What did she know about resentment? She had married her childhood sweetheart, instead of having to hear him say, "I'm sorry, I can't marry you; I've fallen in love with someone else." She didn't have to leave town to escape pitying glances or whispered conversations from family and friends whenever she entered a room.

My mind jerked back to the present when the antique clock struck the half-hour tone for 2:30. I looked at the little girl, checked her pulse again, and found it was almost normal. Her breathing was still regular, but she made no signs that she was coming to.

Wishing that the EMT's would come soon, I looked nervously around the room. It was a room reminiscent of the 19th century when furniture was crafted with meticulous care and design. Somehow, the ancient pump organ, the oak breakfront hutch housing delicate flowered dishes, the frilly, china dolls, and the many museum items comforted me.

My reveries were broken by the rumble of a motor. I stealthily looked out the kitchen window where I could see the one-lane dirt road that led from the highway up to the top of the cliff where the cottage and lighthouse stood. The bright headlights of a large car climbing up the narrow road filled me with fear. I was almost sure that the car was actually the ambulance van, but, in case it wasn't, I had no idea what I'd do.

When it came to a stop, I heard three doors slam. Whoever was out there was making no attempt to be quiet. In quick succession I heard the heavy clomping of shoes on the porch, loud pounding on the door, and a voice calling out, "EMT's here!"

I took the time to look out the small window at the top of door, and I saw three people, one carrying a canvas bag. Since these people were obviously the emergency personnel, I again unbolted the door. I had a vision of my mother's horrified face if she could have seen me this night.

The three people turned out to be two young men and one young women. They were all tall, slim, and efficient-looking. Without any preliminaries, the woman and one of the men immediately rushed over to the sofa where the child was still lying unconscious. They opened the bag, took out a stethoscope, a blood-pressure gauge, and some other instruments, and began working on her.

The other man came over to me and introduced himself. "I'm Jim Billings; my partners are Art Caldwell and Judy Baldwin." Could you answer some questions for us, Miss—Mrs.--Uh?"

"It's <u>Miss</u> Stevens, and certainly, I'll tell you everything I know, which isn't much," I answered, leading him to my desk. He sat on one of the wicker chairs which were placed in front of the desk for people who wanted to ask me questions about the museum or for tired guests who wanted to wait for the rest of their party to see all the exhibits.

"Can you tell me what time the little girl came to your door?"

"Yes, as a matter of fact I can tell you almost exactly. I remember hearing the grandfather clock strike two at the same time I heard the child pounding and sobbing."

"Did she say anything to you when you opened the door?"

"No, she just grabbed my legs and collapsed at my feet."

"Are you sure you didn't hear or see anything else unusual tonight?"

I thought for a moment, then answered, "After I called you, I went over to close the drapes, and I thought I saw a tiny light bobbing above the lake, but I couldn't see anything else because of the fog."

"I see," said Jim Billings. "Yes, it was foggy tonight; do you know if there were any boats in the harbor?"

"No, I was not down at the docks tonight, at all." I answered.

We were talking about some broken-down docks down the hill to the south of the lighthouse. These docks had been built in the 50's by an enterprising businessman from Detroit who had also built a restaurant, laundromat, gift shop, and shower rooms adjacent to them. Now the wooden piers were rotten, some completely under water. What was once a concrete walkway that led to the docks was a jumble of rocks, impossible to travel in bare feet. The restaurant and other shops were deserted because when the businessman died, his whole enterprise died with

him. However, since there were more than 100 miles
between the state docks just south of Silver Bay and the
docks at Randolph City, and since the whole area was
notoriously foggy, boats were forced to take refuge at the
broken piers, tying their boats wherever they could find a
half- way secure post, or they had to anchor out in the bay
and come to shore in smaller boats, called dinghies, that
most large boats towed behind them. Of course, they had
no helpful dock hands or no modern facilities to
accommodate them. Also, no one kept a record of what
boats were sheltered there.

   At that moment the young woman, Judy, announced,
"I think she's coming to, now."

   Jim and I hurried over to the couch, but the other
paramedic, Art, ordered us to stand back so that the child
wouldn't be frightened by four faces staring down at her.

   Her long eyelashes fluttered, and her lids opened to
reveal incredible, bright blue eyes. She looked at Art and
Judy and then at the two of us with wide eyes. Her little
body started trembling, and she started to move up toward
the arm of the couch, apparently trying to put more
distance between herself and the strangers staring at her.

"Hello, little friend," said Judy, gently. "Don't be scared. We want to help you. What's your name?"

Her eyes filled with tears, but she was still silent.

"Please, Honey, don't be scared. We're all here to help you. No one is going to hurt you. Now, will you tell us your name?"

The child's voice was so soft I had to strain to hear her. "I can't tell you my name," she murmured, "I don't know what it is." Then she began sobbing again, frenzied, wrenching sobs that broke my heart.

Chapter 2

All of us stared at the little girl in stunned silence. Finally Judy clutched the child in a firm embrace and softly crooned, "It's okay: it's okay, Honey," until the sobs quieted. Then again there was silence, probably because none of us could believe what we had just heard. Amnesia is a condition that people hear about and occasionally joke about, but probably not many people actually know someone who is suffering from the disease.

Jim Billings was the first to break the silence. "Are you sure you don't know your name, Honey? Now, nobody is going to punish you if you have run away. Can't you tell us your name?"

"I can't remember," said our little stranger in a louder voice.

"Can you tell us what you do remember?" asked Judy.

"I-I just remember running on a path in the woods toward a big building with lights shining on it. It looked like a big ice cream cone." I had never heard a lighthouse described as a "big ice cream cone" before, but I did think it was an apt description.

Then Art spoke to her in a soothing voice, "Well, now, don't worry Princess. Sometimes our minds play tricks on us, and we forget something we don't really want to remember. Just lie here and rest, and your memory will come back--maybe not right away--but sometime."

"But, where am I? What's going to happen to me?" she asked, in a plaintive voice that clutched my heart.

This time I spoke up. "You're in a museum on Silver Bay in Michigan. Does the name 'Michigan' mean anything to you?"

She shook her head slowly. "No, and what's a moo-z-um?"

Again I answered, "A museum is a place where things from many years ago are kept. Like the couch you're lying on is about 100 years old-- those dolls over there are about 75 years; in fact everything in this room is at least 50 years old. I'm Amanda Stevens, and I live here."

"But you don't look very old," she said in complete innocence.

That brought a smile to us adults, in spite of the circumstances. "Well, thank you, young lady. You're right, I'm not too awfully old, but I'm a history teacher, and I like old things."

"Oh," she said solemnly, and she looked around the room, shuddering as one does when sobbing has ceased. The rest of us continued to stare at her in awkward silence, mostly because we were at a loss as what to do next.

Finally, Art stood up decisively and motioned for me and Jim to follow him over to my desk. Judy stayed with the little girl who appeared to be on the verge of tears again.

He began to speak in low tones, "I'm not sure what to do. She doesn't seem to have any physical problems, so we're not qualified to do any more for her. The only thing I can think of is to call the police. I mean, she had to come from somewhere, and it had to be somewhere fairly close because of the way she's dressed. What do you think, Jim?"

Jim shrugged and said, "I don't know. Beats me. But I agree, there's not much else we can do tonight. Maybe the police will find someone who knows something about her tomorrow."

"But, what do we do with her in the mean time?" I asked.

Art shook his head thoughtfully and said, "I don't know that either. I suppose we could take her to the hospital, but that might traumatize her even more. I'm not really knowledgeable about these things, but since I didn't find a head injury or any other injury, I suspect she has had something traumatic happen, something so bad she doesn't want to remember. I think it would be best if she stayed put, at least until tomorrow."

Now my mind began racing full speed. It wasn't that I didn't like children. I taught children about the age of this child in Sunday School, but telling Bible stories to a few little kids one hour every week was very different from having the full responsibility of a child, especially a child with amnesia. And who knows what had happened to her to cause her condition? There were so many questions, so many problems to consider.

The two men were looking at me, waiting for an answer to their unspoken question, and I knew I had to

make a decision. "I-I suppose she could stay here," I
began, "but—what if she starts crying again, or what if she
refuses to stay with me?"

Jim answered gently, "I know this is an awful lot to
ask of you, but I really think she'll be all right till
tomorrow. We'll report this to the Randolph City police
before we leave, and I'm sure they'll be here first thing in
the morning. I imagine they'll send a squad car out to look
around the area, so you won't be in too much danger."

I hesitated before answering, noticing Jim had not
said I would not be in <u>any</u> danger. "Okay, I guess that's
really all we can do," I finally said. Not wanting them to
think of me as selfish, I went on, "It's not that I don't like
kids; I do, it's just…"

"I know," said Art, "this is an unusual case. I don't
want to scare you more than you are already, but please, be
sure to lock up after we leave and don't open the door to
anyone but the police."

"But, I have to open the museum at 10:00," I said.

"Oh, I'm sure they'll be here before that," he
assured. Then, as if to end any other objections, he
suggested we tell the child what was going to happen. So,

we all walked over to the couch where Judy was now holding the child securely on her lap, showing her pictures of her own children and talking animatedly about them.

Art knelt down and looked into the child's eyes, "Honey, we don't know where you live and who your parents are, so for tonight you're going to stay here with Miss Stevens. She'll take good care of you, and then maybe by tomorrow you can remember something. Is that all right?"

Her eyes filled with tears again as she looked from the Art to me. I tried to smile confidently, but I don't think either one of us was convinced I was on top of the situation. However, since she probably figured that she had no other choices, she quietly said, "Okay."

The EMT's gathered their equipment together. Judy gently extracted the child from her arms and laid her back on the couch. Both looked reluctant to be parted from each other, and I secretly wished that Judy could stay with us, but I knew she was still on the job. Finally, after assuring me they would contact the police from their radio in the van, they all said good-bye and left us alone.

I tentatively sat on the chair where I had kept my vigil while the child was unconscious. I found myself at a loss for words, and just managed an awkward, "Well, here we are." I'm sure she wasn't sure what to say, either, so she kept quiet and transfixed me with her incredible eyes.

Again I was the one to speak up, "You know, I can't keep calling you 'Little Girl.' Since you don't remember your own name, do you have a name you'd like to be called?"

"No," she said, slowly, and again she looked close to tears.

"Well, the Bible says something about not forgetting to entertain strangers because we might be entertaining angels without knowing it. Tonight you came to me as a stranger, but you look like an angel. Would you mind if I call you Angela?"

I don't know if she understood all I said about entertaining angels, but she pondered the question seriously. Then she shrugged and said, "Okay."

I was at first irritated by her one-word responses until I remembered the terrifying plight she was in. Finally, an idea hit me. "Hey, I just remembered. My mom sent me some chocolate chip cookies. Would you like some? Are you hungry?"

"No, thank you," she said solemnly.

I sighed in exasperation. I had tried the one magic charm adults everywhere use on children—sweets, and even it had failed to bring a response. "Okay, maybe we should just get to bed. You can sleep right there if you want. There's another bed down here, but it's a museum piece. I mean, it's an old feather bed, and I'm not sure it even has sheets on it, just a quilt someone made a long time ago."

Her only response was to look all around the room, taking in all the old-fashioned artifacts. It occurred to me then that these articles, while comforting to me, might be disconcerting to her. Oddly embarrassed, I then asked her, "Would you like to sleep upstairs with me? I have a big double bed."

Still unsmiling, but looking somewhat relieved, she said, "Yes, please." Someone had certainly taught her manners, I thought.

Then I shyly took her hand, and she slid off the couch. Without another word we climbed the stairs, walked into the bedroom, and crawled in bed. As tired as I was, I didn't go to sleep right away, and I heard her sniffling beside me, probably suppressing more sobs. Finally I heard her even breaths, indicating she had gone to sleep. Just as I was dozing off, I saw lights flash on my ceiling, and I heard a motor. I walked to the window as I had done when I first heard the child at the door, and was comforted to see a police car creeping down the driveway, a spot light shining in the woods. I watched it till it drove out of sight, then I carefully slipped back in bed, trying not to awaken my new little charge. At last sleep overcame me.

The museum didn't open until 10:00 every morning, when visitors usually traveling to Mackinaw Island or camped in cottages in the area would pay $1.50 to view 18th and 19th century relics which were displayed in the cottage and outside on the grounds. Inside the museum, along with early American furniture and farm implements, were fog horns, kerosene lanterns, primitive compasses, and other artifacts, some of which had been recovered from sunken ships years before. Outside the cottage were a huge propeller, stocks used as punishment in Puritan days, and a copy of the liberty bell, which children, and even some adults, loved to ring. The high point of the visit was a walk up the narrow, stone stairs of the lighthouse that ended at a rail-enclosed balcony just under the original light. That light no longer worked, but there were six, bright floodlights surrounding the lighthouse that illuminated it every night. These lights were probably what had drawn my little visitor to my door.

My job was to sit at the desk, take the admission fee from the tourists, and answer any questions they might have about the articles on display or about the Silver Bay area. From research I had done before I took this job I learned that Silver Bay was a natural, horseshoe-shaped harbor on Michigan's east coast, about 60 miles from Mackinaw City. In the early 1800's, a lighthouse had been built on a small hill on the north side of the harbor. The cottage beside it had belonged to the lonely lighthouse keepers, ancestors of Mr. Sanders. In the 1950's, a new, modern, sophisticated lighthouse was built about two miles from the old one, so the old lighthouse and the keeper's cottage, now "modernized" with indoor plumbing and electricity, had become a museum where tourists could explore relics of pioneer boating days in Michigan.

I first saw the area during spring break when my parents and I rented a cottage near the museum. At this time I met the Sanders and learned the procedure I would follow when they left. So, beginning the first Tuesday of my summer vacation I awoke at 8:00, ate breakfast, dusted and straightened furniture and museum pieces, and, from 10:00am till 8:00pm every day except Mondays, put on a friendly face for a steady stream of tourists.

But on the morning after Angela came into my life, 8:00 seemed like the middle of the night. My arm felt like a lead bar as I reached over to turn off the alarm. I decided to let Angela sleep until just before the police came, whenever that would be; she didn't even stir when the loud alarm went off.

As I looked at the slumbering child, I wondered anew what had brought her to my door at the middle of the night. Maybe she would have some answers this morning, I thought. Would she remember me, I wondered, or would she be so frightened, she would be hysterical? I just had to wait and see.

I finally managed to push myself out of bed, and after I showered and dressed in light, cotton tan slacks and blouse, I fixed a breakfast of bacon and eggs, all the time wondering what Angela would like for breakfast--or for lunch or supper for that matter. I wondered what my mother would have fixed for meals that would be nutritional yet appealing to what might be a very picky childish appetite. The child might be so upset that she would refuse to eat anything.

At 8:30 I knew I'd better awaken Angela so that she could eat breakfast before the police would come. I didn't know quite how to awaken her because I feared a repeat of her sobbing the night before. I stood for a while pondering what to do, and then I finally touched her shoulder and softly spoke, "Angela."

She awoke with a start, and her eyes reminded me of the eyes of a deer caught by headlights of an approaching car. She looked around, as if trying to orient herself to the strange surroundings, and then her little body trembled as it had when she first regained consciousness, but instead of loud sobs, she just began to whimper.

I sat down beside her and took her in my arms and tried to soothe her as Judy had done last night. I told her, "It'll be all right, Honey. You're safe here, and pretty soon some nice people are coming to help you." I decided I wouldn't mention the "nice people" were policemen.

After a few minutes her body stilled, but I still cradled her in my arms, possibly for my own comfort as much as for hers. When I released her, I saw that she had a resigned, almost stoic look on her face. I wanted to question her about whether any of her memory had returned, but I didn't want to upset her again. So, my only question was, "Would you like something to eat?"

This time she merely nodded her head. "Let's go into the bathroom and wash your face, okay?" I went on. I had no idea how much I would need to do for her. I knew very little about children, but one characteristic I had observed of all the kids I had ever been around was resentment if adults tried to do things for them that they knew how to do for themselves. Of course, she was too small to reach the faucets on the sink by herself, but fortunately, I remembered a small wooden stool Mrs. Sanders had left in the linen closet, probably to help her reach articles on the top shelf. So, I decided I would simply put out a towel and wash cloth and set the stool in front of the sink and see if she would take it from there. Sure enough, she performed her morning hygiene independent of me, in a ritualistic style. She even hung up her towel and wash cloth on the rack beside the sink.

When she finished, I took her hand and said, "Let's go downstairs. I've got breakfast ready for you."

She obediently walked beside me down the stairs through the living room to the kitchen. I pulled out a chair in front of a place mat where I had set a plate, silverware, and napkin, and I took an egg and two pieces of bacon from the skillet and one piece of toast from the toaster and put them on her plate. She managed to say "thank-you," but she didn't begin eating right away. I didn't know if she was waiting for me, or if she was waiting to say "Grace." I decided to cover all the bases, so I got my food, sat down, bowed my head, and murmured a hurried prayer I had been saying ever since I could remember.

She slowly began eating, but I could tell she wasn't hungry; she was just being polite. My heart went out to her, and I said, "Honey, you don't have to eat if you don't feel like it. I know you're upset."

To my dismay, the sobbing came again, with the same intensity as before. Awkwardly, I went over to her and took her in my arms. Since I didn't know what to say, I merely held her until the sobs subsided to sniffling. Then I said, "Why don't you come out and sit on the couch while I dust the furniture? Pretty soon the po—people who are going to help you will be here."

She shivered slightly, and her arms felt cool to me. I realized she probably needed warmer clothes, but I had none that would fit her. However, I remembered a short, terry-cloth robe I had bought to cover my bathing suit. It would be big on her, but it would be better than the thin pajamas she was wearing. After carrying the child to the couch, I went upstairs and brought down the robe. As I suspected, it fit loosely on her, but she looked warmer after I managed to wrap it around her. She sat on the couch without moving as I threw away the uneaten food, put the dishes in the sink, dusted the furniture, folded the quilt, and got the box for the admission fees from the locked drawer in my desk.

Just as I finished, I again heard a car motor. This time when I looked out the window, I saw right away the familiar markings of a police car. I watched while they parked, and then two uniformed police officers and one young man, dressed in casual civilian clothes, emerged from the car.

I was able to study them in the few minutes it took them to walk up to the cottage. One of the policemen, the driver, looked to be in his forties. He was a large man, not fat, but big enough to make am imposing impression on any lawbreakers I would imagine. The other officer was probably in his mid-thirties, thin but wiry-looking. The young man was probably about my age—mid twenties. He had a casual, almost jaunty manner, and he sported a trim, dark beard, not a bushy, full-faced beard, but a thin fringe that framed the bottom edge of his face.

Since I had no doubts about the identity of my visitors, I opened the door just as they stepped up on the porch. Right away I said, "Hello, I'm Amanda Stevens; please come in."

All three men stepped in, but only the large officer came over to me to introduce himself. He said, "Miss

Stevens, I'm Captain Rogers; this is Sergeant Adams, and this is Bob Wilson. Bob is a reporter for the Randolph Gazette, and we're with the Randolph police department." Since the other officer was looking around, seemingly "casing out the room," and the reporter was preoccupied with adjusting a sophisticated-looking camera he had brought in with him, they barely acknowledged the introductions with a brief nod in my direction. The captain went on, "Is this the child that came to your place last night?" He gestured toward Angela who was still sitting wide-eyed on the couch.

"Yes, I don't know where she came from or who she is, and she doesn't seem to know either."

"So I've heard," said the captain. "Has anything new happened since last night?"

"No, nothing. If she remembers anything else, she hasn't told me. She still seems pretty upset."

"I imagine she is," he said, then he turned to his partner. "Ed, why don't you go over and see what you can get from the kid. I'll question Miss Stevens here, and Wilson, anytime you're ready, you can start taking the pictures." Then to me he explained, "The first thing we'll have to do is put her picture in the paper and on the news. Then we'll need to check through the pictures we have of missing children."

For the first time, Sergeant Adams spoke, "But she couldn't have been missing long, dressed like that."

"Unless she was kidnapped and just escaped last night. Anyway, we've got to explore all possibilities." retorted Captain Rogers. Then he turned to me as the sergeant started over toward Angela. "Why don't we sit here at your desk, Miss Stevens? I need to ask you a few questions."

"Sure," I said, as we both took our places at the desk, "but I don't know what I can tell you."

"Well, I just need to get some background information. For starters, what brings you to Silver Bay?"

Before I answered, I watched Sergeant Adams who was cautiously introducing himself to the frightened child, much as one would approach a wild animal that he wanted to tame. She was obviously frightened, but she wasn't crying or moving away from him. The reporter was looking through the camera lens, but he wasn't pointing it at Angela yet, probably just checking the lighting in the room or something.

"I'm taking the Sanders' place for the summer—you know the regular curators of this museum," I finally said.

"Where are you from, and how did you find out about this job?"

"I live down-state, around Kalamazoo. I teach school there—high school—history, and one of my fellow teachers was up here for vacation last summer. He got to talking to the Sanders and found out they wanted to go out west, to their son's wedding this year, and they needed a replacement. He knows what a history nut I am, and after my engage—or my plans changed, he thought I'd be interested in coming up here. So, I applied, researched the area, got an interview with the DNR, and here I am."

"Okay"—began Captain Rogers, but he was interrupted by blood-curdling screams from Angela. The reporter had finally positioned himself in front of her to take a picture, but apparently the first sight of him and his camera started her screaming. Then she scrambled down from the couch where Sergeant Adams caught her squirming, flailing body in his arms. Shocked, the photographer put his camera down on the couch and approached the child, but the closer he got to her, the more she screamed.

The sergeant motioned for the reporter to back off as he picked the child up and deliberately turned her face away from him. He repeated over and over, "It's all right, Sweetheart. Hush now, it's all right." After a few minutes, she quit screaming, but as during the night before, she still whimpered and shuddered, and the policeman rocked her in his arms.

Captain Rogers called the reporter over to the seat next to him. "How do you explain that, Wilson?" the Captain asked.

"I have no idea," answered the shaken reporter.

"You've never seen the child anywhere before?"

"No, never."

"Well, she sure acts like she's seen you, and she evidently doesn't like what she's seen."

"Maybe it's not me. Maybe she has a thing about cameras," suggested Bob Wilson.

"Maybe," agreed Captain Rogers. "There's one way we can find out, though. Show me how to work your camera, and we'll see how she reacts."

"Okay," the reporter shrugged, "but believe me, there's no reason she should be scared of me." Then he went over to the couch to retrieve his camera, and he began showing the captain how to operate it.

By this time Sergeant Adams had again set Angela on the couch. He was explaining to her about the picture, and this time, when Captain Rogers approached with the camera up to his face, she didn't move. She merely turned her tear-streaked face toward the camera and blinked at the flash.

After taking several pictures, the captain handed back the camera to the reporter, who was trying to be as invisible as possible as he sat at the desk. Captain Rogers then approached the child. "Hi sweetheart," he began, "don't you like Mr. Wilson, over there?"

She peeked around the sergeant who was sitting in the chair by the couch, and again her eyes widened, and her breathing became heavy and irregular. "Now, it's okay.

He won't hurt you. Do you remember why you don't like him?" The captain quickly asked.

She shook her head no, and again she sneaked a look at Bob Wilson, this time without as much fear. He managed to smile tentatively at her, but she looked quickly away.

Captain Rogers then said, "Okay, Honey, we won't let anyone hurt you. Sergeant Adams is going to stay right here with you while I talk to Miss Stevens, okay?" At her nod, the captain motioned for me to follow him into the kitchen.

"I've got to tell you, Miss Stevens," he said, "I've got a lot more questions than answers about this case. I don't know what to do."

"I don't either. Wonder why she reacted that way to the reporter? Do you know much about him?" I found myself suspicious of him, maybe because of the child's reaction to him, maybe because of his beard, maybe because he was a reporter.

"Well, he's a new reporter for the Randolph Gazette, straight out of U of M with a degree in journalism. Cy Davis, that's the newspaper editor, says that even though he's only been working for about a month, he does good work. He must be good if Cy trusts him with a story like this. We've filled him in on what happened last night, but we'll check him out more thoroughly now. I just wish I knew what's going on in that kid's mind. I'm not qualified to deal with this sort of thing."

"Me either. Do you have a psychiatrist who works with your department?" I was probably thinking about all the cop shows I'd seen on TV. It seemed they always had psychiatrists on hand whenever they needed them.

"No, we don't have a very big police department. I know there is a psychiatrist in Randolph City, Dr. Meadows, who moved up here from Michigan State a year ago. I think we could make an appointment for her. But my big problem right now is what to do with her? We can't lock her up. I suppose we could put her in a foster home, but there's a lot of red tape connected with that, and who would be willing to take on a kid who doesn't know who she is or where she came from?"

Again, I felt pressure on me to volunteer to keep the child, but I still wasn't sure. I didn't know if I'd be capable of taking care of her all by myself. What would I feed her?

Would she ever warm up to me? How would she feel about staying with me? How would I be able to keep her occupied while trying to run the museum at the same time?

The captain watched me as I mulled the situation over in my mind. He probably realized what I was thinking. And since I didn't say anything, he continued, "I suppose Ed could take her to his house. He's got six kids of his own, but they're pretty rambunctious little rascals. I'm afraid they might overwhelm the little tike. And we'd have the same thing at a foster home—other kids around might scare her. She needs some place where she feels safe."

No wonder the sergeant was able to quiet the child, I thought. He had plenty of experience with children. However, I agreed with the captain about thrusting Angela in a household with a bunch of boisterous kids. She seemed to be too fragile to handle a situation like that. I realized that I was concerned very much about her welfare, more than I thought I could be. She seemed to be a well-behaved, courteous little girl. Under normal circumstances, she was probably quite adorable.

The captain was still watching me, and I knew I had to make a decision. "Captain Rogers," I said with a sigh, "the child can stay here, I mean if that's okay with you. However, I've got to tell you. I don't know much about kids. I'm an only child myself, and I teach high school, so I'm never around little kids. But it's quiet around here— well, when the museum is closed. But even when it's opened, she won't have to be involved with anyone who comes in, if she doesn't want to be. I just don't know if she'll be content while I'm working."

"Well, Miss Stevens, I don't think she's going to be content anywhere until her memory comes back. But are you sure about keeping her? You've got to remember, she must have come from around here, and if she did run away from someone, that person is probably still around here, too."

"I know; I thought about that, but I guess anyone who keeps her will have to take that chance."

"Okay, thank you for your cooperation. I think this is the best solution. I can get you temporary protective custody of her, and of course, we'll keep in touch with you, and we want you to contact us whenever anything comes up. We've got to go now and get the pictures developed and get Wilson to start on the story before the paper is printed. I'll also call Dr. Meadows, the psychiatrist in Randolph City, and get you an appointment for the child. Is there a time you could go?"

"Well, the museum is closed on Mondays. I could go then, I suppose."

"Right—next Monday then, if the doctor can see you." Then he abruptly turned and walked out of the room to where the child was still sitting talking to Sergeant Adams, and surprisingly, the reporter had pulled his chair over, and Angela was apparently accepting his presence. At least she wasn't screaming or trying to get away.

When Captain Rogers walked into the room, Sergeant Adams stood up and offered him his chair. He sat down, took her small hands into his massive ones, and said, "How's it going, Kiddo?" Not waiting for an answer, he began talking to her in a gentle, matter-of-fact tone. "We don't know why you can't remember anything, but we're going to do anything we can to help you. Until we can find where you came from, you're going to stay here with Miss Stevens. I'm sure she'll take good care of you, and I know you'll be a good girl for her. Also, she's going to take you to a nice lady who will help you. How does that sound?"

"Okay," she murmured. Again I think she was resigned to the fact that she had no other choices.

Then the captain stood up, and the reporter walked over to the desk to get his camera. The three men started to walk out the door, assuring me they would return, when I stopped them. "Wait, I just thought of something. What's she going to wear? I can go buy her some clothes, but she can't go with me in her pajamas."

"I can solve that problem," said Sergeant Adams. "I'll bring some clothes over. I know we're bound to have some that will fit her. I think Mary, our fourth one, is about her size. I can bring you enough to start her out anyway."

"That's fine; Thank you, Sergeant Adams," I said.

After all the good-byes were said, I was again alone with the little girl. "What have I gotten myself into?" I wondered. I looked over at her. She was certainly a pretty little thing; she had dark, curly hair, dimpled cheeks, and she still had her baby teeth. But what did I know about her? I didn't even know her birthday, how old she was, whether she preferred playing with dolls or playing ball. Could she ride a bicycle? Did she know how to read? Was she allergic to anything?

Then, in the midst of all the questions, a startling revelation dawned upon me: she needed me. Suddenly, when that thought hit me, I was overwhelmed with a new tenderness for the child. It was the greatest feeling in the world, one I had never experienced before. I thought, "This must be somewhat the feeling a new mother has when her baby is put in her arms, and I didn't even have to go through labor."

My musings were interrupted by the sound of a car coming up the driveway. I looked at my watch, surprised that it was already 10:00. I turned to the child and said, "Angela, you can sit right where you are, or you can go back upstairs and lie down if you're still tired. Whatever you want to do."

Still unsmiling, she fixed her solemn stare on me and said, "I'll just stay here."

I wondered if the car carried tourists or people searching for the child. I figured until this mystery was cleared up, I would be suspicious, or at least curious, of every new person who came to my door. This time, though, the people were tourists, a couple about my parents' age, who, when they saw Angela, tried to draw her into a conversation about their grandchildren. They seemed rather disconcerted when she only answered in monosyllables and refused to smile. However, I didn't think I should explain her situation, nor did I have time. Other visitors were coming in the door, and there really wasn't a lull in the stream until noon, when I closed the door and put the wooden sign on it that told everyone, "Closed Till 1:00."

However, just as I was walking into the kitchen, mentally inventorying my food supply, I heard a knock on the door and a voice call out, "Police, Miss Stevens."

I opened the door to the two policemen and the reporter, just as I had earlier that day. The reporter hung in the back, stealing a glance over at Angela, who was still in the same position on the couch. Sergeant Adams was carrying two large, plastic garbage bags, and he said, "I've got the clothes I told you about, and also some toys I thought might perk her up a bit."

"That's nice of you, Sergeant," I said. I wasn't prepared to either clothe or entertain a child here. I do have some food, though. I was just about to make some lunch. Have you all eaten?"

"No," answered Captain Rogers, "but are you sure you have enough?"

"Absolutely, but I warn you—it's nothing fancy, just bologna sandwiches and iced tea. Oh—and some cookies."

"Sounds great to me, what about you, Wilson?"

For the first time, he really looked at me and addressed me, "It's fine with me, but do you think—uh— I'll be welcome by everyone here?" He again glanced at Angela.

Sergeant Adams answered, "We'll see what we can do." Then he approached the quiet little girl. "Hi there, Kiddo, remember us? I've got some presents here for you, and since Miss Stevens said she was going to feed us, why don't we all go into the kitchen, and you can see what we've got for you. Now, Mr. Wilson wants to come with us, and he told us he wants to be your friend. Can he come with us?"

Angela looked at the reporter. She still looked frightened, but also rather bewildered, as if she were trying to figure something out about the man. Finally, she nodded her head and allowed the sergeant to take her hand and lead her into the kitchen. Since the table was pushed up against the wall, Bob Wilson and Captain Rogers pulled it out to give us more places at the table. Then I told them to bring in the two chairs at my desk while I started fixing the sandwiches.

Captain Rogers began talking about the case to me while the Sergeant was positioning his bags in front of Angela. "I'm afraid we haven't found out any more than we knew this morning. I guess none of your guests offered any information this morning, right?"

"No, of course they all saw Angela, but none of them appeared to know her."

"Angela, why Angela?"

I was rather embarrassed as I began to explain. "Well, there's a passage in the Bible about entertaining strangers—that we might be…"

"We might be entertaining angels unawares, right?" interrupted the reporter.

"Yes," I had failed to keep the shock out of my voice.

"How--?"

"How do I know that scripture? Even reporters occasionally read the Bible, Miss Stevens." He said, evidently amused.

"Of course, I'm sorry, I just…"

"That's all right. People in the 'liberal media' don't always have a very good reputation with the 'religious right'—and sometimes for good reason, I'm afraid."

Sergeant Adams saved me from further embarrassment by beginning his gift presentation.   All of us watched him as he dug into the bags. Angela was quiet, still, but I think he even had her interest. The first article he brought out was a frilly pink shirt, then a pair of denim shorts. They looked to be the right size, but of course I couldn't be sure. The sergeant continued to pull clothes out of the bag, and he found other shirts, slacks, tops, underpants, and one dress. There was also one pair of rather holey tennis shoes with a couple pairs of tube socks. Mrs. Adams had certainly been generous, and I thanked her husband for what must have been a sacrifice for the family. How could any family afford to feed and clothe six children considering today's prices?

After I had looked at all the clothes, Sergeant Adams dug into what must have been the toy bag. He brought out a beat-up game of "Sorry," explaining that some of the "men" that were supposed to be moved around the board were missing, so we'd have to substitute with buttons or something. Next he brought out a large, crayon scribbled Walt Disney Fairy Tale Book. He then produced a coloring book and crayon box so new looking that I wondered if he would get in trouble from his children when they discovered they were gone.

It seemed that Sergeant Adams had a flair for the dramatic. He took out one toy at a time, slowly, trying to increase Angela's anticipation with each gift. Although she didn't display the hilarious excitement most children would, her interest was evidenced by her wide eyes glued to the sergeant and his bag of toys. I had a feeling the good officer was keeping till last what he considered the piece de resistance.

When he did finally bring out the last gift, Angela's reaction was dramatic, but certainly not what we expected.

The toy was a doll, about the size of a two-year-old child, with dark, curly hair almost identical to Angela's. The doll, meant to be like a soft, cuddly toddler, had been very popular with little girls last Christmas because it was so realistic and beautiful. The one that Sergeant Adams was offering Angela was in good condition except for two streaks of red crayon that someone had drawn down its face.

We were looking at the doll while Sergeant Adams was mumbling something about his two girls being tomboys and not taking to dolls, when suddenly Angela let out a piercing scream that chilled my blood. All of us in the tiny kitchen were so immobilized with shock that none of us tried to stop her as she ran out the back door still screaming her piteous screams.

Chapter 3

Bob Wilson, the first to recover from the shock, bolted out the door like a jack-rabbit. He spurred the rest of us to action, and the policemen and I rushed out after the reporter. We must have looked like a crazy chase scene, so popular on TV. But there was nothing funny about this chase. I was afraid Angela would fall and break her leg or that she would dart in front of a car coming up the narrow road to the cottage.

My worries were useless however because Bob Wilson's long legs easily reached the child, and he caught her in his arms, trying to quiet her screams with soothing talk. But Angela wanted nothing to do with him, and she tried to wiggle out of his grasp. Finally, when I got to them, she broke loose and rushed into my arms. Her screams changed to sobs, like the ones I had heard at 2:00 in the morning. I knelt down and held her until the sobbing subsided. The three men stood around us, concern written all over their faces.

After a while I asked, "Angela, do you want to go back to the cottage? Everything's all right now." When I mentioned the cottage, Sergeant Adams quickly but silently raced up there, probably to put the doll out of sight.

Angela nodded her head. As I stood up, she put her hand in mine, and we walked up the hill followed by Captain Rogers and Bob Wilson. I looked back at the men in bewilderment. Should we force Angela to look at the doll and get her to try to remember why she was so frightened by it, or should we take it away and never mention it again? I decided to follow the latter course, mostly because I didn't want the child to be upset again. I also decided that I would start keeping a journal and record all the events that had taken place since Angela had come to me, and all of Angela's reactions to these events. Maybe the psychiatrist that Captain Rogers had talked about could find some clues to her past from the details in the journal.

By the time we got back to the cottage, it was past one o'clock, and a car was coming up the hill, probably the first visitors to the museum. Picking up a tee shirt and shorts outfit, I turned to Angela and said, "Why don't you go upstairs and get these clothes on, Honey? I'll be right down here if you need me."

After she left, the three of us stood in the kitchen, looking at each other until I remembered lunch. I had managed to make some sandwiches before Angela's outburst, so the men sat down at the table while I walked to the door to greet the new visitors. They were again an older couple, and by the time I had shown them around the cottage and had sent them outside, the policemen and reporter were getting ready to leave and Angela was downstairs dressed in the clothes that looked like they had made for her.

Bob Wilson approached me while the policemen were talking to Angela. "I know you don't have time right now, but I'd like to keep in touch, maybe ask you some more questions."

"I don't really know what I can tell you, other than what you know already," I answered more sharply than I wanted to.

"I know, but I'd just like to keep involved with the on-going investigation of this story. It's very intriguing, don't you think?"

"I suppose, but it's also tragic for the child. The last thing she needs is for her story to become a media circus.

And, by the way, how do the police feel about your 'involvement.'"

By this time Captain Rogers had joined our conversation. "It's all right, Miss Stevens, Wilson has promised to be sensitive about your and the little girl's privacy, and after her hysterics yesterday, we checked him out. Of course, if he gets out of line, just tell us and we'll reign him in."

"Okay," I murmured reluctantly. For some reason, I was prepared to do battle with this man.

Captain Rogers went on talking to me as the others started out the door. "We'll see you later, Miss Stevens. We have men knocking on doors of houses all around the shore to see if anyone saw anything last night. No one has reported any child missing. We'll just have to follow all the leads we can and hope for a break. Just keep in touch with us if anything happens. Take care."

Just as he was going out the door, new visitors were coming in, a young couple in their early twenties. The loving way they looked at each other, and the protective arm he put around her shoulders, told me they were a newly-wed couple, most likely on their honeymoon. Ever since my engagement had ended, couples like these had always made me feel sad, but now that Angela had come into my life, I had so much on my mind I hadn't really had time to think about Paul or Janelle, his new girl. Therefore, I was able to greet the couple warmly, feeling only the slightest twinges of envy. I showed them around the room, pointing out the most popular items, but they were clearly more interested in each other than the relics of the past.

There weren't as many visitors in the afternoon as there had been that morning. All during the day, Angela sat on the couch, occasionally coloring in the book the sergeant had brought her, but mostly she just stared into space. I kept watching her out of the corner of my eye to see if any particular visitor affected her, but she had no particular reaction to any of them.

Between the hours of 4:00 and 5:00, I closed the museum so that we could have supper. I had managed to get Angela to eat a half of a bologna sandwich and drink a glass of milk, but nothing else. If Angela had not been with me, I would have probably fixed myself another quick sandwich for supper because food hadn't been very important to me for months. Therefore, my cupboards and

refrigerator were practically bare. I managed to scare up
one can of soup and a couple hot dogs, half of which
Angela ate with the same lack of enthusiasm she had
shown for any food so far.

I was fascinated with this child who had been thrust
into my life. She was certainly not like the boisterous
children I had taught in the primary Sunday School
department at home. She reminded me of myself as a
child. I was always so intense and serious that I sometimes
had a hard time relating to children my own age. Of
course, maybe she was normally boisterous and even silly
and giggly, but no child would be exuberant under these
circumstances.

"Hey Angela," I asked when I had dried the last dish
after supper, "how about a tour of the museum and
lighthouse--it's on the house--no charge."

"Okay, Miss Stevens," she shrugged.

"Since you've already seen the living room, I'll
show you the bedroom where the old feather bed I talked
about is, and then we'll go down to the cellar. Down there
you'll see a lot of farm tools that pioneer men used about a
century ago." Angela looked confused, so I tried to

rephrase my sentence. "Pioneer men and women are people who built homes in Michigan about 100 years ago. Come on, and I'll show you, and by the way, do you think you could call me Amanda?"

"Okay," she said seriously.

We saw the bedroom which was mainly a large feather bed with an old quilt as its cover, a tall, solid oak bureau, a roll-top desk on which sat a quill pen and ink well, and a chart showing the areas on the Great Lakes where ship wrecks had occurred.

We had to walk outside to get to the cellar stairs. I was apprehensive about the effect the dimly-lit, damp cellar would have on my skittish little visitor, but she walked down the steps without any hesitation. Like most children, she was only mildly interested in the farm implements, but one article did catch her eye. It was an ordinary, black metal tool box--in fact it wasn't even a museum exhibit. It had been left by Mr. Sanders in an inconspicuous corner of the cellar, and I assumed it was filled with wrenches, screwdrivers, hammers, etc. It reminded me that the Michigan Parks and Recreation department had put ads in the Randolph City newspaper to hire a handyman to do some of the heavy work around the grounds, and I realized after only one week that I needed the help. The mowing, trimming, raking, and general maintenance were going to be a bit too much for me to handle alone.

While I was thinking about a possible co-worker, Angela was gazing in silent fascination at the tool box. Since I was afraid she would become hysterical again, I put my arms around her and suggested lightly, "Angela, let's go out and climb to the top of the lighthouse. It's such a beautiful day, I'll bet we can see all around the lake."

I had to give her a little tug to break her concentration, but finally she turned and walked up the stairs out into the bright sunlight with me. The view from the top of the lighthouse was well worth the climb up the winding, hand-chiseled, stone stairs. Lake Huron was calm, and the sunlight brought out the grey-blue of the water. When we came back down, Angela behaved more like any child, pulling the rope that rang the bell and sticking her head and arms in the stocks.

In my best school-marm voice, I began explaining about how the stocks had been used in colonial days to punish offenders of the strict Puritan laws. As usual I really became involved in my subject, and I didn't even notice that a car was coming up the driveway until it was pulling into the parking space beside my car. If Angela had noticed the car, she had been too polite to interrupt me.

"Well, Angela, looks like we're getting some more visitors." I announced unnecessarily. Angela said nothing, just merely looked in the direction I was pointing.

We walked over to the cottage to greet the visitors who turned out to be Judy Baldwin, one of the EMT's, with another couple in their late twenties or early thirties. They both had wavy, dark hair and tall statures. We drew near each other, almost in slow motion. The couple seemed frightened to approach us. When we finally came face to face, the woman looked at Angela with incredibly sad eyes and said in a plaintive voice, "Jenny, is that you, Baby?"

Chapter 4

My head began to swim and my heart was thudding so loudly I couldn't hear anything else. Could these two people be Angela's parents? It would be wonderful to give this tragic couple some happiness, but of course, we wouldn't want Angela to be shuttled off to complete strangers. I looked at the child for some flicker of recognition on her face, but she only looked puzzled.

"Miss Stevens," Judy said, "I want you to meet Tom and Lorna Summers. I met them four years ago, under very tragic circumstances, and I called them this morning about the little girl."

The husband, Tom, explained, "You see, Miss Stevens, our little girl, Jenny, was kidnapped four years ago when we were on vacation up in Mackinac City. The police never found her or any trace of her. Since then, we've kept in touch with Judy, who was one of the people who helped search for Jenny. She promised to call us if any child was found under mysterious circumstances like this."

Lorna, the grieving mother continued with the story, "Our daughter Jenny had--has--dark curly hair and big, blue eyes like this child. Jenny was only two when she disappeared, but we have a computer image of what she might look like now, and this child looks similar, but there's one way we can tell for sure."

"I don't understand how--" I began.

"What we're trying to say, Miss Stevens, is that our child had--has--a distinguishing birth mark on her back—a dark, circular spot around the small of her back. This birth mark seems to run in the Summers' family. I have one and so do my father and my two sisters," said Mr. Summers.

"We could see it ourselves if we examined her, and if it is there," continued Lorna Summers, "but we want to be very sure, and we also thought you might be reluctant to let us examine her alone. We have brought a picture of her when she was new born which shows this mark clearly." She fumbled in her purse and brought out a worn, wrinkled photograph of a small, naked baby lying on her stomach on a lacy blanket. I could see a definite mark on the baby's back. I hadn't noticed a mark on Angela's back, but I hadn't really looked at her body without any clothes on it.

"Yes, well thank you for your consideration," I mumbled, as I looked at the precious picture. I wondered how many other pictures they treasured of this lost child. Then I turned to Angela, "Sweetheart, would you let Judy look at your—uh—back to see if you might be the little girl of this man and woman?"

"I-I guess so, but will it hurt?" Angela asked tearfully.

"No, Honey, I won't hurt you," promised Judy, and she walked over to the front door of the cottage and held it open for us.

I turned to the Summers and asked, "Do you folks want to come in and wait? Feel free to look around, and make yourselves at home. We'll be with you in a moment."

"Thank you, Miss Stevens, we stopped at this museum the other time--the time Jenny--the last time we went to Mackinac City," Mrs. Summers falteringly stated.

My heart broke for the tragic couple standing clutching each other's hand. Their despair made my problems seem insignificant.

"Where's a good place to examine her?" Judy asked, interrupting my thoughts.

"Oh, probably the bedroom down here. There's a door we can close." I decided to go into the bedroom with them, mostly because I didn't know what to say to the Summers. Angela walked obediently into the room with us. "By the way," I added. "I'm calling her Angela because—well—because I like that name, and she can't remember her real name."

Judy displayed her professional manner as she bent down to Angela and said, "Okay now, Angela, will you hop up on the bed after Miss Stevens helps you take off your top? Lie on your tummy, and I'll give you a back rub."

With an amusing little shrug Angela lifted her arms while I slipped the tee shirt off. I noticed that the child had obtained a golden tan while she had probably been wearing a one-piece bathing suit with spaghetti straps that had tied at the back of her neck. Her body was lean and wiry and clean looking, a body obviously well-cared for.

I boosted her on top of the high feather bed, and she rolled over onto her belly. Judy had been studying the photograph, so when Angela was ready, she looked at her back while gently pressing her fingers along the spine, all the time teasing Angela by saying, "Now doesn't that feel good, Little One? I bet you'd have to pay a lot to get a back rub like that at a health spa. Are you ticklish?" Angela giggled softly as she tickled her under her ribs. It was the first sound approaching a real laugh I had ever heard from her.

"Now Angela, you can get down and get your shirt back on. I didn't find the mark on this baby in the picture, so I'm almost positive you're not their little girl. But I think we should give you a complete examination, Pumpkin, your heart, lungs, blood, teeth--the works. I take my kids to a nice young doctor who has an office in Randolph City. He has all the equipment we'll need there to give you a thorough going over." Then she turned to me while Angela was dressing. "The museum is closed all day on Mondays, isn't it? Could you take her to the doctor then?"

"I think Captain Rogers is going to try to get us an appointment with the psychiatrist that day," I answered.

"Oh, sure, well maybe you could see both doctors that day. The offices are in the same building. Would that be all right?"

"All right with me, but do you think it would be too much for Angela?"

"I'll get back with you on that. I'll talk to the doctor about it, okay?"

"Sure," I agreed, and Angela just looked solemnly at the two of us.

Judy sighed and said to me, "Now, I've got the odious task of dashing those poor people's hopes once more. Hanging's too good for kidnappers as far as I'm concerned; I think I'd go out of mind if someone took my kids," she added. Then she walked out promising me that she would call when she had talked to the doctor.

As I helped Angela put on her shirt, I started talking to her about the "Mackinac Island" that was written on it, shamefully admitting to myself that I was deliberately stalling to avoid facing the dejected Summers. I explained to her that Mackinac Island was a resort island in Lake Huron. Then I explained about the Great Lakes and ended up showing her the chart that pinpointed all the known shipwrecks on Lake Huron. Again, whenever I was upset about situations around me, I started delving into history.

I must have been explaining the chart well because the child showed a half-way active interest in what I was saying. Of course, her interest spurred the school teacher in me to talk more and more. In fact, I got so involved in my subject I forgot that I had originally been avoiding the Summers. Therefore, I was surprised to hear voices coming from the front yard.

"Angela, we'd better go outside. I think we have some last-minute visitors. They just made it in the nick of time; the museum closes in ten minutes."

We hurried out to the front yard, but instead of finding museum visitors, I was disconcerted to see the Summers talking to the reporter. His face registered genuine concern, and he was busily writing down the information they were telling him and promising to ask his editor if he could revive the story in the hopes of finding their child.

Shamefully, I walked up to the couple, with Angela crouching fearfully behind me, and told them how sorry I was that their child was still missing. We all muttered polite good-byes, with the reporter promising to do all he could do to help find their child. After they got into the doctor's car and pulled away, I turned to him and snapped, "Do you think you should raise their hopes like that? Do you really think you could find their child when no one else, including the FBI, could find her after four years?" I was already engaging in battle with this man, and he had only been in my presence for a moment.

"Hey, I didn't make any promises I can't keep. I told them I'd talk to a friend of mine who's a private eye, but that's all I could do. If you think they looked like their hopes were raised, maybe they were just encouraged because I listened to them. You see, I really care about them, and I guess my concern came through."

I felt my face redden from the sting of his rebuke. "Well, I care, too!" I shouted indignantly, but even as I spoke the words I realized that I had consciously avoided them instead of showing my concern as the reporter had.

"I didn't say you don't care," he quickly asserted with a disconcerting twinkle dancing in his eyes. Then, with a smile, he changed the subject, "Now, let's get to your and little Angela's story."

"I don't really have a story to tell you, but I'd like to ask you some questions. Why is Angela so frightened of you when she hasn't shown fear of any other strangers she's met, and why are you so interested in this whole deal when I've told you over and over you've already heard everything that we know?"

"Well, I don't know the answer to the first question. I assure you, I've never seen this little girl before I took her picture. Now, as to the second question--I'm interested in people, all people. I like to know backgrounds on everybody I write about. Most of the information I get I never use, but it's all interesting to me. Do you think we could go in and sit down and talk about all this?" he asked with another one of his disarming smiles.

I was not ready to let down my defenses toward this man. "Could your 'interest' be a high-class form of nosiness?" I asked, ignoring his appeal to go inside.

"Maybe I am just nosy, but I'd rather be nosy than apathetic. I believe people are too isolated from each other. We're afraid to get involved with each other or care too much, for fear we'll get hurt."

I was appalled to find tears welling in my eyes. I knew too well the hurt of caring too much. I quickly turned my head to hide my tears and stammered, "May-Maybe we'd better go in. Looks like we might have some rain. I don't think we'll have any more visitors."

Bob Wilson's eyes pierced through mine showing me I hadn't fooled him by my abrupt change of mood. But he didn't say anything while he followed us into the cottage. Part of me wanted to confide in him about my broken engagement, but I was afraid he'd laugh at me. I was sure he wouldn't understand about broken engagements or broken hearts. So, I was determined not to let him find out any more about me than was necessary for his story. And Angela's reaction to him still bothered me. Did he know more about her than he admitted, I wondered. Maybe he had devious reasons for his great interest in her story.

In spite of my suspicions of him, I managed to ask him if he wanted a glass of iced tea and some cookies. He immediately accepted and strode into the kitchen and straddled a kitchen chair, making himself right at home.

I nervously served him the tea and cookies and gave Angela some milk, while she sat at the opposite side of the table staring at him with a frightened gaze. He chattered away about the weather, the cookies, the tea, and other mundane issues, apparently oblivious to the child's stare. He didn't really ignore her because he included her in the conversation, but he seemingly wasn't bothered by her reaction.

When I finally sat down at the table, the reporter asked, "Where are you from, Amanda? Or—may I call you Amanda?"

"Well, yes, but how did you know my first name?"

"Simple, I asked the policemen. You know I had to have it for the story, anyway."

"Oh yes, the story. You know I haven't even read it yet." In fact I'd been so involved with Angela and the Summers I hadn't even checked the mail or picked up the paper, both of which were in mail boxes at the beginning of the driveway up to the cottage.

"I didn't really know how to write it. I used your name, but I didn't say that you were at the museum cottage. I just said a cottage on the lake. Aren't you afraid of living here with the child all alone?"

As I looked at his face, I tried to determine whether he was truly worried about my safety or if he was trying to find out if I was going to be alone for some diabolical plan he might have. "I'm not going to be alone much longer," I assured him with more confidence than I felt. "The Recreation Department is going to send someone to be a handyman--you know--help me with mowing, raking, heavy work. He'll sleep in the shed out there."

"Oh well, that'll be better, I suppose. When is this handyman coming?"

"He could be here any day. The state park officials are thinking that a college guy will want the job for a summer. Since most of the schools are out now, someone will probably be hired soon."

"Good, I hope everything works out well. Now, you didn't have time to answer my questions yesterday, so tell me, what's a nice girl like you doing in a place like this?" he asked with a ridiculous grin on his face.

I smiled back in spite of myself. "I expected a more original line from a writer. But, to answer your question-- I'm a history teacher at a high school down in southern Michigan, and one of my colleagues told me about this job, and since I love museums, I took it."

"Weren't you afraid you'd be lonely out here all summer away from your family and—friends?"

I noticed an almost imperceptible hesitancy before the word "friends," or maybe I just imagined it. I had to be more cautious because his questions were becoming more personal. "I actually see more people here than I would at home. You see, I live with my folks in the country, and since I'm an only child, I don't see many people around our place during the summer."

"But what about friends? I would think you'd have loads of friends, especially male friends. How about it, isn't there someone special pining away since you are going to be stuck up here all summer?"

I wasn't able to keep from sounding flustered when I answered, "There—there—is no one—that is—sure—I have friends, but no one is 'pining away' because I'm here."

Again his eyes pierced through me, seemingly x-raying all my secret thoughts, but thankfully he didn't pursue the subject. Instead he pushed out his chair and announced, "I really have to go. I've got lots to do. Even a small town like Randolph City has lots of news, especially during the summer." As he stood up, he cupped his hand under Angela's chin, "I hope everything works out for you,

Kiddo. You're a sweet girl. You take good care of Amanda here, okay?"

Angela scooted back from him, almost spilling the milk I had given her. Sensing her fear, Bob stepped back and looked at her speculatively. He looked as perplexed as I was, but was he an expert actor? Was he involved in Angela's mysterious past?

Finally he walked to the kitchen door and said, "Well, so long, ladies. I'll be seeing you around. If anything comes up, just give me a call. This nose of mine will travel anywhere for news." With a jaunty salute, he sprinted out of the cottage, revved the motor of his red-striped sports car, and roared down the hill.

I looked over at Angela and saw her eyelids drooping. "You're awfully tired, aren't you, Sweetheart?" You go upstairs and put your pajamas on. I'll be up as soon as I straighten up in here and count the museum money we got today. You can crawl in bed and turn on the TV up there if you like. Just pull out the bottom button on the set."

After I put the dirty glasses in the sink, I went to my desk and began balancing the money I had in the box with the number of visitors I had recorded. I vaguely heard noises from upstairs--the patter of Angela's feet on the wooden floor, the music of a familiar TV advertisement, and the creaking of the bed springs. I didn't expect the next sound I heard. Angela began screaming again, not piercing screams like when she had seen the doll, but this time she was shouting, "No, no don't do it! No, no!"

I rushed upstairs to see a trembling Angela, her eyes riveted to the TV where a seedy-looking character was shooting at some policemen on a dark boat dock along an ocean front. I quickly turned off the TV, silently scolding myself for not monitoring the programs before I had told Angela to turn it on. I rushed to her and held her in my arms, gently rocking her as I would a baby. After a few minutes the trembling subsided, and I could feel the tension ooze out of her, and finally Angela was asleep. I continued to hold her for a few more minutes because she would shudder occasionally in her sleep, and I wanted to be with her to prevent any more hysterics.

When I was sure she was all right, I walked downstairs and finished my bookkeeping. I really wanted to read Bob's story in the paper, but I wasn't eager to walk down the driveway now that it was dark. I stood debating for quite a while before I finally summoned the courage to go to the mailbox. As a precaution, I walked to the small, closet-like pantry right off the kitchen where I picked up a large steel flashlight that was hanging on a hook by the door. I figured it would make a good weapon, if necessary, as well as a provider of light. In my sheltered life, I had never before had to think about having a weapon in my possession just to walk to the mailbox.

I really needed the flashlight tonight because clouds covered the moon and any stars that would be visible. I couldn't shake off my apprehension of what could be waiting for me in the dark woods to my left. The wind rustling through the trees made eerie noises, and there were animal sounds that mocked my fears.

Finally, after what seemed to be an eternity, I came to the mailbox. I was shining the light inside the box to make sure I wouldn't miss anything when I heard a noise behind me. I whirled around and bumped into a dark form hovering over me. I could never remember what happened next. I must have screamed because I vaguely remember hearing screams, and I must have dropped my flashlight to run because somehow I can remember tripping and falling as I ran to the top of the hill. I was only a few feet from the cottage when the man caught me.

Chapter 5

The man grabbed my arm and held me firmly while he tried to get his breath. Finally he managed to say, "Miss Stevens, I'm not going to hurt you. Please listen to me."

We had reached the area that was lighted by the floodlights, so his features were vaguely distinguishable. I figured he was probably in his fifties because the little bit of hair he had left was turning white, and his face was creased with lines that must have taken a number of years to etch. However, there was nothing infirm or feeble about his grip. I was unable to loosen my arm even though my captor was probably only an inch or two taller than I and only about ten pounds heavier than I. Of course, after getting a good look at the man, I didn't struggle as hard because he didn't appear to be the ruthless killer I had imagined him to be.

"Miss Stevens," he panted, "I'm sorry I scared you, but I have something to show you, something about the child."

The fear that had subsided started rising again. In an almost hysterical voice, I asked him, "How do you know my name, and how do you know about the child?"

"Let me start from the beginning. I'm Phillip Jennings, a retired history professor, amateur photographer, would-be author. I'm trying to write a book about early American shipping, and Great Lake shipping is a big part of my research. I became very good friends with the Sanders because I was over here at the museum a lot studying the charts, looking over the relics, and just talking to Mr. Sanders about his lighthouse-keeper ancestors."

"But that doesn't tell me how you--"

"I'm getting to that," he said with a smile and a gasp of air, "but I'm a long-winded professor, and it takes me a while to get to my point." I had to smile then. A long-winded professor, especially a history professor, was someone I could identify with.

"At least I got you to smile," he said, then he let go of my arm and self-consciously began to explain. "Miss Stevens, I want you to know I am not in the habit of grabbing young ladies and holding them hostage. I just didn't want you to go away thinking I meant you harm."

"I'm sorry, too, Mr. Jennings. It's just that it was so dark down there, and I was a little nerved-up, I guess. Go on with your story."

"Okay, as I was saying, I became very good friends with the Sanders, so I knew about their son getting married and about you coming. So, when I read tonight's paper, I realized that the little girl was at your cottage, and I have something I think will be of interest to you."

Then Mr. Jennings pulled a small envelope out of his pocket. I knew I would not be able to see the contents of that envelope very well outside, so I made a decision that I hoped was not a foolish one. "Why don't you come inside, Mr. Jennings?" I asked.

He looked rather nervous as he answered, "All right, if you're sure it's okay with you. I promise I'm safe. You can call the police and tell them I'm here if you wish."

"No, that won't be necessary. If you can't trust a history professor, who can you trust?"

Mr. Jennings chuckled good-naturedly, and we walked to the cottage together, making small talk about our respective careers in history. When we got inside, I offered him some tea, and we walked into the kitchen.

After all the amenities were out of the way and after I had served refreshments, he handed me the envelope and told me to open it. There was a note written in very small, precise handwriting, which I guessed was his, and the note was wrapped around a photo of a small child playing in the sand on a beach and a dark-haired man kneeling down beside the child with his back to the camera. Examining the photo more carefully, I was shocked to see that the child was Angela, but I couldn't tell who the man was.

"Where did you get this?" I gasped.

"That's what I've been trying to tell you. I was going to leave that envelope in your mailbox tonight with that note explaining it. I didn't want to come over here and bother you this late at night, and I had no idea I would see you down there."

When I didn't say anything, he went on, "As I told you, I was—well—am a photographer; I especially love taking pictures of children. The other day, let's see, must have been Thursday, I was looking out my front window (my cottage is right on the beach), and I saw this little girl. She looked so photogenic that I put my telescopic lens on the camera and took this picture. I would have taken more, but right then the telephone rang. It was the library telling me that one of the books I had ordered for my research was in, and I dropped everything and went to Randolph City to get the book. I didn't get back to my house until late that night, and I was gone all day today, but when I got back tonight, I read the paper and recognized the little girl. I have a dark room with all the equipment necessary to develop pictures, so I developed this, and by the time I was finished, it was too late to come over here and talk to you, so, well you know the rest."

"Mr. Jennings, did you get a good look at the man in the picture?" I asked anxiously.

"No, sorry, all I really saw was what's in the picture."

"Let's see, where is this on the beach? Can you see the docks from there?"

"It's right in front of my cottage, sort of the middle of the arch if you think of the harbor as a big horseshoe. On a clear day you can see the harbor, but as you know, it wasn't clear this Thursday. I could only see a few feet beyond the child."

"Hm, do you mind if I keep this and show it to the police?"

"No, that's what I wanted you to do, as I told you in the note. I happen to have an appointment tomorrow morning, so I knew it wouldn't be till afternoon before I could get over here, and I wanted you to have the picture as soon as possible. Do you get the Free Press in the morning? I know the Sanders did."

"Yes, I do, and you're right, I go out and get it every morning before the museum opens." I paused as I suddenly remembered the mailbox. "Oh no, I just thought of something. The main reason I was down at the mailbox was to get the Randolph City Gazette so I could read the story about Angela, and in my fright of you, I left it down there along with today's mail and my flashlight."

"Well, I tell you what, I'll walk you back down there and back here, that is, if you are not scared of me anymore. But, tell me, who's Angela?"

"Oh, Angela is the little girl who came here, the little girl in your picture. That's the name I have given her because she can't remember her real name."

"That's a real shame; you never think about a child that age losing her memory. I hope she gets along all right. You must be a very special person to take her in like this." I must have looked embarrassed because he quickly changed the subject. "Well, how about it? Would you like an escort to the mailbox, My Lady?" He stood up and held out his arm charmingly. Laughing, I put my arm in the crook of his, and we walked in comfortable companionship back down to the mailbox where I had been so terrorized before. Now, I couldn't believe I had ever been so frightened of this man. He was very easy to talk to, and he was so knowledgeable about my favorite subject. I hoped I would get to know him better.

We found the flashlight where I had dropped it, surprisingly still shining. I finally got the mail and the paper, and even though I hated to impose on Mr. Jennings, I took him up on his offer to walk me back up to the cottage. Before he left me, he promised me he would be back the next day with a blown-up copy of the picture. He hoped an enlargement would show more details about the man, and we would be able to find an identifying feature that we had missed in the smaller copy.

When I got inside again, I went into the kitchen to get Mr. Jennings' picture, and then I immediately walked upstairs to get ready for bed, carrying the mail and newspaper with me. I decided I would peruse all these things in the comfort of my bed, that is if I could stay awake.

The bed felt so good when I finally lay down that I let out a sigh of relief that could have awakened Angela if she had not been so sound asleep. I reached for the newspaper on the night stand beside my bed, and a close-up of Angela's face jumped right out at me. As I read the story, I had to admit that Bob Wilson was a very good writer. He wrote factually and accurately, and somehow I could discern an interest and involvement in his writing that many reporters didn't display. Angela's picture had come out very clear, too.

Seeing her picture in the paper reminded me of the one Mr. Jennings had taken. I looked at it closer, this time concentrating more on the man. I couldn't tell much about his height since he was kneeling down, but I could see his dark, wavy hair, and his muscular frame. Then suddenly a thought almost jolted me out of bed. The man in the picture looked very much like Bob Wilson! Had he been lying to all of us? Was there a very good reason Angela was so frightened of him? All those questions burned in my mind long after I turned the light off to go to sleep.

Chapter 6

The next morning was Saturday, but I still had to follow pretty much the same routine that I followed Tuesday through Friday. Mr. and Mrs. Sanders had told me I could be fairly flexible about the museum schedule. "If for some reason, you need more time for shopping or something, close the museum early." Mrs. Sanders had said.

"Yes, and if you have a late date some night, you can open later." Mr. Sanders had said as he winked mischievously at me. I was just instructed to change the hands of a fake clock on a sign down at the gate that announced the opening and closing times of the museum. So far, though, I had maintained the normal schedule.

But this particular Saturday, I decided to close the museum at 3:00 so that I could shop for some groceries and for Angela's clothes. I had money budgeted for groceries, and I doubted that Angela's appetite would add too much to my grocery bill. But her clothes were something else. The only store I could think of that had a good selection of children's clothes was a little one called

"Small Talk," located in a mini-mall in Randolph City. The stores in this mall seemed to cater to rich tourists who had probably docked their luxury boats at the magnificent state docks in Randolph City. When I had seen the price on some of the clothes in stores that carried my size, I was glad I had brought a sufficient wardrobe with me. However, I had no time to hunt everywhere for bargains, so I guessed I would have to dip into the savings I had accumulated for my wedding. It was still with more than a trace of bitterness that I realized I didn't need wedding money anymore.

I was awake before the alarm went off, and I resisted the urge to push the snooze alarm and doze back off to sleep even though I was still very tired. I had wrestled with questions about the picture of Angela and the unknown man even after I had fallen into a fitful sleep. With the thought of the man in the picture came the inevitable thought of Bob Wilson. Even while I was telling myself that it was a relief not to have to answer his questions or have to subject Angela to his seemingly frightening presence today, I realized with some chagrin that part of me wanted to see him. Maybe I just wanted to question him about the picture, or maybe I just enjoyed our verbal sparring.

However I had no time for intense introspection. I had to make out a grocery list and a little girl's clothing list. Besides, I still had to get the museum ready and change the closing time on the sign at the gate. I eased out of bed so that I wouldn't awaken Angela, grateful that she at last was getting the sleep she needed.

I showered, dressed, dusted the furniture, changed the sign, checked the mail, and fixed breakfast in just forty-five minutes. I was looking forward to the shopping trip, and I guess I thought the day would pass faster if I was quick about my chores. Besides it was a day made for activity. The sky was a bright blue, with only a few fluffy clouds drifting lazily by. The temperature must have been in the low 70's, not too hot and not too cold. I had never considered myself to be a morning person, especially a Saturday morning person, but I felt an inexplicable love of life this particular Saturday, in spite of my anxiety over Angela. For the first time in months I was actually hungry, and I fixed myself a big breakfast of eggs, sausage, biscuits (the ones that pop out of cans), juice, and coffee.

I was just finishing my third biscuit when I heard Angela's soft steps on the stairs. She tentatively opened the door to the kitchen, and peered in with wide, frightened eyes. When she saw me, her face lit up with relief. "Good morning, Angela," I said. "I was going to let you sleep in today. You don't have to get up as early as I do."

"Oh, I thought maybe you had left. I thought I was here alone," Angela said tremulously.

I drew her over to my lap and hugged her to me. "Don't worry, sweetheart. I'll be here as long as you need me. If someday you wake up and can't find me in the cottage, I promise I won't be any farther away than the mailbox down at the gate." She rewarded my promise with a hug that indicated the first real sign of affection she had shown me. I realized that I was becoming emotionally attached to this child, probably much more than I should be.

When she released her grip on me, I asked, "What would you like for breakfast, darling?"

"I don't care," she answered, but this time she sat down and looked at the skillets with a little more interest than before.

"Well then, eggs, sausage, and biscuits it is. After you finish eating, go put on one of the outfits Sergeant Adams brought you. I plan to buy you some new clothes today. How would you like to go shopping with me in Randolph City?"

"I guess so, but where's Randolph City?"

"Oh, it's about thirty miles north of here," I answered as I gestured vaguely northward. "It takes about 45 minutes to get there. It's a nice little town with many cute stores that sell everything: groceries, clothes, toys, souvenirs."

She looked puzzled as she asked, "What are soo-ba-neers?"

I was frying her sausage while we were talking, "Well, honey, here's a souvenir right here," I explained as I held up a glass spoon holder on the stove. "See, this has a picture of a big waterfall on it, and it says, 'Niagara Falls' and--

"Hey, I've heard of Ni-gra Falls before," she interrupted excitedly.

My heart started beating frantically. "Think, honey, what do you remember about it? Here look at the picture here on this spoon holder."

She scrutinized the little dish for what seemed to be hours. Finally she shook her head sadly and murmured, "No, I just remember the name. I can't remember anything else."

"It's okay, honey, you will some day." I knew she was frustrated. From all I had learned about child development in my education classes, I was sure Angela was a bright child for her age. I figured she must be suffering to have only snatches of memory come and go like a flashing light.

She was looking so depressed that I quickly changed the subject. "Here, sweetheart, eat your breakfast. When you finish, go upstairs and get dressed. You can take a bath and wash your hair when we get ready to leave, but for right now, just put on any of the outfits Sergeant Adams brought you."

She passively complied, and maybe because she sensed my eagerness to get on with the day, she ate quickly, yet as politely as always. When she finished, she brought her plate to the sink where I was washing my dishes and slid them into the hot, soapy water. Then she picked up a towel and began to vigorously dry the ones I had already washed. "That's all right, darling," I said, "we'll just let them drain this morning because it's almost time for the museum to open. Just run on upstairs and get dressed." She instantly obeyed, and again I wondered if she had always been so cooperative.

I heard Angela walk upstairs, and then I heard her running excitedly down again." Amanda, is this a picture of me?" She was clutching the picture Mr. Jennings had given me. She had evidently picked it up from the night stand by my bed where I had placed it the night before. I wished I had shown it to her and prepared her some before she just came upon it.

"Honey, a man named Mr. Jennings who lives near the beach took this picture of you just a day or so ago. Do you recognize the man, or do you remember anything about when this was taken?"

She stared thoughtfully at the picture for a long time before she answered, "I remember playing with a bucket on the beach, but I don't remember who this man is."

"Well, that's all right, Sweetheart," I said trying to cheer her up. "Like I said before, you'll remember some day." Even though she didn't seem to be comforted much, without another word, she turned around and walked back upstairs where she started to get ready. When I got upstairs, I saw she had placed the picture back where she had found it.

The rest of the morning and afternoon passed by uneventfully. There were no more hysterics from Angela, no heart-broken parents searching for a lost child, no inquisitive reporters asking disturbing questions. However, I registered more visitors that day than I ever had before. I figured that the tourist trade would increase as the season progressed.

At 3:00, after the last guests left, I helped Angela take a bath and wash her hair. Again, I didn't know whether she would be offended if I offered too much help or if she needed more help than I was giving. Between us, we managed to scrub her skin so that it glowed and shampoo her black hair until it was squeaky clean. I only had to brush her hair and blow dry it, and it fell into soft ringlets around her face.

After she was dressed, and after I freshened my make-up and hair do, we piled into my little red Taurus and started off toward Randolph City. I watched Angela out of the corner of my eye to see if she was recognizing any scenery we were passing. But she only displayed casual interest as she gazed at the pine and birch forests that surrounded the highways of northern Michigan. She did show slight excitement when we spotted a doe and her fawn just a few yards off the road, but it was only the normal enthusiasm children show toward animals, especially baby animals.

The sun was an orange ball in the western sky when we reached Randolph City, a quaint tourist town that slept quietly all winter, just waiting to be awakened to bustling activity every summer. Most of the stores in town were decorated with sailing motifs. Almost every one of them had a sign-board in the shape of a ship's wheel or anchor, and the signs bore names like "Davy Jones Locker," "The Galley," "Harbor Lights," and other seafaring nomenclatures. The people strolling the sidewalks looked sunburned and windblown, relaxed and unhurried. The clerks in the stores were smiling effusively as they waited to relieve the tourists of some of their travelers' checks.

The mall had a spacious parking lot where I was able to park just a few feet from the store. I could sense Angela's excitement by the way she was gazing out the window at all the sights, and by the brightness of her blue eyes when she looked over at me. I thought with some amusement that shopping expeditions inspired most every woman, young or old.

A smiling, matronly clerk came to us as soon as we stepped into the air-conditioned store, the front of which contained racks of summer shirts and shorts, all on sale, probably to get ready for the fall clothes that would soon be flooding all stores, although it was only the first of June. The back of the store contained frilly, brightly-colored dresses.

The clerk's eyes lit up like a Christmas tree when I told her that Angela needed a complete wardrobe, and I produced the list I had managed to make when there had been a lull in the museum crowd. "My, you're a lucky little girl to be getting all these new clothes," she said. "Did you grow out of your old ones all of a sudden?"

Angela shyly averted her eyes, so I answered for her, "Well, she doesn't have any old ones. You see, she's--"

"Oh, yes," the lady interrupted, "I recognize her now. She's the little girl in the paper yesterday. I'm sorry, I shouldn't have asked stupid questions." Her plump face turned bright red.

"It's all right," I said and, to relieve her embarrassment, I quickly suggested, "Let's start with the dresses. I think she needs at least two dressy ones."

An hour passed quickly while Angela dressed and undressed and primped and pirouetted in front of me and the admiring clerk. By the time I had reached the end of my list, there was a colorful pile of clothes, including two pairs of shoes, and a pair of warmer pajamas for the nights too cool for the ones she had worn when she came to the cottage. The wardrobe created a stack on the counter about two feet high. Our kind salesperson had helped us find the clothes on sale, and she had given us as many breaks as she could on the others. I wished I could have bought more for Angela because she looked adorable in everything, especially the azure blue clothes that matched her eyes. Since I had transferred my savings to the Randolph City bank, I had no trouble paying for the purchase by check. I was glad to spend money on Angela, but I couldn't subdue a moment's sadness when I realized that my wedding money was essentially gone. Somehow, the loss of that money ended any hopes or dreams I might have about marrying Paul.

The air that met us as we walked out of the store was much cooler than when we had gone in. There would be two or three more hours of daylight left because of daylight savings time. I hoped I could get all my groceries, take Angela out to eat, and get back to the cottage before dark because I was wary of going back through the woods surrounding the cottage in the dark. Therefore, we went directly to the grocery store in the same mall down from the children's store we had just patronized, and we scurried through the aisles so quickly I barely managed to get through my list. Then, instead of going to a restaurant where we would sit and be waited on, we went to McDonald's, only about five miles from the mall. As we approached the golden arches and entered the famous establishment, brightly decorated with all the McDonald land characters, I noticed that Angela appeared to be unfamiliar with the whole atmosphere, a fact that puzzled me. I couldn't imagine an American child who had never gone to McDonald's.

We were just finishing our meal when Captain Rogers and Sergeant Adams walked in. They looked around the restaurant briefly, spotted us at our yellow plastic booth and walked resolutely toward us. "Good evening, Ladies," said Captain Rogers, "we saw your car in the parking lot and thought we'd see how you're doing."

"Hello, Captain," I said, "Won't you have a seat?" I couldn't resist glancing around at the other customers to see if they were staring at us talking to two policemen.

"Well, I think I'll take you up on that offer," sighed Captain Rogers as he scooted in beside Angela, causing her to blush and look down at her new shoes. Sergeant Adams slid in beside me.

"How are you doing, Little Lady?" asked Captain Rogers to Angela. "Are you taking good care of Amanda here?"

To relieve Angela's discomfort, I again answered for her. "Oh, we're doing fine. We just got Angela a brand new wardrobe. She got dresses, shorts, slacks, shirts, shoes--the works."

"Now that's great! I bet you look pretty in every one of them, too. You know, I'd like one of those special ice cream sundaes they serve here. Why don't you and Sergeant Adams go order four of them, my treat."

When Angela looked at me reluctantly, I said, "It's all right, Honey. I'll be right here. Get me a gooey hot fudge sundae with lots of nuts on it, okay?" I could sense that Captain Rogers wanted to talk to me alone, and since the line was long at the counter, I knew Angela and Sergeant Adams wouldn't be back for a few minutes.

Sergeant Adams must have realized the captain's reasoning because he smiled over at Angela and said, "Come on, Sweetie. The Captain doesn't offer to buy anything very often, so we'd better take advantage of his generosity now." Captain Rogers squeezed his heavy frame out of the compact booth to let Angela out. Sergeant Adams took Angela's hand and gently led her over to the counter. She looked back at me as if to reassure herself that I was staying there. I smiled at her encouragingly.

"That tike seems to be attached to you, now. How's she been doing? Has she shown any signs of getting her memory back?"

"I don't know. She reacts to situations--sometimes hysterically, like the doll, and sometimes reflectively--like an ordinary tool box. Just this morning, she recognized the name, "Niagara Falls," but all she could remember was the name. Oh, and by the way, I met a man last night who had taken a picture of her on the beach near the boat docks, and there is a man in the picture with her, and Angela saw the picture this morning."

"No kidding, did she or you recognize the man at all?"

"Uh, no," I hesitated. For some reason I was reluctant to tell him that the man resembled Bob Wilson. It seemed that the policeman noticed my reluctance because he looked at me closer.

There was an uncomfortable silence until finally Captain Rogers asked, "Who was the guy who took the picture?"

Relieved, I answered quickly, "Mr. Jennings, he--"

"Oh yeah, we know Mr. Jennings. He's doing a book on early Great Lakes shipping or something. He's been here digging into old police records from way back. I bet you two really hit it off."

"Yes, we did, but we kinda got off to a shaky beginning." Then I related to him my meeting with Mr. Jennings. The captain laughed, but he understood that it was no laughing matter at the time. I then went on to relate other incidents that had happened with Angela, including her fascination with the tool box and her possible association with the Summers.

As soon as I mentioned the Summers, he again interrupted, "Yeah, we heard about them. That young reporter--Wilson--came by and asked me about that case. I guess he found the story in the newspaper morgue, and my name was mentioned as one of the policemen working on the case. Seems this Wilson would like to dig up the story again." I was glad that Bob Wilson was true to his word and was sincere in his interest. But I didn't know why Bob Wilson's sincerity should concern me.

Captain Rogers was continuing, "Of course, I wish the reporter good luck, but I don't have much hope. The little girl has been missing too long. Besides, we can't help much. We've had a lot of work piled on us all of a sudden. Some GM executive picked his kids up from his ex-wife's place in Dearborn and brought them up here for a vacation on a big cabin cruiser. Well, the coast guard found the boat capsized just off the southern shore of Drummond Island, but no executive or kids. Then we're supposed to be looking for the vice president of a small bank in Wellingham, Ontario. Seems he and his brother, who also works at the bank, ran off with $100 grand of the bank's money. Also, there's a dope ring operating out of Mackinac City with some agents here is Randolph City. On top of all that, the Flint police warned me that there might be a child molester running around in these parts."

I came to attention at the mention of the child molester. "Could this child molester have anything to do with Angela?" I asked.

"Possibly, I thought of that too. Of course, we don't know too much about this guy. It seems a little girl accused this guy of molesting her, but when it came to actually pressing charges, she backed down, so if we would really press him, even if we knew where he is, we could be charged with harassment."

He paused thoughtfully, then changed the subject and went on as if he were thinking aloud, "What really baffles me is why no one has reported her missing or identified her. We've knocked on doors all along the coast from twenty miles south of Silver Isle to Mackinac City, and no one recognizes the little girl from the picture we've shown of her. Mr. Jennings must have been gone when we were combing his neighborhood." When I nodded my head, he continued, "No one saw anything unusual the night she came to you, except one guy in a cottage about a mile from your place saw a bright glow on the lake--like a fire--about 3:00 in the morning. But so far that's all we've got."

"I wish I could help you more," I said. "Maybe the psychiatrist will be able to learn something more. Oh did you manage to get us an appointment?"

"Yeah, I did, and Judy Baldwin called me to tell me what you both had talked about—the doctor and all. I guess she had talked to the doctor, and he thinks the child could handle both appointments in the same day. The psychiatrist's appointment is at 1:00, and the doctor's is before that, at 11:00. Think that would be all right?"

"I guess so. Judy told me the two doctors were in the same building."

"Yeah, not too far from the police station. I'll show you the building when we go over to our station, that is if you can come with me tonight. I want you and the child to come over to get her finger-printed. You may know, a lot of parents have agreed to let their kids be finger printed because of all the kidnapping that's been going on. Do you think Angela would mind being finger printed? Maybe her prints are on record somewhere."

"That would probably be a good idea. She's been very cooperative so far."

"Good, why don't you come over to the station right after we finish our ice cream?"

Before answering I looked at my watch. "I really wanted to be home before dark. I'm kinda scared of going back through the woods after dark."

"Let's see, it won't get dark till about 10:00, so you've got about an hour and a half. I tell you what, we'll give you a police escort home, and we'll check out the cottage before you go in."

Just as I was agreeing to the plan, Angela and Sergeant Adams came back to the booth. After they sat down and we had begun devouring our sundaes, I explained to Angela about the finger printing idea, and as I predicted, she passively agreed.

When we finished our ice cream, Angela and I got into the back of the police car and rode over to the station. I didn't know about Angela, but I was fascinated by all the gadgets in the car--the wire partition that separated the criminals from the police, the radio crackling messages that only the officers could understand, and the button that would switch on the siren.

The policemen parked in their designated spot by the gray stone city building that housed the police station and city jail. I guess I expected a huge, bustling room swarming with officials questioning suspicious-looking characters, so I was surprised to see a small room with three ordinary desks, each flanked by green filing cabinets. The only objects in the room even suggesting police trappings were a glass-enclosed gun case housing six rifles and a bulletin board holding wanted posters.

Only two men were present in the room. One looked to be in his early twenties, his wiry, athletic body dressed in a khaki uniform. He was lounging back in his swivel chair with his feet propped up on the desk. The other man was Bob Wilson, who was perched on the young man's desk with his long legs draped over the front. I expected the young policeman to jerk to attention at the arrival of his superiors, but he maintained his casual position and only nodded his head when the captain introduced us to him.

Bob Wilson smiled broadly, his black eyes twinkling mischievously. "Well, you really caught some ornery looking characters this time, Sergeant," he said in a fake cowboy accent. "What did they do, rob a bank?"

I couldn't help but smile, but Angela was not amused. She again cowered behind me, but at least this time she didn't scream. I would have given anything to know why Bob Wilson terrorized her so.

Captain Rogers watched Angela's reaction, and he asked Bob, "Son, are you sure you've never seen this child? She acts like you're the bogey man."

"I know," Bob answered. "I'm beginning to get a complex. Could it be my beard? Has she reacted to anyone else who has a beard as she has to me, Amanda?"

I noticed the officers glance at each other knowingly when the reporter called me by my first name, so I answered a little sharper than I would have otherwise to dispel any conclusions they may have jumped to. "I don't think she's seen anyone else with a beard. I can't remember any museum guests with beards."

"I guess the men you see are clean-cut, flag-waving Americans who have the decency to shave every day, right?" His question was made in a mocking, humorous tone, and he was still grinning his bold, infectious grin.

Probably to steer us away from a dangerous topic, Captain Rogers quickly told the young policemen, named Jim Lawson, and Bob Wilson about the finger printing idea, and Sergeant Adams coaxed Angela out from behind me to his desk where the finger printing set was kept. Since the three policemen were solicitous and attentive to

Angela she lost some of her reticence and began to demonstrate normal childlike curiosity at putting her fingers in the black, mud-like putty and then transferring her prints on the paper.

"I hope this finger print idea works, but I just can't figure why no one has reported that little tike missing," Bob Wilson said as he walked over to where I was standing.

"No, I can't either," I said absently as I watched Angela daintily sticking each of her fingers in the putty.

"You know, this reminds me of something that happened to me when I was about eight or nine. One day a little stray puppy followed me home from school. He was a dog like Benji--a Cockapoo I think--and I fell in love with him and he with me. Of course, I begged my folks to let me keep him, and they agreed, but my father told me that I had to put an ad in the paper describing the puppy because he was sure someone had lost it. The ad had to stay in for one week.

"Well, I'll tell you, that was the longest week in my life. Every time the phone rang I jumped. When no one claimed him by the end of the week, I thought I was home free, and the two of us became best buddies. But then after about three more weeks passed, a man came with a picture he had taken of the dog just before he had been lost. There was no denying that it was his dog. You see, he hadn't seen my ad when it was first put out because he and his wife had been at the Mayo Clinic getting treatments for their son who was dying of cancer. He told me that normally he would let me keep the pup, but his son was devastated without him. So, of course, I gave him up. I think that was the saddest day of my life."

I could feel hot tears sting my eyes. "I don't know why your story reminds you of Angela's. She's hardly a lost puppy."

His eyes pierced into mine. "No, of course not, but I can tell you already love that little girl more than you want to admit, even to yourself. And I think, deep down, you're hoping no one will come for her."

Bob had expressed the very thought I had been trying to deny. I protested vehemently in order to deny the fact that he had correctly analyzed my feelings. I was surprised that part of me was enjoying this excitement, and I realized that I was "falling in love" with the child. "That's not true. I hope Angela regains her memory and finds her family. I just want her to be happy."

"I know, Amanda," Bob said as he gently patted my shoulder. "I shouldn't have said anything, but I just don't want you to get hurt. I have a feeling that you've already been hurt, just recently."

I flinched as if he had physically struck me. "Oh, and are you a mind reader as well as a reporter, Mr. Wilson?" I asked sarcastically.

"I think all good reporters have to be mind readers in a way, but I've made you mad again. Forgive me," and he bowed gallantly, like a knight to his lady.

I turned my head quickly and brushed away my tears because Angela and the policemen were coming over my way. "Well, I guess that's that. We'll escort you home now, ladies," said Captain Rogers.

"O-Okay," I stammered, "Just take us back to my car and then you can follow us back home."

"Is it all right if I come along with you?" Bob Wilson asked the officers. "I came over here tonight to see if I could sniff out a news story. Maybe something will develop along the way."

"You can come, but I doubt if anything is going to happen. We've had a slow night."

We all walked out to the police car in silence, apparently each involved in our own thoughts. After Captain Rogers pointed out the professional building where the two doctors' offices were across the street, the two policemen sat up front and Bob Wilson scooted in beside me and Angela in the back. I was very aware of the masculine smell of his cologne, and I was strangely disturbed by the feel of his arm up against mine. I hadn't sat this close to a man, other than my father, since my fateful drive with Paul when we broke up, and I was dismayed to realize that my heart was thumping like a silly school girl's. As soon as we got to the parking lot where my car was parked, I rushed out of the police car with a mixture of relief and reluctance. I couldn't understand the feelings Bob Wilson provoked in me.

Captain Rogers called out to me before I got into my car, "Miss Stevens, stay in your car until we have a look around your place."

"All right," I answered as I slid into the front seat and unlocked the other door for Angela. She seemed tired and was even quieter than usual. I watched my driving carefully all the way back; after all, I was being followed by two policemen.

When we got to the winding, dirt road that led to the museum, I slowly inched the car toward the cottage, not knowing what to expect. The trees and bushes that added such beauty in the daylight looked ominous at night. As we passed the huge, black ship's cannon, positioned about twenty feet from the back of the cottage, I thought I saw someone running toward the entrance to the cottage. The policemen must have seen him, too, because all of a sudden they threw open their doors and started running, one in the direction after the intruder and the other in the opposite direction. I heard one of them say, "Stop, or we'll shoot!"

I stopped the car and scooted over to Angela and took her in my arms. She was trembling violently as if she had a chill. I spoke more soothingly than I felt, "It'll be all right, Angela, it's probably just some man who got lost and got scared when we pulled up."

I couldn't see much--all I could hear was running feet. Then all three seemed to converge at one time in front of the spotlights beamed on the lighthouse. I gasped when I finally saw the alleged intruder. He had light hair, was about six foot one, and had a thin, wiry build. I was sure the man was Paul.

Chapter 7

"Angela," I cried, excitedly, "It really is all right. I'm sure I know that man. He's my fia-friend. Come with me and we'll meet him."

She and I both got out of her side of the car, and I took her hand and practically dragged her up the hill. Bob Wilson was also getting out of the police car. Evidently they had told him to wait until the danger passed.

As we were running up the hill, I called out to the officers, "Wait, don't hurt him. I know him. He's Paul Morris, my--friend. He was just looking for me. I'm sure--" I stopped mid-sentence because when I reached the three men, I discovered to my dismay that the stranger was not Paul--just a man who had similar physical characteristics as he. I was bitterly disappointed and embarrassed, but I was also curious about the real identity of the intruder.

"You really know this man, Miss Stevens? Then why were you running away, Son?" Captain Rogers asked.

Before he could answer, I said, "Captain, I don't know him after all. He just looked like someone I used-- someone from home I knew--know." I could feel Bob

Wilson's eyes scrutinizing me closely, and I stepped out of the glare of the spotlights into the darkness to hide my face which I was sure was red.

"I really wasn't sneaking around," the man's voice betrayed his fear. "I just came here because I saw the ad in the paper asking for a handy man around here. I see you have a sign up on the window, and I wanted to apply."

"Why did you run, then?" asked Sergeant Adams.

"I guess I was scared. I was just going to go up to the cottage and wait for whoever was in the car, but then you yelled, 'Stop or we'll shoot,' and I didn't know you were police, so I ran."

The officers looked less suspicious and the captain modified his tone when he asked, "What's your name and where are you from?"

My name is Greg Rothman, and I'm from a little town in Wisconsin. I go to the University of Wisconsin during the winter, but during the summer I try to get odd jobs at marinas or boat docks because my dad has always owned boats, and I grew up with them. You can check all this out. I've got my driver's license, social security card, and other identification papers with me.

"Well, we will check them out. Why don't we all step inside and get better acquainted," invited Captain Rogers.

As soon as I unlocked the door, we all trooped inside. The two policemen quickly moved from room to room, bursting through the doors and scanning every corner of the cottage. The handy man applicant looked very bewildered. I was sure he already regretted stopping at the cottage.

After the kitchen had been searched, I offered to make coffee for all my visitors. Then I asked if the men would mind carrying in the clothes and groceries I had bought. I felt a delightful sense of power as I watched four men do my bidding.

Angela stayed right beside me everywhere I went, but I could see that she was tired, so as soon as I started the coffee perking, I took her upstairs, helped her into her pajamas, and tucked her in bed. I held her closely trying to reassure her that everything was all right, and when I did lay her down, she instantly went to sleep.

When I came downstairs, all the men were in the living room, and Captain Rogers was explaining to the bewildered Mr. Rothman the reason for all the precautions.

"So you see why we took out after you the way we did. And we're going to have to check out your credentials carefully because we have to protect that little girl up there from all possible dangers."

"I understand, Sir," said the newcomer, as he opened his billfold, "Here's my driver's license and social security card, and here's my student ID card from the university. Also, you can call Professor Brink at the university and Mr. Thomas who was my former employer at the last marina I worked at in St. Ignace, if you want some references.

"Okay, Son, here, you keep your cards. The pictures look like you as much as any identification pictures look like the people they are identifying. Do you have numbers where I can call those two people you mentioned? If you're going to start working here, we'll need to clear you soon."

"Sure, I have them written down here somewhere," he said, smiling.

As he again searched through his billfold, I suggested that everyone come into the kitchen for some snack cakes I had bought and for some coffee. Bob Wilson and Sergeant Adams came in right away, and Captain Rogers and Greg Rothman followed soon after Greg had produced the numbers asked for. I was becoming an expert in ordering men around for now I had Bob and Sergeant Adams pull out the table so that the four men could sit around it. After I put out the cakes and poured the coffee, I sat on a stool next to the counter.

Instead of entering into the conversation the men were engaged in, I found myself giving the two young bachelors a single girl's appraisal. I automatically compared both of them to Paul, and I realized why I had mistaken Greg for him. All three men were just about the same height, but Greg and Paul were both blonde and blue-eyed, while Bob had jet-black hair and snapping black eyes. Of course, the most noticeable difference between the men was that Bob sported a beard and mustache, and the other two men were both clean-shaven. If I had been making a preference between Greg and Bob based only on looks, I would have chosen Greg. Maybe I just didn't like

Bob's beard, but probably I liked Greg's looks because I had always been attracted to blondes. In fact, I had always wanted to be a small, delicate blonde myself, instead of the tall, big-boned brunette I actually was. I wasn't fat, but I certainly didn't have the fragile, helpless look I desired.

I was so caught up in my appraisals that I didn't hear the captain talking to me, "Miss Stevens, Miss Stevens, are you still with us?"

I felt my face flush as I stammered, "I'm sorry, I-I guess I was thinking about someone--something else."

Bob Wilson looked at me with a smirk, and Captain Rogers went on. "I was just saying, here we are deciding that Mr. Rothman is going to work here if his credentials check out, but you're the one who's going to be working with him. Do you have any objections to his being hired for this job?"

"No," I answered, probably too hastily, "I'll be glad for his help, but I think the Parks and Recreation Department has the final say."

"Sure, but our input will have a lot to say about who gets hired," stated the captain. "By the way, I don't think you've met Miss Stevens, formally at least. Mr. Rothman, this is Miss Amanda Stevens, and this is Mr. Bob Wilson, reporter for the Randolph City News."

Greg Rothman nodded politely to Bob Wilson, but he turned to me with a smile that could have been in a toothpaste ad; it left me a little dazzled. "I'm very glad to meet you, Miss Stevens. I was wishing like crazy a little while ago that I was this Paul you thought I was."

"Actually it's just your build and hair that are like his, but I was pretty embarrassed when I found out you weren't Paul."

"Oh, don't be. I must have fairly common features. A lot of people think I'm someone else. Now what brings you up to this desolate area, Miss Stevens?"

"Please call me Amanda," I requested, and Bob Wilson raised his eyebrows and started coughing as if he were choking on his coffee. I ignored him and continued, "Well, I'm a school teacher down south of here, and a man I teach with knows the Sanders--the regular caretakers of the museum. He told me that they were going out west this summer for their son's wedding, and they needed someone to take over for them for the summer. I love history--that's what I teach--so I thought this sounded like an ideal job, and I applied and got it."

"I'm sure I'll really like this job, if I get it. I didn't know that my boss would be a pretty school teacher."

I blushed and glanced at the other men. The two officers were trying politely to hide their smiles, while Bob Wilson was scowling. I was surprised at his reaction. Could he be jealous, I wondered, but dismissed the thought immediately.

For once, Sergeant Adams broke the silence. "Well, Captain, we better get going. We've got some work to do tonight. Did you have a car, Son?" he asked Greg.

"No, I have a motor cycle, but I left it down at the entrance to the road that comes up here because I didn't know exactly what the road would be like on up. So, I'll just walk down and get it. I'm staying at a cottage in Randolph City. By the way, is there any place I can stay if I get this job?"

"Yes," I answered, "there's a small shed out back that is equipped with a bed, a two-burner heat plate, a refrigerator, and a bathroom."

"Sounds good to me," he said. "I hope I'll be seeing you soon, Amanda." He and the policemen pushed their chairs back and started for the front door; all of them murmured thanks for the refreshments and said conventional good-byes. Bob Wilson still sat at the table with a scowl on his face.

"Are you coming, Wilson?" called the captain from the living room.

"In a minute," he answered, and then he looked at me with his piercing eyes. "I would watch my step around strangers if I were you--especially this one. I don't trust him."

I was startled, "Why not?"

"Oh, I don't know. Why was he sneaking around here? If he wanted this job, he could have gone directly to the Department of Parks."

"Maybe he wanted to look the place over before he decided to apply," I suggested, then I continued in a sharp voice, "You know, you seem to contradict yourself. Just yesterday you were preaching to me about caring about people and getting involved, but twice tonight you've warned me not to get too involved."

He looked a little abashed, "Yeah, I guess you're right. I know you can't help but get involved with little Angela. I admire the care and love you've shown her, and I don't think you should stop just because you're going to be hurt when or if her real family comes. But this Greg Rothman--I would be careful not to trust him too far. I still say he was sneaking around."

Bob Wilson was probably the most exasperating man I'd ever met. "Mr. Wilson," I said firmly, "I'm a big girl and can take care of myself quite nicely, thank you. From now on, if you don't mind, I'll pick out my own friends and involve myself with whomever I please."

Instead of being angry, Bob's eyes began twinkling and he grinned his infuriating grin. "Oops, I've done it again. It's 'Mr. Wilson' again. I'll bet you're quite a school teacher; you probably don't allow a bit of nonsense in your classroom. But I've got to go or I'll miss my ride. See ya later, Teach." Saluting jauntily, he bounded out of the room and out the door, leaving me with anger and amusement churning together. I thought I would probably never be able to figure out this man.

I put the dishes in the sink and put away the rest of the groceries. Then I walked upstairs quietly and got ready for bed in the dim light of the night light I had bought after the first night I had stayed in the cottage. Just before I lay down, I remembered to lay out one of Angela's pretty new dresses because I wanted her to go to church with me the next morning. I wondered if she had ever been to church before--if she were Catholic, Protestant, or Jewish. There was so much about this little girl that was a mystery. I pondered the questions about Angela, about Bob, and about Greg for a long time before I finally went to sleep. Just before I drifted off, I realized I had forgotten to mention Mr. Jennings' picture to Bob or show it to the police.

Sunday morning dawned bright and clear--a day that made me feel like saying, "This is the day that the Lord hath made." I had dreamed about Paul again, but Janelle wasn't in the dream. In fact, it was happy and romantic, but as I was savoring the joy in the dream, I was jolted awake when I remembered that Paul had been transformed to Greg Rothman about halfway through it. As soon as that thought hit me, I could almost hear an audible inner voice warning me that Greg Rothman was not Paul, and I'd better not try to make him into Paul. Strange, the inner voice had sounded a lot like Bob Wilson.

However, I couldn't waste much time in speculation this morning if I was going to go to church. I gently woke Angela, "Get up, Sweetheart, it's Sunday morning--time for church."

She stretched lazily and yawned just like a little kitten. "Do we have to get the museum ready this morning?"

"No, Honey, the museum doesn't open till 2:00 today. We're going to church. Do you know what church is?"

"Sure, it's a place where we pray and sing and listen to stories about Jesus." I turned to her in surprise. She had just answered all of my questions I had about her religious background. She had evidently been to church--a church that taught about Jesus. It was strange that she remembered some things, but one part of her mind seemed to be blocked out.

We both showered, primped, curled, and put on pretty summer dresses. I was amused to watch Angela mimic me in all I did to get ready. After we looked as good as we could, we ate some sweet rolls I had bought at the store. It wasn't a greatly nutritional breakfast, but it was quick and tasty on a hurried Sunday morning.

About five miles from the cottage was a little white wooden church, complete with a steeple and bell. The bell rope was being pulled by one of the teen-age boys in the church, and the peal was sending out a cheerful invitation for miles around. I had only been to this church once before; the only other Sunday that I had been at the cottage, I had tried a larger church in Randolph City, but I liked the smallness of this one. Besides, it was much closer, and I could get back to the museum easier.

Angela held tightly to my hand as we walked in. Sunday School must have just dismissed because there were many people milling around in the foyer outside the heavy glass doors that led to the main sanctuary. We had just barely crossed the threshold when an elegant lady with a beautifully polished smile came toward us with an outstretched hand. She was dressed in a soft, dainty dress, white with bright tiny daisies sprinkled over it. A green linen jacket matched the leaves on the daisies. Daisy-patterned necklace and earrings completed the ensemble. "Good morning, ladies," she said, as she gently took my free hand in her soft, impeccably manicured one. "I don't think I have had the pleasure of meeting you before. I am Sandy Thomas."

I smiled back while Angela squeezed my other hand more tightly and quietly withdrew behind me. "I'm Amanda Stevens, the caretaker at the old lighthouse museum, and this is---"

"Oh yes," said our greeter when she got a good look at Angela, "the little girl in the paper." Her smile diminished ever so slightly, and she hurried through her speech. "It's so very nice to have you both here today. Please come again. I'm sorry, I have to go now; there are some more new people coming in." The lady's change of manner really didn't bother me. I realized she was probably just uncomfortable being confronted with a little girl who was shrouded in such mystery. She really didn't know what to say that wouldn't sound nosy or tasteless.

Others turned to look at us as we walked toward the sanctuary, but most were busy chattering or gathering children together before the worship service. As I opened the heavy glass doors that separated the foyer from the sanctuary, I heard the organist softly playing the organ, and the sweetness of the music combined with the quiet of the room brought a welcome peace to my spirit. There were only about twenty pews on each side of the red-carpeted center aisle, and only a few parishioners sitting in them, mostly senior citizens whose class evidently met in the sanctuary. These people nodded at us as we walked down the aisle, but then I saw them look at Angela and start whispering to each other. I was sure many of them recognized her from the newspaper story.

The service should have been uplifting, but I couldn't keep my thoughts corralled in the spiritual realm. I kept looking at Angela. She seemed to know some of the songs--at least the choruses. When the pastor asked us to pray, she sweetly bowed her head and folded her hands, and I could see her lips move in a whispered prayer. I felt guilty; I should be praying that Angela's memory would return, and that she'd find her family, but I had been pretty lax with my praying ever since my broken engagement. I didn't admit even to myself that I blamed God for Paul's leaving me, but sometimes I would think, "Why did God send Janelle to our church at all, or why can't God show Paul the mistake he is making?"

As soon as the benediction was over, Angela and I started to leave, but a tired-looking lady, with a wrinkled, slightly askew attire brought on by trying to control four lively youngsters through the service, stopped me and introduced herself as Mrs. Robertson. She was honestly curious about Angela, and she came right out and asked if she was the little girl in the paper. Soon other people were crowded around us, and I began to become a little irritated. "After all," I thought, "Angela is not a side-show freak at a county fair." But the people weren't trying to be unkind. I suppose Bob Wilson would say they were just concerned. I was probably too sensitive.

We managed to get out the door of the church where we shook hands with the pastor. He and his wife had come over to the museum the day after my first Sunday at his church. He was a kindly man in his fifties, tall with black hair sprinkled liberally with gray. His wife looked like a Norman Rockwell painting of the perfect pastor's wife. She was a sweet, grand-motherly woman with auburn hair, not yet turned gray, and eyes as blue as a summer sky. There was nothing showy or pretentious about this couple, just common, God-fearing, grass-roots people that inspired their flock to be the best they could be. The pastor talked to both Angela and me, and she reacted to him about the way she had the policemen and the doctor. I was beginning to formulate Angela's personality as that of an outgoing, friendly little girl. Her present shyness was probably due to her amnesia.

As I turned from the pastor to walk down the five stone stairs in front of the church, I stopped dead in my tracks. There at the bottom of the steps was Bob Wilson in light blue slacks with a short-sleeved, pale blue striped shirt, open at the neck. He was grinning from ear to ear. I walked down the stairs with Angela again gripping my hand and said, "What are you doing here?"

Bob laughed so loud that people turned and stared at him. "Why, I'm here for the same reason you're here. I went to church."

"You were in church, here? I don't believe you. I didn't see you."

"I was about four rows straight back from you. If you don't believe me, ask Pastor Thomas. He knows I was here."

I looked back up at the pastor who was smiling indulgently at us. I was still shocked. "How did you know I was going to be here today? I never told you what church I go to."

"Well, I don't want to deflate your ego, but I've been going to this church for about a month. I was gone on assignment the Sunday that must have been your first Sunday to come. My pastor at the church I attended when I was in school knows Pastor Thomas, and he suggested I come here."

I must have still looked shocked because he guffawed again. "You're still surprised aren't you, Amanda? I bet you never expected a reporter, especially a bearded one, to go to church unless there was a story in it. Everyone knows that all reporters are loud-mouthed jerks who would sell their own grandmothers for a story."

I felt justifiably rebuked. "I'm sorry, I guess I did have a poor opinion of reporters--especially bearded ones." I grinned what I hoped was an apologetic grin.

Bob's eyes softened. "It's all right. I think your conservative, mid-west hang-ups are refreshing. You're so honest; I can read your face like a book. For instance, I know that you're a little suspicious of me because of little Angela there, but I can also tell that you're kinda pleased when I come around."

He had done it again. I would just get around to liking him, and his arrogance would turn me off again. I spoke in an angry whisper so no one could hear me, "I think you're reading too much between the lines of that book. At least you're right in the first statement you made. I am still suspicious of you because of Angela." I looked down at the child who was staring at Bob with the same frightened eyes she always had when he was around, and I thought of Mr. Jennings' picture.

I went on in the same belligerent tone, "And by the way, I saw a picture the other night that a man who lives along the shore had taken of Angela and a man who looked a lot like you. You wouldn't know anything about it, would you?"

Suddenly he became very serious. "No, I swear, I never saw this child until I took her picture at the cottage. Who is this man, anyway?"

I hesitated for a second, wondering if I was giving too much information, but I didn't see any harm in telling him about Mr. Jennings and his photography hobby and the book he was writing. Bob looked thoughtful when I finished. "Maybe he knows more about Angela than he's saying. I hate to nag, but you've got to be careful of strangers, Amanda."

"Does that include you?"

"Okay, you got me there. Maybe it does, right now, but I think it's time to change my stranger status. I think both you and Angela need to get to know me better. Today is a gorgeous summer day--a day just crying out for a picnic. Why don't we have a picnic--the three of us?"

His friendliness again was working its spell on me, and I discovered I was genuinely disappointed to say, "Oh, I can't today. I've got to open the museum at 2:00, and since I closed early yesterday, I should be on time today."

"I can fix that. I'll go down to Kentucky Fried Chicken and get a bucket of chicken with all the fixings.

Then I'll bring them over to your cottage, and we can eat at the picnic table in the backyard. How about it? It'll be my treat."

"I guess it'd be all right." I hesitated as I looked down at Angela.

"Listen, if you still think I have ulterior motives, I'll make sure you've got witnesses." Then to my utter embarrassment, he bellowed out to all the parishioners who were still talking to each other in the church yard, "I want all of you to know that these two pretty ladies are going to have a picnic with me, so if anything happens to them, you'll all know they were with me last."

The people turned and looked at us and laughed. I wished that I could fall into a hole. I was ready to tear Bob Wilson from limb to limb, but when I glared up at him, he was grinning impishly as he made the classic male chauvinist observation, "You know, you're really cute when you're angry. I'll go get that chicken now, and I'll meet you at your place before you can say, 'Pass the biscuits.'" Once again he left me exasperated, yet amused. I was sure of one thing--the picnic was not going to be dull. Life around Bob Wilson could never be boring.

As soon as we got home, Angela and I scooted upstairs quickly to change into picnic clothes. I had tried to build enthusiasm in her for the picnic with Bob Wilson all the way home from church. All I had managed to do, however, was get a passive acceptance from her. But I was aware of an excitement I hadn't felt for months--maybe forever. I had to admit to myself that while I had enjoyed being with Paul, I had never felt the excitement with him that was described in romantic novels. "Maybe," I thought, "Paul and I had known each other for so long we had missed the thrill of the first infatuation of a new romance." I was surprised to be thinking of romance and infatuation in connection with Bob Wilson. I supposed that the excitement stemmed from his exasperating personality and our inevitable confrontations. I was certain there was nothing romantic, in the sense of love, connected with my feelings for him.

My thoughts were jerked back to the present when Angela asked, "Are these clothes all right for me to wear, Amanda?" She was holding a pair of white shorts and a red and white striped shirt.

"Sure, Honey, those are fine. It's so warm today, I think I'll wear some shorts, too." I figured Bob would probably stop at his house in Randolph City to change clothes since that was where the nearest fried chicken place was located.

After we dressed, Angela and I went down to the kitchen to find paper plates and cups, plastic knives, forks, spoons, and the plastic table cloth. I made a pitcher of iced tea and a pitcher of Kool-aide. I was pretty sure, if Angela was like most youngsters, she wouldn't like iced tea, but was she like most youngsters? I didn't know.

Angela and I carried our picnic gear outside and began setting the table. The sunshine felt warm and delicious while a soft breeze rustled through the trees--a perfect day for a picnic. I found myself humming a popular song as I worked. Angela was looking cheerful in spite of herself. Suddenly a shadow was cast over the table, and I felt hot breath on the back of my neck. I whirled around and was startled to find myself face to face with Greg Rothman.

"Oh," I gasped, "You startled me! I didn't know you were there."

"I'm sorry, I didn't mean to sneak up on you like that. I was just looking around at where I hope I'll be spending a lot of time."

The word "sneak" jarred into my mind. Wasn't it Bob Wilson who had accused Greg of sneaking around? But Greg's explanation was perfectly logical to me. I was sure he needed to see the area where he would probably be working. "Oh, that's all right," I answered. "I just didn't hear you. Did you park your cycle down at the road again?"

"Yeah, I wanted to hike through the woods. And besides, I was afraid maybe you and the little girl might sleep in late on this Sunday morning, so I didn't want my cycle to awaken you."

"That was thoughtful of you, but we woke up fairly early to go to church."

"I might have guessed that you are church-goers. I used to go quite a bit with my folks, but when I was in school, I never seemed to find a church I liked as well as mine at home. Where do you go?"

I told him about Pastor Thomas' little white church in the woods. He looked genuinely interested in my description. "That really sounds ideal," he remarked with a twinkle in his eyes. "Maybe if I get this job, I can go with you sometime."

I felt my face flush again. I wished I could be more sophisticated around men. "Sure, that-that would be fine," I managed to stammer. Our attention was diverted from the subject of church to the sound of the motor of a car coming up the hill.

"Is that a tourist coming to the museum, already?" asked Greg.

"No, it's only Bob Wilson. He went to Kentucky Fried Chicken to get us a picnic dinner. Have you eaten? I don't know how much food he got. Maybe I can get you something--" By this time I was thoroughly embarrassed.

"Don't worry, Amanda. I had a late breakfast. I just came to look the place over. Could I see where I'll be bunking--that is if I get this job?"

"Sure, I'll go get the key to the shed. You can check out all the equipment out there too. The lawn mower and weed cutter and all that stuff is in there."

I started toward the kitchen where the key hung on a peg near the back door just as Bob Wilson stalked up toward the table with two large white bags bearing the familiar picture of Colonel Sanders. As I suspected, he had changed into shorts and a T-shirt.

"Hello, fellow chicken lovers." His mouth had a half smile on it that didn't reach his eyes. "Well, hi there, Rothman. What brings you here on a nice Sunday afternoon?"

"Oh, I thought I'd just check out my new home, and of course I don't mind getting another look at my pretty lady bosses," he said as he winked at me and Angela who was diligently folding napkins in neat triangles.

I could feel a humiliating blush again creep up my face, so I quickly started talking rapidly to hide my embarrassment. "Well, Bob, it looks like you got enough food to feed a small army there. Greg said he had a late breakfast, but we could probably persuade him to join us. Angela, set another place at the table. Greg, you can manage at least one piece of chicken, can't you?"

"Well, I--" Greg began.

"Amanda, maybe Mr. Rothman has other plans. We don't want to make him feel obligated if he needs to go somewhere else." Bob interrupted with a scowl on his face.

"Well, actually, I'm free for the rest of the day, and that chicken does smell good--even through the bags. But are you sure you have enough?" Greg asked with a rather appealing bashful grin.

"Of course, we have enough." I gushed enthusiastically. "I think Bob bought enough chicken to feed us, plus all the visitors to the museum, for two days."

"It's really not that much. There's a big bucket there, but it's not full of chicken. But you can stay, Rothman, if you want. There'll probably be enough." I glared at the reporter while he talked. I couldn't understand why he was so uncharitable. The thought again crossed my mind that Bob was jealous of Greg, but, as before, I quickly dismissed the idea.

For the next two or three awkward minutes, we went back and forth in polite arguing, with my stubborn insistence that Greg stay, Bob's half-hearted assurance that we welcomed him, and Greg's weak protests that he didn't want to impose.

Finally, Angela tiptoed behind me and gently grasped my hand and pulled me toward her indicating that she wanted to whisper something. I had to listen very closely to hear her say, "Amanda, could we eat now? I'm awfully hungry."

I had to smile as I turned to the men and said, "What do you say we eat now and argue later? We ladies are hungry."

Both men chuckled, and at last we all sat down. The conversation for the first part of the meal consisted of requests to have the biscuits, gravy, slaw, salt, pepper, butter, and all the rest passed. For the first time in months, I was thoroughly enjoying myself. The food was delicious; the weather was perfect, and the companionship was superb. A girl doesn't often have two handsome men to dine with.

During the course of the meal, Bob Wilson seemingly started to lose some of his animosity toward Greg. After all the food was passed, our first topic of conversation was the weather, and soon we were comparing the gorgeous summer day to the bitter winter we had just experienced in Michigan. Bob turned to Greg and said, "Was your winter in Wisconsin bad, this year, too?"

"Oh yeah, we had a real humdinger of a winter. I thought the snow would never melt."

Bob raised his eyebrows in a quizzical expression that I couldn't interpret. Then he said, "Say, speaking of Wisconsin--You went to the University in Madison, right?" Greg nodded his head in agreement, and Bob went on, "What did you think of Jeff Miller's record this year? Did you know him? I heard he was the talk of all the pros this year."

Greg looked away and hesitated just a split second before answering. "Oh, I heard of him, of course, but I didn't know him personally. I'm afraid I'm not much of a football fan."

A curious expression again came over Bob's face. "But--oh, yeah, I guess you did suggest that boating is your bag. Do you sail or motor?"

Greg's wonderful smile returned as he said, "Sailing is my favorite. My dad has owned sailboats since I was five years old. He started with a sixteen footer and kept buying bigger until his last one, which was a forty footer."

"You say his last--doesn't he have it any more?" I asked, not wanting to be left out of the conversation.

"No--well, you see, my parents both died in a car accident last year, and just this spring I sailed their boat up to a little town in the Upper Peninsula where I sold it to a friend of my folks. Then I bought my motorcycle, and I crossed over the Big Mac Bridge and traveled down the coast. I'm awfully glad this job came along. I had to send the money from the boat back to the University to pay for college debts. There wasn't a large amount of insurance money, and it seems it does take quite a bit of that green stuff to live, eh?"

Bob Wilson asked, "Have you lived in Wisconsin all your life? I noticed you have a slight accent and that 'eh' sounded very Canadian."

Greg's face seemed to redden, or maybe I just imagined it, but he laughed and said, "Oh, I was afraid of that. While I was in the UP, I met a Canadian fellow, and we bummed around together. I think his language rubbed off on me."

"Yeah, that can happen, I guess," said Bob, but his voice sounded suspicious and perplexed. An uneasy silence followed with each of us lost in our own thoughts.

Therefore, I was glad to see Mr. Jennings walking up the driveway.

"Hello, Mr. Jennings," I shouted out, shocking both Bob and Greg who were sitting across the table from me with their backs to the driveway, "Come on up and join us." I looked at Bob's face when he saw our visitor, but his expression was simple curiosity without any sign of recognition.

Mr. Jennings didn't appear to recognize anyone either as he approached our table. I made all of the introductions and told Bob and Greg how I had met him. "Let me go up and get the picture," I suggested at the end of my story. As I got up from the table, Bob began questioning Mr. Jennings in his reporter-like fashion. He didn't seem to fear anything that Mr. Jennings might reveal, and I thought that either he was not the man in the picture or that he was an excellent actor.

When I was half-way up the hill, I turned around to find Angela running to catch up to me. I realized with chagrin that I had just broken the specific rule Captain Rogers had laid down for me--letting Angela get out of my sight and leaving her with people I didn't really know. I

guess I still had a lot to learn about mothering. "I'm sorry,
Angela, I didn't mean to run off from you. Come with me
and we'll get the picture."

She looked at me and asked plaintively, "Do you
think Mr. Jennings will be able to help me get my
remembry back?"

Not wanting to raise her hopes only to have them
dashed again, I answered cautiously, "Well, Honey, last
night when he showed me the picture, he said that he had
never seen you before he took the picture, and he really
didn't get a good look at the man in it."

"Oh," she said dispiritedly, "but why did he take my
picture anyway?"

"I guess he enjoys taking pictures, especially of
children, and since you are so pretty, he especially wanted
your picture."

Her face brightened slightly, as any girl's does when
she's told she's pretty. Then she became very serious,
"Amanda, do you think the man in the picture looks like
Mr. Wilson."

I felt my heart pound, but I tried to answer casually,
"It's kinda hard to tell, Honey. We can only see his back,

but I wondered the same thing myself. Did you hear what he said when I asked him about it today at church? He still claims he never saw you before that first day he came to the cottage." By this time we had reached the bedroom, and without any more comments, I picked up the picture and we walked back down to the picnic table where the men were still sitting. I showed the photograph to Bob who then passed it on to Greg without making any comment.

"Where was this taken, Mr. Jennings?" asked Greg as he carefully scrutinized every detail of the picture.

"In front of my cottage, on down on the beach. I live about 100 yards on a hill above the beach."

"And you didn't see the man's face?" This time Bob asked the question.

"No, only his back, I'm afraid. And it seems this fellow has a pretty average build."

Greg voiced the words we were probably all thinking, "Yes, he's built like either Wilson or me, but of course, he does have dark hair."

Bob glared at Greg and harshly stated, "Lots of guys have dark hair, and hair can be bleached, you know."

Greg smiled, but there didn't seem to be much warmth in his smile. "Sure, I realize that. Nothing personal, eh?" Then he abruptly changed the subject. "I guess I've stuffed myself enough, and I'd better get busy doing what I was going to do in the first place. Amanda, can you get me that key, and I'll look at the shed and the equipment."

I scooted off the picnic bench and started up the hill toward the cottage. Greg came along behind us, and he casually rested his hand on my shoulder as we walked together. He was courteously thanking me for the invitation to dinner, but I was so flustered from the touch of his hand that I barely heard what he was saying.

When we got to the cottage, Greg took the keys and sauntered off to the shed. Then I remembered that I had again left Angela down at the table with Bob and Mr. Jennings, but this time she hadn't followed me, probably because they were both talking to her. I couldn't see how she was responding to them because her back was toward me. I rushed back down to hear Mr. Jennings ask her, "Do you remember if you know how to read, Angela?"

She nodded her head solemnly. "Yes, I remember reading in school."

We all looked at her with undivided attention, and Bob Wilson said, "That's great, Honey. Can you remember anything else about your school--like your teacher's name or the name of the school?"

After a breathtaking moment, she said, "I think my teacher's name was Mrs. Pauley, yeah, that's right, but I can't remember the name of the school."

Bob smiled at her with a tenderness I didn't know he possessed and said gently. "That's all right kiddo. I just wish I had the key that could open up that closed door in your head."

Angela was looking so uncomfortable under his gaze that I decided to break the spell. "Angela, could you bring down a garbage bag from the kitchen? I keep them in a box under the sink." As was her custom, she immediately jumped up to do my bidding, and Mr. Jennings volunteered to help her find them. She seemed to accept his company without any protests, so I didn't object either.

I began to gather all the dishes together and put caps on all the cartons containing leftovers. As I was bustling with the clean-up duties, Bob was helping himself to a second piece of the cherry pie he had bought.

"Thank you for the dinner," I said. "It was very delicious. I hope you're not angry that I invited Greg."

"Well, I was a little put out at first. You know, when a guy offers a dinner to a lady and she invites another guy along, the first guy might have a right to get upset."

"I know, but I just didn't think it would have been very polite to eat in front of him, and--

"Oh, it's all right. I'm not mad, just worried."

"Worried? About what?"

"I just don't trust Greg Rothman, if that's his name, now more than ever."

My surprised retort was canceled by Angela's and Mr. Jennings' return. All of us busied ourselves throwing away the paper plates, cups, and napkins we had used. Just as we started to carry everything up to the cottage, Angela shyly crept up to me and whispered, "Amanda, may I go swing on that swing in the back yard?"

She was talking about a simple tire swing that evidently Mr. Sanders had hung from a giant pine tree in the back yard. When I gave her permission to go, Mr.

Jennings suggested, "I'll push you on the swing, that is if it is all right with you, Amanda."

I saw no reason to refuse to let Mr. Jennings be with Angela. I was sure he would not harm her, and anyway the swing was in full view of the kitchen window where I would be washing dishes. Mr. Jennings seemed to delight in Angela's company, so I told him that he was welcome to push her in the swing.

Bob and I carried our garbage and dirty dishes up to the cottage, and he put away the leftovers as I washed the ice tea and Kool-aide pitchers. As soon as he finished, he looked out the back door at the swing. "Mr. Jennings certainly seems to enjoy kids, doesn't he? I just hope he doesn't have any ulterior motives."

"Boy, you don't trust anybody, do you?" I asked, but I continued before he could reply. "Actually, I only let her go out there with him because I can see the swing from this window."

"Yeah, I figured that. And to answer your question, I don't think you can be too careful as far as Angela is concerned, but I'm starting to lecture again."

"Yes, you are, but please tell me, what did you mean that you mistrust Greg now more than ever?"

"Well, for one thing, Wisconsin had a very calm, mild winter--the mildest in years."

"So, what does that have to do with your not trusting Greg?" I exclaimed.

"If you remember Greg said that Wisconsin had a terrible winter this last year."

"Well, a mild winter to one person might be a terrible one to another. Some people really hate winter, and all coldness is bad for them, but I hardly think Greg's evaluation of the winter is suspicious."

"But that's not the only problem. Another thing, Jeff Miller is not a football star."

"What?" I asked incredulously.

"When I asked Greg what he thought about Jeff Miller's record this year, he said he didn't know very much about football, but Jeff Miller is a six-foot-seven freshman who played center for the University of Wisconsin's varsity basketball team this year. He scored more points in one year than any other basketball player in the history of college basketball."

"So what! I'd never heard of him either. A lot of people aren't sports fans--even men."

"Yes, but you don't claim that you attended the University of Wisconsin last year. I saw the news reports of the big celebration they had for this guy in Madison. There were posters with his picture all over town and the campus, plus they had a big parade for him. Why, a guy would have had to be blind, deaf, and dumb not to know about this guy--if he indeed was in Madison last year."

"Maybe he has him mixed up with someone else. You know how you can hear a name and put that name on another face. Or maybe Greg wasn't on campus during the celebrations. You heard him say that his folks died last year. Maybe he was home during that time. I think you're nit-picking myself."

"I could be too suspicious. I guess it's an occupational hazard, but I do think I've seen more real life than you in your sheltered, mid-west environment."

"Probably so, but I hope I never get so sophisticated that I become so cynical and suspicious of everyone. What happened to the caring, compassionate person you told me about yesterday?"

"Okay, maybe you're right. I guess I'm prejudiced against Rothman because I just don't like him somehow, an attitude that isn't exactly Christian, I suppose. I just wish I could command the same loyalty from you that he is getting. I wonder if you like him so much because he looks like this Paul you knew at home."

Again he had triggered my anger. "I'm not defending Greg because he looks like Paul; I just don't like to see anyone attacked before he is proven guilty."

"Except me." For the first time, Bob had lost his amused, teasing manner, and he looked and sounded really angry as he continued, "You were ready to have me hanged just because the little girl was scared of me."

"Well, you've got to admit that she didn't react to Greg the way she did to you."

"Yes, I guess, but I can't explain that. I wish you'd believe me. I have never seen that child before."

"Okay, I'm sorry, but--" I broke off talking as Greg walked up to the door.

"Say, Bob, could you help me a minute? I need to push the lawn tractor out of the shed to work on it. I can't seem to get it started."

"Sure," he said and both men stalked out the door. I stood at the door watching them, but I was not really comprehending what I was seeing. My mind was busy rehashing the argument that Bob and I had just had. Although I wanted to believe that I was not interested in Greg, I had to admit I was thinking about him more than I should.

I was still standing at the door when Greg and Bob pushed the mower out to the top of the hill. When they began to tinker with the motor, Mr. Jennings sauntered up the hill to help investigate the problem. After a minute or two they managed to get the mower started, and they let it idle while Greg went back to the shed to get another tool. The last time I looked Bob was standing beside the mower, and Mr. Jennings was walking toward the display of stocks. If the phone had not rung, I might have seen exactly what happened, and I would have been spared the suspicion and anxiety of the weeks to come.

The person on the phone happened to be Judy telling me that Angela had an appointment with a Dr. Johnson, a medical doctor, at 11:00 the next day, before her appointment with the psychiatrist, Dr. Meadows. I thanked her, but told her that Captain Rogers had already given me the information and had also shown me the large medical building in Randolph City where the two doctors' offices were located. Our conversation took only about five minutes; then just as soon as I hung up, I heard a blood curdling scream coming from Angela. Terrified, I rushed out to see her lying on the ground with Greg on top of her.

Chapter 8

I can't remember how I got from the back door of the cottage to where Angela and Greg were, but suddenly I found myself clutching her trembling body close to me, and I don't know whether my heart or hers was pounding louder. Finally I was calm enough to ask, "What happened?"

Angela's voice sounded shrill when she said, "That thing there almost hit me."

I looked on down the hill where she was pointing and saw the lawn mower rammed against a tree, and I almost fainted. Evidently Angela had climbed off the swing and was walking toward the cottage when the mower somehow started rolling down the hill toward her. The machine was large enough to injure any adult in its path, and I was certain it would have killed Angela.

By this time Bob and Mr. Jennings had reached us, and it was Greg's turn to relate his part of the adventure. "I had just adjusted the carburetor, and I wanted to take the mower for a test run, so I set the brake--I'm sure I did--and I started walking down the hill to see if there were any large rocks or anything in the path. Just as I reached the little girl, I looked around because the roar of the engine sounded a lot closer. The mower was almost on top of us, so I grabbed her and we both rolled away."

After listening to Greg's story, Bob ran down to the mower and looked it over. In a moment he stormed back up to where we were still standing and shouted at Greg, "The brake isn't set on that, Rothman. I thought you said you set it."

"I'm sure I set it. Maybe the brake is defective," asserted Greg.

"Or maybe you didn't really set it!" Bob accused.

"Now what do you mean by that? By the way, you were up there too. You could have easily run over and released the brake while I was walking down the hill."

"Why would I want to do that?" asked Bob, "Besides, Mr. Jennings was up there too. You know I didn't go over to the mower, don't you?"

Mr. Jennings looked very uncomfortable when he answered, "I'm sorry, gentlemen, but I didn't see anything. I was looking at the stocks and imagining what it would have been like to be in them for hours, and as usual my imagination took over, and I didn't realize what was going on until I heard the little girl scream."

Bob and Greg were glaring at each other, then Greg said, "Well, how about it, Wilson? Did you release that brake?"

"Of course not! Did you really set it?"

"Yes, I did!" Greg almost spit the words out.

I finally managed to find courage to speak up. "Come on, Guys, maybe the brake doesn't work right like Greg said. The important thing is that no one was hurt. Now, I think Angela and I better go up to the cottage; it's time to open the museum."

All of us walked up to cottage in silence, but I could almost reach out and touch the oppressive tension amongst us. In spite of what I had said in my peace-making speech, I wondered if the brake had released by itself. If not, who was telling the truth? If Greg had deliberately released the brake, why did he push Angela out of the way? On the other hand, if Bob had released it, why did he purposely draw attention to the fact that it wasn't set? Since he was the first to the mower, he could have set it again before the rest of us got there. Instead of unraveling mysteries, the events of every day brought more and more.

I really didn't have time to dwell on the situation, though, because as soon as we reached the cottage, the first guests were pulling into the parking space. Angela and I rushed inside so that I could set up the guest book and the money box where I collected the entrance fees. When the visitors came in, a young family with two small children, I made them welcome, explained a few of the articles in the room, and involved myself in the routine of running a museum. Angela got her coloring book and crayons off of the top of my desk where I was keeping them, and she proceeded to create Crayola masterpieces for the rest of the day. I didn't know where Bob or Greg went; neither of them had come into the cottage. Mr. Jennings had briefly popped in and said good-bye to us when I was conducting my tour.

There were more visitors to the museum that beautiful Sunday than there had been since I had taken the job. Therefore I didn't have much time to ponder over any of the day's events. The last visitors didn't leave until 8:00, and as soon as they were out the door, Angela and I went in to the kitchen to have some cold, left-over chicken and potato chips. Angela was especially quiet through the whole meal, and I wondered if she was still upset by her accident and just didn't want to discuss it. But when I saw her eyelids drooping, I realized she was just tired. Of course, even extreme fatigue didn't supersede her normal politeness, for, after she finished eating, she carried her dishes to the sink and offered to help me wash and dry them.

"Thanks anyway, Honey," I said, yawning, "but I'm too tired right now to tackle these dishes. We'll take care of them in the morning. There are just a few anyway." Then she and I climbed the stairs, and I tucked her in bed. Thanks to the resilience of children, her brush with death didn't keep her from going to sleep almost as soon as she lay down.

I stood for a minute and looked at her as she slept. I was again awed by the child's beauty, but suddenly the horror of her close call with the runaway mower dawned upon me. I had a vision of Angela's perfect little body lying mangled and bleeding under the wheels of the machine. Suddenly I found myself sobbing, and my body shook uncontrollably. I lunged downstairs and threw myself on the couch and wept. I guess the terror of the whole weekend had finally caught up with me. I felt I had lived a whole year since that Friday morning that Angela had banged on my door.

In a few minutes, my sobbing and trembling subsided. I lay quietly on the couch and was just settling down when I was jolted by someone knocking at my door.

Wiping away my tears, I walked to the window where I opened the curtains a crack to see who was there. It was Bob Wilson, and now I had to make the decision of whether to let him in or not. Telling myself that his knocking would awaken Angela, I decided to open the door just a little bit, but left the bolt in place. "What are you doing here?" I hissed at him as he stood impatiently on the other side of the door.

"I'll tell you if you let me in. I promise I won't hurt you. If you want, I'll wait till you call the police and tell them I'm here, but I've got to talk to you."

"I guess you can come in, but you can't stay too long because I'm tired." I stated.

He bustled in and looked around the cottage.
"Where's Angela?' he asked. "I was wondering how she
was taking her accident, or near accident."

"Oh, I think she's handling it better than I am," I
said, and I turned around quickly to try to hide the tears
filling my eyes again, but I was not quick enough to evade
the sharp eyes of Bob Wilson.

He came up behind me and put his hands on my
shoulders. "Hey, what's the matter? Is everything just now
crashing down on you?"

I turned to him in surprise, "How did you know?"

"I told you, I'm a mind reader. I'm also a good
listener. Come over here and tell me all about it." With
that, he put his arm around my waist and guided me over
to the couch where he sat down close beside me and took
my hands in his.

His kindness touched me, and my chin started
quivering, and again the tears started flowing. Before I
knew what was happening, he enveloped me in his
muscular arms and held me close to him. I found myself
pouring out all my troubles in sobs that were probably
almost incoherent. "Bob, I'm so frightened. I mean, what

do I know about being a mother, especially the mother of a
child suffering from amnesia? It's such an awesome
responsibility; her life is in my hands. When I think about
what almost happened today, I--"

"Now wait," Bob interrupted, and he took my face in
his hand and looked directly in my eyes, "What happened
today was certainly not your fault. I think you're doing a
terrific job. Besides, her life is not really in your hands,
you know."

"What do you mean?"

"Well, I don't know where Angela's earthly father is,
or even if she has one, but I do know she's got a Heavenly
Father who's watching over her, and I'm sure He'll protect
her, and you too, if you just ask."

"I guess I just don't feel I can ask God anything right
now."

"Why, I know you must be a Christian, aren't you?"

"Yes," I said hesitantly, "but I haven't felt close
enough to Him since--uh--for a long time, and I feel guilty
right now."

"Guilty, but what for, or maybe you don't want to
tell me?"

"No, I don't mind telling you, but I'm surprised you don't already know. You've already lectured me once about it." He still looked puzzled, so I continued. "What I'm talking about is my feeling for Angela. I want her to find her family and be happy, but I don't think I can stand giving her up. It seems impossible that I've only known her for two days. I know, you warned me not to get too attached, but it's too late."

"Believe me, I understand. Even though Angela thinks I'm the monster from the deep, she has become very important to me, but so have you. That's why I've been playing big brother and lecturing you. I just don't know what I'd do if something happened to Angela, or you." Slowly, tentatively, he pulled me closer to him, and he tenderly brushed away the tears that lingered on my face. I knew he wanted to kiss me and, instead of resisting, I found myself longing for his kiss, and when our lips met, I matched his fervor with a passion I didn't realize I was capable of. For an exhilarating moment, I forgot that Angela was frightened of this man, and I forgot my exasperation with him, and I gave in to the excitement that had taken over every other emotion.

Bob looked at me with pleasant surprise, but when he started to kiss me again, I drew back, reluctantly regaining my composure. "No Bob, I-I don't think you should. Angela might wake up, and--"

Bob sighed and smiled sadly, "I should have known Miss Prudence would return. You know, you need to let yourself go. For a few minutes there, you were just really going with the flow, living on the wild side."

"I don't know what came over me. I'm not used to kissing men that I hardly know."

He laughed heartily. "I would venture to say that you aren't used to kissing many men, except for this mysterious Paul. Don't get me wrong though, your lack of experience hasn't hurt your style at all."

"There you go again with that incredible ego of yours. I suppose you have a wealth of experience with women, and you think you could teach me a lot." I retorted.

"I don't think I need to teach you anything. You're doing great on your own."

My face must have turned beet red because he laughed again. "You fascinate me, Amanda. One minute you're a prim, blushing school teacher, then you're a fiery, spirited fireball, and now I've found that you're a warm, passionate lover."

"I think you're making fun of me."

Bob suddenly became serious, "No, I'm not, Amanda. I didn't mean to make you mad. Maybe I should change the subject. Where's Rothman?"

"I don't know. I haven't seen him since this afternoon when you accused him of not setting the brake."

"It wasn't set, Amanda, honest. I'd like to believe that the brake is defective or he just forgot to set it and didn't want to admit it, but I just don't know."

"Where were you when the mower started down the hill?"

"Believe it or not, I saw a weed in the flower bed back behind the cottage, and I went over and pulled it up. I didn't know anything was wrong until Angela screamed."

"But you were close enough that you could have released the brake when Greg started walking down the hill."

"I suppose so, but I didn't. I wish you could believe me. You must have watched too much TV. In real life it's not always the fair-haired, all-American boy who's the hero, and the dark-haired, bearded guy who's the villain."

"I know. Now it's my turn to apologize. I don't really think you or Greg were trying to harm Angela."

"Do you think Mr. Jennings had anything to do with the mower?"

I don't really think so; he seems to be very fond of Angela, and he seems to be so gentle and kind. That's what I hate about this mystery. I don't know who I can trust anymore."

"I'm not trying to be a preacher now, but I know One you can trust, and for what it's worth, I'm praying for you and Amanda."

"Thank you, Bob. I'm going to get back on speaking terms with Him myself."

"That's great! And by the way, I still think you're a great kisser. Lock the door when I leave, okay?"

Again he had left me confused. He was such a complex man. Even though he teased a lot, when he was serious, he was so compassionate and sensitive. He seemed sincere about his relationship with God, but was he just a superb actor? I didn't know, but I did know that I had some business to do with God myself, so before I crawled into bed, I knelt down to pray.

It was a real prayer, not the empty, meaningless phrases I had uttered every night since I could remember. I asked God to forgive me for my bitterness over losing Paul; I thanked Him for bringing Angela into my life, but I prayed that I would be able to give her up if and when her real parents were found. Then I prayed for our safety, and I prayed for Greg and Bob and my relationship to both of them. I even prayed for Mr. Jennings because he seemed to be rather lonely and sad. A very comforting peace settled over me like a blanket my mother used to tuck around me as she kissed me goodnight. I knew now that although I might face more terrors ahead, I was not alone.

Chapter 9

The morning sun had already turned the bedroom into an oven by the time Angela and I awoke. I looked at the clock and was startled to find that it was 9:00. I never bothered to set the alarm on Monday's when the museum was closed. As soon as I moved, Angela turned over and gave me her customary grave look.

"Good morning, Princess," I said. "Did you just wake up, too?"

"No, I've been awake for a little while. I didn't want to bother you."

I reached over and squeezed her close to me. "Oh, you could never bother me. But, we better get moving. You have a doctor's appointment today at 11:00, and then another one right after that."

"What're the doctors going to do, Amanda?" Angela asked in a trembling voice.

"Oh, I think the first one will put on his stethoscope and listen to your heart, and he'll probably use a little light to look into your ears, mouth, and nose. He'll check you all over, something like Judy did when she checked to see if you had a mark on your back. I think the other one will just talk to you."

"Do you think they'll get my remembry back?" she asked.

Again, not wanting to have her be disappointed any more than possible, I spoke as honestly as I could, "I really doubt if either one of them can get you memory back right away, but I think you will start to remember more and more on your own until you will finally remember everything again. Now, what do you say, let's get going."

We both bounced out of bed and headed for the shower. I helped her take a quick bath, then she dressed herself in clothes I had suggested for her to wear while I showered. I tried to hurry her more than I had the day before because I wanted her to eat a good breakfast in case the doctor asked her what she had eaten. Therefore during her relatively long breakfast, I had a little time to update the journal so that I could take it along.

Finally we were on our way by a little after 10:00. The sun was hiding behind a dark cloud signaling a rainstorm, but the air was still as oppressive as it had been in the bedroom that morning. I predicted that we were in for a big storm, but Michigan weather is always changing and hard to predict.

About ten miles along the way, we passed a two-story, white frame farm house, with green shutters and a rambling porch that skirted the entire front. There was a sign out in the front yard that I recognized as a "century sign." In my best school teacher manner, I asked Angela, "Did you see that sign in front of that big white house we just passed, Angela?"

"Yes," she said quietly.

"That's a sign that says that the people who live there right now are the descendants, or grandchildren, maybe even great-grandchildren, of the people who built the house in the first place, one hundred years ago. The house where my parents and I live in southern Michigan is a century home. My great-grandfather built it, my grandfather got it after him, and my father after him. If I don't go back there to live after Mom and Dad die, it'll go to someone else. It's really a nice house."

I stopped lecturing when I saw Angela put her hand up to her face as if to brush away a tear. I glanced over at her, and sure enough, tears were rolling down her cheeks. "What's the matter, Angela?" I asked in alarm.

"I don't know who my parents are. I don't know where I live or anything about myself. I wish I had my remembry back."

I wanted to reach out and hold her, but I couldn't while I was driving and we were both strapped in our safety belts. I could only try to comfort her with words. "Oh, Honey, sometimes I forget how hard it must be for you not to know anything about yourself. I'm sorry I went on about my past like that, but I bet when you do remember your parents and grandparents, they'll be just as nice as mine are." I realized anew how selfish I had been to wish for everything to go on as it was just because I wanted Angela to stay with me. I resolved to do anything in my power to help her regain her memory.

Angela seemed to be comforted, and after a few more minutes we reached Randolph City. I concentrated all my attention on finding the medical building where the doctors' offices were. I was grateful I had already seen the building because I found it without any trouble, an unusual accomplishment for me, generally a klutz with directions.

The building was an impressive three-storied red brick structure with meticulous, colorful landscaping all around it. There was a large parking lot on the left side of the building where I parked my Taurus. I noticed that my car was the smallest one there. Most of the others were larger, newer, and more luxurious. Suddenly, I began to worry about the bill for the examinations, especially the psychiatrist's. I had brought a checkbook along, but I wasn't exactly wealthy. I had never even thought to ask for money to help take care of Angela because I had not thought she would be with me very long, and I wasn't officially her foster parent. But, of course, there was no turning back now. Even if I had to take out a loan to pay for the doctors' services, I figured I would manage if they would help my little visitor.

Angela had quit crying, but she looked frightened as she unlatched her seat belt and opened her door. I really couldn't blame her. Probably anyone, of any age, is apprehensive about a doctor's appointment, and Angela had two of them. I noticed she walked slower than usual up to the building, almost like a criminal walking to the electric chair.

The two glass doors at the front of the building opened into a large room, carpeted with plush, but durable carpet and furnished with leather chairs and couches. On all the tables and in the corners of the room were healthy-looking potted plants of all varieties and shapes and sizes. A huge chandelier with maybe one hundred tiny, golden lights hung down from the ceiling. At the other side of the room was a tall, oak counter where an attractive blond girl sat talking on a phone. As soon as we walked up to the counter, she finished her conversation and directed us to a hallway behind her where we would find stairs that led to the doctors' offices, both of which were on the second floor. We walked up a flight of stairs, carpeted just like the lobby, and down a narrow hallway with solid wooden doors on both sides. The doors all bore names, each followed by at least three initials.

Dr. Johnson's office was the second door on the right. As I turned the handle with my free hand, Angela squeezed my other so tightly that I was afraid my circulation was being cut off. The reception room for Dr. Johnson was almost a scaled-down replica of the lobby downstairs, with the same type of leather furniture, the same carpeting, and similar plants, but without the chandelier. There were about six other people in the room, mostly women with small children.

Angela and I walked up to a glass-enclosed cubicle, and another attractive blond slid back the glass door and said, "Hello, welcome to Dr. Johnson's office, what is your name?"

"My name is Amanda Stevens," I stated, "and this is Angela. I think Judy Baldwin called for this appointment."

"Yes, Miss Stevens. You and the little girl may have a seat, and the doctor will be with you in just a few minutes. But, in the meantime, Miss Stevens, could you fill out this information sheet for us?" She handed me a clip board holding a blue piece of paper.

"I don't really know what information I can give you;" I answered, "do you know about Angela's amnesia?"

The wide, practiced smile the young girl had cultivated for her job dimmed slightly as she said, "Yes, I know you won't have a great deal of information about the child, but just fill out anything you can. For instance, if she has seemingly had an allergic reaction to anything, note that. Also you would be able to tell us if she has had any medication since she--uh--came to you."

"Okay, I'll do the best I can, I promised." Then, noticing a sign regarding prompt payment for services rendered that was posted on one of the glass panels, I asked, "Will you accept my check for the payment today? I have an account at the Randolph City bank. About how much do you expect this visit to cost?" I was speaking as quietly as possible because I was a little reluctant to let everyone in the room know about my financial worries, and I didn't want Angela to think I didn't want to spend money on her.

"The payment is being taken care of, Miss Stevens," the receptionist assured with her professional smile back in place. "Just have a seat and we'll call you when the doctor is ready to see Angela."

I was relieved but puzzled about the bill. I wondered if the police had secured some state funds for Angela, or maybe Judy Baldwin was paying the bill. I was sure the receptionist in the psychiatrist's office would tell me the same story, so I relaxed a little.

Angela and I sat in two adjourning seats right across from the receptionist's cubicle. Before I started filling out the information sheet, I turned to reassure Angela who was still fiercely gripping my hand. "It's okay, Angela, you can let go of my hand. I think I'm going to need it to write." I reached for a Walt Disney story book on the glass-topped table next to me. I remembered that Mr. Jennings had found out that Angela had been to school, but I didn't know how much she could read. "Here, Honey, I don't know if you can read this or not, but do the best you can, and I'll finish reading it to you as soon as I answer these questions." She handled the book with the skill of a normal beginning reader. Watching her read, I was certain that she did know some words, but I could tell she was sounding out some more difficult ones by the way her mouth moved. I was anxious to evaluate her abilities for myself when I would finish the information sheet.

However, I never had the chance because as soon as I had supplied the meager information I could about Angela, the nurse called for us to come into one of the offices to wait for the doctor. I was instructed to undress Angela down to her panties and then help her up on the examining table. As I was helping her, I realized again how frightened she was. I thought that the doctor wouldn't even need a stethoscope to listen to her heartbeat because I could almost hear it myself.

The doctor finally came into the room, and he was nothing like I expected. He was probably only three or four years older than I, and he looked like a movie star, with sandy, wavy hair and deep blue eyes. His well-developed muscles didn't seem to go along with a man who had spent at least eight years studying medical books. He was so young that I wondered if he were experienced enough. Then I remembered what my mother had told me a few years before, "One of the hardest thing about growing old is that doctors, dentists, lawyers, even preachers look like your sons." Dr. Johnson was indeed young enough to be my mother's son, but I was glad he wasn't. "He's much too handsome to be my brother," I thought, chuckling to myself. Then I saw the familiar band of gold around his ring finger on his left hand, and all romantic thoughts vanished before they could really begin.

The doctor was thorough and professional, yet he was able to put Angela at ease, or at least, more at ease than she had been when she first walked in the office. I was uncomfortable and embarrassed when he checked her for signs of child molestation, and Angela was much braver than I when the nurse came in with the needle to draw blood for her blood test. She whimpered just a little bit, but I had to turn my head, and I was appalled to discover tears welling up in my eyes. When it was finally over, I looked over just in time to see the doctor and the nurse exchange an amused glance in my direction. "I guess you can tell I'm not an old pro at this mothering business."

Dr. Johnson smiled warmly, "Oh, I don't know. I find that some of the most experienced mothers can't watch the needle going in. Besides, you've been taking really good care of this little girl; I can tell." Then he turned to Angela who was watching the nurse put on her bandage with normal child-like curiosity. "Angela, would you let Mrs. Smith help you get dressed so I can talk to your--uh--Amanda for just a minute. I promise she'll come here after you as soon as you're dressed."

Angela didn't look too happy at the prospect of my leaving her, but the nurse didn't give her too much time to protest. She quickly started gathering her clothes, chattering gaily to her the whole time. I walked out the door with the doctor who guided me to his office across the hall from the examining rooms.

The doctor's office didn't seem to have a comfortable, lived-in look; it fit the doctor like a pair of shiny new shoes. Of course, he had impressive diplomas on the wall, but they were conspicuous in their spanking whiteness, not at all yellowed with age. There were thick, scholarly medical books on the shelves, also new-looking, and they only filled a fraction of the shelves that lined the wall behind the doctor's desk. The desk itself was neat and orderly, one corner containing a well-balanced stack of manila folders with computer-labeled names on the front of each, and another corner with one lone prescription pad sitting right next to a gold, ballpoint pen that had probably been given to the doctor for his graduation from medical school. The most noticeable object on the desk was a picture of a beautiful, blond-haired girl, radiant in her bridal gown. When I looked at the picture, I felt a twinge of sorrow. Janelle would probably make a radiant, beautiful bride, too. I wondered how all the wedding plans were coming along, but my thoughts about the wedding were more of curiosity than sadness. I noticed that my broken engagement was causing less pain every day.

The doctor broke into my thoughts by indicating a plush, leather chair in front of his desk where I was to sit. He sat in his swivel chair across from me, and began talking to me in a professional, factual tone of voice. "Angela is basically a healthy child," he stated. "I did hear a slight heart murmur, however, but I don't think it is serious. Sometimes heart murmurs are hereditary, and the child eventually outgrows them. I didn't find any evidence of molestation, either physical or sexual. Except, I did notice some bruises on her stomach and some scratches on her legs, but these looked recent. Can you tell me anything about them?"

He had caught me off guard, and for a moment I floundered for an answer. "Uh, I-I'm not sure." Then it came to me. "Oh yes, the scratches on her legs, I figure, were made by briars in the woods when she came to my cottage that first night from wherever she came from, and the bruises are probably from an accident--or near accident--that she had yesterday." I went on to tell him about the lawn mower and about Greg's rescue of her.

The doctor's perfect countenance clouded with a frown. "Are you sure that was an accident?" he asked.

"Well, no, I guess with a child in Angela's circumstances, you can't really be sure of anything. I try to make sure I watch her carefully."

"Oh, believe me, I'm not criticizing you. I think you're doing a marvelous job in what must be a frightening situation. I'm sure Dr. Meadows will go into the subject more, but does she seem to be especially frightened of anyone in particular?"

I was surprised at my reluctance to tell him about Angela's reaction to Bob, and when I did, I played down her apparent fright quite drastically. "Well, she seems to be more shy and withdrawn around the news reporter and photographer for the Randolph newspaper, Bob Wilson. However, he has a beard and he's dark, and he's a big-built man, so maybe he's just not the sort of person she's used to."

"Possibly, but maybe he looks like a person she is very frightened of. Dr. Meadows should be told about her reactions to all the circumstances you've been able to observe." His tone of voice suggested a lecture, as if he thought I were trying to hide something.

For that reason, I became very defensive. "Oh, I intend to tell the doctor everything. I have kept a journal since she first came to me so that I could better remember what has happened and Angela's reactions to all of it."

Again the doctor smiled his reassurance. "That's very commendable, Miss Stevens: Angela is very lucky she picked your door to come to in the middle of the night. Now, you probably have your appointment with Dr. Meadows soon. If you have any questions, don't hesitate to call. But, one thing I wanted to ask? Do you have a first-aid kit at the cottage? And how extensive is it?

"Yes, there's one there, but what do you mean about 'how extensive' it is?"

"Well, I just wondered if you had a bee-sting kit— you know—in case the little girl gets stung and is allergic?"

"Yes, now that you mention it, there is some medicine and a hypodermic, and I do know how to use it. I took a first-aid course before I took the job."

"That's great. I'll let you know if there's something unusual about the blood tests, and of course, I'll tell the police her blood type. I guess you'll just have to play the rest by ear. If she has a reaction to certain foods, just stop giving her the foods. Again, feel free to call with any questions you might have. And, Miss Stevens, I hope the mystery ends soon with a happy ending."

Since my dismissal cue had been given, I rose from my chair, thanked Dr. Johnson, and walked across the hall to where a fully dressed Angela was talking with the friendly nurse, well as much as she ever talked. She seemed to have lost a little of her shyness, but she was still very quiet. The nurse had evidently broken down some of her walls, though, because even though she grasped my hand when the nurse lifted her down from the examining table, it wasn't with the same fervency she had shown on the way into the office. Also, as we walked toward the waiting room, Angela turned and shyly waved to her new friend.

Since it was already 12:15, we hurried down the hall to Dr. Meadow's office and opened a door to a waiting room quite different from the other rooms I had seen in the building because of its bright colors. The chairs were the same style as the others except they were bright red, blue, yellow, and green. Since Dr. Meadows specialized in children, one whole wall supported three colorful bookshelves with many thin, bright children's books, some of which sported titles like, "You are a Special Person," or "Baby Sisters Can Be Fun." Part of the shelves were devoted to puzzles of all descriptions.

I had a feeling that the doctors in this building had somehow cloned one blond receptionist to make all the rest because the one in this office was also blond and pretty. I wondered if the want-ad for the jobs had read, "Brunettes need not apply." This receptionist also had a beautiful smile and professional manner as she instructed me to fill out yet another form, slightly more detailed than the other one in the area of emotions and behavior. However, the receptionist's desk was not enclosed in the glass cubicle that seemed to act as a fortress in the other office. I suppose that a closer communicative atmosphere was desired in a psychiatrist's office. And, indeed, Angela did seem calmer here, for she went to the shelves to pick out a book without my suggesting it.

She read her book while I diligently filled out what I could of the inevitable form until a tall professional-looking woman opened the huge, oak doors behind the receptionist's desk and called Angela's name. Again she grasped my hand, and we headed for the door. However, the woman, who must have been the doctor's secretary, stopped me. "I'm sorry, Miss--uh--," she consulted the chart, "Stevens, but you will have to wait out here until Dr. Meadows is finished interviewing the child." This stern, forbidding secretary seemed to be the antithesis of the motherly, kind nurse who had soothed Angela's fears in the other office. She was ram-rod straight in stature with dark hair pulled tightly back in a bun at the back of her head. She wore thick, horn-rimmed glasses that seemed to magnify piercing, dark eyes.

Angela started cutting off my circulation again with her vise-grip, but I could tell that this sentry-guard secretary was not going to back down. I knelt down and took the child's shoulders in my hands, "Angela, Honey, I'm sure Dr. Meadows is just as nice as Dr. Johnson, and I promise I'll be right here all the time. You just have to be a big girl and go with this lady."

"I'd rather have you come with me, Amanda," she said.

"I know, Honey, but maybe the doctor can help you better by talking with you alone. Now, I promise, I won't leave. I'll be right here when you get back." She nodded her head and turned to the tall, severe secretary, who closed the door firmly, and for the first time in almost a week, Angela was out of my sight.

I wandered around the waiting room, picking up some of the magazines Dr. Meadows had displayed for the parents of his patients, but I couldn't find any that really interested me. Since there was no one else in the room, I couldn't even take up any of the time by making small talk with fellow waiters. Finally, I decided to look over the journal once more to see if I had forgotten anything.

The time dragged on, and the journal reading took only a small fraction of it. I was so antsy that I started reading the children's books, and they proved to be more captivating than the magazines. I could get the gist of the subject matter without thoroughly concentrating. At last, after five books, the door was opened, and Angela and the nurse came out. The look Angela gave me brought tears to my eyes. She ran to me and flung her arms around me as if she had been gone for days. I held her and searched her face for changes in her condition. I was so anxious to find out if the doctor had been able to get her to recall anything.

Her face revealed nothing, however, and just as I was beginning to ask Angela about her encounter with the doctor, the secretary spoke up, "Miss Stevens, the doctor would like to speak to you now, if you'll follow me." She again opened the door and stood impatiently waiting for my compliance.

"But what about Angela?" I asked, probably a little defiantly.

"Miss Baker will watch her while you're gone. I'm sure she'll be perfectly all right." She indicated the blond receptionist who immediately rose from her desk and came over to Angela. This time Angela was not so reluctant to be separated from me as I was from her. She and the receptionist seemed to quickly find a puzzle that engrossed both of them.

I walked toward the door with probably as much anxiety as Angela had had. I wondered if Dr. Meadows would be even more forbidding than his nurse.

The door which the nurse held open led immediately into a large, airy office, with panels of windows covering the opposite wall. The color scheme in here was a soft mauve, and the pictures and decorations displayed a lightness I hadn't expected. There was another oak-paneled door off to the left of the room through which the secretary disappeared. The doctor's plush chair was turned toward the window until I walked in. Then when the occupant of the chair did turn toward me, I'm afraid I gasped in shock. Dr. Meadows was a woman!

I don't know why I was so surprised. I guess, even in the days of women's lib, most people naturally assume that a man will be the doctor, and a woman will be the nurse. It was a credit to Captains Rogers' updated thinking that he never mentioned the fact that the "young psychiatrist in Randolph City" was a woman. I doubted that Bob Wilson would have been so modern.

Dr. Meadows was a small, pretty woman in her mid-thirties. She had sea-green eyes and soft auburn hair that curled around her face. She smiled good-naturedly when she saw my reaction, probably having become accustomed to similar reactions in her profession. "Have a seat, Miss

Steven," she offered as she indicated a chair in front of her desk. "I hope we didn't make you wait too long."

"No, well, I was wondering about Angela, of course, but--"

"Yes, I can tell from talking with her that you and she have a great rapport. She is very fond of you, and I can tell already that you are smitten with her. Now, I'd like to talk to you about Angela and everything's that has happened, and I must tell you that our conversation is being recorded, and my secretary will also have access to the recording later. Is that agreeable to you?"

I nodded mutely.

"Well, I'm sorry to say that I really didn't learn too much about Angela's past. I'm sure of only one thing--that she has had a deep trauma of some kind, something so tragic that her mind is refusing to remember it." She paused to let her words sink in.

"Sometimes children who are molested or otherwise abused block out the abuse, often even creating another personality to deal with the incident. However, I don't think Angela has been abused. I think she has witnessed something that has happened to someone else, and this incident was so horrifying that she has blocked it out."

"Do you think that maybe whatever happened could have happened to her parents?"

"That's very possible, but of course, I have no way of knowing. And, I'm a little wary of trying hypnosis on her for fear she would have too severe a reaction if she were forced to recall this supposed incident."

"You're probably right," I said, even though I had no idea if she were right or not.

"Could you tell me exactly everything you can think of that has happened to Angela or any of her reactions since she came to you?"

I was waiting for that question. "Well, yes, as a matter of fact, I have been keeping a journal since the day after she came, and if you don't mind, I'll consult that." As I was talking I lifted up the notebook from under my purse on my lap and opened it to the first page.

"Excellent," she exclaimed, and I'm sure I must have been beaming.

"I guess being a detailed, exacting school teacher sometimes pays off," I said in an embarrassed tone.

She smiled warmly, and began looking at the book. For the next half-hour, we read, discussed, and analyzed all the entries in the journal. Finally, when we came to the end, I closed the book and stood up. The doctor also came to her feet and stretched out her hands to take hold of mine.

"Thank you, Miss Stevens, for your detailed account. Some biological parents who have been living with their kids for ten years or more don't have as much information as you do. I know Angela is in good hands. Although I can't make much sense out of her reactions to the doll and the tool box, I'll have my secretary make notes of our conversation, and we'll go over them later. Also, I don't want to frighten you, but please watch the child carefully, even if it means being a little over-protective. I'm not sure the lawnmower incident yesterday was an accident. Anyway, we'll keep in touch; I'll call in a few weeks, that is, if nothing is resolved by then. Also, if anything happens that you think I should know about, call me, any time, day or night."

I thanked the doctor and left the office with a lighter spirit. The doctor inspired confidence. I thought she had certainly chosen the right profession. I was gratified with her praise of the care I was giving Angela.

When I walked into the waiting room, Angela and the pretty receptionist were working on another puzzle. They were so engrossed in their task that neither noticed that I was watching them. Finally I said, "Angela, Honey, are you ready?"

She looked up and smiled for the first time since I met her. The receptionist looked rather embarrassed as she stood up, trying to collect her professional manner again. "Angela is a very smart girl, Miss Stevens," she said. "She could find the puzzle pieces easier than I could." I was absurdly pleased with her comment, even though I really had nothing to do with Angela's intelligence.

"Thank you for watching her, Miss Baker," I said. Then, although I was almost certain of the answer to my question, I asked, "Do I owe anything today for the appointment?"

"No Mam, the bill has been taken care of," Miss Baker assured me, smiling. She then put her hands on Angela's shoulder and fondly said, "Good-bye, Sweetheart; you come back and see me, will you?"

Angela nodded, but I suspect she really wondered how she would be able to come back unless I would bring her. It was easy to see that the child had made another conquest, and the receptionist looked reluctant to see her go. However, the phone on her desk rang, and we took our leave as she answered it.

We walked out to a beautiful, sunlit day. All the dark clouds that had threatened us all the way over had evaporated. Again Michigan weather had reversed itself. Just as we were approaching the car, a police car carrying Officers Rogers and Adams swung into the parking lot over to where we were standing. The policemen greeted us warmly and asked us to go have lunch with them. Looking at my watch and noticing the rumblings of my stomach, I realized we were rather late for lunch, and I imagined that Angela was more than ready to eat also. Therefore, I readily accepted their invitation, and again Angela and I found ourselves in the back of a police car.

This time we were taken to a small cafe sandwiched in between a gift shop and a drug store on the main street of town. The cafe specialized in pizza, so predictably, the decor was Italian, with red-checked table cloths on the tables. The place was permeated with the smell of oregano, tomato, and cheese. By this time my stomach was rumbling so loudly that I was afraid I would be embarrassed in front of the policemen. I hoped that the two pizzas we ordered from our young, preppie waitress would be delivered quickly. However, we were told we would have at least twenty minutes to wait, but when the officers began talking, I managed to forget my hunger and concentrate on their information.

Captain Rogers began, "Amanda, we've checked on young Rothman's references, and they checked out okay. He indeed went to the University of Wisconsin last year, but he did not live on campus, and his parents did die last year, and he did work at a marina. So, we talked to the DNR, and they're giving him the job. Do you have any objections?"

"No," I said slowly, "only--I wonder--"

"What is it? Asked the Captain. "Has anything happened to make you suspicious of Rothman?"

"No, not me. I mean, well, Bob Wilson said something that made me wonder." Then I recounted my conversation with the reporter about the mild Wisconsin

winter and the basketball star that Greg had called a
football star. I also told them the arguments I had given
Bob.

"Hum, I think your reasoning was valid. I mean,
Rothman probably hates winter because he can't be out
sailing, which he seems to love, and any winter would
seem bad to him. As for the basketball star--since Rothman
didn't live on campus and apparently has no interest in any
sports other than sailing, he might have missed the hoop-la
the university had for this guy. Also, he did miss part of
last year because of the death of his parents, and, as you
suggested, maybe it was during basketball season. I'll ask
Rothman about it though."

Sergeant Adams spoke up, "Do you think Wilson
could be blowing this up for his own ulterior motives?"

"What do you mean?" I asked, and I immediately
regretted bringing the subject up because I was oddly
reluctant to get Bob in trouble with the police.

"Well, at the worst, Wilson could be involved in the
little girl's past, and he could be trying to throw suspicion
off himself and onto someone else. But, of course, he
could have another reason for wanting you to suspect

Rothman." At this, Sergeant Adams smiled impishly at his partner.

I could feel the familiar blush creeping up my face, and although I had an idea what the policeman was talking about, I asked, "What other reason?"

"Come on now, Miss Stevens, it's obvious those two young bucks are competing for the attention of a certain pretty lady."

Now I knew I was probably as red as the tablecloth. "Thank you, Sergeant, for your compliment, but I think their mistrust of each other goes beyond jealousy, even if there is jealousy there. Yesterday, after the accident, I thought they were going to come to blows."

"Accident, what accident?" asked Captain Rogers.

"Oh, yes, I forgot that you haven't heard about it yet." Then for the third time that day I recounted the lawnmower incident.

"Whew, I'm glad you're all right, Honey," said Captain Rogers. Then he turned to Sergeant Adams and suggested that he take Angela over to the counter and watch the cook roll out the pizza dough and throw it in the air. I knew that he wanted to talk to me alone, and I rather suspect that Angela knew it, too, because she went with the sergeant without any protest. When they were out of earshot, Captain Rogers asked, "Amanda, what did you mean when you said Wilson and Rothman almost came to blows?"

"Oh, they both blamed each other. Bob accused Greg of not setting the brake, and Greg accused Bob of releasing the brake when he was walking down the hill."

"What do you think happened?"

"I don't know," I admitted. "I suppose either of them could be right. Even Mr. Jennings is not off the hook because he was standing near the mower just before it started rolling down the hill. I really think, though, the brakes just gave out."

"You're probably right, but in a mystery like this, any 'coincidence' is suspect. By the way, speaking of Mr. Jennings, has anything 'developed' with that picture you were telling us about?" He grinned sheepishly and added, "Sorry, no pun intended."

I smiled dutifully and answered, "No, but Mr. Jennings told me he was going to enlarge the picture so that we might see some identifying mark on the man that we might have missed on the smaller picture." He had no comment, so I went on," Before the accident, Mr. Jennings started asking Angela if she remembered anything about school, and she did remember going to school and her teacher's name, but she couldn't remember anything else. In the doctors' offices today I could tell she was reading, but I don't know how well she reads." Then I filled him in on the two doctors' visits and when I finished, the waitress came with our steaming hot pizzas, and Angela and Sergeant Adams rejoined us. I was so hungry that I had to make myself wait in a ladylike manner for the two pedestal platters to be set on the table before I grabbed a big hunk for myself. I think Angela was hungry too, because her eyes were big and round as I pulled a sliver of the pie off for her. However, she hesitated and looked up at me expectantly before she picked it up. Guiltily, I realized she was waiting for prayer to be said, and I had almost skipped it. "Angela," I said, "would you like to pray for us?"

Sergeant Adams had his slice half-way up to his mouth, but he laid it back on his plate as Angela bowed her head and said, "God is great; God is good, and we thank

Him for this food. Amen." Then we all began to dig in,
Angela as much as the rest of us.

When we finished, the men insisted on paying the
bill. Angela and I were standing near the door of the cafe
waiting for the police when a heavy set, gray-haired man
appeared at the large picture window next to the door. He
had on faded jeans and a dirty, holey tee shirt. His hair was
dirty and unkempt, and his face bore a bushy, speckled-
gray beard.

Angela had her hand in mine as she casually gazed
around the room. Suddenly, she caught sight of the man at
the window, and she gasped. "Turtle man, that's turtle
man," and before I could stop her, she tore away from me
and bolted for the door.

Chapter 10

By the time the door closed on Angela, the police were at my side. The old man looked first at Angela, then at the police rushing out the door, and he began to run. By this time I was out on the sidewalk where I caught hold of Angela and pulled her out of the way of the pursuing policemen.

The man was surprisingly agile for his weight and age, and the police had a difficult time catching him. Angela was again clutching my hand as we waited to see what would happen. I bent down to her and asked her in the calmest voice I could manage, "Honey, who is this 'turtle man'? Tell me what you remember about him."

"I remember he found a turtle for me, and he gave it to me, and we made a hole for it to live in, she answered.

"Do you remember where all this happened?" I noticed that I was trembling and my heart was pounding.

She shook her head slowly, "No, but there was lots of wet sand there and water. He had a cup and he put water in the hole where we put the turtle, and we built a wall around the hole with sand and rocks so the turtle couldn't get out."

Soon the panting policemen arrived with the old man shuffling along in between them, each policeman grasping one of his arms. Eventually they managed to pull him over to where Angela and I were standing, and even in the midst of all the confusion, I was amused by the stares we were attracting from the many tourists who were milling around on the street.

"Now, tell us your name, Mister, and tell us what you know about this little girl," said Captain Rogers.

"My name is Edwards, Jim Edwards, but I don't know nothing about this girl. I never seen her before," he stated in a quivering voice.

"But you're turtle man," wailed Angela. Don't you remember our turtle?"

The old man's face turned fire engine red, and he shouted vehemently, "I don't know what this kid's talking about, I tell you. I ain't never seen her before."

"Angela, honey, what do you remember about this man?" Captain Rogers asked in a voice much more gentle than the one he had just used to question Edwards.

Angela repeated the account she had just told me in the most determined voice I had heard her use. I could imagine her frustration. Finally she remembered someone from her past only to have him deny ever seeing her.

"Well, Mr. Edwards, I think you'd better come with us. We need to ask you a few questions," ordered Captain Rogers.

"What for? Why can't you believe me? I don't know nothing about this kid."

"We just need to ask you some questions. To start with, why did you run when you saw the little girl?"

"Cause she was yelling at me about turtles, and then you guys banged out the door, and I was scared. I mean-- wouldn't you be?"

"Maybe, but let us ask the questions," said Sergeant Adams. "You come with us now."

"Am I arrested, then?" the old man asked.

"No, we want to have a friendly chat, but if you make any trouble, we'll make it more official," said the sergeant.

"Okay," Edwards shrugged, "but I can't tell you nothing I don't know."

We all walked to the squad car. Angela was still staring at the man, but as I watched her, big tears watered her eyes and started rolling down her cheeks. I put my arms around her and muttered, "It's okay, Honey, it's okay."

Captain Rogers said, "I tell you what, Amanda and Angela, you sit up front with Sergeant Adams, and me and Mr. Edwards will sit in the back."

We piled into the car as the policeman ordered, and now the people were really staring, but Angela seemed oblivious to anything going on around her. She sat in between Sergeant Adams and me, her eyes unblinkingly peering straight ahead. The policeman patted her hand and said softly, "Now don't you worry, Angela, we'll get this guy to talk. If you remember anything else about him at all, you tell Amanda to call us."

"I don't know why he says he doesn't know me. I remember he was nice to me," Angela cried, not even bothering to wipe away the big tears that rolled down her cheeks.

"Well, we'll find out, don't worry." the kind policeman said.

There was no noise except the crackling of the police radio until we reached my car. As I opened the door, Captain Rogers said, "We'll come over later on, Amanda. Take care and remember to call us if anything happens."

"I will," I promised. "Thank you for lunch." Angela and I walked over to the car which was sitting right in the middle of the lot in the hot sun. When I unlocked Angela's door, the hot air rushed out at us, almost knocking us down. We quickly rolled down the windows on our way toward home with the wind blowing through our hair. Angela was very quiet, and I decided not to intrude on her thoughts. Besides, I had some heavy thoughts of my own. The incident with the old man was possibly a signal that Angela was soon going to regain her memory. I had an idea that I thought might help her more as soon as we got back. The terrain around the abandoned docks was sand and rocks, much as Angela had described when she was telling her story. I wondered if we could find the "home" she said she and the old man had made for the turtle.

It was still the middle of the afternoon when we reached the cottage, and since the museum was closed for the rest of the day, I decided that Angela and I would walk down to the docks and search for the hole she and Turtle Man had dug. When I told Angela my plan, she readily agreed, probably hoping to prove to herself that the incident had really happened. After I helped her change into play clothes and I put on more comfortable walking shoes, we started off.

Although the temperature was probably in the mid eighties, we were kept fairly cool by a soft breeze that blew off the lake. All along the pathway to the docks, the wild flowers grew in colorful profusion, and the tall pine and birch trees towered over us creating a natural arch, like the ceiling of a magnificent cathedral. There was one sailboat on each side of the broken down pier that jutted out into the lake from the northern shore of the cove. The people that owned them must have also gone for a walk because no one was around either boat.

Angela held my hand as we cautiously stepped over the large stones that made up the surface of what was once the walkway. Both of us were looking down at the ground intently searching for evidence of a turtle's home. Finally at the end of the dock next to a wide, wooden pier, Angela stopped and exclaimed, "Amanda, here it is! See it?"

Sure enough there was a definite hole in the ground surrounded by a wall made of stones and mud. One part of the wall had collapsed, so the resident of this sand castle had evidently left. We both bent down to examine our discovery more closely, and I spied something green floating in the miniature moat that had been dug out right at the base of the wall. When I gingerly picked up the green object, I exclaimed to Angela, "Look, Angela, here's some lettuce. You must have gotten this to feed the turtle. Do you have any idea where you got it?"

She shook her head slowly, "No, but I know there was a turtle, wasn't there? Why did that man lie?"

"I don't know, Honey. Maybe he's just scared about something. Is there anything else you remember about all this?" I asked, indicating the whole area around the hole.

Angela looked gravely at the dock, the lake, the sailboats, and the home she had built for what was probably a cherished turtle. "I just remember digging the hole and building a wall, and Turtle Man and me taking turns holding the turtle until we got his house all built."

"Well, maybe something else will come to your mind later on. But we should go back to the cottage. I just remembered that I had better do some laundry for us. Okay?"

Angela nodded her head in a preoccupied way. She obviously had more on her mind than laundry. As we started toward the cottage, she asked, "Amanda, do you think I'm starting to get my remembry back?"

"Probably so, Honey. I know how hard it is for you to wait, but I think you'll remember everything in time." She gave me another smile, like the one in the doctor's office, as we trudged back up the hill.

When we got back, I went upstairs to unload the wicker laundry basket that sat in the corner of my bedroom. I was surprised at how quickly it had filled since Angela's clothes had been added to the pile. Since the Sanders did not own a washer or dryer, we had to drive to a hot, crowded little laundromat placed in the middle of cluster of stores, hyperbolically dubbed a mall, about ten miles up the road toward Randolph City. A small grocery store and a drug store flanked the laundromat, and an all-purpose hardware store that advertised live bait was two doors down. I was glad to see that there were only a few cars in the graveled parking lot because I figured the laundromat would not be crowded. The only other time I had been here almost every washer was being used, and the place was unbearably hot and noisy.

After I parked my car, Angela and I carried our clothes in. She had a small basket while I carried a large one that contained all the wet, heavy towels. As soon as my eyes adjusted to the dim lighting after the bright sunshine, I was relieved to see that there were only two other people in the laundromat, a middle-aged woman folding a large pile of clothes on the folding table, and a man with his back toward us and a large book in his hands. The man looked familiar, but it wasn't until Angela and I had sorted our clothes into three washers that I realized the man was Mr. Jennings. I debated whether I should go over to talk to him because he seemed so engrossed in his reading, but the matter was taken out of my hands as soon as Angela spied him. "Amanda," she shouted over the noise of the machines, "that's Mr. Jennings over there. Let's go over and talk to him." She surprised me by her suggestion. Again I figured she normally had an outgoing personality, and she would probably exhibit it more as time went on. The only person she really seemed frightened of was Bob Wilson, and strangely, this fact bothered me more than it should have.

We walked to the back of the store where uncomfortable plastic chairs had been placed next to the large grimy picture window that looked out on a wooded, rustic scene to the east of the stores. Mr. Jennings sat in the middle of the three chairs, so absorbed in his book that he was apparently oblivious to the scenery out the window. Angela eagerly rushed over to him, while I followed a little more slowly.

"Hi, Mr. Jennings. Guess what, Amanda and I found the home Turtle Man and I had built for our turtle, so Turtle Man lied when he said he didn't know me, and--"

"Whoa, slow down, Little One, I'm afraid I don't know what you're talking about. Hello, Amanda. Do you think you can interpret for me?" asked Mr. Jennings.

"Hello, Mr. Jennings," I said, a little embarrassed. "Are we bothering you? I don't want to keep you from your reading."

"No, that's all right. I'd much rather talk to you lovely ladies than read this ponderous book on Great Lakes history. Besides, I've got to hear about 'Turtle Man' and a turtle's home and all the rest."

I quickly filled him in about Mr. Edwards and his running from the police and the turtle and our discovery of his home. Every once in a while, Angela would interrupt my story when she felt I was leaving out something important. Finally at the end she said excitedly, "So, Mr. Jennings, maybe I'm getting my remembry back."

"Sure, maybe you are, Honey. I hope so." Then turning to me he asked, "But why do you think this Edwards denied knowing the child?"

I looked at Angela whose enthusiasm had dimmed a little with Mr. Jennings' low key response, and I answered carefully, not wanting to give her false hope nor dash her hope completely. "I think maybe he's been in trouble with the police before, and he was scared to admit to anything."

"Oh, I see. Well, they'll probably get him to tell the truth, but Angela, don't be disappointed if he can't answer all your questions. You're going to remember everything some time, I'm sure, but I think it's going to take some time."

I couldn't criticize Mr. Jennings' caution. After all, I had often said the same thing to Angela, but I wondered if we adults did children a favor by throwing cold water on their enthusiasm in order to shield them from disappointment. Angela's bright eyes clouded, and she murmured, "Okay," in a soft, sad voice.

Then, Mr. Jennings voice became animated. "Say, I just thought of something. Do you think this Edwards is the guy in the picture with Angela that I took?"

"No, I don't think so," I answered thoughtfully. "Edwards is much, well, fatter than the guy in the picture, also much older. His hair is white while the guy in the picture has dark hair."

"Oh well, it was a thought. You know, I've been meaning to blow up that picture to see if we can see the guy in more detail, maybe find a scar on his hand or something. When we finish here, we'll go over to my house and work on it. Okay?"

"Sure, I guess we can. We don't have to be back at any set time."

"All right. But I think my washer is done. I guess I'd better get busy." Since my washers were finished soon after Mr. Jennings', the next hour was spent drying, folding, and stacking clothes. It was obvious from watching Mr. Jennings expertise that he had done this job many times. He even helped us out when his clothes were all neatly stacked in the huge straw basket he had brought. Then, he helped us carry our two baskets out to the car where we packed them in the back seat since there was no room for them in the trunk.

"You follow me, Amanda," Mr. Jennings instructed me." My house is only about five miles from here."

I nodded and obediently followed his black, dignified Buick out of the parking lot. In just a few minutes we turned onto a quiet, tree-lined street that ran in front of one-story cottages with gleaming white siding, the backs of which all faced the beach of the horseshoe bay called "Silver Bay."

Mr. Jennings' cottage was much like the others, a small front porch with wooden posts and railings, a green-tiled roof with green shingles, and a neatly-trimmed lawn bordered by brightly colored petunias, marigolds, and pansies.

Mr. Jennings hadn't bothered to lock the door, but he gallantly opened the door for us and invited us to be seated before he went back to his car for his basket. I was surprised to see that he was an impeccable housekeeper because I imagined him to be a rather absent-minded professor, concentrating exclusively on the past. His couch and chair were early American, with pictures of buildings like Mount Vernon making up their patterns. He also had a wooden rocking chair with red, ruffled pads to make the seating more comfortable. The floors were hard-wood, and they were polished to a gleam that one usually only could see on a floor-polish ad. One wall was taken up by a brick fireplace and hearth; the fireplace was enclosed by a black iron grating and sparkling glass doors, bordered with equally sparkling brass. The opposite wall held book shelves that reached from the floor to the ceiling and stretched from the front door to the arch wall that separated the living room from what I assumed to be the dining room because of the round, oak table and chairs and large breakfront hutch that dominated the room.

Probably the most noticeable objects of his decor were pictures, seemingly hundreds of them lining the walls and the fireplace mantle, and there were a few on the oak

end tables and coffee table at the end and in front of the

couch. And the pictures were all of children, all different

and in various poses. He had portrait-type pictures where

children were sitting sedately staring at the camera,

dressed in frilly dresses or tailored suits. Other pictures

showed children in jeans or swimsuits chasing sea gulls on

a beach, examining a dandelion in a green and yellow

meadow, or playing in the sand, as in the picture he had

taken of Angela.

The biggest, most prominent picture was over the

fireplace; it was a professional-looking photograph that

had been done in oil and framed in a wide, wavy, wooden

frame. The subjects of this picture were a pretty, dark-

haired lady flanked by two cherubic children, a boy and a

girl, both of whom were about three years old. They were

posed on a dark blue velvet settee with a light blue

background. The woman had on a lacy, white silk dress,

which matched the little girl's dress. Both dresses looked

like the style worn by royalty in the 30's or 40's. The little

boy had on a powder blue, striped suit with short pants.

They were all smiling serenely, but I fancied I saw pain or

sorrow in the woman's eyes. From the size and position of this particular picture, I surmised that this trio were special people to the photographer, who I imagined was Mr. Jennings. But who these people were and what significance they had in his life I didn't know.

I was standing gazing at the picture, so engrossed in my speculations that I jumped guiltily when Mr. Jennings came in the door. "I'm sorry, Amanda," he said. "I didn't mean to startle you." He set his basket of clothes on the floor in front of him.

"That's all right. I was just admiring all your pictures, especially this one," I pointed to the portrait over the fireplace. "Are you the photographer of all these?"

"Yes, but that one was oil-painted by a professional studio after I supplied the original photograph."

"They're all beautiful! Are these all children that you know?"

His face was clouded with a frown that was uncharacteristic, at least of what I had observed about him so far. His voice sounded sullen and almost angry as he answered. "No, most of them I don't know. However, the ones in the big picture--I--uh--they are--were my children.

They were twins, and they--uh--died about a year after that picture was made."

I felt like a person who had barged into a private room, uninvited. "I-I'm sorry," I stuttered. "I didn't realize."

"Of course, you couldn't know, but I'd rather not talk about it, if you don't mind. Now, how about a nice, cold drink? I've got some lemonade in the refrigerator." His sunny disposition returned as he looked over at Angela who was sitting on the couch.

Embarrassed, I mumbled, "Yes, I would like some. How about you, Angela?"

"Yes, please," she answered simply.

Mr. Jennings picked up his clothes basket and walked through the living room and the adjoining dining room and disappeared into a hallway off to the right of the dining room. Since I heard noises from the other side of the bookcase wall, I assumed that he was in his bedroom putting his clothes away. Soon he appeared in the dining room again and this time walked to the back of the cottage where there was a polished, white refrigerator visible in the doorway.

Angela and I sat in silence as we listened to our host getting glasses from the cupboard and pouring the lemonade. I didn't know what Angela was thinking about, but many thoughts were running through my mind. How did Mr. Jennings' children die? Why was he so reluctant to talk about them? Was the woman in the picture his wife and the mother of his children? Was she still alive, and if so, where was she?

"Here you go, Ladies," Mr. Jennings said when he returned bearing a silver tray with two tall glasses filled with ice and yellow liquid. "I hope you like this. I must confess that I don't squeeze the lemons and make it from scratch; I buy the mix."

"That's all right. I do too," I said, as I took my glass off the tray, "and I'm so thirsty that just about anything liquid would be fine for me." It was more than fine; after the hot laundromat, it was divine. I tried to sip politely, but I'm afraid I ended up gulping it down. Out of the corner of my eye I noticed that Angela was making quick work of hers too, so in just a few minutes we both had empty glasses.

I looked up rather sheepishly to find Mr. Jennings standing with the empty tray in his hands grinning affectionately at us. "Could I interest you in another glass?" he asked.

"Well, if it wouldn't be too much trouble. Can you handle another glass, Angela?"

"Yes please" she said again.

"It's no trouble at all," our gracious friend said. "Here, let me have your glasses, and I'll fill them again."

Again he walked out to the kitchen and returned with the refilled glasses. After handing them to us, he stated, "I'm going to work on that picture now. I have a dark room at the back of my studio. Just make yourselves at home, and I'll be back in a jiffy." Then he stooped down to the bottom shelf of his book shelves and brought out a voluminous, leather-covered picture album and handed it to me. "Here, you might be interested in looking at some more of my pictures. Some of these go back quite a few years."

I gingerly opened the album, scared that I would rip the pages or damage the pictures. Angela scooted over closer to me and held the bulk of the album in her lap. I noticed that there was no dust on the cover or in the pages even though it was probably rare that anyone looked at it. Mr. Jennings would put most women to shame with his meticulous housekeeping.

The pictures started out in black and white, and the first few were blurred and indistinct. The quality gradually improved as we kept turning pages, and after about the fourth page, all of the prints were in color. Many of the pictures were of children, a few of the twins in the portrait. However, there was more of a variety of subjects in his album than on his wall. There were some pictures of adorable puppies and kittens, some tranquil scenery pictures in all seasons, and pictures of adults, especially pretty young women who looked like covers in glamour magazines. There were even some pictures of fires, floods, and automobile accidents, such as one would see in news magazines. A whole section of the album was taken up with what I guessed were the photographer's personal family snapshots. There were pictures of people who looked as if they were Mr. Jennings parents, some who could be his siblings, and many shots of what was probably a family reunion. One of my questions was answered when I came across snapshots of the young woman in the fireplace portrait in a wedding gown with a very young Mr. Jennings. The look in her eyes in the wedding pictures was complete joy, none of the haunting sadness I thought I detected in the portrait.

After we had looked at about the first thirty pages, Angela told me she had to go to the bathroom. Not wanting to search an unfamiliar house, I asked probably the most common and possibly most futile question an adult ever asks a child: "Can't you wait?"

"No," she answered, a little panic entering her voice. "I guess I had too much lemonade."

"Okay," I sighed. "Let's see if we can find it." I closed the book slowly and very carefully placed it on the end table next to me. Then I took Angela's hand and headed toward the hallway that Mr. Jennings had gone to when he put his clothes away; it was the only place the bathroom could possibly be. However, this tiny hallway was surrounded by four solid oak doors, one on each end and two in the middle, and they were all closed.

Mr. Jennings' bedroom must have been the end room on my right because it was the one on the other side of the living room wall. Also, having viewed the cottage from the outside, I was sure that the end room on my left was the studio and dark room, because the cottage did not look wide enough to accommodate a room that would serve that purpose. So, the bathroom had to be behind one of the two middle doors. But which one?

I felt like the young man in the story of the "Lady and the Tiger" as I crept toward one of the two doors. Just as I was turning the knob, Mr. Jennings burst out of his studio and snapped, "What do you want?"

I let out a small scream and let go of the door handle as if it were red hot. Trying to compose myself, I stammered, "I--we--Angela has to go to the bathroom, and I--uh--was just looking for it."

"Of course." His tone softened considerably. "I'm sorry. I--well--I have a lot of junk in that room, and I'm--uh--really embarrassed to have anyone see it. The bathroom is right here." He opened the door for us grandly, like a doorman in an elegant hotel.

"Thank you," I said, only slightly mollified by his apology. I really didn't believe that he didn't want us to see the room just because it was cluttered. For one thing, I couldn't imagine any room in this immaculate house being other than perfect. Also, his anger seemed too extreme if he were only concerned about sloppy housekeeping.

The bathroom was as spanking clean as the other parts of the house, but I barely saw it. My mind was occupied by lots of questions. Up to this point in my life, everything and everyone had been open and above-board. Suddenly, I was faced with one mystery after another, and the people I had met, except for the police, all seemed to be hiding something. Even though I had to admit my life was more exciting than it ever had been, I wanted the mysteries cleared up for Angela's sake.

When we came out of the bathroom, Mr. Jennings was waiting on the couch in the living room closely examining a glossy, 8 x 10 picture. "Come in," he invited. "I finished the picture, but as far as I can see, there is nothing unusual about the man that would identify him."

He handed the picture first to me and then I lowered it so that Angela could see it. He was right; I found nothing helpful in the enlarged picture. There was only the head and one hand visible on the man, and I could see no scars or birthmarks on either.

Angela was staring at the picture, obviously concentrating with all her might. "Does this bring back any memories, Honey?"

"No, except I think that was the place where the turtle was, but I'm sure that's not Turtle Man."

"I don't think it is either," I agreed. "But maybe Mr. Jennings will let us take this picture with us, and if you look at it more, you'll remember something about it."

"Sure," he answered," but could I see that again?" When we handed it to him, he almost stared a hole through it. Finally he said, "You know, I don't want to accuse anyone of anything, but that certainly looks like Bob Wilson."

A shock wave went through my body, and I found myself defending the reporter vehemently. "You can't really tell, only seeing his back. Besides, you only met him once, didn't you?"

He looked at me curiously. "Well, yes, but his build, and his dark hair--well I still think he could be the man in the picture, but I could be wrong."

I tried to calm down; really I had no right to be so upset anyway. "Yeah, I guess he could be the man. Of course, you heard him, he denies ever seeing Angela before the police brought him to the cottage to do the story. I just wish I could know the truth. I don't know who to trust."

Mr. Jennings handed me the picture, and I put it in the side pocket of the large, denim bag I carried with me everywhere I went. "I know how frightening this has all been to you," he said. "I wish I could be more help. Just think, if the phone hadn't rung when it did, I would have gone down to the beach and met Angela. It's funny how such little, insignificant events can have catastrophic results in your life." As he talked, his eyes looked as if they were seeing events far away and long ago.

I hated to disrupt his thoughts, but I felt we had to get back to the cottage. After seeing Mr. Jennings' house, I had a tremendous compulsion to go home to vacuum and dust. My watch said it was already 6:00, so I announced, "Mr. Jennings, I think Angela and I better get going. I have some work to do before tomorrow."

He abruptly came to attention. "Sure, I didn't mean to hold you up, but could I ask a favor of you?"

"Of course," I said, "if I can."

"I need to come over to the museum for just a few minutes. You see, the book I was reading when you two came into the laundromat was telling about a certain kind of fog horn used by ships in the late 1700's. There is a distinctive mark, sort of a manufacturer's seal, on them, and I wanted to see if any of those at the museum had these marks."

"Sure, you're welcome to come over. I won't even charge you the full visitors' fee," I said smiling.

He smiled back, "Good deal. I'll just ride with you ladies then walk back, if that's all right. I need the exercise."

Normally I would not have thought twice about a nice man like Mr. Jennings riding with us, but after his suspicious behavior with the closed room, I felt a slight uneasiness creep into my voice when I answered. "Uh-- sure--I guess that would be all right, but--uh--my car is certainly not as nice as yours--and--"

One look at his face told me that he was aware of my discomfort. He gallantly tried to get me off the hook. "Well, on second thought, I don't know how long I'll be over there if I do find what I'm looking for, so maybe I'd better have my car over there. I'll just follow you."

Utterly ashamed of myself for hurting a man I had begun to consider my friend, I tried to apologize. "Oh no, there's no use for you to take your car. It's not very far; just come on with us."

"You're sure?" he asked, looking deep into my eyes.

"I'm sure," I answered, then breaking away from his intense scrutiny, I turned to Angela and said, "Are you ready, Kiddo? We've got to get home and clean the cottage a little bit." She nodded her head, and soon we were off. Mr. Jennings insisted that he would sit in the back, even though I told him that there wasn't much leg room in the back of my little car. However, since we were home in just a few minutes, I don't think he was greatly discomforted.

Immediately when we got into the cottage, I went to work putting away clothes and vacuuming the rugs. When Angela asked me what she could do, I put her to work dusting, a task she seemed familiar with. Mr. Jennings examined all the ship horns we had and was very happy to find the mark he was looking for on one of them. Thus, none of us heard Greg come to the back door a little while later because we were all engrossed in our various tasks.

I was bending over picking up a paper clip from the rug when suddenly Greg appeared right beside me and said, "Amanda, I-- "Startled, I jerked back, almost knocking Greg down in my fright. "Oh, you scared me," I gasped.

"I'm sorry. I didn't mean to sneak up on you. I knocked on the door, but nobody could hear me, I guess, with the sweeper running."

By this time I had turned off the sweeper and Angela and Mr. Jennings had stopped to listen to our conversation. "That's all right. I hope I didn't hurt you when I rose up like that."

"No, no harm done. Hello, Mr. Jennings, Angela." said Greg. "Hey, maybe I came at the wrong time. I didn't know you were all so busy. I just wondered if you and Angela would like to go to Randolph City and get a bite to eat, and you're welcome to come too, Mr. Jennings."

"That's really nice of you, Greg," I answered, "but I know I'm stuffed from all the pizza we had at lunch, and I think Angela might be too. I was just going to fix some

Chapter 10   225

sandwiches here tonight for us. Of course, I can't speak for Mr. Jennings. By the way, you're all welcome to share our sandwiches."

"That sounds good to me," said Greg, "if you're sure it's not too much trouble."

"Good, now how about you, Mr. Jennings?"

"Well, I generally never turn down a meal I don't have to cook myself, but I will only eat here on one condition."

"What's that?" I asked.

"I want you all to call me Phil. I know I'm older than the rest of you, but I'm not that old. If you don't want Angela to call me by my first name, maybe she could call me 'Uncle Phil.'"

"Okay, Phil," I said tentatively. It seemed almost disrespectful to call him by his first name because he seemed like one of my professors at college. Also, I was still wary of him because of his past that he refused to talk about.

However, we all moved toward the kitchen, and by the time we were digging into the sandwiches, chips, and pop, we had reached a measure of comfort with each other.

Greg asked Phil about his book, and somehow they got on the subject of photography. I extolled the pictures I had seen in Phil's house and in the album. Then Greg said something about the fine quality in the picture of Angela that he had taken. Then he asked, "Have you been able to find anything else in the picture that would help solve our mystery here?"

"No," I began, but was interrupted by Angela.

"I might be getting my remembry back soon," she blurted enthusiastically to Greg. While I wanted Angela to be encouraged, I was afraid she was building too much on her remembrance of Edwards. After never saying more than a few words to anyone but me and possibly the psychiatrist, she was opening up to a relative stranger, the second in one day.

Greg must have been surprised too because he choked on the cola he was sipping. After a moment when his coughing subsided, he smiled his toothpaste ad smile. "Well, that's great, S--Sweetheart, but how do you--or--what makes you think your memory is coming back?" I didn't realize Greg was so concerned about Angela's situation. He seemed to be genuinely pleased and interested in her news.

"Because I saw Turtle Man today and then Amanda and I found the house we had built for the turtle and even food we had given him and everything."

Since Greg looked totally confused, I explained to him about the events of the day. "I guess the police are questioning this guy right now. He was still denying that he had ever seen Angela when we left them." I told him.

"Well, I hope they can get him to talk. I wonder how much he knows."

Just then I heard a car outside. I went to the back door as the familiar black and white squad car reached the end of the road. To answer Greg's question, I said, "We may find out now. Here come the police."

Three doors of the police car were flung open and out jumped Officers Rogers and Adams plus Bob Wilson. I could not deny a tingling excitement that came over me. I had not seen Bob since the night before when he had kissed me. I wondered if he would act any differently toward me.

I went to the door just when the three men reached it. We all went through the ritual of greeting, and Bob's greeting didn't seem to be any different than it ever was. I figured that he was used to kissing women, and I was making too much of it because I was so inexperienced with romance.

I invited the policemen and the reporter into the kitchen and again offered some food. All three took me up on my offer, so I started fixing sandwiches and pouring pop while they pulled up chairs, getting one extra from the living room. The three new arrivals began talking to Greg, Phil, and Angela, and the police were very interested in seeing the picture Phil had taken. In the midst of my preparation I sent Angela to get the picture from my bag which was sitting on my desk in the front room. I noticed that as soon as both officers looked at the picture, they immediately looked at Bob. He must have noticed too because his eyes took on the stormy expression I had noticed before in some of our heated encounters. Also, the exchange between Greg and Bob, while surfacely polite, seemed to be seething with constrained hostility.

After the police had questioned Phil about the picture, not mentioning the resemblance between the man in it and Bob, Greg said, "I just heard that we might have an end to this mystery soon. What's the good word, Officers?"

Sergeant Adams looked at me with a frown on his face, the same look I would give a misbehaving student in my classroom. "How much did you tell him, Amanda?"

My words came out sharper than I intended because I was on the defensive. "I didn't bring the subject up. Angela told Greg about her so-called 'Turtle Man' herself. As a matter of fact, she told Mr.--uh--Phil, too."

"Okay, I'm sorry. I didn't mean to scold you. I just want you to be careful who you're talking to before you say that Angela's getting her memory back. Someone is not going to be too happy about the news."

"I didn't mean to get Amanda in trouble, but let's face it, we're all concerned about the situation here. I'm sure we'd all like to know what you found out from Angela's 'Turtle Man.'"

Captain Rogers answered," We didn't find out too much from him, directly. He still insists he doesn't know the child, but we did run a check on him, and it seems he has been arrested before for suspected child molesting. You remember, Amanda, I told you the other day about him. The Flint police warned us to watch out for him."

It was as if a bomb had dropped in the little kitchen. All of us stared at the policeman, even Angela, but I did not think she understood what he was saying. She was just interested in any conversation about her Turtle Man. Greg was the first to break the silence. "Golly, so I suppose you put him in jail?"

"No," he said slowly, "I'm afraid we couldn't. You see, I said he was arrested for suspicion of child molesting, but they had to release him because the child he allegedly molested wouldn't testify, so charges were dropped."

"So you just let him go?" I gasped.

"Well, what else could we do? He doesn't admit to even knowing Angela, but even if he's lying, according to Angela, he didn't harm her."

"But what if--" I began.

"I'll tell you what," the Captain interrupted, "we're going to post a policeman here all night. He'll stay out in the squad car where he'll be able to watch the back door and front door and all the windows. You'll be safe for tonight. Then we'll see what we can do. I'm sorry, I wish we had more men, but we don't."

"I'll be glad to stay here a couple of nights to watch over things, Captain Rogers," Bob offered.

Immediately Greg responded, "I don't think that will be necessary. I'm here all the time. I can handle things." His firm tone of voice and the scowl on his face defied any rebuttal from Bob.

The three older men watching the exchange were trying very hard to suppress grins. Captain Rogers cleared his throat before he said, "Gentlemen, you are very generous to offer your services, and we may have to call on you, but anyway, tonight Officer Larsen is on his way over to watch the place all night."

I tried to be grateful for the protection I was getting, but I was still frightened thinking about an alleged child molester still walking around free. "I appreciate everything you're doing, Captain. I just wish you could have learned something from Edwards--was that his name? I'm sure Angela really did remember him. We even found the home she and this man made for her turtle."

"Oh yeah, where?" asked the policeman.

I related our afternoon exploration, and all the men listened with interest. After I finished Bob asked, "Does this guy, Edwards, live around here?"

"Yeah, he has a little cottage on Cypress Street-- about a mile north of here."

"So, that means he could have very well been over here the other day, and he could come here again easily?" I asked, trembling.

Before the officer could answer, Greg asked, "But what was he doing over at Randolph City? Do you think he's been following Amanda and the little girl?"

"I don't know," said Captain Rogers, "he might have been, but he said he had gone up there to get some groceries, and he was looking in the window of the pizza place because he was trying to see the prices."

"How did he get there? Does he have a car?" asked Phil.

"Yeah, he has an old, beat up 1960 Chevy. It's not much, but I guess it gets him around. In answer to your question, Amanda, yes, he could come over here, but we'll have a man here tonight, and we'll figure out something else after that. At least you know what he looks like, and I really don't think he'll bother you. He seems pretty scared."

None of us talked much after that; we all seemed involved in our own thoughts. Instead of solving mysteries, the appearance of Edwards had posed more unanswered questions. I looked over at Angela, and again my heart went out to her. Her face was a study of sadness and frustration."

After a few minutes of small talk about the weather and other mundane subjects, we all heard a car climbing up the driveway. It was another black and white squad car, and the young policeman Larsen, whom we had met at the station, was the driver. As soon as he positioned the car in the parking lot where he had a clear view of the cottage, he walked to the door where he was greeted by Sergeant Adams. He was introduced to all the others, and after refusing my offer of food, he took his post in the car. Soon after that, the policemen offered Phil a ride to his home, and, along with Bob, they all left.

By this time Angela and I were standing hand-in-hand in the living room saying good-bye to all our guests. Greg came up to us and put his arm around my shoulders.

"I'm going out to my room," he said. "I'm working on a thesis for my Master's, so I have a lot of typing to do. I wish I had a computer, but all I have is an old-fashioned type-writer. You'll probably hear it a lot this summer when you're outside." Then he added, "Don't worry, either one of you, everything will be all right. I'll be right out back if you need anything." He gently squeezed me to him, then walked out the front door to the police car. Apparently he was offering Officer Larsen his help, if needed, and telling him where he would be.

Angela and I busied ourselves with the dishes, and then I helped her get ready for bed. As I tucked her in, I bent down and kissed her rosy cheek. "Go to sleep, Sweetheart," I said. "Try not to feel bad about Turtle Man saying he doesn't know you. It's just that he's been in trouble with the police before, and he's scared of something."

She smiled sadly and said, "All right, Amanda, but you believe me, don't you, that I really did know him?"

"Sure I do, Honey. Maybe he'll decide to tell the truth later on. But, now, go to sleep, and we'll see what tomorrow will bring."

I started to pull the covers up around her when she sat up in bed. "Could I pray first, Amanda? Will you pray with me?"

I knew what people mean when they say they are cut to the quick. I should have been the one to suggest prayer. Maybe the simple trust and dependence that children had in God were the qualities Jesus wanted us to copy when He said we must become like children if we wanted to enter the kingdom of Heaven. Even after my talk with Him the night before, He had to remind me that I had to depend on Him.

Angela and I both knelt down by the bed, and Angela unashamedly began praying, "Jesus, help me get my remembry back, and help Turtle Man to tell the truth, and help Amanda not to be afraid. Thank you. Goodnight, Jesus."

I quickly brushed away my tears as she climbed back up into bed. After I tucked her in, I crept downstairs to get a drink of milk. The police car was prominently illuminated by the mercury pole light that stood by the parking lot. I could also hear the regular click-clack of Greg's typewriter, so, with the knowledge that two strong men were on hand ready to protect me and trusting in the One who was mightier than all, I was no longer really frightened when I went up to bed.

I slept well, too, and when the alarm went off, I found myself more than ready to face a gorgeous Michigan summer day. Angela, also, seemed to be in good spirits as she and I showered, dressed, and readied the museum for tourists. We had just finished breakfast when I heard a car pull up in the driveway. I looked out the window and recognized my two friends, Officers Rogers and Adams. They walked up to Officer Lawson who was still sitting in the police car. I was idly wondering how anyone could sit in a car all night without falling asleep when I caught sight of the policemen's faces as they headed toward the cottage. I knew right away that something was wrong, and I began bracing myself for an emotional blow.

Before they even reached the door, I opened it and called out unceremoniously, "Is something wrong?"

They looked shocked but didn't answer until they stepped up on the porch. Then Captain Rogers soberly announced, "Amanda, we just found Edwards dead in his house this morning."

Chapter 11

My legs started to buckle under me, and I barely managed to find my voice to ask, "What happened? How did he die?"

"It was apparent suicide. We found him in bed with a bullet in his head." Just as Captain Rogers finished speaking, Angela crept up behind me, looking frightened and confused.

I bent down to her and gently took hold of her hands. "Honey, I'm sorry to tell you, but Turtle Man died last night."

"Died? Oh, poor Turtle Man! Who killed him?"

I was shocked by her question, and the policemen looked as surprised as I. Captain Rogers said, "what makes you think anyone killed him, Angela?"

She shrugged her shoulders and said, "I don't know, but did he ever say he knew me?"

"No Honey, I'm sorry. The last time we saw him was yesterday at the police station." Then he turned to me to further explain. "We got a call about him from the paper boy this morning. He had found him when he accidentally threw the paper into the bushes right under Edwards' bedroom window. After he picked it up, he just casually glanced in the window, and he saw--well, he saw a grisly sight."

"How come you think it was suicide?" I asked.

Captain Rogers glanced at Angela before answering, and he probably carefully weighed his words because of her. "Uh, well, we found his--uh--weapon on his body, and there were powder burns on his hand, and we found this note.

At this, he unfolded a dirty, smudged piece of tablet paper with an almost illegible scrawl covering it. I had to study the writing carefully before I could decipher it. The note said, "I don't deserve to live. I have hurt small children. I don't want to hurt them anymore."

Something was wrong with the note. Somehow it just didn't sound like Edwards, but I couldn't say why I thought that. After all, I had only known Edwards for about ten minutes. The feeling I had, though, was so strong that I asked, "Are you sure this is his handwriting?"

"As sure as we can be. Of course, we didn't get much of a chance to get to know him, and the only writing we could find in his cottage were signatures on receipts, food stamp orders, and stuff like that. I don't think Mr. Edwards was very literate."

"That's it," I cried, "that's what's wrong with this note. It sounds too literate. You're right, Edwards didn't seem very educated to me. I remember his poor grammar, but this note is grammatically perfect, even spelled right, in spite of the scrawled handwriting."

"I understand what you're saying Amanda," said Captain Rogers, "but I don't think we know enough about Edwards to determine whether this is his note or not."

"I suppose so," I shrugged. "It's just so frustrating. Here was a man who might have told us something about Angela that could unlock this mystery, and now he's dead."

Captain Rogers spoke gently, "I know, but we'll have a break in this case soon; I just feel it in my bones. Well, try to have a good day, ladies, and don't let this get you down. I told Officer Lawson to go home. I guess you won't be needing any protection from Edwards any more, will you?" He asked with a wry smile. With that the two policemen plodded wearily out the door.

Again my job left me no time to muse over the disturbing news I'd been given, for just as soon as the officers left, some visitors pulled up in the driveway, and after them came two more cars. In fact, we were busy with guests practically all morning. I was amused watching Angela guide the tourists around the cottage. In just the few days she had lived with me, she had learned almost as much as I knew about the items of interest in the museum.

At 11:00 Greg appeared at the back door with a tablet of paper in his hands. He called out to me as I sat at my desk in the living room, "Hey, Boss Lady, is this a good time to discuss finances with you?"

"Sure," I replied. "We seem to have a lull in the visitor traffic right now. I guess you need to order some things, right?" The Parks and Recreation Department in Michigan paid Greg's and my salaries, and I was told to deposit all the proceeds from the museum fee in the Randolph City State Bank, but until the deposit could be made, I kept all the cash in a small safe hidden behind a seascape picture on the living room wall. I also had the authority to write checks to order anything for the maintenance of the cottage, lighthouse, and property.

"Right," said Greg as he pulled up a chair beside me. I took out an order blank which had been supplied for me by our main office in Lansing. To my dismay, I found concentrating on lawn and garden supplies very difficult with Greg sitting so close. How long would I act like an adolescent around men, I wondered.

Near the end of our consultation, Angela put down her coloring book she had been working on and asked if she could go outside to play. I was reluctant to let her because of what had happened the last time she had been out, but realizing I couldn't keep her in forever, I gave her permission with the time-worn warning, "Be careful."

After she left, Greg said, "She is certainly a cute little girl, and she is very fond of you."

"Well," I said, "the feeling is mutual."

"I'm amazed when I watch you with her," he continued.

"Why?"

"Because you're so good with her. Have you had lots of experience with little kids before?"

"No, I'm very new at this mothering business. Of course, I teach high school kids, and I have taught Angela's age group in Sunday School, but one hour a week is certainly different than twenty-four hours a day."

"Well, Angela seems happy with you--as happy as she can be under the circumstances. I think you make a great mother, Angela."

Again I could feel the hated blush come to my face. "Thank you, but Angela makes me look good. She's an easy child to care for."

"Oh, don't be so modest, Amanda." As he talked he slipped his arm around my shoulders. "Most women in your place would have shipped the kid off to a foster home the first night she came, but you're a loving, caring person. That's one of the things I like about you, but it's not the only thing."

Like a slow motion movie, our faces drew closer and closer together. Our lips were about to touch when suddenly the door burst open, revealing an astonished Bob Wilson. "Oh, excuse me," he said. "I'm sorry if I interrupted something."

"You could have fooled me," murmured Greg sarcastically.

"I am sorry," said Bob with a smile that was very close to a sneer. "I'll come back later if I've come at a bad time."

"Of course not," I said hastily, "we were--uh--were just ordering some lawn and garden supplies. Greg, why don't you write down the last two items you want, and I'll write the check after we add up all the stuff we need. By the way, there's a calculator in the top desk drawer."

With as much dignity as I could muster, I stalked out of the room toward the back door leaving Greg and Bob glaring at each other in undisguised hostility. Angela was swinging in the tree swing, so I didn't bother her. Instead I looked at my watch and decided it was lunch time. Since I could hear the low murmur of the men's voices in the living room, I figured they must have reached at least a measure of civility. I walked back into the room and asked, "Would you gentlemen like some lunch. I make a pretty mean tuna salad."

Bob looked at Greg and then at me, and he smiled rather sheepishly. "It seems eating here is getting to be a regular event. Are you sure I won't be imposing?" he asked with a humility that surprised me.

"Oh, don't be silly," I answered lightly. "I'd rather fix lunch for four than for just Angela and me. It makes it more worth the effort."

I turned and began busily preparing lunch. Bob sauntered out to the kitchen and leaned against the door frame with his arms folded against his chest. He asked me, "Did you know about that man, Edwards, being found dead this morning?"

"Yes, I answered, "The police were over here this morning and told us."

Greg walked up and stood beside Bob and asked, "Did I hear you talking about Edwards?"

"Yes," I spoke up, "I forgot you hadn't heard. Edwards was found dead in his bed this morning--apparent suicide."

"No kidding. Who found him?"

This time Bob answered, "A paper boy who had accidentally thrown his paper in the bushes underneath his bedroom window."

"Poor kid," said Greg, "a head blown off by a gun can be a pretty grisly sight. Did he ever admit knowing Angela?"

"No," I answered, "he left a note, but all it said was that he had hurt little children and didn't deserve to live."

"Well, he probably didn't." stated Greg, sternly. "A guy who would molest a little child is nothing but scum."

"I guess you're right," I said, "but I don't really think he harmed Angela."

"Why not?" asked Greg.

"Well, for one thing, the doctor didn't find any evidence that she had been molested, and Angela has nothing but good memories of her 'Turtle Man.'"

Bob spoke up, "I tend to agree with you Amanda. I've also been thinking that his alleged 'suicide' came at a regular convenient time for someone who doesn't want Angela's past to come back."

As he talked, a shudder crept over me. It was frightening to imagine that someone had killed Edwards in cold blood just because of his connection with Angela. There was another thought nagging at the back of my mind, but it wouldn't crystalize. Anyway, since lunch was now ready, I invited the men to sit down, and I went to the door and called Angela in.

During lunch, we didn't mention Edwards, probably because all of us were trying to protect Angela. Instead Bob brought up a subject almost as uncomfortable to me. He directed his piercing eyes toward me and asked, "Tell me, Amanda, if it's not too personal, who is this Paul you took Rothman for the first night he came?"

I wished I could crawl under the table. I didn't know if Bob was deliberately trying to embarrass me in front of Greg or if he was showing his reporter's "concern" for other people's lives. Greg's eyes showed normal curiosity and sympathy. I decided to tell them the whole story, and I was surprised that I could do so without experiencing most of the emotional upheaval I had gone through at first.

Both men listened intently while I recited my love story from the church nursery to the disastrous lakeside talk in Paul's car on Christmas night when we had ended our engagement. After I finished, Greg reached across the table and patted my hand. "Well, you're better off without a creep like that. I'm sure he's already sorry he let you get away from him. I know I would be."

His tender words brought tears to my eyes, and I smiled at him in appreciation. But when I looked at Bob, I saw such a scowl on his face that I immediately became angry. "I take it you don't agree with Greg?" I demanded sharply.

"Well, yes and no," he said. "I do agree that you're better off without Paul, but I think Paul is better off without you, too."

"Thanks a lot!" I shouted as I jerked myself up from the table.

"Now wait, let me explain. I don't think you and Paul were really ever in love. I think you were just comfortable with each other, sort of like old shoes. Maybe you would have had a dull little ho-hum marriage, but I'll bet Paul and this Janelle will have a July 4th fireworks marriage. I admire Paul. What he did took lots of courage."

"I suppose you're entitled to your opinion," I retorted. "Now, if everyone is finished, I'll start cleaning up this mess before we get any more visitors." I began clattering dishes together and throwing silverware in the sink with a bang. Greg and Bob quickly got up from the table and silently picked up the leftover food and drinks and put them away. Angela sat watching us all with wide, frightened eyes. She didn't understand what was going on, but I'm sure she knew I was angry.

I turned on the water, squirted the soap into the sink, and was just about ready to start washing when a car started climbing up the driveway. I immediately recognized Phil Jennings' car, and wanting to ease the tension in the room, I said, "Looks like Mr.--uh--Phil. Maybe I'd better go greet him."

"Sure, Amanda, go ahead. We'll finish up in here," Greg offered.

I walked into the living room and almost collapsed in my chair by the tourist desk. I was trembling with anger from Bob's remark. How dare he suggest that Paul and I were never in love! Everyone knew we were meant for each other, everyone except Paul apparently. All the time these angry thoughts were churning in my mind, I couldn't completely suppress the fact that I had never felt the excitement from Paul's kisses that I had experienced with Bob's one kiss. I finally decided that Bob was exciting to me because he was my verbal adversary, and getting him to kiss me was like winning a battle.

My temper had cooled considerably by the time Phil came to the door. He was carrying about five books with covers that must have once been brightly colored, but were now dulled with age. "Hello, Amanda, I thought I'd bring these books for Angela to look at," he began to explain. "They are children's books that my ch--that I found in my house. They're old, but they are still interesting, at least I think Angela will like them. Would you allow me to read at least one of them to her? We'll sit in here right in front of you."

He looked so pathetic that I couldn't have refused him even if I had wanted to. "Sure," I said. "I really appreciate your thinking about her. She has taken to you in a big way. I guess I will have to take you up on your offer to stay right in front of me when you read to her, though. I'll be glad when this mystery is over. I'm getting tired of not being able to trust anyone."

"I know, it must be hard. Where is Angela now?"

Again I realized I had let her get out of my sight. I could hear Bob and Greg in the kitchen, but I hadn't heard her. But fortunately, I had no need for worry, because Angela walked into the living room at that moment, followed by Greg and Bob. The latter strode over to me with a folded dish towel folded on the curve of his arm which he had extended in a mock imitation of a butler. "Is there anything else we can do for you, Madam?" he asked with a fake English accent."

I had to smile in spite of myself. "No," I answered meekly, "thank you all for doing the dishes." Before I could say anything else, I heard a car approaching, immediately followed by another. "Looks like I've got to get busy," I said. "It seems visitors either come all at once or not at all."

"We'll stay and help," again Greg offered, "although I don't know what I can say about these old relics. I'll just sorta stand around here and see if there's anything I can do."

Phil spoke up, "Angela, I brought you some books to look at. Why don't we sit over here on the couch and look at them. When these guests leave, I'll read one to you. Is that all right, Amanda?" I nodded my consent, and they walked over to the couch and soon had their heads bent over the books.

"I'll stay too, but I just want to get a free guided tour. You realize I've never heard your spiel about all this stuff," said Bob. I was rather uncomfortable at the prospect of saying my 'spiel' in front of someone I considered to be rather cynical about the relics in the museum, but I didn't have time to object because the other guests were already at the door.

First there was a family of five, two weary-looking parents with three boys who were probably all under six years of age. As soon as I collected the fees, all three boys bolted immediately to the ships' horns which they quickly learned to operate, a feat that delighted them and dismayed their parents. While I was trying to bring some order to the situation, two more people came in, a young couple who I surmised were newlyweds by their loving expressions and touches. Thankfully, since they were so absorbed in each other, I hastily greeted them and then turned them over to Greg while I endeavored to pry the boys away from the horns and thus regain a semblance of the dignity that should reign in a museum.

I had just captured everyone's attention with my speech about the very first light house operator when chaos again took over with the next two guests who walked in. They were a middle-aged couple dressed in very loud, flowered, matching shirts, and shorts that were the color of the brightest fuchsia flower on the shirts. The woman sported a straw sombrero and sequined sunglasses shaped like a butterfly's wings, and the man wore the inevitable 30 millimeter camera around his neck. My first impression of the couple was unkind, but I couldn't help but think of the nursery rhyme about Jack Spratt and his wife because the woman was what one might tactfully call portly, weighing at least 200 pounds. The husband, however, was thin as a reed; I felt that if he turned sideways, he would disappear.

The size of the woman caused everyone in the cottage to turn and look at her, but her personality kept her the center of attention. She began talking as soon as she walked in the door of the cottage, and she dominated the conversation the whole time she was there. In one breath she told us that her name was Lucinda Parsons, but her friends called her Lucy, that her husband's name was Frank, and he was an avid fisherman, but he agreed to take her sightseeing for one hour a day if she would let him go off in the small motor boat they had towed behind their car from Dearborn. After all that, she began flitting around the room exclaiming over each museum piece as if she had discovered the eighth wonder of the world.

Phil and Angela were still sitting on the couch looking at the books, and Phil caught my eye and smiled. Greg and Bob entered the room just as Lucy was extolling the magnificent workmanship that had gone into the ancient organ, and they too were smiling at this remarkable woman. Suddenly, Lucy turned toward the couch and spied Angela. For a split second she was silent, then she began, "Oh, what a darling child! She's gorgeous, and I know I've seen her before. I never forget a face. I've seen that child before."

Immediately, Bob, Greg, and I bolted over to her side. Bob was the first to speak, "Are you sure you've seen her before?" He gestured toward Angela who was taking the whole scene in with a bewildered expression on her face.

"Mrs. Parsons," I cried, "it's very important that you remember where you've seen her. You see, she has amnesia, and we're trying to find some clue to her past."

"Well, I declare," she exclaimed, "I just can't think where I've seen her, but it'll come to me. I'm always recognizing people I've seen before, and, if I can't remember them right away, I just think awhile, and it comes back to me, doesn't it, Frank?"

"Yeah," said her husband, simply.

"Do you recognize the little girl, Mr. Parsons?" asked Greg.

"Nope," he answered with no further elaboration. Apparently he was as taciturn as his wife was talkative.

I walked over to Angela and asked, "Honey, do you recognize that lady?" I asked pointing to Lucy as she approached us.

"No," she shook her head solemnly, "I've never seen her before."

"Mrs. Parsons--" I began.

"Call me Lucy, dear," she interrupted.

"Lucy, would you be willing to wait here until the police come? There are two policemen in Randolph City who are working very close with this case, and I'm sure they'll want to ask you some questions."

"I'd love to help in any way I can, but do you think they could come over to our cottage this afternoon and talk to me there? You see, Frank met an old man who lives near our cottage, and they made a date to go fishing at 2:00, but I'm not going. I hate fishing, and I hate boats because I can't swim, and I use these times when Frank fishes to sit on the beach and write because I'm a writer of sorts. Anyway you tell the policemen to come over any time after 2:00, and meanwhile I'll be thinking where I saw the little girl."

"Okay," I said, as I rushed over to the phone, "I'll call them. Tell me where your cottage is."

"We're staying at the Lakeview Cottages on the opposite shore of the old boat docks. Ours is number 9, but I won't be there. I'll be sitting on the beach right in front of our cottage. I'm sure they'll be able to spot me," she stated with a good natured chuckle.

As I started to dial, Bob approached Lucy and asked, "Are you sure, Mam, that you don't recognize Angela, the child, because you saw her picture in the paper last week?"

"No, we only got here yesterday, and we haven't seen any papers for a while, and--" She continued talking, but I didn't hear her because Captain Rogers answered the phone, and I began relating Lucy's story. He told me to tell her they would be over to talk to her at 3:00.

I had become so excited over Lucy's recognition of Angela that I had completely neglected my other guests. However, they all seemed caught up in our drama, so I don't think they were too concerned about the museum articles. After I gave Lucy the message from Captain Rogers, I gathered my wits about me and began pointing out the special exhibits to my guests. Soon they all departed to explore the grounds and the lighthouse, leaving Bob, Greg, Angela, Phil, and me in the cottage.

"Well, maybe we're getting a breakthrough at last," I suggested.

"I wouldn't count too much on it," said Greg. "That lady is such a scatter-brain, I doubt if she knows half of what she's saying."

"Oh, I disagree," said Bob. "Didn't you hear her say that she's a writer? A writer notices people. I personally think she'll be able to tell us something about Angela after she thinks a little while."

"You might be right," Greg conceded reluctantly, but he didn't look convinced. Instead he looked at his watch and turned toward the back door. "I've got some work to do. I'd better get moving," he said.

"Yeah, me too," said Bob, as he headed for the front door. "I've got to see if there is some more news to report besides the ongoing saga of Amanda and Angela."

Phil had not offered any opinion on Lucy's revelation, but now he spoke up, "I guess I'd better go too, Amanda. I haven't spent much time on my book today. I got sidetracked when I found those books for Angela. However, I'll be interested in hearing if our loquacious friend comes up with an answer to our mystery."

After saying goodbye and expressing good wishes about Lucy's meeting with the police, all three men left just as some more visitors were trudging up the driveway toward the cottage, and several more came right after them. I was so busy during the afternoon that I only had fleeting thoughts of the all-important interview that I supposed was taking place on the beach across the bay.

I was standing on the porch when the black and white squad car pulled up the driveway. Even the car seemed sluggish, and when I saw my police friends climb out of the car, I experienced an eerie replay of the catastrophic morning. The policemen had the same shocked, distressed faces and the same weariness in their walk as they had when they had come to tell us about Edwards. My heart started to pound, and I automatically looked back in the cottage where Angela was sitting reading her new books, wondering if I could shield her from the bad news I felt sure was coming. Sure enough, as soon as Captain Rogers stepped up on the porch, he lowered the boom, without any preliminary small talk to soften the blow. "Lucy Parson drowned this afternoon. We found her body washed up on the shore of Silver Bay Point."

Chapter 12

I remember screaming, "No, no, it can't be!" Then the whole world became black, and the next thing I remember is coming to on the couch in my living room and looking into the concerned faces of my two police friends and Angela. For a second I couldn't understand what had happened, but all too soon the announcement of Captain Rogers came crashing down upon me again. That vibrant, joyful Lucy Parsons who had captured all our hearts in the brief time we had known her was dead. Even if she hadn't said she recognized Angela, her death would have been a brutal shock to me, but since she had offered some hope of answering some of our questions, her death was also a painful disappointment. I could feel my eyes filling with tears.

Sergeant Adams knelt down beside the couch and took my hand in his. "There, there, Lass," he soothed, "everything will turn out all right."

As soon as I gained control of my voice I sat up and started asking questions. "Do you have any idea how this happened? I remember her saying she didn't know how to swim, so what was she doing in the water?"

Captain Rogers answered, "We don't know for sure. We went to the beach and saw her chair, her writing tablet, and her big bag that she carried sun tan lotion, combs, and stuff like that in. Nothing was put away. It was like she had just stepped away but was coming back right away. There were footprints leading down to the lake, and there was a large stone sticking out of the water just a few feet from the footprints. The rock that was sticking out above the water was the top of a huge boulder that was mostly submerged. Since there was a nasty bruise on her head, we figure she must have stepped onto that stone and slipped, because stones like that are slippery, and she must have hit her head on it, knocking herself unconscious, and then drowning."

"I think somebody pushed her in the water and drownded her," said Angela in a deadly calm voice that made me shudder.

Captain Rogers looked shocked too. "What makes you think that, Honey?"

"Because she said she saw me before."

I was glad that the captain wasn't going to try to pretend that Angela was the only one wondering if Lucy's death had been a murder. He bent down to look her in the eyes and said honestly, "Well, Angela, I admit we have thought about that. I guess if she hadn't said she recognized you, we would have just thought she had had an accident, but since she did say she thought she had seen you before, well, we're going to ask a lot of questions."

"I just wish she had remembered me better," said Angela wistfully.

"I do too," Sergeant Adams joined the conversation, "but I'm sure everything is going to work out fine very soon. It's about time that we're going to start getting some breaks. You'll see."

I smiled at him, grateful that these particular policemen were on the case. We couldn't have found any more compassionate, understanding men anywhere.

Captain Rogers again focused his attention on me, "Are you feeling better, Amanda? I'm sorry I hit you with the news so abruptly. I guess sometimes we policemen don't realize the effect sudden deaths can have on a person who doesn't see them every day."

"No, it's all right. I don't know what happened to me. I've never fainted before in my life. I guess that Lucy was just so full of life, and I became attached to her in the short time I knew her, and--oh, I can't explain it."

"I think I understand," said the captain. "I didn't meet her at all, but just talking to her husband, I realized she must have been a special person."

"Oh no! I forgot about him," I was dismayed at my insensitivity. "How is he taking it?"

"Pretty hard. It's funny, just looking at the two of them--well, they looked like they would have been the most miss-matched couple ever, but I could tell they had a really good thing going. I've had to announce many deaths of spouses to the survivors, and I can detect real grief, and I know Mr. Parsons is really suffering."

"That's so sad. Is there anything we can do for him?"

"No, he's on his way back home to start the funeral arrangements. Of course, the body won't be released till tomorrow because of the autopsy."

There didn't seem much to say, and for a few moments the only sound in the room was the ticking of the grandfather clock, reminding us that time marches on regardless of the disastrous events that happen around us. I was the first to break the silence. "Would you gentlemen like to join us for supper? I asked, desperately wanting to return to a sense of normalcy. "I can't promise a seven-course meal, but I can stir something up that will at least be filling."

"Oh, thank you anyway, Amanda," said the Captain, "but we have to get on our way. You sure you're both all right?"

Angela nodded her head when he looked at her, and I said, "Yes, we'll be fine. Thank you for your concern."

They both stood up and started for the door. "We'll see you later. If you need us for anything, just call."

Angela and I walked to the door with them and said our good-byes. We stood watching them until their car disappeared down the driveway. As soon as I had locked and bolted the door, Angela clutched my hand and whimpered, "Amanda, are you okay again, really?"

I bent down and drew her trembling little body close to mine. "Sure, Honey, I'm fine. I'm disappointed and sad, but everything will be all right."

"Are you scared," she asked in a barely audible whisper.

"Well, yes, I am, a little," I admitted. Then without even thinking of my next words, I found myself saying, "You know, Jesus knows we're scared, and He wants to help us. Would you like to pray?"

I felt her nod her head, so we walked hand in hand to the couch where we knelt, and this time I led out in prayer. "Dear Lord, Angela and I need your help. We are frightened and sad. Please take care of us, and help us not to be so scared. Jesus, also help Mr. Parsons in the grief he has over his dear wife. Please help Angela to get her memory back, and protect us both, we pray. Amen."

Before we stood up, Angela flung her arms around me, buried her head in my chest, and sobbed. Instinctively, I knew this was no time to say anything. I just held her tightly and waited till her tears were spent. When at last she was quiet, I dried her eyes with my shirt, and we silently walked into the kitchen and began dinner preparations. I looked out the back window for Greg, but I didn't see him or hear his typewriter anymore, so Angela and I had a quiet meal alone. After dinner I tucked her in bed and read her a story from one of the books Mr. Jennings had brought. When she fell asleep, I went back downstairs to finish my book work.

I was diligently concentrating on my work when I was startled by a knock on the back door followed immediately by Greg's voice calling softly, "Amanda, it's me, Greg. Can I come in?"

"Sure," I said as I walked to unlock the door I had carefully locked before.

"Hello, I hope I didn't frighten you. I saw your light, so I figured you were still up."

"Yeah, I've been catching up on some book work. You know the government. Everything has to be written in triplicate. Have you eaten yet, or can I get you something?"

"No--or--yes, I've eaten already in Randolph City, and no, you don't have to get me anything. I've been working all day on my thesis. I'll be so glad when that's over."

As we talked, we slowly moved toward the living room where we both sat on the couch. "What are you writing about, Greg? I asked.

"Economics," he answered unenthusiastically.

"You don't sound very happy with your subject," I observed, laughing.

"Oh, it's all right, I guess. I know that subjects like economics are important if you want to make the big bucks, but it can be deadly dull. What I'd really like to do-- oh, I'd better not tell you, you'll probably laugh."

"No, I won't. Tell me."

"Well, I'd really like to be an actor." He looked like a timid little boy, afraid that I was going to ridicule him.

"I think you would be a very good actor," I said honestly. "Have you done any acting before?"

"Oh, just in high school, well, a little in college, too. But my father said he wouldn't pay for my college if I went into drama full-time, so, well, a guy has to eat, eh?"

"Oops, your Canadian friend is coming through again."

Greg blushed. "Yeah, you know, I started out teasing my friend about his 'eh,' and it became part of my speech."

"I know what you mean. My mother is from the South, and one of her expressions I used to tease her about was, 'I reckon,' and now I have found myself saying it, too."

"That explains your 'southern hospitality.' I don't think I've ever been over here when you haven't offered me something to eat."

It was my turn to blush. "Yeah, you're right. My mother always taught me that you offered guests something to eat or drink even if you only had a glass of water to offer."

Greg smiled and put his arm around my shoulders. "Well, I was kinda hoping I would be considered a regular fixture around here, not a guest." His lips drew near mine, when suddenly, like an instant replay, we heard the clomp of heavy footsteps on the entry way and a vigorous pounding at the door.

Sure enough, when I opened the door, I was not surprised to see Bob Wilson, his tall frame filling the doorway. "Hi there," he said jovially, "I was in the neighborhood and thought I'd drop by."

"I've got to say this for you, Wilson, you've got incredible timing." Greg growled.

Bob looked puzzled, but then he grinned as Greg's words apparently registered. "Uh oh! I must have interrupted something again. I'm so sorry." The sneer on his face refuted his apology. "I guess you've heard by now about Lucy Parson's death?" He asked, abruptly changing the subject.

"No," gasped Greg. "How did that happen?"

"I guess I forgot to tell you," I said, and I looked over at Bob who had a mocking gleam in his eyes. I knew he was thinking that we had other things besides Lucy's death on our minds. "Lucy apparently drowned today."

"Oh no," said Greg, "did she talk to the police before she--uh--died?"

Bob answered this time, "No, it happened before they got over there to see her. Rather convenient for someone who might have been concerned about what she had to say, don't you think?" His eyes seemed to bore into Greg when he asked the question.

"Why are you looking at me like that, Wilson?" Greg asked in undisguised hostility. "Are you implying that I had something to do with her drowning?"

"You tell me, Rothman. All I know is that yesterday and today two people have been implicated somehow in Angela's past, and now those two people are dead."

"So what does that have to do with me? It might be that Edwards really did commit suicide because he was scared out of his mind that the police were going to nail him for child molesting, and I remember Lucy saying she didn't know how to swim, so her death was probably an accident."

"Maybe, but it just seems too coincidental."

There was an uncomfortable silence while the two men glared at each other. Finally Greg blurted out, "You know, I could be pointing some fingers at you. The police have checked out my credentials, and Angela doesn't have a fit every time I come around like she does with you."

"I can't explain that," Bob admitted, "but I know I'm innocent. I just don't know about you."

"Well, believe me, I'm not losing any sleep just because you don't trust me. Just as long as Amanda does."

Afraid that they were going to come to blows, I finally spoke up, "Come on guys, you're not going to solve anything this way. We need to work together to find an end to this mystery."

Bob looked mollified. "I'm sorry, Amanda. I didn't mean to make a scene. My apologies, Rothman, I guess I don't have any real reason to suspect you."

Greg relaxed, "It's all right. I guess all of us are nerved up after what's been going on." After another pause, Greg said, "I've got to go, Amanda. It's been a long day, and I've got to organize some of the notes I made today. Oh, by the way, could you open the museum about an hour later tomorrow? I've noticed that some of the lighthouse railing spikes are loose, and I'm going to have to weld them. I got some welding equipment from the DNR office today when I was in town." He was talking about railing around the top of the lighthouse that consisted of wrought-iron spikes, about an inch apart, welded to three steel circular rods placed at the top, middle, and bottom of the railing.

"You've had some welding experience?" asked Bob.

"Yeah, at boat docks where I've worked. It's one of those jobs that are not exactly thrilling, but somebody has to do it."

"I guess so," agreed Bob, "and talking about work you have to get done, I've got to go develop some pictures. I'll see you later."

I said good-bye to both men and bolted and locked both the front and back doors after them. So many questions were swirling around in my head that I was afraid I would never get to sleep. Was Lucy Parson's death an accident? Did Mr. Edwards commit suicide? Could I trust Greg and Bob? Both of them? Neither of them? And what was Phil Jennings hiding in the room I almost blundered in? I couldn't find the answers to any of these problems, but for once, I took a lesson from Angela, and in simple childlike faith, I committed all of them to the One who knew everything. After that, I fell into a deep, peaceful sleep quickly.

The next few days were uneventful, though busy. I never realized how much extra work a little girl could bring. I had to do laundry more often, and I was more concerned about making nutritious meals. Before Angela had come, I had just nibbled on junk food whenever I felt hungry, so Angela's presence was beneficial to my health.

My care and concern for Angela had improved my emotional outlook, also. I hardly ever thought of Paul anymore, and I hadn't had a dream about him since the night Greg came. I felt rather guilty that Angela's misfortune was the reason I was no longer brooding over my lost love. I even felt a little selfish in that my life was more exciting now than it had ever been, and I wondered if my offer to keep Angela was made with the purest of motives. That was the reason I was uncomfortable whenever anyone complimented me on my care of the child.

To give myself credit, though, I was worried about Angela, her immediate safety and her future. I wondered if she would regain her memory before I had to go back to school in the fall, and if she didn't, would the authorities allow me to take her with me when I left. I knew that my mother would gladly watch her while I was at school even without talking to her. I had not been able to tell them about Angela or anything that had happened since she had come because they had gone on vacation to tour the New England states, and I did not know how to contact them. It was just as well, though, because I knew they would have worried themselves sick. I also knew they would fall in love with Angela if they ever would have the opportunity to meet her.

In the midst of all these speculations, life went on. Tourist business at the museum was probably at its peak, especially since the weather was being so cooperative. Every day the sun shone brightly in clear, blue skies. The visitors were mostly landlubbers, though, because the boaters spent all their time on the lake, warmed by the friendly sun and propelled by the gentle breezes.

I didn't see Bob the entire week after Lucy's death, but I saw Greg often. In fact, Greg ate with us every night, and one night he took both Angela and me out to a posh restaurant in Randolph City and treated us to a delicious steak dinner with a sumptuous salad and dessert bar. He didn't try to kiss me again, but in every other way he acted like a young man who had "come courting," bringing bouquets of beautiful wild flowers, complimenting every outfit I wore, and laughing at all my jokes.

I had mixed feelings about his attentions. Part of me liked them; I guess I would have been crazy not to. However, another part of me was unaffected, almost bored, by his overtures. The night after the steak dinner when Angela had gone to sleep, I lay in the bed wide awake analyzing my feelings toward Greg. I realized that I was glad to see him when he came around, but if he wasn't around for a while, I didn't really miss him. Greg seemed to agree with everything I said and everything I did. He liked the same kind of music, books, or TV shows I liked, or at least he said he did. I should have been happy to find someone with the same interests as mine, but I felt something was missing.

Suddenly, I realized what it was, and I sat up so abruptly that Angela stirred in her sleep. I missed the verbal sparring Bob and I always had together. In fact, I missed Bob, and the realization of that fact astounded me. Bob appeared to be as different from me as ice cream and hot sauce, but maybe that was the attraction. I had never met anyone like him in my "mid-west, conservative upbringing." I missed the mischievous twinkle in his eyes when he was teasing me. I remembered the half-amused, half-angry look on his face when he interrupted Greg in his attempt to kiss me. Was that why he was staying away, I wondered? Did he think I was in love with Greg, and since he disliked Greg so much, he didn't want to see me anymore either? Maybe in his distrust of Greg, he thought Greg and I were in some diabolical conspiracy that was connected to Angela's past.

I knew I would have no peace unless I could talk to Bob, but if he wasn't going to come over to the cottage anymore, I wondered when I could talk to him. Then in the dark bedroom, an idea burst through my thoughts like a light. The day after tomorrow would be Sunday, and if Bob was at church, I would invite him to a picnic dinner, without Greg this time, and I would try to explain that Greg and I weren't having a romance, at least as far as I was concerned. I felt sure the words would come to me when I needed them. I finally fell asleep formulating my plans.

The next morning, a sunny Saturday, I awoke with an eagerness to start putting into practice the plans I had made the night before. At 5:00, after I had entertained many guests at the museum, I put the "closed" sign on the gate at the end of the driveway, and Angela and I got ready to go grocery shopping. I planned to really splurge and have sirloin steak, baked potatoes, Italian salad, brown and serve rolls, and I planned to make a luscious, chocolate cake from a recipe my mother had given me.

Just before we were about to leave, Greg knocked on the back door of the cottage. When I let him in, he smiled warmly and asked, "How would you ladies like to go to Roger's City with me and get a pizza? It'll be my treat."

I didn't really know what to say. I didn't want to hurt Greg's feelings, but I didn't want him to see food I was going to buy at the grocery store because it would obviously be more than Angela and I could eat alone. I must have made him curious about my plans anyway, though, by my faltering answer. "Well, that's nice of you, Greg, but--well--we--uh--Angela and I were going to the store, and--uh--well, we might be there for a while--and, I don't want you to have to go with us. I tell you what, I'll get those frozen pizzas from the deli at the store, and we'll heat them up in the oven here when we get back."

"Well, why don't I come along with you? I have a little shopping to do myself. Then we can go to the pizza place and get a good pizza. I'm not too fond of those frozen things."

Again I didn't know what to say. "Oh, you probably have more important things to do. Let's see, maybe I could get the things you need at the store and then I'll go to the pizza place and get one of their pizzas to go. It'll stay warm until we get home, I'm sure."

Greg looked at me curiously as he answered, "I don't mind going with you. In fact, I need a break; I've been working all day. I'll just come along, that is, if you don't mind."

I'm sure my face must have displayed my embarrassment. "No, of course not. I-I just didn't want you to have to be bored in the grocery store, but I'll be glad to have your company. Are you ready to go?" I had to quell guilt feelings because what I had just said wasn't exactly the truth, at least the whole truth. I began to realize how difficult it was going to be to have a private picnic with Bob without Greg's knowing about it.

All the time we were in the grocery store, I played a ridiculous game of cat and mouse with Greg. I had managed to get away from him when we had first entered the store by taking Angela to the restroom; then when we came out, I looked for him in the various aisles. If I saw him at the end of one aisle, I would go to another one. Finally I spied him at the check-out counter, and I deliberately waited until he was checked out before I went up. Luckily, he went out to the car without seeing my purchases.

I was considerably more relaxed at the pizza parlor, and Greg and Angela and I seemed to be enjoying ourselves, gaily talking about insignificant matters. We were in the same restaurant where we had encountered Mr. Edwards, and if the place brought back any bad memories for Angela, she didn't show it. I deliberately sat with my back facing the window that poor Edwards had peered in because I was afraid I would keep imagining his face there. I also made sure Angela was facing away from it too.

Suddenly, just before the pizza arrived, Greg got up in his seat, reached over, and rubbed his thumb gently over my cheek, right under my eye. "I'm sorry," he said, "but there was a smudge on your face." Then he sat down and glanced surreptitiously at something behind me. I turned around just in time to see Bob Wilson glaring at us through the window. I was dismayed that he had again witnessed a romantic-looking scene between Greg and me. I tried to smile at Bob and beckon him in, but he quickly turned around and disappeared up the street. After that I wasn't very hungry for my pizza, and I was annoyed at Greg. I think the whole scene had been staged to further alienate Bob from me, to make him think that Greg and I were "going with each other." I was more determined than ever to have that picnic with Bob to clear up the misconceptions he must have about my "attraction" to Greg.

When we drove home that night, I must have shown my irritation because Greg didn't linger long with us. He said quick good-byes, and, I suppose, spent the rest of the night in his room. I got to work baking the cake, letting Angela lick the beater, and preparing anything else I could for the dinner the next day. Then I spent half the night awake, wondering just what I was going to say to Bob.

Sunday was as gorgeous as the other days of the week had been, but I knew as soon as I woke up in the hot bedroom that it was going to be a scorcher. Angela and I dressed as coolly as we could and still be appropriate for church. I felt excitement building up inside of me, and I knew my excitement came from the thought of seeing Bob, but I tried to tell myself that I was just eager to clear up a misunderstanding and restore friendship with him. I kept hurrying Angela along, telling her I wanted to get a good seat near the window of the small, un-air-conditioned church. I don't know whether she bought that or not, but as usual she quietly obeyed.

We pulled into the parking lot fifteen minutes before Sunday School was over, so we walked into a quiet foyer where only one man was standing with his back to us. He turned around when he heard us enter and came over and greeted us warmly, "Well, hello, you ladies look cool and comfortable in this heat. I'm Dan Morrison, and I want to welcome you to church today. You've been here before, haven't you?"

"Yes, we have. I'm Amanda Stevens, and this is Angela--" I broke off abruptly since I could not supply a last name for Angela.

Mr. Morrison was a big man, undoubtedly at least six-three and weighing well over 200 pounds, but his warm smile and twinkling eyes told me that he had a big heart as well. "Yeah, I recognize this little lady from the newspaper," he said looking down at Angela. Then he turned to me, "Any good news about her mystery?"

"No, I'm afraid not, but thank you for asking."

"Sure, we'll keep praying for you both." Then he bent down laboriously and talked to Angela. "You look mighty pretty in that pink dress."

Without any prompting from me, Angela said, "Thank you. Amanda said it was the coolest thing I had except for my bathing suit, and I couldn't wear that to church." She giggled charmingly, almost normally, causing Mr. Morrison and me to laugh with her.

Rising up, our greeter said to both of us, "I tell you what, since you're my special friends and since I'm an official usher today, I'll take you to the coolest spot in the sanctuary." He gently took my arm with one hand and held Angela's hand with the other one, and led us to the third pew from the front, right next to a screened window. As soon as we sat down we could feel a faint breeze probably drawn in by the giant floor fans on both sides of the platform. Before he left us he gave me a bulletin and gave Angela a Sunday School paper geared for her age level. She seemed to be immediately interested in it. I guiltily wondered if I should have brought her to Sunday School, but even in church I was reluctant to be separated from her while she was in her class and I was in mine. The future again loomed before me. If Angela's memory never returned or if we never learned more about her past, would she be able to go to school? There were so many things to worry about that I was surprised I hadn't already developed ulcers.

In a few minutes, however, a petite lady, probably in her early fifties, came in through a door at the back of the platform and sat at the organ. She began playing the old, familiar gospel song, "His Eye Is on the Sparrow." I felt a peace come over me because I believed the song was meant for me. God knew I needed to be reminded that if God is aware of every little sparrow that falls to the ground, how much more was He aware of Angela and me. Even the bulletin was a reminder of God's love of children. The outside picture was of a little girl in a green meadow surrounded by brightly colored tulips. I prayed that life would someday be that serene for Angela.

When I began reading the inside of the bulletin, my eyes immediately picked out Bob Wilson's name. He was going to sing a solo that morning. I had no idea he had musical talent, but I did realize he had a rich, mellow speaking voice. He sounded like a TV or radio announcer.

Soon I heard that very voice behind me saying, "Good Morning, Mrs. Dawson, how's the world treating you today?" I turned around to see Bob talking to an elderly lady sitting two pews back from us. I couldn't hear her side of the conversation because she had such a quiet voice, but her face clearly showed her pleasure in the attention this young man was giving her.

After a while, Bob finished his conversation and started down the aisle. My heart was a trip hammer as I rehearsed what I was going to say when he came to our pew. However, when he did reach us, he returned my smile with an icy one of his own, nodded slightly, and walked quickly up to the platform without another glance at us.

My heart sank, and I could feel hot tears welling in my eyes. I was sure then that he thought I was in love with Greg, and I desperately wanted to convince him that he was wrong. I never stopped to wonder why Bob's opinion was so important to me; I just resolved more fervently to set everything straight at the picnic.

My thoughts were interrupted by a loud buzzer that evidently signaled the end of Sunday School. All this time Angela had been engrossed in the paper Mr. Jennings had given her, so she jumped when the buzzer rang. She looked up at me and grinned sheepishly.

"That paper must be really good;" I said, "I don't think you were aware of anything going on around you."

"Yes, this is a good story."

"I'll bet you're a good student. You really read well."

"Thank you, I don't know. I guess I was good, but I can't remember my school."

"I know, Pumpkin, but you'll remember soon, I'm sure.

The quiet was broken in the little church by people of all different ages coming through the glass doors at the back. Some babies were howling as their hassled mothers wrestled them in their arms. Teenagers filed in, as usual more girls than boys, and they were giggling, chomping on chewing gum, and showing off to the opposite sex. Then some children rushed in, punching and pushing each other. One little boy kept glancing at Angela and then whispering to another boy standing with him. I looked down at Angela just in time to catch her looking at the boys with a barely perceptible smile. When she saw me watching her, her face turned scarlet. I tried to pretend I hadn't noticed her little flirtation, but I couldn't hide my grin. She was saved from further embarrassment by the appearance of Greg standing at the end of the pew.

"May I sit here?" he asked.

Emotions that were not exactly appropriate for church rose within me. I was still a little angry with him because of the scene I felt sure he had staged at the pizza parlor the night before, and I was afraid he would ruin my plans of inviting Bob to my picnic alone. However, I couldn't very well refuse him the right to sit wherever he wanted to in church, so I said as graciously as I could, "Sure, this is supposed to be the coolest spot in the church today."

"That sounds good. Today is really hot." He was obviously chafing under the discomfort of his light gray suit and red silk tie. He didn't look too accustomed to dressy clothes. I remembered that he had told me he had gotten out of the habit of going to church. However, I could tell he had been in church before. He knew most of the hymns we sang, and his voice was a high tenor, just like Paul's. When the pastor read the scripture for the day, he took out a very new Bible and turned right to the book and chapter without looking in the table of contents.

Just before the sermon, Bob walked up to the pulpit and began to speak in a quiet voice, more serious than I had ever heard him. "Sometimes, even in a Christian's life, trials come and the days are long. I've chosen this song for some friends of mine who are going through some hard times right now." Although he didn't look at us, I had a feeling we were the people he meant. His song was, "A Brand New Touch," and if Bob did mean for it to minister to me, he certainly succeeded. His voice was tender, yet dramatic. I was convinced he knew what he was talking about. One part of the song is, "Oh Lord, you know I need a brand new touch; my strength from yesterday is gone."

Again my eyes spilled over with tears, but I didn't even bother to wipe them away. I felt closer to God than I had felt for a long time, but I also felt close to Bob. I forgot all the doubts I had had about him, and I knew I would never be happy again if he were suddenly out of my life.

I was so caught up in my emotions that I forgot that Greg was even sitting by us until he leaned over and said, "Quite a voice."

"Yes," I answered, but I didn't even look at him, keeping my gaze on Bob instead.

Bob finished his song, and it seemed he glanced back at me, though I couldn't be sure. I wished that Greg had not come to church today, but then chided myself for having such uncharitable thoughts. I was hoping that Bob would come down and sit by us since there was a lot of room on the pew, but when he walked off the platform, he went to the other side of the church.

My thoughts could not be corralled throughout the whole sermon, so I have no idea what it was about. I felt like a race horse at the starting gate, so eager was I to have the benediction pronounced. Finally the last amen was given, and I was ready to bolt out of the pew over to Bob's. However, I had to stop and make small talk with those around me, all the time trying not to scream, "Let me go; I have to talk to Bob." Even Greg was an obstacle. He stood right at the end of the pew and kept pressuring me to have dinner with him at a new restaurant he had found.

I tried to be as gracious as I could, but I'm sure some of my impatience must have seeped into my voice. "No, Greg, you've bought enough meals for us, and I have some things at home ready for us. Besides, I--uh--have some things I have to do today, and I just don't have time to go out." That wasn't a lie; I just failed to mention that the "things" I had to do included cooking a dinner for Bob and clearing up misunderstandings he might have.

Finally, Greg reluctantly accepted my refusal, and I managed to escape from him when he stepped out into the aisle to talk to a young couple who were welcoming him to the church. I immediately glanced over to the place where Bob had been sitting, but to my dismay, he wasn't there. I scanned the entire sanctuary, but Bob was nowhere to be seen. Clutching Angela's hand I rushed out to the foyer, managing to give the pastor and his wife a quick handshake and murmur a polite greeting, but I still did not see Bob anywhere in the foyer. Then I bolted out the door and searched for him amongst the small crowd who were taking advantage of the sunny weather to stand around and talk. Still, no Bob. Finally I glanced out to the parking lot where I spotted Bob walking toward his car with a pretty, blond teenage girl by his side.

I was hesitant about approaching them, but I did want Bob to come to my picnic, and I knew I wouldn't be able to get hold of him later. So, again with Angela in tow, I barreled out to the parking lot. I got to the car just as Bob was unlocking the door on the passenger side. Both of them turned toward us as I rushed up to them, completely out of breath. Bob gave me only a trace of a smile and said politely, "Hello Amanda, Angela, isn't it awfully hot to be running a race?"

I don't know when I've felt so foolish. The teenager was glaring at me with all the hostility of a competitor. My words seem to stick in my throat. "Uh--Bob--uh--I was wondering--" I looked at the girl and Bob. Neither one was giving me much encouragement. "Well, I'm having a--a picnic today--outside--I mean out by the cottage--and--er--well, would you like to come?"

Bob looked at the girl and then answered me. "That's nice of you, Amanda, but Holly's family has invited me to dinner today, so I'm afraid I'll have to decline." The triumphant look on the young girl's face left no doubt about who Holly was.

I tried to be as nonchalant as possible even though I desperately wished I could quietly disappear. "Well, I'll have to give you a rain check, I guess. You have a nice dinner, both of you."

"Oh, we will," crooned Holly. Then turning to Bob in a proprietary manner, she said, "I guess we'd better go, Bob. My folks will wonder what has happened to us." With the grace of a victor, Holly allowed Bob to open the door for her, and then she slid in and sat down primly, smoothing her lacy white dress under her. With Angela still holding onto my hand, I turned around and stalked over to my car with what I hoped was at least a shred of dignity.

The beautiful day was lost on me. I struggled with a potpourri of emotions--humiliation, anger, disappointment, even jealousy, but finally the one emotion that emerged strongest was anger. He had no right to treat me so coolly just because he had seen me with Greg a couple of times, I thought. After all, I had the right to see anyone I wanted to. Therefore, when I saw Greg standing by his motorcycle, I pulled my car up to him and invited him to the picnic. He accepted happily, but I thought he looked rather confused since I had previously turned down his invitation claiming I had too much to do.

As soon as we got home, Angela and I changed into shorts, and I went into the kitchen and started getting the meat ready for the grill and putting the last touches on the other food. Greg arrived at the cottage only minutes after we did, and as soon as he changed, I put him to work starting the charcoal. In the midst of all our preparations, Phil Jennings came over bringing more books for Angela, and I invited him to stay knowing I had enough food. I immediately set him to work setting the picnic table while Angela and I carried out the food. Finally, when the meat was medium cooked and the rest of the food was on the table, we sat down to eat. Angela asked if she could pray, and her prayer was so simple, yet meaningful, that it brought tears to my eyes.

I'm sure Greg and Phil, and even Angela, thought the picnic was a great success. The food was good; the weather remained clear, and we were even blessed with a soft breeze from the lake that kept us cool in spite of the high temperature. Greg and Phil talked about a variety of topics--photography, sailing, history, motorcycling, etc. I tried to enter into the conversation, and they both tried to include me, but my mind wasn't quite there. I couldn't quit thinking about Bob, as hard as I tried. Even to my own ears, my laughter seemed hollow and forced. I don't know if I fooled the others or not.

After dinner, Phil gallantly offered to help clean up, but Greg insisted we could manage alone. The older man smiled and winked at me, letting me know he was aware of Greg's ploy to get rid of him. As soon as it was tactfully possible, Phil left, and Greg, Angela, and I cleaned up the picnic mess.

When we put the last dish in the cupboard, Greg looked at the clock on the wall and said, "Amanda, you've got one whole hour before the museum opens. Want to go for a walk along the beach?" Since I could think of no reason to refuse, I agreed, and we started off down the hill by the cottage to the beach.

Most of the beaches along the coasts of northern Michigan are extremely rocky, with hardly any sand, and the beach at Silver Bay was no exception. We had to carefully watch our step so that we would not stumble or slip on the stones that had been smoothed by centuries of lake water washing over them. Once I did stumble and to keep from falling, I instinctively reached out for Greg's hand, but when I tried to release my hand after the danger had passed, he wouldn't let go. Not wanting to hurt his feelings, I kept my hand in his for the rest of the walk.

We walked to a sliver of land that was almost perfectly perpendicular to the coastline, about one mile northeast of the cottage. I was somewhat afraid for Angela to venture out on this tiny peninsula because the rocks here were especially slippery, and there were gaps where the land had been completely washed away. However, before I could tell her not to step on the land, she effortlessly skipped to the very tip of the peninsula. Greg and I followed her at a slower, more careful pace.

Soon, Angela bent down and picked something up. "Look, Amanda, what I found," she cried.

By this time Greg and I had reached her. She was holding a dirty, soaked, horseshoe-shaped life preserver. Even though it was ragged and muddy, we could make out some faded letters on one side of the preserver at the top of the arch. The letters were, "W ND S NG."

"Where did this come from?" I asked to no one in particular.

"It was right there," said Angela pointing to a large rock that was wedged into the north side of the peninsula. The life preserver must have been caught in the tiny cove created by the rock and the land.

"I know where you found it, Honey," I said. "I just wonder where it came from originally."

"Well, obviously a boat," said Greg, rather caustically I thought. Then his tone softened. "I mean-- somebody must have dropped it overboard from a boat and neglected to pick it up, eh?"

Although I heard his "eh," I didn't comment because I was so absorbed in Angela's discovery. "I wonder what these letters stand for-- W ND S NG?"

"Wind Song--that spells Wind Song," said Angela. Startled, I looked at the child. Her eyes were wide, and she appeared to be in a kind of trance.

I knelt down and took her hands in mine. "Honey," I said softly, "How do you know those letters say 'Wind Song'?"

She didn't seem to hear me at first. Then she came back from wherever her troubled mind had taken her. "What did you say, Amanda?" She asked.

"I wondered how you knew these letters say 'Wind Song.'"

"I don't know," she shook her head slowly. "I just remember that word from someplace."

I turned to Greg excitedly. "Do you think this could be another clue?"

Greg answered quickly, "No, I don't think so. It's not too hard to figure out that these letters could spell Wind Song, and Angela is a bright little girl."

"Sure she is, but I don't think a little girl her age could figure that out without having seen it before." I turned to Angela. "Honey, do you remember ever seeing this cushion before?"

"I think so," she said. "I remember looking at something like it and hearing the name Wind Song somewhere. I just can't remember."

I turned to Greg and exclaimed," I think we should take this cushion to the police."

Greg shrugged, "I suppose so, but don't be too disappointed if nothing comes of it."

"But I think that Angela was on a boat named 'Wind Song.' Maybe it can be traced somehow."

"Possibly, but do you have any idea at all how many boats are named 'Wind Song'? That's one of the most popular names of sailboats."

"I guess you're right, but I'm still going to show the police this cushion and mention Angela's reaction to it."

"I'll tell you what, I've got to go to Randolph City tomorrow morning, so I'll show it to them and tell them all about it."

I started to protest, but since I knew I had no valid reason for an argument, I gave the cushion to Greg, and we followed Angela off the peninsula. It was almost time to open the museum, so we headed toward the cottage, Angela skipping a few yards ahead and Greg and I strolling along at a leisurely pace.

Just as we reached the bottom of the hill in view of the cottage, Greg suddenly dropped the life cushion, turned me around to him, took me in his arms and kissed me. The kiss was not passionate or tender, but violent, almost savage. I pushed away in anger and looked up at the cottage to see if Angela had seen us. Fortunately, she was still walking up the hill with her back to us, but someone else was watching us. Bob Wilson was standing at the door of the cottage with a scowl like a thundercloud on his face.

Chapter 13

This time I was furious! I felt like slapping Greg because I could tell by the gleam in his eye that he had seen Bob, and he had staged the whole kiss for his benefit. Now I had no hopes of convincing Bob that there was no romance between Greg and me. I stalked up the hill as quickly as I could, and if my face was a true indicator of my anger, it must have been flaming red. I quickly reached Angela who was completely oblivious of anything that had happened, and the two of us approached Bob together.

My mind was racing to come up with some explanation to tell him about what had happened, but even if I could have thought of what to say, I had no time because Greg had already caught up with us. He was again carrying the floatation cushion which was hung over his left shoulder. "Well, Hello there, Wilson," he said jovially, "Long time, no see."

"Yeah, well, I've been kinda busy lately," muttered Bob with a face that still hadn't smiled.

Finally I managed to say something, "I really enjoyed your song today, Bob. It really spoke to my heart."

Bob's eyes softened a bit, "I'm glad. You're the friends I was talking about who needed the song."

It was as if a huge anchor had been lifted, and my spirit soared. How remarkable that those few words could have made me so happy! Again Greg intruded into my ecstasy, "Yeah, why didn't you tell us you could sing like that? Do you have anything else you're hiding from us?"

"Let's put it this way, Rothman, I don't have any more secrets than you do." Bob's tone bristled like a frightened porcupine. "By the way, what do you have there?"

"Oh this?" asked Greg, as he held out the cushion in front of him. "We found this down on the beach, and Amanda thought it might be a clue because Angela was able to read the name on it."

Bob looked carefully at the faded letters, "Hm, 'W ND S NG.' That must have been Wind Song," he concluded.

Greg looked at me triumphantly. "See, it's not too hard to figure out those letters." Then he turned to Bob. "Angela said the same thing you did when she saw them, and Amanda thought she might have been on a boat named

Wind Song for her to be able to figure that out. She thinks we should show the cushion to the police.

I was still more than a little angry with Greg, so my tone was sharper than I intended. "Well, you've got to remember, Bob is much older than Angela. I just thought it was significant for a child her age to be able to figure that out without any prior knowledge of that name."

"I agree," said Bob, "but don't get your hopes built up too high, Amanda. Wind Song is a very popular name for boats."

"That's just what I told her," exclaimed Greg. "Imagine the two of us agreeing on something."

I laughed nervously, but the men glared at each other. Finally I said, "Would you guys like to come in? I've got to open the museum soon, and I need to get my money box out and get ready."

They both agreed, and true to my upbringing, I offered them some ice tea. Greg winked at me and teased, "Southern hospitality again, eh?" Then when Bob looked puzzled, he said to him, "Oh, it's a private joke."

"I see," said Bob. "Yes, Amanda, I'll take some ice tea if it's not too much trouble."

I went into the kitchen to pour the tea, and when I got back into the living room, the men were making small talk about the weather and other mundane subjects, almost congenially. I served the tea and started getting my materials ready to open the museum, while Angela sat on the floor at my feet coloring in the book Sergeant Adams had brought her. Greg and Bob sat in two folding chairs adjacent to the front corners of my desk.

Almost nonchalantly, Bob pulled out a folded piece of paper from his pocket and said, "The reason I came over here today is this."

When he handed the paper to me, I saw that it was a Xerox copy of a newspaper report with the headlines: "Famous Photographer Convicted of Manslaughter in Death of Family." Under the headlines was a picture, and even in the blurred copy, I clearly made out the features of a young Phil Jennings."

"No, there must be a mistake," I cried. "Tell me this is not a picture of Phil Jennings."

Greg reached over and took the paper from my hand. "It certainly looks like him," he stated.

"I'm afraid it is," said Bob. "Listen to what the article says." Bob took the paper from Greg and began to read: "'Phillip Jennings, photographer of the rich in East Manhattan, was convicted yesterday of manslaughter in the head-on collision involving his car and his wife's car on the highway five miles from their posh estate in New Rochelle. The accident resulted in the deaths of his wife, 28-year-old Elaine, and their twin son and daughter, Phillip II and Patricia, both three years old. The two children were pronounced dead at the scene of the accident, and Mrs. Jennings was rushed to New Rochelle hospital where she died minutes later from excessive internal injuries. Jennings received a concussion and a few bruises, but was able to leave the hospital after treatment. Police said that a blood test done on Jennings at the hospital revealed a blood-alcohol level double the legal intoxication limit.'"

I shook my head. "Phil Jennings--drunk? I can't believe it."

"Wait, there's more," said Bob, and he continued reading, "'Jennings was a famous photographer who did many portraits of Wall Street business tycoons and their families. However, police have found evidence that links Jennings with a child pornography ring, allegedly run by organized crime.'"

I was too shocked to speak, and apparently Greg was too. Bob went on, "I won't read the rest of it, but the story I got from this news story and others written when all this happened goes like this: Jennings started out as a legitimate photographer in a little studio in New York. He specialized in portraits, and his work was so good that he became rather famous, and soon, like the article said, he became the photographer for the New York elite. Unfortunately, the business, although probably very lucrative, must not have been enough for Jennings. Anyway, he got involved with a Mafia boss who got him into child pornography, and I guess he really got into the big bucks. In the meantime, he married this Elaine, who was the daughter of one of the biggest Wall Street tycoons in New York, and they had the twins mentioned in the paper."

I interrupted, "I saw a portrait of them when I was in Phil's house the other day. It must have been one of his portraits. The woman was gorgeous, and the twins were adorable. I can see why Phil's pictures were so popular. He really did good work."

"Yeah, since I've been researching all this, I've come across some of his work in Life Magazines and other places, and as a photographer myself, I can tell you he was a master. However, I've also seen some of the porn pictures, and they made me sick. I can't understand how a person with such a great gift could turn it into something so dirty and sordid."

Greg joined the conversation, "Was his wife in on the porn business?"

"No, and that's what led to the tragedy. I guess she found some of these pictures, and she confronted Jennings with them the night before the accident. He refused to stop, and they had a big fight, but she really didn't take any action until he left for the studio the next day. Then she packed herself and the kids up, got in the car, and started out for her parents' house. Before she left, though, she picked up an envelope of the pictures she had found because Jennings had threatened to take the children away from her if she tried to leave him, and I guess she wanted some proof she could use against him if he tried."

"I can't believe this monster is the same man we just had dinner with," I exclaimed. "He seems so gentle and kind, now."

"I know," said Bob, I always thought I was a great judge of character, but Jennings really had me fooled. Of course, we're leaving out the possibility that he changed."

"Finish your story," said Greg, "Did the accident happen when they were leaving?"

"Yeah. I guess the butler at the house was in on the porn thing, and he called Jennings when he saw his wife was going to leave. There was evidence in the envelope that would have incriminated him, so he was anxious to stop her. Well, anyway, the butler stalled Mrs. Jennings as long as he could, but she finally left. They were just five miles from home when they came across each other. I don't really think Jennings deliberately tried to kill them, but he was so drunk that in trying to stop them he crashed into them and ran them off the road down a steep cliff. I guess Jennings had been drinking ever since the fight the night before."

"So, did he go to prison?'" asked Greg.

"Yeah, for ten years, but all the reports ended with his going to prison. I don't know anything about him after that, except what he has told us. I couldn't find any of his pictures after his conviction either.

After a moment of stunned silence I asked in a quiet voice that I hoped Angela wouldn't hear, "So, you think this --uh--business that Phil was in could have something to do with --well, you know."

"Yeah, it has crossed my mind. Unfortunately my line of work exposes me to some of the sordid side of life. In fact, in college, I did extensive research on the porn industry, and I still have nightmares where I see the faces of little kids that have been dragged into it. I can tell you, I wouldn't be surprised if a kid who had been forced to pose for some of those sick things would want to block it out of her memory."

Afraid that Angela was hearing too much, I suggested that she go outside and play on the swing. I think she realized that she was being sent away, but she complied without argument, as was her custom. I turned my chair so that I could watch her out the window.

As soon as she was out of earshot, Greg spoke up, "I'm sorry to be antagonistic, but I don't buy any of this."

Bob's scowl reappeared, "What don't you buy, Rothman?"

"For one thing, what made you start digging up stuff about Jennings and how did you so conveniently come across this story?"

Bob's black eyes glared unblinkingly at Greg as he answered. "Well, Rothman, it's no secret that through this whole thing you've suspected me, and I've suspected you. But the other day as I was thinking about the case, I decided to change my tactics a little. I mean, I know I'm innocent, and I decided to go on the assumption that you were innocent, too."

"Oh, thank you so much. I'm indeed grateful," said Greg with a sarcastic sneer.

Ignoring him, Bob went on, "So, I asked myself who else besides you, me, and Amanda, was a part of Angela's life and had been here when the police told us about Edwards and when Lucy said she recognized Angela, because I really believe those deaths are related to this whole thing." No one said anything, so Bob continued,

"So, thinking back, I realized that Jennings had been here all those times, and since I have easy access to microfilm copies of old newspapers, I looked his name up and found this story."

"That's another thing, Wilson," Greg was almost shouting, "if Jennings really was involved with the Mafia, why wouldn't he change his name and identity? And, if he was connected with Angela some way, why would he walk up to Amanda and show her a picture he had taken of her?"

"To answer the first question, there was no point in his changing his name. The Mafia bosses were powerful enough to cover their involvement so that they were not affected by Jennings' arrest. Now, as to why Jennings would make himself known to Amanda, I figure he had to find out for himself how much Angela remembers, and maybe he's waiting for a time to--uh--eliminate the possibility of Angela's memory returning."

I shuddered and automatically looked out at Angela, who was blithely swinging on the swing. "I can't fathom Mr. Jennings trying to hurt anyone, most of all Angela, but there is a mystery about him." Then I told them about going to his house after being in the laundromat and about the locked room he was so upset about when I almost blundered in.

Greg shook his head, "I still can't believe it."

"What? Do you think I made up the whole thing? Where did you think I got this story?"

"You're a newspaper reporter. You could have made up the story and used a computer or something to print it up like a regular news story."

"Oh, and where would I have gotten his picture?"

"You're also a photographer, I'm sure touching up a picture you have taken of Jennings would be no problem."

Bob sighed and turned to me, "I'm not going to convince your friend, Amanda, but I hope you believe me. Just be careful around Jennings, please. I'm not making this up."

I winced at the phrase, "your friend." I desperately wanted Bob to know that Greg was just a friend, not anything more as his tone of voice seemed to imply. However, all I could do was just dumbly nod, accepting his warning.

Bob rose up abruptly, "Well, that's why I came over here. I'm going to show this to the police, but if I were you,

I wouldn't confront Jennings with this. If he's guilty of anything, he might do something crazy if you tell him what you've found out."

"Then again, he could deny the whole thing which would make it his word against yours, eh? Asked Greg.

"Yeah, I guess he could, but it's up to you, Amanda, whom you choose to believe." At this, he gave me his soul-piercing look, and turned around and stalked out, his shoulders slumped dejectedly.

Greg and I sat staring at the front door, maintaining an uneasy silence for a few moments. Finally Greg spoke up, "So, what do you think about Wilson's story?"

"I don't know. It's hard to believe that Phil Jennings could be involved in something so sordid, but then again, I can't help but think about the locked room he was so protective about. Also I did see his photographs and the portraits of his wife and twins."

"Seems to me there could be lots of reasons for him not wanting you to go into that room. Maybe it was just a mess, and he was embarrassed for you to see it. And as for his wife and kids, Wilson could have easily found out about them. What did Jennings say had happened to them when you were over there?"

"He said they had died."

"Well, there are many ways they could have died."

"Yeah, I suppose you're right. And if the room that was locked was a mess, I'm sure he wouldn't have wanted me to see it because he is a very meticulous housekeeper. But his reaction seemed more than embarrassment."

"As bad as I hate to admit it, I think Wilson was right when he said not to confront Jennings with this. Let's just let the police handle it, that is, if Wilson does show them the story." He smiled wryly, but before I could retort, Angela came in and asked if she could get a drink of Kool-aide. I went into the kitchen and helped her, and by the time we were finished, the first visitors were pulling up in the driveway, and Greg was gone. The rest of the afternoon was spent with many visitors. In fact, there was no break until closing time when Angela and I finally were able to sit down, have a light supper, and get ready for bed.

Since the day had been so hot, and we had spent much of it outdoors, I felt we both needed a good bath. I let Angela go first, and as I was helping her undress, my mind went back to Bob's story about Phil Jennings. As hard as it was for me to believe that he was involved in child pornography, I found it even harder to believe that Angela had ever been subjected to anything that demeaning. She seemed as every other normal little girl would be about her naked body, natural and unashamed. But how would I know what a little girl would do if she had been in child porn? I wasn't really certain how 'normal' little girls would act in all circumstances because I had never been around little children much. There were so many questions and mysteries. I wondered when they would all be answered, or even if they would all be answered.

In spite of my musings, Angela and I went to bed soon after our baths, and when we had both said prayers, mine silently including the new information about Phil, we both went quickly to sleep, probably as a result of our early rising and long walk during the day. The last thought on my mind as I drifted off to sleep was how I could explain to Bob about Greg's kiss.

The next day was cooler, probably because of the rain we must have had during the night as evidenced by the puddles in the driveway. Today was Monday, my day off, so Angela and I had a leisurely breakfast after which we strolled down to the beach where I stretched out in a green-netted lounge chair to read a novel I had brought with me from home, and Angela played in the sand. At noon my stomach began reminding me that it was time to eat, so I called Angela to me, and we gathered our belongings, including some prize rocks Angela had found, and started toward the cottage. However, remembering that the mail must have already come, we left our stuff at the cottage and walked down the driveway to the mailbox.

The first few pieces of mail I shuffled through held nothing unusual, certainly nothing alarming. There were bills, one letter from my mother, and the ever-present junk mail. However, the last piece was a plain, 5 x 7 manila envelope with my name and address spelled with letters and numbers cut out from newspaper print. There was no return address and no stamp which meant the envelope had been hand-delivered by the sender.

I must have drawn in my breath or made some sign of fear, for Angela asked, "What's wrong, Amanda?"

I tried to cover up as best I could, "Oh, nothing Honey. I just got a funny-looking envelope here that kinda took me by surprise. It must be an advertisement or something." I don't really know if the answer satisfied her or not because my mind was preoccupied with a peculiar sense of foreboding.

Somehow we got back to the cottage, and after making sure Angela was involved with her coloring book, I opened the envelope with clumsy, trembling fingers. Inside was a plain piece of notebook paper with some more cut-out letters that spelled the message: "Come top of lighthouse 10:00 tonight Come alone News about child TELL NO ONE."

I was dumbfounded. It all seemed so melodramatic. As an avid fan of mystery books and TV shows, I had heard of characters getting letters like this, but that was fiction. I never dreamed it could happen to me. Hundreds of questions bombarded my mind. Who could have sent it? Why meet at the top of the lighthouse? Why was it supposed to be so secret? Should I ignore the warning and tell the police?

I was in a fog the rest of the day, mechanically cleaning the house, cooking for Angela, and washing the ever-present dishes. I'm sure Angela noticed my preoccupation because several times I would realize she had said something to me, and she would have to repeat it since I hadn't been listening. It seemed the hours dragged on interminably. Ironically, nobody came to the museum that day. I didn't even see Greg. I probably would not have been able to keep the letter from him or Bob or the police, but none of these people came around.

Finally it was 9:30. I still had not decided what to do. Angela was already in bed, and everything inside was so quiet that the noises of the insects and animals outside were magnified. I kept imagining that I could hear footsteps running through the woods. In fact, when I looked out the picture window in the front of the cottage, I thought I saw the shape of a person streak across the front lawn. Since the flood lights shone on the lighthouse, anyone or anything around the cottage was indistinguishable at night.

I tried to concentrate on my book work, then read the paper, then answer my mother's letter, but I couldn't get my mind off the note. What if I didn't go, and this was going to be the only chance I would have to find out about Angela? I had promised myself and Angela that I would do everything possible to help her find her past; was this something I had to do to fulfill that promise?

Finally I knew I had to go, frightened or not. Maybe I should defy the warning and call the police before I left, I thought, and I made myself walk over to the phone and pick up the receiver. Then I had some more misgivings. What if the person was listening outside and would run if I called? At last, with my heart practically beating out of my chest, I picked up the flashlight again from the pantry and walked out the back door toward the lighthouse.

The sky was clear with thousands of stars visible, and the moon was a bright globe hanging right above the shed where Greg lived. As I passed the shed, I heard the clacking of Greg's typewriter, an old, manual typewriter he had found when he came to the museum. He had remarked that he did not have the funds nor the time to purchase a computer or word processor, so he was grateful for the antiquated yet workable typewriter. When I heard his typing, I considered stopping and asking him to come with me, but when I flashed the light on my watch, I saw that it was already 10:00, and the note had said, "Tell no one."

I crept across the yard looking behind me every few minutes. The flashlight only illuminated a narrow path in front of me, so I was thankful for the moonlight, and then the floodlights illuminating the lighthouse. Finally when I reached the lighthouse, I pulled open the heavy wooden door at the bottom, evidently scaring little animals whose footsteps I heard scurrying away in the darkness. I swallowed hard and began my ascent up the narrow, winding, stone steps. These steps were perilous enough during the day, but at night they became eerie, almost evil. I felt as if they were leading me down to a medieval dungeon instead of up to what had been a helpful, lifesaving beacon.

After what seemed hours, I reached another wooden door at the top of the lighthouse. I slowly pulled it open, so frightened now that I was afraid I would faint. I crept out slowly, flashing my light all around. Seeing nothing, I stepped over to the rail, and then suddenly, without warning, I was grabbed from behind by a person taller and stronger who clasped his leather-gloved hand over my mouth, and my flashlight flew over the rail, crashing on the rocks below. I was sure my attacker was planning for me to follow it to the same disastrous end.

Chapter 14

I prayed a quick prayer of "Lord, help me," and I began to fight. I'm sure the Lord must have been helping me because I fought with a fierceness I never knew I possessed. I managed to twist myself around in his arms, and I kicked his legs, pounded his chest, and even sank my teeth in his shoulder.

When I bit him, he let out a yelp and released his grip on me. I took advantage of that one second of freedom and pushed him with all my might. To my great astonishment he fell backward with a thud, hitting his head on one of the steel posts that made up the railing around the balcony.

He lay very still, and I saw that he had a hood over his face, but since I didn't know if he was unconscious or not, I didn't stop to remove it. My only thought now was that I had to get out of there fast. I threw open the door and started down the stairs. First, I tried standing up and running down them as I would descend a normal staircase, but after almost falling, I realized that I would have to turn around and crawl down, a process that seemed to take hours. I kept glancing up, terrified that the door at the top would start to open. To my immense relief, the door stayed closed, and I finally reached the bottom door. As soon as I opened it, I bolted toward the cottage, stumbling over twigs and rocks I couldn't see in the dark. I had run only a few feet when I suddenly crashed into someone running toward the lighthouse. I screamed hysterically until I heard Greg say, "Amanda, it's me. It's all right. What are you doing out here?"

"Oh Greg," I exclaimed breathlessly, "I've been attacked! There's a man up at the top of the lighthouse. I think he's unconscious. I've got to call the police."

He grabbed my shoulders and held me tight. "Slow down. Tell me what happened."

"I don't have much time. There's a man up there. He tried to kill me, but I managed to push him, and his head hit one of the posts on the railing."

"Okay, you go call the police; I'll go and deal with the man."

"No," I screamed, "If he is conscious, he'll kill you."

"Don't worry, I'll be all right. Just go back to the cottage. Don't come out here again."

I ran to the cottage, but as soon as I got inside, I thought about Angela. What if my attacker had an accomplice who had planned to do something to Angela while I was being disposed of at the lighthouse? I don't even remember how I got from the kitchen to the bedroom. All I remember is the tremendous relief I felt when I saw the child sleeping peacefully, her little chest rising and falling with even breaths.

All I wanted to do was collapse and sob until the panic drained out of me, but I still had to call the police. I quickly walked back downstairs and dialed the now familiar police number. The phone rang twice, but the voice that answered was neither Captain Rogers nor Sergeant Adams. Instead it was the young voice of Officer Larsen.

"Is Captain Rogers or Sergeant Adams there?" I asked in a trembling voice I barely recognized as my own.

"No, I'm sorry. They are both off duty this evening. May I help you?"

I tried to hide my disappointment and realize that my two trusted policemen couldn't be at my beck and call twenty-four hours a day, but I really wanted to talk to one of them instead of this young man I barely knew. However, I took a deep breath and began my story. "This--this--is Amanda, Amanda Stevens. I--I was attacked tonight by a man who tried to push me off the top of the lighthouse, but I pushed him down on the--uh--floor, and he hit his head--and I think he's unconscious--and--"

"Hold on, Miss Stevens, did you know this man?"

"No, he had a black hood over his head, and after I knocked him down, I was afraid to lift it up because I--I didn't know if he was really unconscious or not."

"That was the smart thing to do. Now, how about the little girl? Is she all right?"

"Yes, I just checked on her, and she's sound asleep."

"That's good. Do you have anybody there with you?"

"Greg, my--uh--the handyman that lives in the shed out back, is out to see if he can catch the man."

"I wish he had waited for some of us. He needs to be with you, not trying to be a hero. Well, just sit tight, and don't open the door to anyone except the handyman. Be sure you know it is the handyman before you let him in. I'll call the Captain, and I'm sure he'll be over as soon as possible. Try to calm down."

"All right, Officer, thank you," I said, a little calmer now that I knew my policeman friend was coming.

I had just hung up the phone when I heard a pounding at the back door. Again, my heart leaped up to my throat, but I sighed with relief when I heard Greg say, "Amanda, it's me." I walked to the kitchen and looked out the window until I could indeed identify Greg.

"Did you find him? Are you all right?" I blurted out my frantic questions before the door had closed behind him.

"No, when I got to the top of the lighthouse, there was no one there. I went all around the balcony, but I have to admit I didn't explore much anywhere else. Going to the top of the lighthouse was an impulsive act, and besides, I thought the guy was unconscious. But when I didn't find him knocked out cold on the ground, I realized he had to be somewhere close by, and I guess I lost my nerve. I just bolted back here.

"I don't blame you; I'm just glad you're safe. I called the police, and I think they'll be over soon. Could you--or would you mind staying with me until they come?"

"Of course, I'll stay with you. No one could make me leave. Is Angela all right?"

"Yes, she's asleep. When I think of what could have happened, I mean, what if the guy had had an accomplice who got to Angela while I was up there? Oh, I've been so dumb!" Suddenly, the terror of the whole episode engulfed me, and great, agonizing sobs escaped from somewhere deep inside me. I was barely aware of Greg putting his arm around me, leading me to the couch in the living room, all the while soothing me with words that I heard, but didn't really comprehend.

When I began to come to myself, I realized that Greg's comforting moves were becoming more than brotherly. He was kissing my ear and my neck, and his hands were beginning to roam in a way that made me extremely uncomfortable. I pushed myself away, angry that he should take advantage of my vulnerable state to make a pass at me. At least I thought it was a pass, but I was so inexperienced with men that I wasn't really sure.

I was even less sure when I saw the hurt look on Greg's face when I pushed him away. He said, "I'm sorry, Amanda, I was just trying to comfort you. I didn't mean anything."

Again I felt like a naive 12-year-old. "I'm sorry, too, Greg," I mumbled. "I guess I'm just a bundle of nerves. Don't pay much attention to anything I say or do tonight."

"Of course," he said with his glorious smile, "I know you've had quite a shock. Let me go fix you a cup of hot tea. That's what my mother always did when any of us had a crisis."

"Thank you, but I can get it." I started to get off the couch.

"No, let me wait on you for once. You know, northerners can be hospitable too. Now do you take milk, sugar, lemon, or what in your tea?"

"I take two teaspoons of sugar, please. It's another habit I acquired from my southern mom."

"Okay, just sit tight, and I'll bring it out here to you. Don't worry, I'm sure I'll be able to find everything, and I do know how to boil water."

I smiled at him, but I again started to get off the couch. "Hey," Greg protested, "I thought I told you to sit tight."

"I'm going to, but I feel a little chilly. I was going to get a quilt from the chest in my room."

"I'll get it. I think I can manage that besides fixing tea. You need to learn how to let people take care of you." With that, he stole up the stairs, quietly, and came down quickly with the same quilt I had put around Angela that first night when she was unconscious.

Gratefully, I lay down on the couch and let Greg tuck the quilt around me, and magically my fears seemed to dissolve, and my trembling subsided. I imagined that even though the creator of that quilt was no relative of mine, the love and care put into it was enveloping me now. I could understand why a little child would pick out a special blanket and carry it around everywhere with him.

In a very few minutes Greg brought me a steaming cup of tea on a charming silver tray I had seen in the cupboard, but had never used. He sat in the Victorian chair that matched the couch and sipped tea he had made for himself. He didn't question me about my ordeal, probably feeling I wasn't ready yet. Instead we talked about mundane things: the weather, supplies he needed for the yard, insects that were threatening to kill the flowers, and other superficial matters.

I had just set my tea cup on the coffee table by the couch when I heard a car motor outside. "I hope that's the police," I said.

"Well, we won't open the door until they identify themselves. You just stay where you are."

Greg walked over to the door, and soon we heard two car doors slam and loud footsteps rushing to the door. A voice called out, "Amanda, open up, it's the police." I didn't need an identification card this time because I recognized the voice of Captain Rogers.

Greg unbolted the door, and the two policemen rushed in. Without any preliminaries, they came over to the couch where I was still lying and began questioning me. "What's this I hear about you getting attacked, Amanda? Are you all right?"

"Why don't you gentlemen have a seat," suggested Greg, as he carried the two chairs by my desk and set them near the couch.

"Thank you, Son," said Captain Rogers as he positioned his large frame on the straight back chair. "Now, Amanda, let's hear your story from the beginning. But first, are you all right?"

"Oh, I guess I'm okay--just a little shaky," I answered in a trembling voice.

"Well, tell us quickly what happened, and we'll go out and look around."

I took a deep breath and began. "It all started when I got a letter in the mail. Uh, let me show it to you." I started to get up, but again, Greg stopped me before my feet hit the floor.

"Stay there, Amanda, I'll get it. Just tell me where it is."

"The top right hand drawer of my desk," I said.

Greg found it and handed it to Captain Rogers. Sergeant Adams leaned over to read it too. After a minute Captain Rogers looked at me and spoke in a stern voice, "I guess I don't have to tell you what a chance you took to go off and meet this fellow all by yourself. Promise you'll tell us if anything like this comes up again."

"I will," I said contritely. "I just was anxious to learn something about Angela, and I was afraid he wouldn't tell me anything if I weren't alone."

"Okay, so I assume you went to the top of the lighthouse at 10:00."

"Yes, I--"

"Wait," the captain interrupted, "where were you at 10:00 tonight, Rothman?"

"Uh, I was in my room typing my thesis, but when I heard Amanda scream, I ran out toward where I heard her voice, and I ran right into her. Then I told her to come inside here, and I went to the lighthouse, but I didn't see anyone."

I didn't remember screaming, but before I could question Greg, Captain Rogers asked, "Can you verify that, Amanda?"

"Yes, well--I didn't see him until he ran into me, but I heard his typewriter going when I walked past his shed."

"Okay, sorry I interrupted," said the captain, "Now, go on, Amanda."

"All right, as I was saying, I made sure Angela was asleep, and I climbed to the top of the lighthouse, and suddenly this guy grabbed me from behind." I paused to take another deep breath because as I articulated the events, my feelings of terror again welled up inside of me.

Sergeant Adams noticed my distress and gently spoke, "Okay, Lassie, you're all right now. Captain, let's go out and see what we can find."

"Right, Ed, but first, Rothman, do you have anything to add?"

Greg glanced at me apologetically, then looked at the policemen and said, "I kinda hate to bring this up, but I saw Bob Wilson's car hidden out in the woods a few hours ago."

"No," I heard myself shout, and my heart began to pound furiously. "The guy wasn't Bob, I know he wasn't."

All three men looked at me curiously, and I silently cursed my open-book face. I knew they could tell that my emphatic protests were attempts to convince myself as well as them. Greg's declaration had brought to surface the fear I had been suppressing since my attack. Now, I could no longer fool myself. The man could have been Bob; he was the same size, and I admitted to myself something I had refused to think about before--the man smelled like the cologne I had smelled on Bob many times.

Captain Rogers' voice interrupted my thoughts, "Where did you see his car, Son?"

"It was in the woods off to the east of the driveway. It was pretty well hidden, but I found it because I was looking for some dirt to fill in around the flowers in the bed out here. I figured I could get some really rich soil because the land there is rather swampy."

Captain raised his eyebrow and exchanged glances with Sergeant Adams. "Have either of you seen Wilson tonight?" he asked.

"No," I said quickly.

Greg's response was a little slower, "No, just his car. I wondered why it was hidden in the woods."

"Okay, maybe you can come with us and show us where you saw it. Amanda, you stay in here and be sure and lock the doors. We'll be back after we look around a little."

"All right, thank you. Please be careful."

"We will. Now, Mr. Rothman come with us, if you would. I think we have an extra flashlight for you in the car."

As the men stalked out, I hurried to the front door and bolted it securely. I picked up the tea cups and headed for the kitchen. When I walked into the room, I noticed the door leading to the pantry was ajar, and since I couldn't remember opening it, I proceeded to investigate. My hand just barely touched the doorknob, when a man's hand reached out and pulled me into the dark pantry, knocking over a broom and mop in the process. For the second time that night, unbelievably, I found myself struggling with a tall man dressed in dark clothes.

Chapter 15

My first thought was, "I'm going to explode. I can't take any more!" But I noticed that I had more confidence and less fear this time, probably because of my apparent victory in my first attack. I struggled fiercely, but I couldn't twist myself around and fight him as before because he seemed to be holding me more securely. I tried to scream, but my captor had his large hand clamped firmly over my mouth.

Then I noticed it. It was the distinctive smell of the cologne, the smell I would always associate with Bob. I still held on to the hope that this man wasn't Bob until I heard his voice. Then my heart sank, and I no longer struggled. Nothing seemed to matter now that I knew it was Bob Wilson who was trying to kill me.

I fell limp in his arms, and he must have thought I had fainted because he turned me around and shook me gently. "Amanda, Amanda," he whispered hoarsely. When he saw I was conscious, he said, "Don't worry, I'm not going to hurt you. I just want to talk to you. I'm sorry I scared you, but please, can we go inside and talk?"

"You, you--" I started to shout, but he again clasped his hand over my mouth.

"Please be quiet. I've got to talk to you. I promise I won't hurt you. If I had wanted to hurt you, I could have easily strangled you already. Please just let me come in and talk to you, okay?"

I nodded my head slowly, but he kept his hand clasped over my mouth until we reached the couch in the living room. He gently set me down, and he sat down right beside me and laid his head back against the couch and closed his eyes for a moment. I was dismayed to realize that hot tears were rolling down my cheeks. I said in a pitiful voice, "It was you. You tried to kill me!"

"No, Amanda, you've got to believe me. I wasn't the one who tried to push you off the lighthouse tonight."

"But, how did you know I went--?"

"I heard the police and you and Rothman talking." He paused, touched the back of his head gingerly, and winced with pain. I looked at his head and saw that his dark hair was matted with blood, right at the spot where my attacker's head had hit the lighthouse railing.

"How can you sit there and deny you were the man? Are you going to tell me you hurt your head shaving or something?" I asked sarcastically.

"No, I did get hit on the head tonight, but it didn't happen the way you think. Let me start at the beginning."

I must have still looked skeptical because he threw his hands up as if I were holding a gun on him and said, "Look, I have nothing to hide. You can search me if you want; in fact, that might be fun." His eyes were twinkling almost as they had when he had teased me before, and in spite of my suspicions, I found myself ready to listen to him.

When I didn't protest any more, he began his story. "All right, today I got this letter from you in the mail." As he talked, he pulled out a crumpled piece of paper from his pants pocket. "But wait, would you trust me enough to go to where we can watch for the police. What about the bedroom down here; isn't there a window in there?" He took my hand and started pulling me toward the bedroom.

Wondering if I was again being an idiot, I walked with him, and we stood at the window in the dark. I said, "I didn't send you a letter."

"I know that now, but when I got it, I thought you were genuinely asking for my help. You see, it says that you wanted to meet me at 9:30 tonight in the lighthouse."

He handed the letter to me, but since I couldn't read it in the dark, he told me what it said, "Dear Bob, I need to talk to you about things I have found out about Angela. Please come over tonight and meet me inside the lighthouse at 9:30."

Bob continued, "So, I hopped in my car at 9:00, and I came over here. I parked my car in the woods because I didn't want anyone, especially Rothman, to know I was here. Anyway, I got within a few feet of the lighthouse when I was conked on the head by someone, and I went unconscious. When I came to, I was in the bushes on the other side of the lighthouse, and there was no one around. I started toward the cottage, but I looked in the window and saw you and Rothman sitting here, and since I still didn't trust him, I decided to do some spying. I was able to open the pantry window and crawl inside the pantry. By the way, we need to make sure we lock that window. Anyway, I was listening right behind the door to your story, and as soon as the police left I waited for you to walk into the kitchen so I could talk to you without you screaming and letting the police know I was here."

"But don't you think you're hurting your chances of the police believing you by hiding from them, that is if you are really innocent."

"Yes, I know I am, but if the police locked me up right now, I'd have no chance to find the real killer."

"That may be true, but why are you still hanging around here? I mean, why didn't you get out of here as soon as you heard the police were suspicious of you?"

Bob's face turned red, and he spoke so low I could barely hear him. "I had to talk to you, to convince you that I'm not the one who tried to push you off the lighthouse." When I didn't speak, he went on, "I know you'll never feel the same way I feel about you, but you can't believe I'm a murderer."

My heart was pounding as I asked, "How do you feel about me, Bob?"

"Do I have to spell it out? I love you, and I'm going to keep on loving you no matter how you feel about me. Haven't you figured that out yet?"

I couldn't believe I had heard him right. "Well, lately, you haven't exactly overwhelmed me with your attentions. You have barely given me the time of day."

"That's because lately, every time I've seen you, you've been in a clinch with Rothman. I love you, but I'm not going to grovel for you if you obviously want someone else."

"I thought reporters were supposed to be able to separate fact from fiction."

"What do you mean?"

"Those 'clinches' you saw me and Greg in were not my idea. In fact, I didn't encourage them at all. Greg staged them for your benefit, I think."

"But why should he do that?"

It was my turn to be embarrassed. "I don't know, maybe he figured out how I feel about you."

Bob put his hands on my shoulders and grinned boyishly. "How do you feel about me?"

I looked directly in his eyes and voiced out loud what my heart had been trying to tell me for days, "I love you, too. I've been trying to deny it, but I'm more sure of that than I am of anything else."

To my surprise, Bob let out a whoop and almost crushed me in his arms. "I thought I had women all figured out, but you really led me a merry chase. I have a feeling that life with you will never be dull; that is, you will marry me, won't you?"

I started giggling, "I might have known a proposal from you wouldn't be conventional. Of course I'll marry you. Somebody has to keep you on the straight and narrow." We both laughed then, but soon Bob's lips found mine, and we kissed with a tenderness, and yet a passion that I had never known before. I forgot about the mysterious stranger that had terrorized me a few hours before, and I forgot that this man that I was kissing had enough evidence against him that Perry Mason wouldn't have taken his case. All I knew was that I was in love, for the first time in my life, and no matter what would happen next, I would always be in love with Bob Wilson.

As if he were reading my thoughts, Bob managed to say between kisses, "You sure you have no doubts about me? I mean, it looks pretty bad for me."

"I know it does, but I believe in you with all my heart. I know you wouldn't hurt me or Angela."

"I wish I could convince everybody else of that, especially Angela."

I couldn't stand to hear the sadness in his voice. "She'll come around, Darling, I'm sure she will, when she regains her memory."

His voice was light again, "'Darling,' I like that. Say it again."

The word had come so naturally that I hadn't noticed it. I said it again, and then again, and we both laughed like giddy children on a merry-go-round. Then we kissed and reveled in our new-found love.

I could have stayed like that forever, but surprisingly, it was Bob who became serious. "Honey, as bad as I hate to end this love-fest, we've got to talk about what happened tonight, and I'm sure we don't have much time before the police come back. Since we both know it was not me up on that lighthouse, we've got to figure out who it was because you and Angela are in danger until we do, and if something happens to either one of you, I'll--"

"I know," I sighed as I leaned my head on his chest. "I wish I could be more help, but I have no idea who it could have been."

"I was sure it was Rothman until I heard that he ran into you right after you got down. He couldn't have been up at the top at the lighthouse and then have been down in time to meet you."

"That's right."

"Do you remember anything about the man that might help? His size, his clothes, his voice--or did he speak at all?"

"No, he didn't say anything. He was about your size, but of course, that's a pretty average size for a man. Oh, there is one thing, but you're not going to like it. He smelled like you--that is, the cologne you wear. I had noticed it on you before, and then I noticed it on the man at the lighthouse, and you have it on now."

"Wow, the noose around my neck keeps getting tighter and tighter. Sounds like somebody's trying to frame me, even going to the trouble to find out what cologne I wear. But who and why?"

"I don't know who, but the why seems pretty obvious. If you are suspected, then he will be off the hook."

"Yeah, but there are other people that he could pick on. That's why I was sure it was Rothman. He has more than one reason to want me locked up." We were both silent for a while, then Bob said, "Have you seen Mr. Jennings since I showed you that news article?"

"No, he hasn't been over here, but I just can't seem to suspect him. I mean, I believe that news article, but he must have changed. He seems like such a sweet man."

"I know it's rotten to have to suspect everyone, but we have to if we're going to get to the bottom of this. The most baffling part about this whole mystery is that no one has come forward to identify Angela, well, except for Lucy Parsons."

The mention of Lucy's name cast a shadow over my joy. "I just wish she had lived, even if she had never been able to remember where she'd seen Angela. It's strange how a person who comes into your life for only a few minutes can make such an impact."

"I know. By the way, speaking of Lucy, I went to see her husband last week."

"You did? How's he doing?"

"Not very well. I could tell he was lonely. You know how quiet he was when they were both here?" I nodded my head. "Well, he about talked my leg off when I visited him. I asked him where he and Lucy had vacationed the last few years, and he not only told me, but showed me hundreds of slides, mostly of Lucy in every place they've visited in the last five years."

"Why did you ask him about his vacations?"

"For two reasons: one, his loneliness. He seemed to enjoy talking about their vacations together. I think he and Lucy really had a good thing going, and I think it helped him to remember their good times together."

"I think that's one reason I fell in love with you."

"What is?"

"Your concern for others, you know, what I called 'nosiness.'"

"After all that, I hate to admit that I had another reason for my visit other than cheering up a lonely widower. You see, I am firmly convinced that Lucy actually saw Angela at one time, and I figured it must have been on one of their vacations because if she had lived around where Lucy lived, then Lucy would have remembered right away. Anyway, I was hoping that Mr.

Parsons' pictures might connect with the little I know about

Angela."

"Did it?" I asked eagerly.

"Not at first, and not directly. But the name of one

of the places Mr. Parsons mentioned was very familiar to

me. It was a little town in Canada called Wellingham.

Have you ever heard of it?"

"No, it doesn't ring a bell."

"Right at first I couldn't think where I had heard of it

either. For two days after I talked to Mr. Parsons, the name

of that place nagged at my mind. Then I looked up some

news reports that had come over the wires around the time

Angela came here. And there it was."

"What?"

"The name of the town. It seems the day before

Angela came knocking at your door that the president of

the Wellingham bank and his brother had disappeared

without any trace. That same day, the vice president called

in the bank examiners, and they found that a million

dollars, in Canadian money, were gone too, without a

trace."

"But what do you think this has to do with Angela?"

"Well, the bank president had a wife and a six-year-old child who are also missing."

I shook my head. "No, it's not possible. Angela couldn't have parents who are bank robbers."

"No, I agree it doesn't seem likely. I know it's a long shot, but, just to make sure, I called the newspaper up there, and they were going to try to find me a picture of the family or some more information about them."

We were again quiet, contemplating all that happened in the warm companionship that lovers share. Suddenly, though we heard a noise outside and saw the beam of two flashlights coming through the woods. Then we were able to see two men emerge from the woods into the parking lot. Bob stepped back from the window to avoid being seen if they beamed the flashlights toward us. I continued watching and reported to Bob, "I think it's Greg and one of the policemen, but they're not coming here. They're headed for the lighthouse."

Bob was right behind me. "You say you only saw one of the policemen?" I nodded my head and Bob said, "Probably the other one is watching my car. I think I know how to get out of here without anybody seeing me, but I'm not going to tell you where I'm going, so you won't have to lie if they ask you."

I threw my arms around him, "But, you're hurt. How can you tramp through the woods with your head aching, without a car especially? Why don't you hide in the basement?"

"No, they will search the basement soon, and I don't want to get you in trouble. I'll be all right. As for my head hurting, I'm so happy that I can't even feel it anymore. Just remember, I love you." He gave me a quick kiss, left the bedroom, and sprinted into the kitchen. I heard the back door open, but then all was quiet.

There was a potpourri of emotions churning inside of me. I was frightened, for Bob and also for myself and Angela. I also felt guilty because I was aiding and abetting a murder suspect in his get-away. But over-riding all the other emotions was pure ecstasy. I knew then that the feelings I had had for Paul couldn't have been love because they were nothing compared to what I felt for Bob. I couldn't be still. I felt like laughing and jumping and shouting all at the same time. However, I knew I had to control myself when the police came back in. I couldn't let them suspect that Bob had been here, so I walked back out to the living room and sat on the couch, trying to assume the demeanor of a woman in shock, not one in love.

Soon I heard the tramp of feet on the porch and the very familiar voice of Captain Rogers called out, "It's me, again, Amanda, Captain Rogers. Would you let us in?"

I was shaking like a leaf, sure that my face would give me away. I knew I could never be a real criminal. With trembling fingers I unbolted the door and let the captain and Greg in. It did seem that the policeman scrutinized me more carefully than usual, or maybe it was my imagination. Captain Rogers was holding two articles, which he had encased in plastic bags. One was a dark cloth of some kind, and the other looked like a gold piece of jewelry. I had a momentary curiosity about the articles, but I was more concerned with hiding my secret meeting with Bob. To cover my guilt, I began talking quickly and loudly. "Well, what did you find? Where is Sergeant Adams? Did you see anyone out there? Where could that man have gone when Greg came up? What do you have in those bags, Captain?"

"Hey, Amanda, one question at a time," laughed Greg.

"Yeah," said Captain Rogers, "Let's sit down and we'll tell you what we found." We all went to the same places we were before except I was sitting on the couch instead of lying on it.

Captain Rogers began, "We didn't see anyone out there, but we did find this hood. Does this look like the one your attacker wore?" He took a pair of tweezers from his pocket and carefully pulled the hood from the bag. It looked like a pillow case that had been dyed black, and there were holes cut out for where the person's eyes and nose would be. As he turned it around slowly, I noticed a small tear in the back. Even the hood smelled of Bob's cologne, and I hoped they wouldn't notice.

"Yes," I answered. "That looks like the hood, but of course I can't say positively that it's the one my attacker wore."

"No, I realize that. Anyway, we found it at the bottom of the lighthouse, in the corner back of the stairs. My guess is that the culprit came down there right after you got down, and he hid in the small crawl place behind the stairwell when Rothman came in."

"I guess that could have happened," I said, "but he must be a lot better on those stairs than I was. It took me forever to get down them."

"It probably seemed longer because you were so frightened," said the Captain.

"I suppose you're right."

"Now, to the rest of our discoveries. We also found Bob Wilson's car where Mr. Rothman told us it would be. Sergeant Adams is watching it in case Wilson tries to get in it tonight."

I made no comment, but I silently prayed that he would not ask if I had seen Bob tonight. My face felt flushed, and I caught myself drumming my fingers nervously on the arm of the couch.

After a slight pause, Captain Rogers continued. "We did happen to find this on the floor of Wilson's car." As he talked he took his tweezers and pulled out a sparkling gold chain with a heart-shaped locket on the end of it. With the tweezers he managed to pry the locket open and show me the picture inside. I almost fainted when I saw the tiny picture. It was of a beautiful, dark-haired child, about two or three years old. The child could have certainly been a younger Angela.

"Oh my goodness," I gasped. "This looks like Angela! Did you say you found this on the floor of Bob Wilson's car?" My voice was squeaking, and I was trembling so much that I hid my hands behind my back for fear that the captain would notice.

"Yeah, it's rather incriminating, don't you think?" asked Greg almost gleefully.

My mind was searching frantically for an explanation, and soon I found one. "I suppose it is, but it doesn't really prove anything, does it?" I mean, the little girl looks like Angela, but it could be someone else. This child is much younger than Angela is now, and you know how quickly kids change. Even if it is Angela, couldn't someone have put that locket in Bob's car to implicate him in all this?" I could sense the wariness of the men as I talked. I wished again that I knew how to hide my feelings better.

"I guess that's possible," agreed Captain Rogers. "Well, tomorrow we hope we'll know a little more. I'm sending an officer down to Lansing with the hood and necklace where they have equipment to check for fingerprints, hair follicles, blood—"

"Blood?" I cried. "Why do you think they'd find blood?"

"Well, did you see this little tear in the back of the hood?" I nodded, and he continued, "We found a tiny piece of this same material on the bolt of one of the posts on the railing. You know how the railing is made up there-- the steel meshing is bolted onto those heavy iron posts that are about four feet apart. We figure this fellow conked his head on the bolt that juts out, and I'm sure his head would be bleeding, sort of like when you hit your head on an open cabinet door."

My mind flashed back to the sight of Bob's dark hair matted with blood, but again I didn't want to believe Bob was my attacker. "But I don't understand; if he wasn't unconscious, why didn't he come after me right away? And if he was unconscious, how was he able to come to in enough time to manage rushing down dangerous stairs in the dark before Greg got to him?"

"I know it seems pretty strange, but stranger things have happened. Anyway, I've got to go. Sergeant Adams will be around here watching Wilson's car, until I can bring a replacement for him, but we won't be bothering you anymore tonight. We will be back tomorrow, and by the way, Amanda, Rothman is going to lock the lighthouse door, so tell your guests it's off limits. We're going to see if we missed anything."

"Okay, I hope you find something."

"I hope so too. Meanwhile, be careful, Amanda. Don't go off on anymore expeditions without checking with us. Remember you not only have your own safety at stake, but also the little girl's. So, I hope you will tell us everything." His voice was so emphatic that I was certain he knew about Bob. Only my strong conviction in Bob's innocence kept me from spilling out the whole story.

"I'll be careful, Sir," I promised.

Just then the grandfather clock struck 1:00. As if by signal, both Captain Rogers and Greg stood up. The captain said, "I'd better go. I have to be here early tomorrow morning. I've found that there is a better chance of finding evidence if there's an investigation as soon after the crime as possible. Amanda, I've asked Greg to stay here tonight--downstairs here on the couch. I'm sure we can trust him. I'll feel better about you if I know there's a man here to watch over you."

Greg smiled wryly as he looked over at me. "I don't know, Captain, it seems Amanda can take care of herself. I mean, you can't say she lacks courage."

"Well, Son, maybe you can make sure she behaves herself." He smiled at me as if he were a kind father who had just scolded me for my own good. I wondered if he had another reason for posting Greg in the cottage, like maybe keeping me from meeting Bob? Again, though, I decided my guilty conscious was making my imagination run wild, and the good policeman only had my safety in mind. Anyway, I wasn't going to argue.

Captain Rogers spoke again, "Oh Amanda, would you do me a favor? My throat is as dry as a desert. Could I bother you for a glass of ice water?"

"Sure," I said quickly, relieved that he wasn't asking something more difficult, like asking me about Bob's whereabouts, "you can have water, or I have some ice tea or pop in the refrigerator, too."

"Water will be fine, and I hate to be picky, but do you have some ice for it? I really don't like tap water without ice in it.

"Sure, just a minute. Greg, would you like something?"

"Yes, could I have a glass of ice water, too?" he asked.

I was glad both men stayed in the living room while I went into the kitchen so that they couldn't see my shaking hands. As I got the ice from the freezer I involuntarily looked over at the pantry door and wondered where Bob was now. I was having a rough time dealing with all the evidence that kept mounting against him, but the love in my heart refused to believe he was guilty. I kept telling myself that the evidence was just circumstantial, a term I used to hear on lawyer programs on TV, and I was convinced that it could all be explained.

When I came back to the living room with the water, the captain and Greg were over by the couch, and again, I had the feeling that they were looking at me suspiciously. It seemed that I had interrupted a conversation about myself when I had walked in, but at the time, I relegated these feelings as nothing but paranoia.

Captain Rogers drank his water and walked wearily out to the car. Just as he was leaving, he said, "Amanda, don't be alarmed if you hear noises in the basement. I'm going to see what I can find down there. Rothman, will you get me the key?"

"Sure," Greg agreed as the policeman walked out the front door, and then Greg walked toward the kitchen and said to me, "Amanda, I'll be right back. I'm going to go get my sleeping bag and my pillow. You just go on upstairs to bed; I'll lock all the doors when I come back."

"Greg, you don't really have to stay here if you don't want to. I don't imagine I'll sleep anyway, and I don't really think the man is still around tonight."

"You can't be sure. I'll be glad to stay here, and don't worry, I'll be a gentleman."

"I'm not worried. I just don't want to impose on you."

"You won't be imposing. I just don't want anything to happen to you or Angela. I just wish I could have found

Wil--uh--that guy tonight when I went up to the top of the lighthouse."

I heard the beginning of the name Wilson, but I chose to ignore it. I didn't want Greg to know that Bob had been here tonight, and I was afraid that if we really started debating Bob's guilt or innocence, my secret would come out. Instead I said, "I still can't figure out how he got down so fast. I kept looking at the door to see if it opened, and it didn't."

"Well, it was awfully dark in there. Maybe you looked down at the stairs or something, and he opened it without your seeing him."

"Then why didn't he finish his attack on me. He could have finished me off easily then."

"I don't know. Maybe he changed his mind, or maybe he was afraid I was coming. Who knows what goes on in the mind of a killer? Well, I'd better get going if either one of us is going to get to sleep tonight."

I laughed to myself after Greg left about his hope for sleep figuring there wasn't much chance I'd get to sleep tonight. I was still too nerved up. I went through all the mechanics of changing clothes, brushing my teeth, washing my face, and finally crawling into bed. Angela was still sleeping peacefully, and I was so glad she didn't know what had gone on this night.

I was tired, more tired than I ever had been in my life, but my mind was racing full speed. Pictures, like slides on a screen, kept flashing before me. There was the dark man trying to push me over the railing, Greg running into me on my way to the cottage, Bob pulling me into the dark basement, Captain Rogers looking at me suspiciously, but most of all Bob kissing me and telling me that he loved me. Tonight had been the most terrorizing night of my life, yet it was also the most wonderful. I caught myself smiling to myself, and the irony of my exhilaration in spite of the fact that I had almost been killed made me want to laugh. Of course I didn't want to wake Angela, but it was hard to control my emotions.

Greg must have come back in when I had been in the bathroom. I vaguely heard him checking all the doors and windows, and then he must have settled down on the couch to sleep because I no longer heard him walking around. I appreciated his willingness to protect me, but I really felt uneasy with him around. It wasn't that I mistrusted him, but I didn't want him to get the idea that I needed him around all the time. I liked Greg, but I knew I could never feel anything more than friendship for him, even if Bob were out of the picture.

I started to turn off the light, but just then Angela rolled over toward me, and I gazed in wonder at her beautiful face. Where had this lovely child come from? I was beginning to think she was that angel I had jokingly named her after because she had seemingly appeared from nowhere. Then I started thinking about the locket the police had found in Bob's car? Should that be shown to Angela? Was the child in the picture really Angela, and if so, would she recognize herself if she were shown the picture? The one question I didn't deal with was--why was the locket in Bob's car?

I had only written sketches in my journal during the preceding days, so, since sleep seemed to be eluding me, I decided to update the events that either directly or indirectly would affect Angela. I recorded the frightening events on the lighthouse, but I didn't write anything down about Bob for fear that someone else would read it. Instead, I relived our love scene in my mind where no one else could see. I went over everything he had said, the ecstasy I had experienced when he had kissed me, and the future we would have together. But thoughts of the future broke the spell of my sweet reveries because it was so uncertain. Would we ever find my attacker? Would Angela regain her memory? I knew I couldn't ever get to sleep if I tried to figure out all the answers myself. Thankfully, the dangers and turmoils I had gone through since Angela had come into my life had done something good for me; they had taught me where to take my problems. I took out a piece of paper and wrote out all my worries, fears, and even guilt, and I presented them to God. It wasn't long after that that I fell to sleep, content that everything was going to be all right.

My sleep, although peaceful, had come too late, so I wasn't ready to get up the next morning when the alarm rang, but I still had a job to do. I lay still for a moment, and let the events of the night before wash over me. I was still in a blissful euphoria when I thought of Bob. I could still feel his arms around me and his lips on mine. Then I remembered my terror on top of the lighthouse. Right then

I breathed a prayer of thanks that I was alive to face a new day.

The alarm rang again, and Angela stirred a little when I reached over to turn it off. Then she opened her incredible eyes and smiled at me, and once again I felt a surge of love like an electric shock go through me. I mentally thanked God for protecting her in spite of my foolishness the night before.

I leaned over and kissed her cheek and said, "Good morning, Darling. Did you have a good sleep?"

"Yes, did you?"

"I had a good sleep when I finally got to sleep, but it was pretty late when I got to bed."

"Why?" she asked.

I again didn't know how much to tell her. I knew she would be terrified if she heard the whole story, but she would realize something was wrong when she saw Greg sleeping downstairs, if he was still there, and we wouldn't be able to hide the police activities from her. "Well," I began, "uh--Greg thought he--uh--saw or heard someone over at the lighthouse last night, and we called the police. Greg slept on the couch downstairs last night, just to make sure everything would be all right, and the police are coming over here this morning before the museum opens to see if they can see any evidence that anyone was there."

Surprisingly, she seemed to ignore the frightening possibility that a stranger had been lurking around, and she asked an unexpected question, "What is evidence?"

"Let's see, how can I explain? Well, they're going to see if there are fingerprints or footprints or something up there of someone who wasn't supposed to be there."

She looked puzzled, "I don't understand."

"Hm, do you remember when the police had you stick your fingers in that mud when we went to the station?" She nodded solemnly. "They were getting your fingerprints because, you see, there are designs on the ends of our fingers, and nobody has the same design. So, if you had ever had your fingerprints taken before and we had found the record of them, then we would know exactly who you are. And if the police find some fingerprints of someone up on the railing that they have a record of, they will know who was up there."

"But a lot of people were up there yesterday."

I was beginning to learn how hard it was to answer a child's questions, especially a bright childlike Angela. "Yes, that's true, but maybe they'll find some prints of someone they know could not have been a tourist."

"How do they get the fingerprints off the railing?"

"I don't know for sure; I think they put a powder or something on them that make them show up. Then they take a picture of them, and they'll send the picture to Lansing or somewhere they can be checked." As I talked, I got out of bed and started gathering my clothes to take into the shower.

Angela also got out of bed, stretched like a tiny kitten, and asked, "What is 'Lanzing?'"

"Lansing is the capital of Michigan, the state we are in right now. I asked you once before if you had ever heard of Michigan, and you said no, but do you remember now?"

She nodded her head. "Maybe, but I can't remember where I heard it."

I stopped gathering the clothes and went over to a small, wooden bookcase the Sanders had in the corner of the room where I had placed my history books when I had moved in. I pulled out the book we had used the previous year and turned right to the page showing a map of the United States with their capitals and major cities highlighted. "See, this is the state of Michigan," I said as I pointed to the mitten-shaped state on the map. "Here is where we are, and here is Lansing. You see the lake out here is Lake Huron; it's one of the five Great Lakes."

Angela looked at me excitedly, "I've heard of the Great Lakes."

"You have? Let's see, the names of them are Lake Huron, Lake Michigan, Lake Superior, Lake Erie, and Lake Ontario." I pointed them out on the map as I named them.

"On—tar—o, I've heard of that!"

"Yes, Ontario is not only a lake; it's a province in Canada."

"Canada! I remember Canada. That's where I live."

Now I was as excited as she. That explained why she didn't seem familiar with McDonalds, although I knew there were McDonalds in the big cities in Canada. I figured she must have come from a small town in Canada, and I remembered what Bob had said about the two brothers who had embezzled from the bank in Wellington, a small town in Ontario. "Do you remember the town you lived in?" I asked eagerly.

Her forehead was wrinkled as she thought. Finally she said sadly, "No, I can't think of anything except Canada."

"Well, that's a first step, though. Tell me, does the name 'Wellington' mean anything to you?" I was holding my breath. In one way, I wanted her to say that Wellington was her home town, but in another way, I did not want to think about her being connected to bank robbers.

Again she shook her head sadly, "I'm sorry, I just can't remember."

"That's okay, Sweetheart, but we'd better get busy. After all, we're working girls, right?"

"Right," she smiled her special smile, and we both started to get ready to go downstairs.

It didn't take us long to get dressed and start the day. It was hard to believe that the routine events of life could go on in spite of my close brush with death the night before, but I knew that when I got downstairs, I would have to make breakfast, do the dishes, dust the furniture, and set up my desk to receive the museum visitors. Greg was busy folding his sleeping bag when we reached the bottom stair. He turned around and smiled charmingly, as if it were the middle of the day instead of the morning after only a few hours sleep. "Hello Ladies, how are the most beautiful ladies on Silver Isle this morning?"

Before I could answer, Angela piped up, "I remembered something. I remembered Canada."

Greg stopped folding and stared at us incredulously, "That's great, Honey. What do you remember about Canada?"

This time I answered, "She thinks she lived there. She remembered the name 'Ontario' too."

"Wow, that could mean she's regaining her memory," said Greg, and his smile was more dazzling than ever. "I think we ought to tell the police about this. I'll be with them as soon as they come over, so do you want me to tell them?"

"Okay, yeah, they should be told."

Angela looked up at me and asked, "Do you think the police will know who I am after Greg tells them about Canada?" Since she had first remembered the word, she seemed to say 'Canada' emphatically, probably relishing the sound of something familiar.

I bent down to her, again in the role of dream smasher. "Well, Honey, Canada is a big place. It will probably help them to know, but they probably won't find anything out right away."

"I guess so," she said sadly.

To break the mood, I said, "We'd better get going, Kiddo. What do you want for breakfast?"

She brightened a little, but she was still preoccupied. "I don't know; whatever you'd like," she said.

"Then, let's have some French toast, and maybe Greg would like some too."

"Sure," he said, "but first I think I'd better put up a sign on the lighthouse door telling no one to go up there today."

"Yeah, that's right. I'll tell the guests, too. Just come on back when you finish, and breakfast will be ready."

"All right, thanks," and with that Greg picked up his sleeping bag and walked back to his shed.

Angela and I busied ourselves in the kitchen making the French toast. Angela was very helpful when I was cooking something. I could tell that she had been used to a kitchen, maybe helping her mother fix meals. I still wondered if Angela should be shown the locket found in Bob's car, but I had no control over that decision because the police still had it with them.

It seemed that no matter what I was doing or thinking about, my thoughts always strayed back to Bob. In spite of my fears for him, I felt a thrill go through me just knowing that he loved me. I had never felt this way before about anyone. I was so glad I hadn't married Paul. I was sure then that God had worked all this out for my good, but I had not been able to see it before.

Greg came in the back door just as I was setting a plate of steaming French toast on the table. I poured Greg and me some coffee and Angela some milk, and we ate and talked as if nothing unusual had happened the night before. We were eating the last bites of food when the police drove up. They walked directly to the lighthouse without stopping at the cottage. Greg thanked me politely for the breakfast and then caught up with the officers as they walked across the lawn.

Angela and I washed and dried the dishes, then dusted all the furniture in the front room. I pulled out my fee box and set out the guest book, and soon a car drove up. I thought it was a tourist, but to my dismay, it was Phil Jennings. I didn't know how I was going to treat him after what I had learned about him. Should I confront him with his past, or should I try to act as if everything was the same?

As soon as he walked in the door, I knew I wasn't going to be able to pretend that all was well. When I said hello to him, even I could hear that my voice was edged with hostility. He walked over to Angela who was sitting on the couch reading one of the books he had brought her, and he started showing her a paint-by-number set he had brought her. Angela was very excited about the present, but I'm ashamed to say that I didn't give them much of a chance to talk. As soon as he sat on the couch beside Angela, I was immediately on his heels, hovering over Angela like a mother hen.

Phil looked up at me with a puzzled expression. "How are you doing today, Amanda? You look a little perturbed. Is anything wrong?"

I managed a smile. "No, I'm just tired. I didn't get much sleep last night."

"Oh, I'm sorry to hear that. Was something worrying you?"

"Yes, I guess you can say that," I said in the voice of a shrew. Then I put all pretense aside and decided to confront him with my suspicions. "Phil, you haven't always been a history teacher, have you?"

His face got red, and his eyes became wary. "No, but why do you ask?"

Now I was on the defensive, not quite as eager to confront as before. "Oh, I guess all those pictures I saw over at your house, well, they looked so professional. I just wondered--"

He looked me straight in the eyes without flinching, "Yes, you're right. I was a professional photographer at one time."

Now that I had come so far, I had to plod on. With my heart pounding I said, "I noticed that many pictures were of children. Did you specialize in children's pictures?"

He cleared his throat, and his face was grim. But just as he was about to answer, we heard the police and Greg walk up on the front porch. There was so much tension now between Phil and myself that I was relieved that the awkward interrogation was interrupted. When I let them in, I started gabbing foolishly to hide my discomfort, "Well, good morning, Gentlemen. How's the weather out there? I hope you both got some sleep last night. I certainly didn't get as much as I wanted."

Captain Rogers didn't smile. With a sternness that sent my heart plummeting, he ordered, "Amanda, would you sit down over here, please?" He indicated my desk chair. He and Sergeant Adams sat in the two chairs in front of the desk, and Greg sat on the couch with Phil and Angela.

Still without a smile, the captain turned to Phil and said, "Maybe you'd like to take Angela outside for a few minutes, Mr. Jennings."

"No," I almost shouted. "I don't think--"

Captain Rogers interrupted, "It'll be all right. Mr. Jennings, please do not leave the yard out here where we can see you right out the window. Angela, would you go out and play on your swing with Mr. Jennings?"

Both Angela and Phil looked bewildered. Angela nodded her head slowly, and Phil said, "Sure, let's go Angela." Then he looked at me and said in a stiff voice, "She'll be quite safe with me, I assure you, Amanda."

I felt miserable. Phil had no doubt now that I was suspicious of him, and I had no doubt that I had fallen from the good favor of my police friends. I tried to convince myself that I had no idea what had changed their attitude toward me, but I knew deep down that they had somehow figured out that Bob had been with me last night. I sat very still like a lamb waiting for the slaughter.

As soon as Angela and Phil were outside, the captain began, "Amanda, you remember last night I showed you the hood your attacker must have worn, and the locket we found in Wilson's car?"

I nodded silently.

"I also told you that we were going to send those two items to Lansing to be analyzed for blood type, hair follicles, and fingerprints. However I didn't tell you that we had a third article we sent to the lab for the same tests." As he said this, he pulled out of his pocket what looked like a typed report of some kind. He continued, "The third article we sent was the doily that goes on the back of your couch. Did you notice it was missing?"

Immediately I looked over at the couch. Sure enough the lacy doily someone had obviously crocheted with great care was gone. "No," I mumbled, "I didn't notice, but I don't understand."

"Last night when we were here, I saw a stain that looked like a blood stain on that doily. I confess I asked for that glass of water mostly to get you out of the room while I took it and put it in another plastic bag I had with me." He paused, probably to see if I would react, but I wouldn't have been able to speak if my life had depended on it.

"Anyway, we have the lab report now. As we expected, Amanda, the blood and the hair follicles on the hood match perfectly those found on the doily. In other words, the man who wore that hood was the same man who must have sat on that couch and leaned his head against the doily. Do you want to tell us who that man was, Amanda?"

Chapter 16

I will never be able to describe the despair I felt that moment. I was plunged into a dark cell of agony, far removed from the others sitting just a few feet from me. I don't know how long the police tried to get my attention, but finally I became aware that all three men were standing around me, calling my name, patting my hand, and gently shaking my shoulders.

"Amanda, are you all right?" the authoritative voice of Captain Rogers brought me back.

When I nodded my head, he sighed, and all of them sat back down and looked steadily at me. "Now, Amanda, are you ready to answer some questions?"

"I guess so," I said in a voice so strange that I actually looked around the room to see who had spoken.

"Okay, let me ask you again, who was the person who sat on the couch last night after we went outside?"

"It was Bob, Bob Wilson," I whispered. I was surprised I could get the name out.

The captain wasn't in the least perturbed, as if he had known the answer before he asked the question. "Do you know where Wilson is right now?"

"No," I said, then I raised my head in time to see a look of skepticism pass between the two policemen. "Really, I don't know. He told me he wasn't going home, and he wouldn't tell me where he was going so I wouldn't have to lie if you asked where he was." I felt a fresh stab of pain when I thought of his kiss right after he had made that statement.

"Amanda, what did he tell you that would make you let him in and not tell us that he was here?"

I swallowed hard and managed to relate Bob's story the way he had told it to me. I didn't tell about his trip to see Frank Parsons, his investigation about the two brothers in Canada, nor about his suspicions of Mr. Jennings. I had all I could do to tell his explanation of the wound on his head, and I figured all the rest he said was a smoke screen to make himself appear innocent. When I finally finished, I covered my face with my hands and said, "How could I have been so stupid?"

"You're not stupid, Lass," soothed Sergeant Adams. "There's no crime in falling in love with someone. You did fall in love with Wilson, didn't you?"

I nodded again. There was no use denying the obvious.

"But there is a crime in hiding evidence," interjected Captain Rogers. "Amanda, I don't want to make you feel worse than you feel, but I must stress to you the importance of telling us everything. Our job is to protect you, but we can't do it with only half the information."

"I know; I'm sorry, but I really did believe him."

"I know you did, and I understand what you're going through. After all, police are human too. But I want you to tell me if and when you see him, if you can."

"Sure, I will, Captain. I just hope nothing happens to Angela because of my foolishness."

"Now that you know about Wilson, you won't be easily fooled again. If he comes around, maybe you should try to pretend you still believe him, you know, go along with him until you can get to a phone and call us."

"I don't know whether I could do that," I thought of being in his arms again knowing that he was plotting my death. It would take an academy-award actress to pretend nothing was wrong, and I had just proved that I was no actress at all with my clumsy questioning of Phil.

"Well, Rothman is going to keep his eyes open for him. He said he'd stay close around here and keep watch.

I looked over at Greg and felt my face burning with shame. I had rebuffed his honest approaches and had fallen for the lies of a murderer. How could my instincts have been so wrong? True, I had been wrong about Paul, at least about his feelings for me, but Paul had not tried to kill me. Before this summer, I would have claimed that a murderer would always give himself away, that his evil character would surface, and it would be obvious to everyone that he was a criminal. Now, I realized the true meaning of the scriptures I had learned as a child about the heart being "deceitful and desperately wicked." I realized then that all of us were capable of evil, even murder.

My reveries were broken by the scuffling of the chairs as the policemen got up to leave. They gave some instructions to Greg that I really didn't hear; then they turned to me and kindly said good-bye without further rebukes.

I was ashamed to face Greg, and he was apparently sensitive enough to understand my discomfort because he smiled at me and said very simply, "I've got some work to do, Boss Lady. If you need me, give me a call." Then he left quickly, thoughtfully giving me solitude to deal with my anguish.

I sat at my desk, so numb I couldn't even cry. I wished desperately that I knew where Bob was. I wanted to confront him, to have him explain away all the evidence against him. Most of all, I wanted him to take me in his arms and assure me that he loved me, that he never tried to hurt me, and that we were going to live happily ever after.

My thoughts were so dark that I resented the bright sunshine and blue skies outside. I couldn't understand how the birds could go right on singing and the flowers could keep right on blooming as if nothing had changed. I envied Angela swinging happily on the swing with Phil pushing her, and in the depths of self-pity, I forgot that she was suffering too, not knowing who she was or where her parents were. My despair was so great that I resolved never to entangle myself in romantic relationships. Falling in love was too painful. I was going to devote myself to Angela and her welfare.

I was just about to get up and go out to join Angela and Phil when I saw Angela jump off the swing and the two of them start walking up the hill toward the cottage. I had no idea what I was going to say to Phil after the cool reception I had given him, but it turned out that I didn't have to worry because he merely left Angela off at the door and went on toward his cottage. I figured I must have really hurt him, and that was one more sorrow added to my misery.

Still sitting at my desk, I tried to plaster the brightest smile I could muster on my face when Angela came in, but she wasn't fooled for a minute. "What's wrong now, Amanda?" she asked. "Did the policemen tell you someone else got killed?"

"No," I said, and I was sad that a child as young as Angela would be acquainted with so much death. I then made a quick decision. I figured that she would have to be warned about Bob Wilson, and hard as it was going to be, I was the one who would have to do the job. "Sweetheart, there is something I have to tell you. The police examined the evidence I told you about this morning, and they have figured out that Bob, Mr. Wilson, is a bad man. If you're ever outside, away from me, and you see him coming, run to me as fast as you can."

She looked confused. "But you really like Mr. Wilson, don't you?"

I had to smile in spite of my pain. It seemed nothing had escaped her. "Well yes, I did like him, but now I know he's dangerous, and we can't trust him." I turned my face from her to hide the tears that were filling my eyes. I felt as though I was betraying him, an absurd thought after all of his deceptions.

"Okay, Amanda," she said quietly, "I'll stay away from him." She then crawled up on my lap and hugged me around the neck. With this gesture, I wondered who was the adult and who was the child. She was instinctively offering the comfort I desperately needed at that moment. I couldn't stop the tears from flowing, and she kept her arms around me while I cried. She even offered me a Kleenex when my tears subsided.

I don't know how long this scene would have lasted if we had not heard a car pulling up the driveway. That car

contained a boisterous family of five that filled the cottage
with such noisy activity that my problems were
temporarily forced out of my mind. They were the first of
a moderate stream of visitors that day, and my thoughts
were kept off Bob, except for when a tall, dark man would
be among the visitors, or anyone with a deep, hearty laugh
would catch my attention, or whenever there was a lull of
five minutes or more.

Finally the long day was over, and I put the closed
sign on the gate at the driveway entrance. Angela and I had
a quiet supper, or at least Angela did. I pushed my food all
over the plate and finally threw most of it away, going
against all the thrifty, unwasteful lessons that had been
ingrained in me since early childhood.

Angela tried to carry on a conversation with me, but
she finally gave up when she would have to say my name
two or three times before I would respond. She finally
asked if she could watch some TV, and after finding a
good, decent Disney movie on one channel, I allowed her
to crawl into the bed and watch it while I went downstairs,
sat on the couch, and stared into space. I turned on only
one light, my desk lamp that had a decorative anchor on

the lamp stand that turned to activate the on/off switch. The only sound in the room was the ticking of the grandfather clock and the wind outside that seemed to be heralding an approaching storm.

I knew I could not stop myself from thinking about Bob, so I let my mind wander back in time, like a slow-motion movie, from my first sight of him until the night before when I had declared my love for him. I remembered seeing him at church that first time and the glorious picnic we had had after church. I remembered his concern for the couple who had thought Angela might be their kidnapped daughter. I remembered his song in church, and I couldn't imagine a person who could sing with so much spirit being a cold-blooded murder. Then I started thinking about the murders, or what I was almost sure were murders--Mr. Edwards and Lucy Parsons.

I tortured myself trying to imagine how he had managed to drown Lucy when she herself stated that she never went into the water. Then I let my mind dwell on the pathetic man, Edwards. I saw in my mind Bob holding a gun to the poor drunk's head and pulling the trigger, but then the picture in my mind became blank. Thankfully, I had no experience with what a man's head would look like when part of it was blown away with a gun. All I knew was that it must have been a grisly sight.

The phrase "grisly sight" stuck in my mind. Who had said something about feeling sorry for the paper boy who had found Edwards because "someone shot in the head is a grisly sight"? I mulled the question over and over for several minutes, and then I remembered. It had been Greg who had said that the day we had found out that Edwards was dead.

I then remembered that something had bothered me that day, and it seemed to be in connection with Greg's statement. Now I concentrated on the whole episode starting with the policemen's announcement to me about Edward's death. I remembered that Angela and I had been the only ones here when they told us, and I remembered trying to comfort her. Then I remembered that Greg had come over and we were sitting at my desk writing orders for lawn supplies. Then Greg had said something about not wanting to be a guest in my house, and he had leaned over to kiss me. I was overcome with bitter-sweet nostalgia when I recollected that Bob had burst into the room just before Greg's lips had touched mine.

Then my memory became fuzzy. It seemed that I went quickly into the kitchen to hide my embarrassment and Bob had followed me. I remembered his standing in the doorway with his arms folded against his chest talking to me. At some point in our conversation I know we had started discussing Edwards. He had said something about the police telling him about it, which was most likely a lie because he must have been the one who had pulled the trigger.

I felt a shudder go through me as I again thought about the murder, but I forced my mind back to the scene in the kitchen and the conversation about Edwards. About half-way through the discussion, Greg had walked to the kitchen door, and he had asked what we were talking about. When we told him, he had asked who had found the body, and then he had made that comment about the "grisly sight."

All of a sudden it hit me why that statement had bothered me so much and had nagged my subconscious like a tiny splinter just under the skin. I couldn't remember anyone ever telling Greg how Edwards had died. How could he have known that Edwards had been shot in the head? Of course, there was probably a very logical explanation. Maybe Bob had said how Edwards had died, or maybe Greg had just assumed that Edwards had been shot. It was all academic now anyway, but I still couldn't fully dismiss my question. After pondering the question for a while, I finally decided I was clutching at straws, still trying to divert suspicion from Bob by casting it on someone else.

Now the wind was furiously howling, and I heard the rumble of thunder in the distance. I went to the large front window and pulled the curtain. Just as I did, a jagged line of lightning lit up the sky, heralding the beginning of a summer thunder storm. Oddly, the approaching storm lifted my spirits a little. Every clap of thunder and bolt of lightning seemed to echo the rage and frustration inside me, and I felt I was giving vent to my feelings in a vicarious way, a way that would not be destructive to anyone around me. I stood and watched the black clouds rolling, the trees flailing in the violent wind, and the sheets of rain pelting the window.

Watching the forces of nature lash the land and wind all around me, I began to think about God, the creator of the winds, thunder, and rain. I thought about the familiar story of Jesus stilling the storm when He and His disciples were in a boat on the Sea of Galilee. I desperately needed the storm in my own heart stilled. I didn't want to become the sour, bitter woman I was after my broken engagement with Paul. I had been angry then, at Paul, Janelle, and even God, but I hadn't admitted it until that night Bob had found me crying and had comforted me. Now I had been dealt a more terrible blow than I had ever experienced, and I didn't have Bob to comfort me. Could God comfort me and give me the ability to forgive? I decided to take everything I was feeling at the time to my Heavenly Father. I admitted my anger this time, and I asked God why He had allowed me to be hurt twice by two men I cared so much about. I cried and beat my fist against the couch where I was kneeling, all the time trying to muffle my sobs so that Angela wouldn't hear me.

Finally, after what seemed to be hours, a peace came over me that is still hard to describe. Somehow I knew everything was going to be all right. I was able to forgive Bob, and I even prayed for him, as well as for Greg, Phil Jennings, the police, Angela, Lucy Parson's husband, and everyone else that came to my mind. When I got up off my knees and looked out the window, I noticed that the storm outside had become as calm as the storm that had raged inside of me. There was only a light drizzle left when I went up to bed and fell into a deep sleep beside Angela who appeared to be in an untroubled sleep of her own. I must have slept so soundly that I didn't even hear the other storms that I later learned had kept coming all through the night.

I was not awakened by the alarm as usual in the morning, but by Angela shaking me and saying, "Amanda, wake up. There's someone knocking at the door."

It took me a while to awaken enough to know what was going on, but then I heard the knocking Angela described. I turned to look at the alarm only to find my electric digital clock was blank, registering nothing, and I realized the power must have gone off during the night, and that was why the alarm had not gone off. In panic, I looked at my watch and was horrified to find that it was already 9:30. I immediately surmised that I had forgotten to put the closed sign on the entrance gate, and that the person knocking at my door was a persistent visitor wanting to see the museum.

I jumped out of bed and grabbed clothes from my dresser and closet haphazardly. My first thought was to send Angela to the door to tell the person I would be right down because no one would care if a little girl greeted him in her pajamas, but then I figured that making Angela open the door to a stranger might be a dangerous move. I decided I would have to hurry to make myself as presentable as possible. I rushed into the bathroom to wash my face, but no water came out of the spigot, and being a country girl, I realized that the pump on the well would not work without electricity. I told Angela to get up and get ready, and I told her not to try to flush the toilet or run water.

At last I was ready, or as ready as I was going to get, and I opened the bedroom door and ran down the steps as fast as I could without falling. When I reached the bottom, I realized that there was someone at the back door, not the front. Then I heard Greg's familiar voice, "Amanda, are you in there? Are you all right? Amanda? Angela?"

Relieved that I didn't have to face a total stranger, I rushed into the kitchen and unlocked the door. Greg's face looked anxious and concerned, and I was gratified that he seemed to care so much for our welfare. When I opened the door for him, I saw a thick wall of gray fog all around us. I couldn't even see the shed where Greg stayed. The temperature must have dropped at least ten degrees since the night before because the air was much cooler. When Greg stepped into the kitchen, he grabbed hold of my hands and said, "Thank goodness you're okay. I imagined all kinds of things when you didn't appear this morning."

"I'm sorry. The power must have gone off last night, and my alarm didn't go off. I thought you were a tourist coming to see the museum."

"I doubt if there'll be a lot of people around today. That was quite a storm last night; in fact, there was a tornado spotted about thirty miles south of here. Power is out all over, and even the phones are out."

"That must have been a worse storm that I thought, or were there lots of storms? I was still down here when the first one went through, but I must have slept through the rest of them."

By this time, Angela was standing beside me dressed in the same clothes she had worn the day before, probably the quickest ones she could find. "What storm, Amanda? I didn't hear anything."

"Well, you must have slept very soundly last night. I'm glad because you might have been scared of all that thunder and lightning." Then I turned to Greg, "I can't offer you anything but cold cereal and cold orange juice. All the appliances in here are electric. I just hope the power is not off for long because I don't want the food spoiling in the refrigerator."

"They're working on it right now, I know. I walked down to the docks this morning to see if the boats were all okay, and I saw some telephone and power trucks down the road, but I don't know how long it'll take them. And about that cereal, I think I'll take you up on that. I haven't had anything to eat yet."

I got some boxes down, realizing as I did that I would have to do some grocery shopping soon. There was just a little cereal left in each of the three boxes. I then got out the milk and orange juice from the dark refrigerator, feeling many items to see if they still felt cold. Since everything seemed to be all right, I got out three bowls and tried to serve the cereal as hospitably as if I were serving a gourmet meal.

Oversleeping and rushing to answer the door had made me forget the agonizing events of the night before, but when we all sat down at the table to eat, I remembered other times when Bob had sat at this same table, and the sadness came rolling over me, surrounding me like the fog that had enveloped everything outside. However, I didn't feel the same despair and anger as I had. Instead, the peace that had been my last comforting thought at night was still with me in the morning.

After breakfast Angela asked if she could go upstairs and work on the picture Mr. Jennings had given her. As soon as she was out of earshot, Greg said, "Amanda, are you all right? You had some pretty heavy news laid on you last night. I thought you'd be in the depths of despair. That's why I was so worried when you didn't show this morning. I didn't expect you to get to sleep at all last night, much less sleep through all the storms. I'm surprised at how well you're taking this."

The smile I gave him was not fake or forced. "Thanks Greg. I'm still hurt because I was in love with Bob, probably still am, but I was able to dump all my feelings on God last night, and things don't seem as bad now." Greg looked embarrassed when I mentioned God. Even though he had been to church with us once, I didn't really know his religious beliefs. He was a nice guy, but I knew that not all nice guys were really Christians.

Finally he said, "Well, however you've been able to handle it, I'm glad you're not pining away for Wilson. Losing someone you love, I think, is the worst thing in the world--worse than any illness I know of-especially when you lose the person to someone else." Greg smiled, but his eyes revealed the bitterness that was seething underneath. He stared into space, and I knew his mind had traveled to another time and another lost love. I wondered who had put that look in his eyes. What memories were being dredged out of the past?

Those thoughts led me to think about the puzzling memory I had pondered about Greg the night before. I decided to broach the subject, "By the way, Greg, I'm a little curious about something. Do you remember when we found out that Edwards, the old man Angela saw at the pizza place, had died?"

Greg's eyes seemed to narrow, and he hesitated when he answered, "Well, I sorta remember, but I can't promise how much. A lot of water has gone under the bridge since then."

"Yeah, I know, but for some reason I was thinking about it last night. You and I were ordering supplies, and--"

"Oh yeah, now that I do remember," Greg interrupted with his charming shy grin. "I seem to recall we were just beginning to--uh--well, anyway Wilson burst into the cottage, rather abruptly, I believe."

I again felt the dreadful blush creep up my face and I said, "Uh--right. Well Bob walked into the kitchen with me, and you stayed at the desk finishing the order. Bob asked me if I had heard about Edwards, and when I said I had, we started talking about it. Then you walked up to the door and asked what we were talking about. Bob told you that the police had found Edwards dead, and I don't think he told you how Edwards had died. Anyway, you asked if he had said anything about knowing Angela before he had died, and then you asked who had found the body, and when Bob told you, you said you really felt sorry for him because someone who had shot himself in the head made a grisly sight."

"Yeah, I'm sure it must."

"Oh, I know, but how did you know Edwards was shot in the head? Again, I don't remember anyone telling you how he had died."

Greg's face got very red, and he eyed me suspiciously. "Hey now, you don't think I had anything to do with his death, do you?"

"No, of course not," I said quickly. I was just curious about how you knew how Edwards had died."

"Hm, to tell you the truth, the only real clear memory I have of that day is of us--uh--ordering supplies. I don't know, but I think that Bob said something about Edward's being found with his head blown off rather than just that he had been found dead. Or maybe I just assumed he was shot. From all I had heard about the man, I guess I imagined his death would be a violent one, and yes, grisly. I hope that satisfies your curiosity. I'm sorry I can't remember more."

His tone was rather hostile, and since I didn't want both him and Phil Jennings to think I suspected them, I assured him quickly, "I must have just forgotten what Bob really said. I never have had perfect recall about anything. And of course, it really doesn't matter anyway. From what the police have found out about Bob, he must have murdered the old man, and anything he said that day was just an act. I can remember him arguing with you that Edward's death was murder, not suicide. That must have been a ploy to get the suspicion off him. I'll say this for him; he's a good actor."

Greg seemed to relax a little. "Yeah, I just wonder what his connection with little Angela is. I just hope the police find him alive so that he can clear the whole thing up."

Until that moment I hadn't thought of the possibility that Bob would be killed. I realized that even after his betrayal of me, the thought of his being killed was like a stab in the heart. I was sure then that I was never going to get over Bob. I couldn't even think of ever falling in love with someone else.

My face must have betrayed my thoughts, for Greg said, "You're still hung up on Wilson, aren't you?" I started to protest, but he interrupted. "It's okay, I'm sure the police will do everything possible to keep him alive so that they can get some answers from him." I wanted to say something, but he abruptly snapped back to the present. "I think I'd better leave; I still have some work to do on my thesis. Do you want me to put the closed sign at the gate?"

"Yes, if you wouldn't mind. It wouldn't be very convenient to show people around here without electricity or water. Did you say the telephones are out, too?"

"Right, but I don't know how far an area is affected or for how long."

"I hope they get them fixed soon. I mean, with all that has been going on around here, I feel like a sitting duck with no way to contact the police or anyone."

"Well, for what it's worth. I'm here. I'll try to take good care of you."

I was afraid I had hurt his feelings. "I know you will, Greg. Thank you for staying over here last night. I appreciate all you've done."

"Don't mention it. I'll check on you in a little while. In the meantime, I'll be right out in my room. If you can't see it through the fog, just stand at the back door and yell." With that he grinned and took off for the shed, leaving me feeling guilty about my suspicions of him, my anger toward him, and most of all for my inability to love him as I still loved Bob.

As soon as the back door closed behind Greg, depression again began to hover over me, like a helicopter, ready to land at the first sign of a landing place. I couldn't give it a chance to descend on me. I knew that if I sat still and let my thoughts dwell on everything that had happened, I would be in the same state I had been in the night before. I wished I could have had the museum open, something to occupy my mind. I decided to go upstairs with Angela. Maybe I could read to her while she painted, or if nothing else, I could see if daytime TV had improved from what it had been during my childhood summer vacations. Then I remembered that there was no power, so I couldn't watch TV, and any reading I did would have to be by the light of the kerosene lanterns, museum articles that had a practical purpose.

When I got to the bedroom, I saw Angela bent over in a very uncomfortable-looking position on the floor with her paints and canvass safely surrounded by yesterday's newspaper. Again I wondered how much of her character was instinctive, and how much had been shaped by obviously caring, thoughtful parents. I didn't imagine that many kids would think of protecting the floor when they painted unless they had been instructed to do this. Bitterly I scoffed at the idea Bob had tried to plant in my head about Angela having bank robbers for parents.

After I persuaded Angela to come downstairs to paint at my desk with one kerosene lantern illuminating her canvass, I sat down with one of my books I had brought with me for such a day as this, with another lantern on the end table near my head. It was impossible to concentrate on the words that seemed to swim all over the pages. The little noises around me were magnified, both outside and inside--distant fog horns from ships on the lake, screeching sea gulls who circled over the cottage, the incessant ticking of the grandfather clock, and the occasional creaking of my desk chair as Angela intently painted her picture.

However, I didn't hear a motor from a boat on the lake, nor the footsteps of a fisherman trudging up the hill to the cottage, so when he knocked on the door, both Angela and I jumped as if we'd been shot. I dropped my book, actually throwing it in the air, and I later learned that Angela had jerked the paintbrush all the way across the picture, luckily causing little damage since she had been using white paint at the time.

I managed to collect myself and walk to the door and unbolt it. The first thought that popped into my head when I saw the stranger was, "It's Big Bird from Sesame Street," for the man was decked out in yellow rain gear, from the top of his pointed hood to the knee-high wading boots that covered his feet. He was as tall as Bob or Greg, but he was fatter, completely filling out his plastic yellow suit. Under bushy white eyebrows, he had brown eyes, distorted by thick-lenses of steel-rimmed glasses, and the lower half of his face was covered by a cottony white beard and mustache. The visible part of his face was tanned and creased, and when he opened his mouth, he revealed some gaps where his back molars should have been, and some silver false teeth that had replaced some of his front teeth.

His voice was raspy, obviously a smoker's voice. He held a card in one hand and something he hid behind his back with his other hand. He said, "Howdy, Ma'am. Cap'n Rogers sent me to give you a message. I'm Dick Garrows. Sometimes I'm a deputy, when the Cap'n needs me. You kin see that on my card 'ere."

Sure enough, the card identified Richard Garrows as a sworn sheriff's deputy in the county that the Randolph City police had jurisdiction over. After checking the credentials carefully, I said, "Okay, Mr. Garrows, won't you come in?'

"Thank ye, Ma'am." Before he walked in, he carefully wiped his feet on the mat right outside the door, but he kindly refused to take off his coat or even put down his hood. As he stood in the middle of the room, he looked like a display in the museum, an old salt right at home with all the shipping artifacts that surrounded him. He nodded his head at Angela, and she smiled back at him. I noted her nonchalant reaction to him even though he had a beard, and it made me realize anew that it was Bob that had frightened her, not just his beard.

He didn't seem to know how to begin his mission, so I asked, "Did you say you have a message for me, Mr. Garrows?"

"Uh, yes Ma'am, but--well--would you mind if the little girl, that is--kin I talk to you alone?'

"Sure," I answered, and I started to tell Angela to go upstairs, but she was already gathering her paints and canvass, not asking any questions of why she had to leave.

Mr. Garrows and I silently watched the child as she walked up the stairs and closed the door to our bedroom. Then I turned expectantly to my visitor, and he again hesitated before he began. Finally he said, "I really have someth'n to show you, as well as tell you." With that he held out the hand that had been behind his back and handed me four or five pictures that had been taken with a Polaroid camera. My legs started to buckle under me as I looked at them. They were all pictures of Angela, recent ones, of her in a bathing suit, one of her in jeans, and even one of her in the pajamas she had worn the first night she had come to the cottage.

Chapter 17

I had to sit down, not trusting my legs to support me in my shock. Mr. Garrows stood silently patient while I shuffled through the pictures over and over. Angela was alone in all of them, and the scenery in all the outside pictures was general and vague. One of the Great Lakes was the backdrop of the ones in which she wore a bathing suit and the jeans. In fact the jeans picture was very similar to the photo taken by Phil Jennings; Angela was playing in the sand in both, but there was no tall, dark man in the one Mr. Garrows had shown me.

However, in the picture that showed Angela in the baby doll pajamas she had worn to the cottage that first night, Angela was sitting on a cushion in what appeared to be a very small cabin, most likely the V-berth of a sailboat. None of the pictures was even remotely obscene. Angela was decently dressed, and she wasn't posing in any suggestive or perverted manner. She looked like a normal, happy child having a good time on a vacation.

After examining the pictures for several minutes, I finally was able to ask, "Where did you get these, Mr. Garrows?"

"Well, I'll tell ye. Me and my buddy, we went out fish'n today, and we run across this here boat gone aground off the east side of Charter Island, about five miles east of 'ere. You know where it is?"

"Yes, I've seen it many times from the top of the lighthouse."

"Right, anyways, there weren't no one around the boat so we clumb up in it, and there was a whole bunch of clothes, sleeping bags, food--everthing you'd find on any boat. And in the drawer of the cap'n's desk was these here pictures."

I had to ask a question, but I was afraid of the answer I would get, "Did--did you find any--uh--bodies on or around the boat?"

"No Ma'am, nobody dead or alive was nowhere around. Just the boat and all the stuff inside."

"But you said you had a message from Captain Rogers for me? Does he know about what you've told me?"

"Sure does. We went and showed him the pictures and told him the story soon as we could. That's when he told me to come 'ere and tell you the message. See, he couldn't get ahold of you, what with the phones being down and all."

There was a slight pause, and I was beginning to get impatient. "Well, what was the message, Mr. Garrows?"

"He tol' me to tell you to git yer handyman, Rothwell or Rothmon or sumthun like that, and yer s'posed to bring the lit'l girl to the island where the boat is, and he and Sarge and that psycheology woman is a-going to meet with you 'ere."

"Why does the captain want us to come out in this fog? Isn't it awfully dangerous?"

"I don't reckon it's awful dangerous right now. Cap'n says there's a light on the rowboat you got 'ere, and you'll be able to see fer enough ahead so as not to run into anything."

"But I still don't understand why he wants us to come clear over to the island?"

"I don't rightly know, either. All I know is that after I told all I jist told you, he sent that young policeman over to the psycheology woman, and purty soon, he brung back a note a-saying that she wanted you all to come over to the island. It was sumthun about having everthing jist like it was when the girl come 'ere to you, the fog and all. Also, I think she 'pects her to recollect the boat."

"Does he want us to come right away?"

"Yes Ma'am, soon as you kin git around. Be sure to dress the young'n in warm clothes. We had a cold spell come in after the storm last night."

"Are you going to go back to the island, Mr. Garrows?"

"No Ma'am, I got my work cut out fer me a-help'n git the lights and telephone back a-running. I wish you luck, though. I hope the young'n gits her memry back."

"Thank you, Mr. Garrows. I'll go out and tell Greg about the plan, and then I'll get Angela ready. Thanks again for coming over here to bring the message."

"Sure thing, Ma'am. But I'll tell yur man--Greg--the story, so as how you kin jist git ready. I'll take them pictures and show him, if'n you want."

"That's awfully nice of you," I said as I handed him the pictures. "Tell him I'll be ready in just a few minutes, please."

"Okay, mebbe I'll see you agin. I'm a-going to ask the cap'n how all this comes out. Bye now." With that, Mr. Garrows walked out the front door and turned toward Greg's shed. Remembering I hadn't told him where Greg lived, I opened the door and started to call to him, but I couldn't see him. I hurried to the back window and was just in time to see something yellow disappear through what must have been the door to the shed. I remember thinking how fast he was for a man his age and I wondered how he knew exactly where Greg was without my telling him.

However, I didn't have time to speculate; I had to get Angela ready for a boat ride that might end in the most traumatic episode in her young life. All the way up the stairs, I debated how much I should tell her about what Mr. Garrows had told me. I no longer had the pictures to show her, but even if I had them, it might have not been wise to spring them on her, at least without the psychiatrist around. The psychiatrist--that was my answer. I decided to tell her just enough to answer her questions of where we were going, but I wanted the psychiatrist to handle her reaction to the boat and anything else we would find on the island.

Angela was still working on her picture on the floor again with the newspapers around her. When I looked at it, I was astonished that she was almost finished with it, and she was doing a very good job. She started explaining to me of how she had smeared the white paint when the knocking at the door had startled her, but there was only a small streak left that hadn't been covered by the appropriate paint. Angela had settled into such a routine that I hated to drop the bomb I was about to drop, but maybe I was just afraid of the chance of losing Angela.

However, I had to take that chance. I had to put Angela's welfare over my feelings. When she quit talking about her picture, she looked up at me expectantly. I could put it off no longer. "Angela," I began, "Mr. Garrows, the man who was just downstairs, told me that Captain Rogers wants us to meet him on Charter Island, that's that little island I pointed out to you from the lighthouse, you remember?

"Yes, but why?"

"Well, they--that is--Mr. Garrows and a friend of his have found a--or--something that might help you get your memory back. The psychiatrist, you remember the nice lady doctor you talked to, will be there, too."

Her eyes got very wide. "Oh, Amanda, do you really think I'll remember who I am when I go to that island?"

"I hope so, Honey, but nobody can tell you that for sure. Anyway, we've got to get going. Greg is going to take us over there in the rowboat. I guess it's kinda cold out, so we'd better dress in some warm clothes. Let's put on some jeans, some long-sleeved sweat shirts, and jackets." I was hastily pulling all these articles out of the closet as I talked. Angela didn't say anything as she and I dressed, but I sensed the excitement boiling up inside of her.

In just a matter of minutes we were fully dressed, sitting downstairs on the couch waiting for Greg. I was nervous and jittery; I drummed my fingers on the arm of the couch and kept looking at the grandfather clock whose ticks seemed to get louder with each passing second. I could tell that Angela was nervous, too, because she squirmed and fidgeted, and she also kept looking at the clock even though I know she wasn't able to tell time on it. Finally, I couldn't take it anymore. "Angela," I said, causing her to jump, "let's go see if Greg is ready."

She was more than ready to take up my offer, but just as we were heading out, there was a knock at the back door. Assuming it was Greg, I hurried to the door and swung it open, only to find Phil Jennings, not Greg. "Oh," I said, "I thought you were Greg."

"I'm sorry," said Phil, "I must have caught you at a bad time. I see you're ready to go somewhere."

"That's all right. Come on in." He stepped into the kitchen, and I continued. "You couldn't know, but we are in kinda a hurry. You see, a guy was just here--he's a deputy sometimes for Captain Roger--and he found--" I paused when I noticed Angela was standing right behind me. "Uh--something on Charter Island that may be a key to Angela's mystery. Anyway, Greg's supposed to take us over to the island, and the captain and Sergeant Adams and the psychiatrist I took Angela to are all going to meet us over there."

"In this fog? It seems strange that they would want you to be out on the lake right now."

"That's what I thought, but Mr. Garrows, the guy who was here, said they wanted to have conditions about the same as the night Angela came here. And he also said he didn't think it would be dangerous, and if anyone should know, he should. He looked like he's been on boats all his life."

"How come this Garrows fellow had to tell you all this? Why couldn't Captain Rogers just have called you to tell you?"

"Because of the phones being down after the storms last night."

"Oh yeah? My phone is working. It might have been off during the night because I know the power was off until about 9:00 this morning, but since then I've had both telephone and electricity."

"You must be one of the lucky ones, I guess. We haven't had either all day."

"Huh, that's unusual. It seems that they could restore your power if they did mine; we don't live that far apart. Well, anyway, I won't keep you. I just came over to--uh-- apologize for my rather hostile behavior the last time I was over here."

I smiled what I hoped was my warmest smile. "No, I should be the one who apologizes. You see, someone said something about you to me that caused me to be--well--suspicious of you, but it turns out that I should have been suspicious of that person, not you."

"I'd like to say that you have no reason to suspect me, but there are some things in my past that I'd give anything to blot out. I was going to tell you all about it tonight, but it can wait until you get back. I would like to say, though, that I have not had any connection with Angela except for the picture I showed you of her. And I know nothing about the picture except what I told you."

"I know, and you don't have to tell me anything about your past if you don't want to."

"I want to. It has taken me a long time, but I think I'm finally at the place where I can talk about it. However, now is obviously not the time. I'll see you when you get back. Be careful, and let me know how this all comes out." He knelt down and took Angela's hands in his. "Good luck, Sweetheart. I hope your memory comes back and that it is filled with all good things."

We said our good-byes, and I was left with a lump in my throat. Whatever had clouded Phil's past was certainly all behind him now. He was a dear man, and I was so glad that the enmity between us had been blown away.

After all this, there was still no sign of Greg. I began to wonder if Mr. Garrows had actually talked to him or if he had been gone when the old man went to see him, but I thought surely he would have told me if he had not found Greg. Then I had the horrible thought that something had happened to both of them. I didn't know if it was safe to go out to the shed, but I felt I would go crazy if I had to wait in the cottage any longer. After glancing out the back door, I said, "Angela, let's go over and see if Greg is ready. He should have been over here by now."

I was eager to get over to the island, but by this time I was also apprehensive about what I might find when I got to Greg's room. It was evident that Angela did not share any of my misgivings, for I could hardly hold her back. I was just afraid I was leading her into a dangerous situation.

Since Greg's room was at the back of the shed, we had to walk through a room filled with rakes, hoes, sickles, pesticides, and other lawn equipment, including the large mower that had almost run over Angela the day she was playing on the swing. Without electricity, the shed was dark, and I imagined there was danger lurking in all the shadows.

Greg's door was closed, and when we reached it, I heard music coming from a nearby radio station. I wondered how he could have a radio going with the electricity off. Finally I summoned the courage to knock on the door, and my relief was unbounded when I heard Greg's voice say, "Yes? Who is it?"

"Greg, it's me and Angela. Did Mr. Garrows talk to you?"

The door suddenly swung open to reveal Greg dressed in blue jeans and a thick gray sweat shirt. He answered my question, "Uh, yeah, but I was--uh--asleep when he came, so it took me a little while to get ready. Come on in; I'll be ready to leave in just a minute."

He stepped aside so that we could enter the small room, dimly lit by another kerosene lantern that sat next to a non-working electric lamp on a small, unvarnished wooden table. I saw that the radio was a "boom box" powered by batteries when there was no electrical source; I saw that this boom box would also play cassettes as well as CD's. Along with the bedside table, the room was sparsely furnished with a narrow bed, an old, white chest of drawers made out of the cheapest wood, a card table, and above the table, a crude, wooden shelf that contained a two-burner hot plate, two cheap tin pans, and a simple two-cup percolator, and a long, steel flashlight like a night watchman might use. Under the bed, I saw a toolbox, like the one in the basement of the cottage, and a cardboard storage box. I was impressed with Greg's housekeeping; his bed was neatly made with the sheets and the blankets the Sanders had provided, and there was no dust on any of the furniture. There was a hanger rod on the back of the door on which Greg had neatly hung one summer suit and a red, windbreaker jacket.

Greg pulled out the folding chair that was in front of the card table for me, and he told Angela to sit on the bed. Then he stepped into the bathroom, off to the right of the card table. The bathroom was a little cubby hole containing a toilet, shower, and sink, with a towel rack on the wall beside the sink. On that rack was a washcloth stained with what appeared to be tan shoe polish. I looked at Greg's shoes and saw that, sure enough, they were high-top leather hiking boots, the same color as the stain on the wash cloth. Momentarily I wondered why Greg had put his shoe polish on with his wash cloth, or why he had put it on at all. I guess I was impatient to leave, and I didn't see much need of polished shoes on the island where we were going. Even now I was ready to scream because Greg was slowly combing his hair, peering into the dingy mirror that was on the front of a rusty metal medicine cabinet above the sink. I couldn't understand his need for grooming when we had such an important meeting to get to.

I didn't want to say anything, though, because Greg didn't have to take us over to the island at all. He was only doing it out of the kindness of his heart. So, to take my mind off the waiting, I began to concentrate on the articles on the card table. I figured this table was serving as Greg's desk because it contained a portable typewriter, a small tape-recorder, the boom box, and a stack of neat, professional-looking typed papers, a spiral notebook, handwritten with scribbled notes all over the page, and a stack of blank paper. I asked Greg how he was doing with his thesis, but before he could answer, my hand accidentally touched the button on the boom box that started the cassette player. Immediately the sound of typing loudly clattered into the room.

Greg stalked over to me, smashed down the "off" button, and glared down at me. "What were you doing?" he asked, almost savagely.

"Nothing, I must have accidentally turned on the cassette player."

Greg calmed down, and he smiled as he said, "I'm sorry, Amanda. I just got startled, that's all. I guess the storm, that Garrows fellow, and the thought of taking a trip in this fog has me all nerved up."

"That's okay, but what was that? A tape recording of your typing?"

He stammered in an agitated voice as he said, "Uh, no, that is I--uh--didn't tape my--," then his face brightened into another infectious smile. "Oh, now I know what must have happened. When I was typing the other night, I must have accidentally left the record button on, and I recorded my typing. I sometimes read parts of my thesis out loud, record it on the tape recorder, and then play it back on the boom box, because it has better sound quality than the tape recorder. I must have put that tape in to listen to it, but so many things have come up, I haven't had a chance. I didn't know it was filled with my typing."

"Oh, I see," I said, but I was still puzzled about his initial reaction when he had heard the typing. His reaction had seemed extreme for such a minor incident.

"I guess I'm ready," he said as he grabbed the wind breaker off the hanger. He then reached for the big flashlight on the shelf, turned it on, then blew out the kerosene lantern. Angela and I walked out of Greg's room and the shed with the light from the flashlight illuminating our path. It was still daylight out, since it was only early afternoon, but the fog still hadn't dissipated any, so our visibility was limited. We wound our way down the hill to the little boat resting on the calm lake. On a foggy day, there wasn't much wind, so we wouldn't have to battle strong winds or high waves on our crossing. Our biggest worry was trying to see through the heavy curtain of fog surrounding us.

Greg helped Angela and me step into the boat. I noticed that Angela was very agile in boarding boats. I was almost sure she had had some experience with them in her past. As soon as we were on one of the two benches that transepted the small boat, Angela shivered and moved closer to me. "What's wrong, Honey, are you cold?"

Her voice trembled as she answered, "A little, but I'm mostly just scared."

"I know, Sweetheart, but nothing is going to happen to you. Greg and I will be with you, and Captain Rogers and Sergeant Adams and the doctor will meet us over at the island."

Soon we shoved off, and Greg pulled the string that started the motor gurgling through the water. After Greg adeptly steered out of the harbor, we were gliding across the open lake.

Everything was quiet and peaceful in this world of gray, mocking the turmoil that was churning inside of me. I wished we could be at the island instantly, but I couldn't even see it, so I had no way of knowing where we were. Greg broke the silence we had held since we started, "Amanda, there are some life jackets up in the cuddy cabin at the bow. Maybe you should put one on Angela."

"Yes, you're probably right." The cuddy cabin was a small compartment under the bow of the boat. I reached for a pile of life jackets and pulled them toward me. Just as I dislodged the jackets, a glittering object fell to the bottom of the boat within my reach. When I picked it up, I found it was a pair of sun glasses with frames in the shape of butterfly wings, dotted with cheap jewels of every color. I knew I had seen them before, but it took me a minute to remember. When I did remember, I gasped in shock. The last time I had seen those glasses, they had been on Lucy Parson's face.

Chapter 18

Lucy Parson's glasses! They had to be her glasses. None of my other guests or anyone else I had met had glasses like them. I didn't know what to do. Should I tell Greg or keep my discovery to myself? The way he had reacted to my turning on his cassette player made me scared about how he would react to my finding a dead woman's glasses in his boat. But it wasn't actually Greg's boat. It could have been used by anyone because it was never locked up, at least during the summer.

"Greg," I began hesitantly.

"What?" he answered rather abruptly, without even turning around from steering the motor.

"Look what I found in here--Lucy Parsons' sun glasses!"

He turned then, making the boat swerve off course. "Let me see," he said as he took them from me. He turned them over in his hands and looked at them, glancing every once in a while to steer the boat. "Are you sure they are hers?"

"I'm positive. Those glasses were the first thing I noticed about Lucy--except her size. I've never seen any others like them.

Greg fidgeted nervously in his seat. "How do you think they got in here?"

"I don't know. When did you take the boat out last?"

"Now, what do you mean by that?" Greg asked in the same voice he had used during the cassette incident. I didn't know what had gotten into Greg; he seemed to be in such a surly mood.

"I didn't mean anything by what I said, Greg. I was just trying to figure out when the glasses could have gotten in here."

Greg looked abashed, "I'm sorry, Amanda, again. You have to forgive me. I've had a rotten day." He paused, took a deep breath, then went on, "Let's see, I had it out about a week ago, fishing, but I didn't bother with those life jackets, so the glasses could have been there, and I wouldn't have known it."

"That's true. I have a feeling that Bob is the only one who could tell us. Maybe he lured--" I stopped mid-sentence when I suddenly remembered Angela cuddled up

next to me. "Well, anyway, maybe you get the picture." I
then proceeded to fasten the life jacket on Angela.

"Yeah, I think I do." Greg looked at Angela, but just
before he turned his head, I thought I detected a grin,
almost as if he was recalling a joke he couldn't share with
us. Again I was puzzled about Greg's mood. He was
irritable and jumpy one minute, then amused and even
gleeful the next. I finally came to the conclusion he must
be as jittery as I was about what this night was going to
bring, and that's what made him seem so different.

Greg handed me the sun glasses, and we all fell
silent again. I started thinking about Lucy, trying to
imagine how Bob could have killed someone so vibrant
and full of life. I tried to picture that last day of Lucy's life.
I could almost see her sitting in her lounge chair on the
beach. I imagined Bob coming up to her, maybe telling her
some story to get her into the boat with him, and then Bob
piloting the boat to a point in the lake where the water
would have been over Lucy's head. But then the picture in
my mind would go blank. I could not believe that Bob was
capable of conking Lucy over the head and pushing her
overboard, if that is how she died. Nor could I imagine him

pulling the trigger and blowing off Edwards' head. Most of all, I could not consider the thought that the arms that had wrapped me in tender embraces could be the same arms that had tried to push me over the lighthouse rail to my death. I couldn't be that wrong about a person, I thought. Sure, like Greg had said, I was still "hung up" on Bob, but more than that I believed in him, in spite of all the evidence stacked up against him. Maybe I was experiencing what St. Paul had written in the 13th Chapter of I Corinthians, the "Love Chapter." I couldn't quote it exactly, but I did remember the passages about love being loyal and believing all things. I knew people would call me a fool, but in my heart I was convinced that Bob was innocent.

Of course, my belief in him wasn't enough. We had to have some way to prove his innocence. But how? As soon as I realized the magnitude of my problem, I realized my need for God's help. I was ashamed that I hadn't thought to pray before this, not even before I had left on this uncertain, potentially dangerous venture. Silently, I started talking to the Lord from the depths of my heart, "Oh Lord, forgive me for not coming to you earlier. I don't know what's going to happen today, but I want you with us. Protect us all, and please help Angela, whether she regains her memory or not. And Jesus, you know how I feel about Bob. If he's innocent, as I believe he is, please help us to prove he is. And Lord, help Greg today. He seems troubled and not like himself. Please be with--"

Greg abruptly interrupted, "Just another minute or two and we'll be there. I see the island now." Angela and I turned around and peered through the fog. The island was just a dim shadow ahead of us. I couldn't see a boat or any other distinct objects, though, because even though the fog had dissipated somewhat, it had not completely lifted.

The rest of the trip was spent in silence except for the whir of the motor. Even after my prayer, I couldn't stop the apprehensions that were increasing the closer we got to the island. So many possible disasters tormented my thoughts. My greatest concern was for Angela. What if she went into shock or became hysterical, or what if her past came back, but she couldn't remember anything about me? Tears filled my eyes as I thought about the possibility of my being a stranger to Angela. More than that, I ached with the grief I somehow knew she would feel if and when she regained her memory.

Greg slowed the motor down as we inched toward the island. My heart was almost beating out of my chest when the bow of the boat finally bumped against the rocky shoreline of the tiny cove we had pulled into. I still saw no boat, neither the one Mr. Garrows had described nor the one that had to bring the policemen and doctor over to the island. However, Mr. Garrows had said that the boat was on the east side of the island, so I assumed the side we had just landed on was the west.

Greg and I got out of the boat and pulled it up onto a small patch of sand, no bigger than a sandbox. Then we helped Angela out, and the three of us started to make our way through the jungle-like terrain on the island, Angela and I in front and Greg following close behind. In the fog, the branches of the trees clustered around the beach looked like huge tentacles reaching out to grab us. Our first steps on land scared a nest of quail into frantic flight. I was so edgy that I screamed as they flapped their wings and rose abruptly in the air. Greg grabbed hold of my arm and said, "Don't be afraid, Amanda. I'm right here with you." But somehow his touch was not comforting; in fact, he squeezed my arm so hard that I winced with pain. Then he laughed, but it was not a humorous laugh. My first thought was that he sounded sinister, much like a mad scientist in a horror movie, but I immediately chalked up my wild imaginings to the eerie, unknown environment I was stepping into.

It was obvious that no one had tamed the wild growth of nature on this island, for the foliage was so thick we had to push away branches and prickly vines that would scratch our faces and cling to our clothes. We also had to watch our step because there was no path, and the soft, mossy ground was jutted with jagged rocks and snake-like tree roots, both of which lay just under the surface or on top of the thin soil. Occasionally, we would have to climb over thick tree trunks that had been felled by violent storms. And to add to our discomfort, there were small gnats and flies that buzzed around our heads constantly throughout the whole trip.

I suspected that Angela had met similar conditions when she had come to the cottage that first night, but she had not been protected by a long-sleeved jacket and long pants as she was now. Maybe this trek through the forest was designed to prod her memory of that night, but I still wondered at the wisdom of this whole idea. Although I was trying to help her as much as possible, I could tell she was having a hard time. I wondered if it would better if Greg would carry her on his back, but because of his apparently foul mood, I was scared to ask him.

After what seemed like hours of this rugged jungle travel, we came to a clearing of sorts. There were still many trees and foliage surrounding us, but there was about a fifty yard strip of land that was devoid of big trees or bushes. Instead it was covered with lush green grass and colorful wild flowers interspersed randomly.

Right in the middle of the clearing, I saw a mound of dirt that appeared to have been recently excavated. Instinctively, I stopped dead in my tracks, feeling that something was very wrong. Suddenly I heard a voice, the voice of Dick Garrows who was responsible for our being on this desolate island. He said, "Well, now Ma'am, you and the young'n ain't gonna have to walk anymore. You've come to the end of the line, in more ways than one." He laughed gleefully then, as if he had told a great joke.

I jerked around quickly to find where the old man was, but the only person in sight was Greg, but not the Greg I knew. This Greg was grinning wickedly, and he held a shiny object in his hand. Before I realized that the object was a gun, Angela let out a chilling scream and said, "No, Uncle Roger, please not again!"

Chapter 19

"So, your memory has come back, right Sarah?"

Tears were flooding down Angela's cheeks, and she was gripping my hand so hard it hurt. She had a pitiful wail to her voice when she talked, "Yes, I remember everything. You killed them, Uncle Roger, you killed Mommy and Daddy. Why?"

"I had to, Sarah. Believe me, I didn't want to, but your dad was going to turn me in—his own brother. He wouldn't listen to reason."

This whole scene was so weird; I expected eerie music to start playing and someone would come out of the shadows to tell me I had just entered the "Twilight Zone." The two people I had known as Angela and Greg for weeks were now strangers calling themselves Roger and Sarah. They seemed to be completely oblivious of me, even though the child still had hold of my hand. I wondered if I could get away without Greg--or Roger-- noticing, but I didn't see how I could extricate myself from Angela. Besides I wouldn't leave her alone with this maniac with a gun.

Angela continued her agonizing dialogue with him, "You tried to kill me, didn't you?"

"I thought I had, but you've got to believe me, I didn't want to. In fact, I was happy when I saw your picture in the paper the next day. How did you get out of the boat?"

"I was wondering if my turtle was in his house Turtle Man and I had made him, so I crawled out of the hole in the roof above my bed, and I went over to check on him. When I got back, I saw Daddy holding your tool box; then you took out a gun from your pants pocket, and you shooted them. I ran away as fast as I could, but then when I got to Amanda's door, I went to sleep or something."

"But I saw you all covered up in your bed."

Angela shook her head, "No, that was my doll!"

The pieces of the puzzle were beginning to fall into place. The reason no one had reported a child was missing, Angela's fascination for the tool box, and her violent reaction to the doll with the red crayon mark drawn down the face. No wonder she had blocked it out of her memory. What a trauma for a little girl to have to go through! I wanted to take her in my arms and comfort her, but the man who had caused her agony in the first place was still in control of the situation.

Greg--or whoever he was--became almost gentle as he talked to the child. His kindness to her was in direct contradiction to the gun he was holding and the words he was speaking. "Sarah, I have to kill you now, though. You understand that, don't you? I thought maybe you'd never remember what happened again, but when you remembered old man Edwards, I knew I just couldn't take the chance. I do love you, though. You're so much like your Mommy. You know, your mommy was going to marry me, but your daddy took her away from me." His voice turned hard as he continued, "He always took everything away from me."

Angela--or Sarah--buried her head in my side and sobbed. When Greg had started talking about his brother, another puzzle piece clicked into place for me. I asked him, "Are you the brother of the president of the Wellingham bank up in Canada?"

He glared at me contemptuously, as if I were a bug annoying him, "Yeah, how did you know?"

"Bob did some investigating and found that some money was missing from the bank and that the president, his family, and his brother were missing."

"Well, isn't he the smart one!" he said sarcastically. Then he sneered at me. "Your handsome prince, Bob. Too bad his investigations aren't going to help him or you. He'll never know what happened to his lover; no one will ever know. But the police will be convinced that Wilson is guilty. I'll see to that."

"You mean, he had nothing to do with Angela or any of those deaths?" Even in this desperate situation, I felt an unspeakable joy at the thought that Bob was everything he had claimed to be.

"No, your boyfriend is as pure as the driven snow." I must have displayed my elation at that moment, for Greg continued, "Don't look so happy. He won't be able to help you now, and I've got some plans for him that will insure his ticket to the chair."

He was right. How could I prove Bob's innocence if I were lying underneath the mound of dirt that I was sure Greg had dug for our graves? What could I do? I began to pray silently, but I certainly didn't have time for a long, flowery prayer. I prayed much as Peter had when he was sinking in the water he had just walked on, "Oh Lord, help us. We need your protection now." Immediately, a thought struck me like a thunderbolt. I remembered that I had told Phil Jennings that we were coming to the island, and I believed with all my being that he would tell someone where we were. I knew the only way we could stay alive was by keeping Greg talking. It was to be the most crucial conversation I would ever have in my life. Since he seemed to have a perverse sense of pride about framing Bob, I figured I could buy time by appealing to this twisted egomania of his.

"You know," I began in a voice that was sickly cloy, "I remember saying that Bob was a good actor when I thought he was the one behind all this mystery, but you're the good actor. You've been playing lots of parts these past few weeks, haven't you? Were you Mr. Garrows, today?"

He grinned diabolically and said in the Garrows' voice, "Yes Ma'am. I guess I had you and the young'n fooled. I jist wish that fool drama prof at actin' school could'a seed my performance. Maybe he'd have second thoughts about telling me I wasn't good enough to be an actor."

"Your voice was very convincing, but how did you disguise yourself like that? I didn't recognize you at all!"

"Oh, I learned about make-up and costuming in school. I once played an old man like 'Garrows.' I used tan make-up on my face, plastered on a white beard, mustache, and eyebrows, and I used a special paint to make my teeth appear silver or missing. An added touch was contact lenses to make my eyes brown. Then, for my body disguise, I packed pillows underneath the rain gear to make me look fat. Of course, that make-up job was nothing compared to the one I had to do to become 'Greg Rothman.' And that's where your lover came in handy. Before that fateful night when Sarah came to your door, I had a beard much like good old Bob's, and dark, curly hair like his, too, but I had to do a complete transformation to become Greg Rothman."

"Is there really a Greg Rothman?"

"Was--there really was a clean-shaven, fair-haired Greg Rothman who went to the University of Wisconsin, had a sailboat named 'Wind Song,' and had excellent references from respectable people he had known in his past."

"Did you kill him, too, plus Ang--Sarah's parents, Edwards, and Lucy Parsons?" And you must have been the one who tried to push me off the lighthouse?"

"You've got it all figured out, except I didn't really try to push you off that lighthouse. I was just building a case against your boyfriend. Like when I sent that lawnmower down the hill, and then rushed out and rescued Sarah in just the nick of time."

"How did you get Bob's blood on that hood?"

"Elementary, my dear, there were two hoods, one of which I stained with Wilson's blood from where I'd bashed him on the head and stuffed that hood in the closet behind the lighthouse stairs where the police found it. Then I put the other one on, climbed to the top of the lighthouse, and waited for you. Later, after your attack, when I so courageously volunteered to go back up and 'look for your attacker,' I picked up the hood I had worn, took it out behind my shed and burned it to ashes."

"Okay, how did you get down from the lighthouse in time to run into me before I even got to the cottage?"

"Well now, that took a little practice. Luckily, I had some training in stunt work, as well as acting, in school. I had a good, strong rope tied to the rail on the other side of where we had our little foray, and as soon as you were out of sight, I did a Tarzan impression. I also had to remove that rope during the time I was supposedly looking for the tall dark stranger who had tried to push you over the railing."

"Very clever," I said, all the time shuddering at the evil genius he had used to perpetrate his crimes. "Tell me something else, what was that tape of your typing all about?"

"That was an alibi. I used it twice--once when I 'visited' Edwards, and the night you went to the lighthouse. You know, you would have been better off if you hadn't been so smart. At first I was just going to take care of Sarah, but your questions and your snooping were beginning to bother me."

Angela whimpered beside me, and I held her tighter to me. I felt so sad for her that I couldn't continue to pretend I admired him. I said with all the venom I had been storing up, "You're a monster. I don't see how you could have killed anyone, but especially your own brother, sister-in-law and niece." Just as I got the words out of my mouth, unbelievably, I saw a light flicker in the woods behind Greg. Could it be that someone was coming to rescue us? Yes, the light was stronger now. I had to be the great actor now. I willed myself to keep my face impassive and keep my eyes from staring at the light.

Miraculously, Greg hadn't noticed my excitement. He continued talking, "Hey, I didn't want to kill anybody, but I had to have money. Money means everything. My old man knew that. He was the owner of the Carswell Shipbuilding Company in Wellington. 'A self-made man.' If I heard that once, I heard it a thousand times. 'No one ever gave me a handout,' he'd say, 'I had to work for every penny I ever got. There's no such thing as a free lunch.' So to teach me that valuable lesson, he left his money to a church when he and Mom died in a car accident a couple of years ago."

Allowing myself a glance in the direction of the light, I saw a man just on the edge of the clearing. Working hard to keep the tremble out of my voice, I asked,

"But why did you take money from your brother's bank? Why didn't you go someplace where no one knew you?"

"Two reasons. Good old brother John was the only one who would give me a job in a bank, and also there was justice in taking money from him. After all, he had taken the only woman I ever loved. You know, I met her when I was in acting school. I took her home to meet the folks, and big brother decided he wanted her. By this time he was out of school with a Master's degree in business, on his spiral up the corporate ladder, and I was a reject from acting school. He started writing her, sending her expensive gifts, calling her, and I never had a chance."

Fortunately Greg--Roger--seemed to be so engrossed in his story he had no idea there was anyone behind him. I deliberately held Angela's face against me so that she wouldn't see the light and tip him off. Now I could see there were three men creeping up through the woods. As far as I could tell, they were Captain Rogers, Sergeant Adams, and someone who looked like Bob, only without a beard. I could barely contain the anticipation springing up inside of me.

Greg continued pouring out his tirade against his brother. Strangely, I was beginning to feel like his therapist, not his victim. "Of course, I don't think anyone was surprised when I got kicked out of acting school, least of all my old man. I was never as good as John. He was valedictorian, star athlete, student council president, then model husband, devoted father. He was all my old man could talk about. It was John this, and John that, until I got fed up with it. No one ever knew why those brakes on my parents' car failed."

Even though I was caught up in the suspense of an impending rescue, I couldn't help but react to Greg's last statement. "You mean you were responsible for your parents' deaths too?"

Greg shrugged, "Yeah, but it didn't do me any good. He left his money to a church; course I still have the cash I got from the bank stashed in my tool box." That probably explained Angela's fascination for a tool box. She must have seen the money.

Now the men were only about five feet away from Greg, but he still wasn't aware of anything but the bitterness that must been consuming him for years. My hope was soaring; I believed we could really pull this rescue off without anyone getting hurt. But suddenly, Sergeant Adams tripped on something, and he fell to the ground with a deafening thud. Greg jerked around and fired the gun, luckily hitting no one. Angela screamed, pushed away from me, and ran toward the forest. I started out after her when Greg grabbed me and held me with his left arm as he brandished the gun with his right hand. "Okay, you guys," he yelled, "don't come near me or Amanda will get shot. I've got nothing to lose."

Chapter 20

"Let go of her, Rothman," Bob shouted. Greg kept backing up, dragging me with him. I was struggling to get away, but he was too strong. Bob and the policemen looked on helplessly.

Frantically I tried to think of what I could do. If I pretended to faint, he would still drag me along. I tried to kick him, but I had no control over my feet and could not get them into kicking position. Greg held the gun right to my temple and told the men, "Now, just keep your distance till we get on the boat and away from the island."

I knew it was going to be very hard for Greg to drag me through the forest, but he was a desperate man, determined to escape. My mind was rushing ahead frantically trying to think of a way to make a break from him. At first, I imagined his pulling me into the little boat we had come on, but then I figured he would probably set that adrift and take the police boat which would most likely be bigger and faster. Could I possibly get away from him while he was trying to launch the boat? Of course, all he would have to do was knock me unconscious and carry me on board. I realized that all my resourcefulness would not save me. I cried out to God again, but this time I didn't bother making it a silent prayer. "Oh God, help me," I cried.

At that moment, Greg started falling, pulling me down with him. Instinctively trying to break his fall, he let go of me and his gun, and in that split second, I sprang away and ran toward Angela, who was standing a few feet from us. At the same time, Bob lunged for the gun, picked it up, and ordered Greg to get up. When Greg slowly rose to his feet, Sergeant Adams pulled his arms behind him and clasped handcuffs on his wrists. Captain Rogers proceeded to arrest him and read him his rights.

As all this was going on, I pulled Angela over to me, sat down, and cradled her in my arms. Her little body was racked with sobs. "Go ahead, Honey, cry it out," I soothed. "You have every right to cry."

As soon as Bob saw that Greg would no longer be a danger, he rushed over to us and wrapped his arms around both of us. "I was so scared," he said, "I thought we'd never get over here, and then when that monster grabbed you, well, it was hard for me not to pump him with bullets when I got hold of that gun. He didn't hurt you did he?"

"No, I'm all right now. I just knew somehow that somebody would come if I could stall Greg--Roger long enough. Was it Phil Jennings who told you we were over here?"

"Yeah," he began, but the policemen and Greg were coming over to us.

Captain Rogers knelt down right in front of Angela and said, "It's all right, Little One; it's all over now." Angela's sobs had subsided, and she looked up at him and smiled a tearful smile. Immediately, both Bob and I wiped tears from our eyes, too. Then the captain said to Bob, "Wilson, why don't you take these ladies back home? We'll be over later."

"I'll be glad to, Sir," said Bob. Then as the other men walked off, Bob gave me a squeeze, got up, and took the same position the policeman had just left. He gently took hold of Angela's hand and said," Honey, you're not scared of me anymore, are you?"

To our astonishment, she reached out her arms and wrapped them around Bob. He, in turn, took her in his arms and kissed the top of her head. This time I couldn't control my tears; I didn't even try. We stayed like that for a while until finally, wordlessly, we trudged back through the woods to the boat, but this time, Angela was carried on Bob's strong back. And the trip wasn't anywhere near as difficult as it had been before. In fact, I didn't even notice prickly branches or annoying bugs. The little boat looked like a yacht to me, so happy was I to see it. I suppose the fog was still bad, but it didn't bother me at all. I was riding so high on my blissful cloud that nothing could have disturbed me.

None of us talked much after we got into the boat because of the noise of the engine, or perhaps because we all needed to quietly reflect on our own thoughts. I did show Bob Lucy Parsons' glasses I had found on the boat and I told him, "You know, when I found these glasses, I started trying to imagine you luring Lucy on this boat somehow, and all the rest that must have followed, and I just couldn't see you as a murderer. That's when I knew you couldn't be guilty, in spite of all the evidence against you."

Bob looked over at me and smiled tenderly, "From what the police said on the way over here, there was a bunch of evidence piled up that I didn't even know about yet. They said you were pretty devastated when they told you about my blood being on the hood."

"Yes I was, but after the initial shock, I still believed you were innocent, and I wasn't going to believe otherwise unless you yourself would tell me so."

He grinned impishly and teased, "Does that mean I can do almost anything after we're married, and you'll still have faith in me?"

With a mock severity I said, "Don't push your luck, Buddy." He laughed, then turned his attention back to steering the motor and getting us back on course.

When we got back to the cottage, I made hot chocolate, and we sat around the table in comfortable companionship, like a real family. I asked Bob to tell us how he had found out about our being over on the island. He said, "I came over here today to show you both a picture. It was a picture of you, Ang--uh--Sarah and your parents. A lady in your father's bank had sent it to me. I'd show it to you now, but it's still at the police station.

Anyway, when I got here no one was home, but just as I was leaving, Mr. Jennings came walking up to my car. It seemed he was troubled about what you had told him about the story some old man had told you. He couldn't imagine that the police and the doctor would expect you to take a little girl to such a desolate island on a foggy, cold day. So he tried to call the police to verify the story, but the lines were so busy with people calling in about the storm damage that he couldn't get through. Then he came over here to see if he could talk you out of the wild venture or at least let him go with you, but you were gone. When he told me your story, we both hightailed it to the police station. Since they knew the old man's story was completely false, they figured you were in grave danger. They quickly launched one of the police boats, and headed for the island at full speed. I convinced them that I should come with them, but we left Mr. Jennings to help Officer Larsen man the phones."

"I know I was stupid for believing Mr. Garrows, actually Greg--or Roger in disguise. But Bob, you should have seen him. He looked like a genuine old sailor, and he talked differently, too. He had me completely fooled. Did you know he went to an acting school where he studied not only acting, but make-up and costuming and stunt roles? He told me that he had changed his looks after he kil--uh--got over here to the states." I amended my words when I remembered that Sarah was listening. "He said he had a beard and dark hair like you. Hey, that reminds me, where is your beard?"

Bob smiled, "Why, do you miss it?"

"Yeah, I do. You have to understand that for me to fall in love with a bearded guy was a traumatic event, but I got over the hurdle, and now I have to adjust all over again."

"I can always grow it back, you know. But to answer your question, when I was--uh--hiding from the law, I decided that my beard was too much a trademark for me, and that I could keep a lower profile without it."

"Okay, I understand. I know my parents will probably be happier if you keep it off, but like you said, it was a big part of you. But you decide what you want to do. I'm not going to be a bossy, domineering wife."

He reached over and touched my hand. "Oh sure, that's what they all say until they get you hooked." I smiled back at him, and we were so enthralled with each other that for a moment we even forgot that Sarah was there until she softly giggled at the two love-sick adults making fools of themselves.

Bob turned red, cleared his throat, and said, "Angela, or Sarah, I guess we'd better get used to calling you Sarah. Can you tell us more about your parents? Do you feel up to talking, yet?"

"Yes," she seemed eager to spill out all the facts that had been blocked in her mind for the last few weeks, "My father's name is--uh--was John, and my mother's name was Diane. We lived at 512 Royal Drive in Kingston, On—tar—o.

"Do you have any brothers and sisters?"

"No," she said sadly, and my mother didn't have any either."

I broke into the conversation, "I know your father's parents are dead, but what about your mother's parents?"

"I didn't know them at all. Mommy said her daddy left when she was a little girl, and she doesn't know where he is, and her mommy died before she married my daddy."

I had to swallow a lump in my throat when I realized that this little girl's only living relative was a mass murderer.

I could tell that Bob was as choked up as I was, but he must have seen the need for Sarah to talk, for he gently prodded her on, "Honey, do you want to tell us about how your mom and dad died?"

She sat with a trance-like expression on her face as she recounted the horrors of that night. "Uncle Roger had borrowed this boat, and he said he wanted all of us to go on a trip with him. We got up real early in the morning and got on the boat at a place where there are lots and lots of boats. We were on the boat all day until we got to the place where we tied it up. Then I got off and walked on this real rocky place, and that's when I met Turtle Man. We found a great big turtle, and we built a house for it. Then it got real dark, and Mommy put me to bed in the part of the boat called the 'Zebra' or something."

Bob and I looked at each other in confusion, then Bob said, "The V-berth! Is that what it was?"

"Yeah, that's it. Well, I slept for a while, then I woke up because Daddy and Uncle Roger were talking real loud. Daddy said, 'You have to give that money back'; then

Uncle Roger said, 'Why don't we share it? There's enough for both of us.' Then they said lots more stuff, but I can't remember it. Then I thought about my turtle and if he was all right, so I climbed out of a little window in the roof and went and checked on the turtle. He was still there, so I turned around to go back to the boat. When I looked in the window, I saw Daddy holding Uncle Roger's toolbox in his hand, and I saw Uncle Roger take out a gun, and there was a loud bang and my daddy fell down, and then another bang and my mother fell down. Then Uncle Roger walked to my bed and he pointed the gun at my doll that was in bed with me, and he shot her, too. Then I was real scared, and I ran to where I saw the light."

By this time, tears were running down her face. I reached over and gently squeezed her hand, but I was at a loss as to what else I could do. I wanted to kiss away the hurt and make her completely happy. Even though I didn't want her to go away, I would have given anything to have her parents back.

Bob spoke up after a little pause, "I bet your mom and dad were wonderful people, weren't they?"

Sarah nodded her head, and her eyes shone with pride. "Yes, they always took me to fun places. Once we went to a zoo, and there was this elephant, and he sprayed water all over Daddy with his trunk." She smiled, and a sad, sweet, nostalgic look came over her face.

Then she went on," Mommy and I used to make cakes, and she knew how to put pretty flowers and things on them. Then she'd let me lick the bowls after we were all done. Mommy made the best cakes of anybody in our whole church."

"Did you and your mom and dad go to church a lot?"

"Yeah, we went every Sunday. Daddy led the singing. He could really sing good."

"How old are you, Sarah? Have you been to school yet?" asked Bob.

"Yes, I was in first grade till summer came. I'm six years old." Sarah paused, and a worried frown came over her face. "Do you know what's going to happen to me--where I'm going or do you think maybe I could stay with you, Amanda?"

Those same questions had been formulating in my
mind, too. "I don't know, Honey. You said your
grandparents were all dead, and you don't have any aunts
or uncles, but is there anyone else, a close friend or
someone that your folks were with a lot?"

"They had some friends in the church, and I have a
real good friend named Mary who goes to our church. And
there's Uncle Zachary; only he's not my real uncle. He's
real old, older than my parents. He used to come to the
house with a bunch of papers in his suitcase, and he and
Daddy would talk about things like taxes and stuff."

"Can you remember all of Uncle Zachary's name?"
asked Bob.

"Uh, I think it is Zachary Reynolds."

Bob turned to me, "We'll tell the police about him.
He's probably the one that should be contacted."

Just then, as if on cue, there was a knock on the
door, and Captain Rogers called out, "It's the police." For
the first time in weeks I wasn't dreading a visit from the
police. We told them to come in, and they opened the door
we had left unbolted. By now, the policemen were so
familiar with us that they automatically joined us in the

kitchen, and I began fixing them hot chocolate without even asking if they wanted any. We all waited till they had their first taste of the hot liquid before we started questioning them.

Bob was the first to ask the question, "Well, did Rothman--Carswell tell you everything?"

I was not sure how much Sarah should hear about her uncle's crimes. I knew it was good therapy for her to talk about her parents as Bob had encouraged her to do, but I didn't think hearing about the other murders would be good for her. Captain Rogers must have shared my concern because he spoke to her before he answered Bob, "Sarah, how are you coming with that picture Mr. Jennings gave you to paint?"

"I'm almost done with it," she told him.

"Good, he told us all about it when we took him home a little while ago, and he's coming over later. Do you want to work some more on it so you'll be able to show him all you've done?"

Sarah got up from the table, but before she walked upstairs, she stood right in front of the policeman and said,

"Captain Rogers, what's going to happen to me? Can I stay with Amanda?"

"For the time being you'll be with Amanda. We've already contacted the police department at Wellington. The captain there told me that your family has always been with a law firm--King, Owens, and Reynolds. I'm sure they'll do what is best for you."

"Sarah told us about someone she calls 'Uncle Zachary,' and she said his last name is Reynolds."

"Okay, we'll get in touch with him."

Sarah started to go upstairs, but then she paused and said to both policemen, "Thank you for helping me, Captain Rogers and Sergeant Adams."

We could almost see the officers' hearts melting. Captain Rogers pulled Sarah over to him and squeezed her gently. "I'm glad we got over to that island on time, Sweetheart, but I'm awfully sorry about your parents. I'm sure they'd be awfully proud of you--the brave way you put that log behind the--uh--your uncle to make him trip."

"She did?" I asked in astonishment, "Until this moment I had no idea how he had tripped." You saved my life, Sarah." Then it was my turn to hug her. She seemed to take all this praise in stride, and finally she walked upstairs to continue working on the picture she had left when we went over to Greg's or Roger's shed, a whole life time ago, it seemed.

The captain waited until the child was out of ear shot before he finally answered Bob's question, "I think Carswell told us everything. He's admitted to killing several people; he seems almost proud of it. He went into detail telling how he tried to frame you, Wilson."

"How did he get my blood on the hood, and how did he get off the lighthouse so fast without Amanda seeing him?"

The policemen related the account that Roger had told me about the two hoods and the rope, and then I filled in the detail about the tape of Roger's typing that he had used to make me think he was in his shed when he killed Edwards and when he met me on top of the lighthouse.

"So, there's no question that he killed Edwards and Lucy, too?" asked Bob.

"That's right," said the captain, "he has confessed to both of them. He told us that Edwards had passed out from drinking too much, so he put the gun in his hand, held it to his head, and pulled the trigger, leaving gun residue all over Edwards."

"What would he have done if Edwards hadn't been passed out?" I asked.

"He said he would have gotten him drunk. He was sure it wouldn't have been hard just from what we had said about Edwards that day we interrogated him."

We were quiet, digesting the information we had just been given. Then Bob again broke the silence, "Can you tell us how he got Lucy into the boat with him?"

"How did you know she had gotten into the boat?"

"Amanda found her sunglasses in it on the trip over to the island. I wondered how he could persuade a lady who was so afraid of water to get into a small boat like that."

"He told her that her husband had had a heart attack, and that he would take her to him. Then when he got out into water over her head, he knocked her out with a big rock he had carried on board, and then he pushed her overboard."

"Poor Lucy," I mumbled.

"Yes, all she ever did was have a good memory for faces," said Bob.

At that moment, we were all startled by a knock at the back door. My momentary panic, which was more than just ordinary jumpiness, showed me that the fear and nervousness that had been with me for weeks wasn't going to leave for a while. I noticed a tremor in my voice as I said, "Come in."

My visitor was Phil Jennings, and when I remembered that he had saved our lives by coming over to check on us after we had left for the island, I surprised myself and him by rushing up to him and hugging him. "Thank you for coming over here when you did today. If you hadn't been here, no one would have known where we were."

He looked rather embarrassed, "I'm just glad everything turned out all right, but I think it was providential that I came over here in the first place to hear your story."

His words made me stop and think about the incredible timing of this whole adventure. If I hadn't told Phil about Mr. Garrows' story before we left for the island, if he hadn't related it to Bob before he left the cottage, and if the police hadn't arrived when they did, Sarah and I would be buried in the graves Roger had dug for us. I realized that there were too many 'ifs' in the saga to be coincidental; providential, the word Phil had used, was more accurate. I wondered what Phil's faith was? I knew so little about this man that I would always feel close to. Then I remembered that he had come over to the cottage today to tell me about his past. I knew it would make no difference in how I felt about him, but I was curious anyway.

However, before we discussed anything else, I knew I had to have something to eat because my stomach was reminding me that I hadn't eaten since the cold cereal in the morning, and it was now close to 5:00. I suspected the men were in the same predicament, and when I asked them, they confirmed the fact. I was starting to rummage through the cupboards to see what I could fix, when Bob said, "Why don't we just order pizza? There's a pizza place that delivers just on this side of Randolph City. They can have it here in about a half hour." We all agreed that pizza sounded good, so I sat down again after fixing Phil a cup of hot chocolate.

After taking a sip of chocolate, Phil asked, "How is Angela? Is she coping with this?

"She's doing okay under the circumstances," I answered, "but I'm sure she's going to need lots of tender loving care in the future. By the way, we found out her real name is Sarah."

"Sarah, that's nice. Yes, she will need lots of TLC from now on. I understand what she's going through."

"Phil," I said shyly, "you came over here today to tell me something. Do you still want to? You don't have to, you know."

"I know, but I want to. I think by the way you were acting the other night that you had learned something about my--uh--profession before I became a history professor, right Amanda?"

"Yes," I said, "After that night, I learned I would never be a good detective or actress."

Bob jumped into the conversation, "I found a news clipping about your man slaughter conviction when your wife and kids died."

"Yes, and without even seeing the clipping, I can tell you that it is all true. I did photograph children for the pornography business, and my wife did discover it, and I was involved in the accident that took their lives. I would give anything in the world to go back and change that part of my life, but I can't of course."

He was quiet for a few moments and then continued, "When I was in prison, I changed. I should say I was changed, because it took a Higher Power to turn my life around. There was a prison ministry in our prison, and I accepted the Lord into my life, and miraculously, he forgave me for all the horrible sins I had committed. However, I had a very hard time forgiving myself. Amanda, when you came over a few weeks ago, you tried to open the door to the room you mistook for the bathroom. I know you were puzzled by my reaction. Well, let me show you some pictures of that room; after all, they say a picture is worth a thousand words.

He handed me three five by seven color pictures of various angles of a room that looked like a nursery. In one picture, there were two tiny cradles prominent, draped in a white lacy cover, in the center of the room. Also in this picture, I could see dolls, toy trains, trucks, balls, stuffed animals, and blocks. In the next picture, I noticed an old-fashioned bureau with matching boy and girl outfits from very small sizes to larger sizes. Right next to the bureau, on a wooden rocking chair, I saw a gorgeous, ruffled wedding gown, and even in the picture I could tell how it had yellowed with age. The last picture showed a wall covered with pictures of two very adorable children, from infancy to toddlers, and pictures of the young wife and mother in poses that completely captured the vibrant love that was evident even in this picture of a picture.

Phil was right; these photos told me volumes about a man who had sacrificed the loves of his life to the god of money. All I could say when I handed them back was, "I'm so sorry, Phil." There seemed to be nothing else to say.

Phil handed the pictures to Captain Rogers who in turn gave them to the two other men. He had to clear his throat before he said, "I've never shown that room, or even pictures of it, to anyone before. Maybe now I can lay all the ghosts to rest. I had to show these to all of you because I didn't want you to have to wonder about me. I just hope none of you are offended by me, now."

We all assured him that we still wanted his friendship. Sergeant Adams said, "You're sorry about what you did. Carswell seems to be gloating over his crimes. He even volunteered the information that he had killed the real Greg Rothman and even his own parents."

"Yeah, he told me that, too!" I exclaimed. "He must be crazy." We were all silent for a while, then I asked a question that I was really afraid to get the answer for, but for Sarah's sake, I felt I had to, "What happened to Sarah's par--I mean--where are the bodies of Sarah's parents?"

Captain Rogers answered, "Carswell told us he had completely destroyed the sailboat with Sarah's parents on it. He sailed the boat to the middle of the lake; that was the bobbing white light you saw right after you found the child at your door, Amanda. Then he inflated a rubber dinghy, poured gasoline all over the sailboat, got in his dingy, and rowed out a few feet from the big boat. Then he lit a flare and tossed it on board the sailboat. Of course, it went up like a gigantic firecracker. Then he rowed away, calmly leaving the boat as a burning funereal pyre for his brother and sister-in-law. When he got on shore, he set up a pup tent he had brought with him, and he proceeded to change his appearance. Luckily for him Rothman had a fairly average face, and of course, you really can't tell a lot from identification pictures like he showed us."

Bob asked, "What do you know about the real Greg Rothman?"

"Just what Carswell told us. From what I can gather, the story of Carswell and Rothman makes a fascinating psychology study. It seems that Rothman was a real loner, a poor little rich kid. We still haven't been able to contact his folks. They're off in Europe somewhere. Evidently they haven't even tried to contact their son for months."

"How did Carswell meet him?" asked Phil.

Sergeant Adams took up the story, "Rothman was a student at the University of Wisconsin during the school year, but summers he spent on his sailboat, cruising Lakes Michigan and Huron. Two years ago he came to the docks where Carswell had been working, you know, the place he had the identification from. Well, just for a lark, Rothman got a job there, too. He certainly didn't need the money, but Carswell befriended him, paid some attention to him, and I think Rothman took the job out of loneliness. Of course, Carswell began scheming how he could use this rich, rather naive lad for his own purposes. So, after Rothman went back to school that fall, Carswell went up to Wellington and got a job in his brother's bank. Pretty soon, he started embezzling money, and he wrote Rothman to sail up to Wellington this summer so that they could take a sailing trip. Of course, he really just wanted to kill him and take over his identity."

"How much money did he get?" Bob asked.

"Close to $100,000, U.S. value."

"Wow!" I said, "But why did he take his brother and family on a sailboat trip when he had just stolen that much money? It seems that a sailboat is the slowest form of transportation in the world."

Captain Rogers answered, "For one thing, he didn't steal the money all at once. He gloated over the fact that he could grab little bits of it from the tellers' tills when their backs were turned. Everybody in the bank, especially the tellers, were beginning to smell a rat, and he said that he kept dropping hints to draw suspicion on his brother. So, just when his poor brother was at the breaking point, he suggested a sailing trip to 'get away from it all.' He told his brother to leave all the arrangements to him, and he would tell the vice president where they were going and how long they'd be gone, but of course, he didn't tell anyone anything. By this time, he had already killed Rothman, so he had his boat at his disposal; his brother thought the boat had been rented. He brought them here because there are no dock hands to check him in, also no customs officials."

"He really had it all figured out, didn't he?" I said.

"Yeah, but of course, he didn't think he'd see his niece's picture in the paper the day after he had killed her."

"I bet that was a shock," said Bob. "Sarah told us that he had shot her doll, I guess thinking it was her."

"That's right," said Sergeant Adams, "I know now why that doll I brought her caused her to go into hysterics. It must have looked like hers. I feel really bad about that."

"You couldn't have known," I tried to comfort him. "She must have had little flashes of memory when something happened that would trigger them. Poor little girl, it's a wonder she ever regained her memory after seeing her parents being murdered by her own uncle."

"You know the ironic thing about this whole tragedy is that Carswell seems to love Sarah," reflected the captain.

"Yeah, he told her that he was happy when he had found out she was still alive, but of course, when he said that, he was preparing to kill her again." I paused to summon the courage to ask the question that was uppermost in my thoughts, "You know, Captain, from what we've heard from Sarah, Roger is her only living relative, so do you think I have any chance of adopting her?"

He stroked his chin thoughtfully, "Well, now, they may have a will specifying someone to be her guardian in case of their death, and that person may want her, and anyway you look at it, there will be a lot of legal hassles to deal with. Seems to me your biggest problem is that you're single." He paused and looked over at Bob with twinkling eyes, "Now if you were to get married sometime soon-- well, that would be a different story."

Bob looked at me and smiled tenderly. Keeping his eyes on me, he said, "I think we might be able to deal with that situation soon."

I felt like a butterfly floating high in the air. I was so ecstatic that I don't remember even hearing the pizza delivery boy knocking on the door. I must have been like a sleepwalker as I called Sarah down and served the pizza to my guests. Even now, I have no idea how it tasted; I probably could have eaten the cardboard it came on and not have known the difference.

After we ate, Phil went upstairs to look at Sarah's picture, and we could hear his praise of it all the way downstairs. Soon they both came down, hand in hand, and I vowed that if I had any say in Sarah's future, I would keep in contact with this man who seemed to have become a surrogate grandfather to the little girl. Also, I knew she was helping ease his pain over the loss of his own children. Even though nothing could change the fact that he had caused the death of his family, I thought that God had shown extra-special love by allowing Phil to be the one who saved our lives.

When the last crumb of pizza was devoured, the policemen pushed their chairs out, thanked us for the pizza, and headed for the door. Just before they left, Captain Rogers asked Bob, "Don't you need to come with us? We still have your car at the station, you know?"

"Actually, Sir, that's a car I borrowed from a friend of mine who's on vacation. If you remember, my car is still out in the woods, in hiding." Bob grinned in embarrassment as he talked.

The police grinned, "Oh yes, I'm sorry about that, Son, but you'll have to admit there was a pretty good case against you."

"Yeah, I guess Carswell had several reasons to pick me to frame. According to what he told Amanda, before he disguised himself, he used to have dark hair and a dark beard like mine, well, like mine used to be."

"Oh yeah," exclaimed Sergeant Adams, "in all the excitement I didn't even notice you had shaved."

Again Bob was embarrassed, "I guess you can say that I did a little disguising myself when you guys were hot and heavy on my trail."

Phil broke into the conversation, "Why else did Carswell pick you to frame?"

"Because he realized my interest in Amanda, and he was more than a little interested himself."

Now I was embarrassed as all eyes turned on me. I said, "Oh, I don't think he was all that interested in me. He told Sarah and me that he had loved her mother, and I guess he was very bitter that his brother 'had taken her away from him.'"

"That came out in the interrogation, too. It's sad that a young man who had so much going for him would let bitterness and jealousy ruin his life," the captain reflected, then went on, "Well, we must go now. You realize, I guess, that this case is not all over with yet. I'm going to need all of you to come and make a formal statement about what happened, and you'll all have to go to Canada to testify, but I don't think there will be a long, drawn out trial. So far Carswell is confessing to everything. I hate to see you put through this, Sarah, but you want your uncle punished for what he did, don't you?"

"Yes," she said solemnly, "but will he be able to get me again?"

"No, Honey, he'll be locked up in prison for a very long time, and he'll not be able to get to you." I realized then that in some ways Sarah's agony was just now beginning. She was going to need a lot of patience and tenderness in the years to come.

The police finally left, and Phil left soon after them, promising that he would come over again and bring Sarah

another present. Sarah was grateful to him, but I could tell
that she was exhausted, both emotionally and physically.
Bob must have sensed it also, for he suggested that she go
put her pajamas on, and he told her he would read her a
story. I helped her get into her heavier pajamas I had
bought her since it was still chilly, and she picked one of
her longest books and brought it down to Bob who was
sitting on the couch. I sat next to her, and we both listened
to his deep baritone voice as he read with all the
expression that a news reporter could bring into a story. It
wasn't long before Sarah was fast asleep. I walked up the
stairs right behind Bob as he carried her up and gently
tucked her in bed. Then we both stood and looked at her
angelic face. As I bent down and kissed her cheek, I
thought about the mother who had lavished love and care
on her child for six years. I wondered if somehow she
knew she was being loved and cared for.

After making sure Sarah was sound asleep, Bob and
I walked downstairs, and we fell into each other's arms on
the couch. It seemed there was no one else in the world
except the two of us. The terror and uncertainty of the past
few weeks melted away in Bob's embrace. I felt as if I had

known him all my life; it seemed impossible that he had been a stranger to me only a few weeks ago.

As if reading my thoughts, Bob said, "How do you feel about short engagements? I know I couldn't love you any more than I do now if we had known each other all our lives. However, I know the plan you had for your life; you were going to marry the guy you had met in the church nursery, all safe and comfortable. Are you willing to take a chance on a crazy reporter you've just met?"

"Sure, but I don't think I'll be taking a big chance. When two people have been through what we have together, we learn more about each other than some people do in a life time."

He smiled with relief, "I agree, but I have to ask you, are you sure you're over Paul?"

"Paul who?" I asked, and we laughed as if I had told the funniest joke in the world. Then I went on, "I think you were right; I never did love Paul--at least not the way I love you. I was just used to him."

"Do you think you'll ever get used to me?"

"No," I laughed, "I think you'll always be unpredictable, and I have an idea our life won't always be smooth sailing. I think we'll have some storms along the way."

"Yeah, but just think of the making up after the storm." Once again he enveloped me in his arms and left me breathless with his kisses.

After a while, I broke away and asked Bob very seriously, "What about Sarah? If we could adopt her, would you be willing--I mean--sometimes it's rough starting out a marriage with a child."

Bob gave me another squeeze. "I'm more than willing. I love that little girl, too. I'll do everything in my power to keep her; I just hope we don't run into too many problems."

"We might, but at least we can face them together." In Bob's arms, I had more confidence than ever before.

We sat and talked for more than an hour, making plans and learning about each other. Bob told me that he was the third in a family of four boys. His home had been a lively, boisterous place, filled with laughter. We talked about our religious beliefs, and I was pleased to discover our church backgrounds were almost identical. We had our differences, though. He liked contemporary music--soft rock. I liked easy-listening, mellow sounds. He loved outdoor, winter sports; I preferred the warm fire place. We both decided we were alike in important matters, but just different enough in other areas to make our lives interesting.

Finally, when the sun was painting the sky in back of the cottage with a lovely pink glow, Bob gave me one tender, lingering kiss. Then he slowly rose to his feet. "I think you need to get some rest. I'll be over here again tomorrow--and every day I can. We're going to have a whole life time to spend together."

We walked to the door with our arms around each other. After one more good-bye kiss, Bob walked out the door to find his car he had hidden in the woods seemingly years ago. I could feel his arms surrounding me as I climbed the stairs and got into bed. Just before I fell into a deep, peaceful sleep, I remembered to thank God for His protection and for the love I'd found. Then from the depths of my heart, I prayed, "Lord, you know I'd like for us to have Sarah, but you know what would be best for her. Help me to understand if she's taken from us, but if you want her to be with us, let me be as good--or almost as good--as her real mother must have been. Help Sarah deal with her grief. Thank you, Jesus, goodnight."

EPILOGUE

I can't believe a whole year has gone by since that night that Sarah regained her memory, the night that was almost our last. The few weeks before our wedding was a whirl of activity. I invited my parents up to the cottage the weekend after Roger was arrested. They met Bob and Sarah and were delighted with both. I still chuckle when I remember the look on my mother's face when we told her we were going to be married in about six weeks. I thought we were going to have to give her CPR. As soon as she got home, she got into a frenzy of buying and sending announcements, engaging caterers, making arrangements for flowers and photographs, etc.

I helped all I could, but I was busy with my museum job plus working with Zachary Reynolds to determine Sarah's future. He came down to Randolph City to help in the extradition of Roger to Canada, and afterwards, he came to the cottage to talk to Bob and me.

Mr. Reynolds, who had been the lawyer for Sarah's family since her grandfather's time, was a thin, tall man in his late fifties, with a pinched, Scrooge-type face. At first,

I was afraid he would be cold and unfeeling, but after a few minutes of talking to him, I found him to be a kind, loving, grandfatherly man, who really had Sarah's best interests at heart. It turned out that John Carswell's will had named Mr. Reynolds Sarah's legal guardian, but since he was a bachelor, he was unable to take care of her. There seemed to be no one else that would be able to take custody of her since there were no living relatives or no friends capable of taking on the responsibility. The Carswell's had been close to the Johnsons, a family in their church who had four children, one of whom was Sarah's little friend, Mary. However, they did not feel they could take Sarah in because the mother had serious health problems that made it very difficult for her to care for her own children.

Therefore, after talking in great depth to the lawyer, Bob and I were more hopeful than ever about gaining custody of Sarah. We decided against trying to adopt her because we felt she should keep her parents' name as a reminder that these good people had given her life and had cared for her for six years. However, we still had a lot of red tape to cut through, mostly because Sarah was a

Canadian citizen. Mr. Reynolds represented us at both the Canadian and U. S. immigration officials, and it was determined that Sarah would remain a Canadian citizen until she was old enough to choose for herself which country she would claim.

There were also some problems posed by Sarah's inheritance. Sarah not only inherited all of her parent's possessions, but also she was the sole beneficiary to her grandfather's will. In the terms of the will, if neither of the sons were able to inherit, then the money would go to Sarah on her twenty-fifth birthday. Bob and I decided that any money from Sarah's parents would go into a trust fund until she was eighteen, so Sarah was going to be a fairly wealthy young lady when she grew up. Mr. Reynolds, or his law firm in case of his death, would be the trustee of her inheritance.

Roger had thought that his father had left all his money to a church, but what he didn't know was that there was a secret clause in the will that would give either or both of the sons a large sum of money after they had been gainfully employed for ten years. I guess the senior John Carswell wanted to make sure his sons worked for a living, rather than live off his money. Ironically if Roger had just waited, he would have had wealth without killing anyone, but it probably still wouldn't have been enough.

Fortunately for all of us, Roger confessed to all the crimes, so we weren't put through a long, drawn out trial. However, we did have to go to Canada to testify in his hearing. I was very proud of Sarah; she told her story clearly and calmly, all while her uncle was sitting in the defendant's chair just a few feet from her. During her testimony, Roger kept his head down and stared at the desk in front of him, showing the only hint of remorse he had expressed through the whole trial. At the end he was sentenced to life imprisonment, in fact, five life sentences without hope of parole, in a Canadian prison. The judge took the time to assure Sarah that her uncle would never be able to get to her again. I just prayed that someday she would be able to forgive him.

Every month this year, I have taken Sarah to the psychiatrist in Randolph City, the same one who had attended her when she had amnesia. She advised us to take Sarah to her house in Canada so that she could come to terms with the reality that her parents were gone. So, when we were up in Toronto for Roger's hearing, we took Bob's station wagon, which he had bought in preparation of becoming a family man, and drove the few miles to Kingston where Sarah had lived in obvious happiness with her parents.

Her house was a large, two-storied farm house that her parents had been restoring. The furniture, wall paper, and decorations had a warm, country charm. Maybe I was too imaginative, but there seemed to be a friendly, happy atmosphere lingering in all the rooms of the house, especially the kitchen and family rooms which both had large, open fireplaces back to back along the wall they both shared.

Sarah ran from room to room showing us around, pointing out toys or other objects that would bring back happy memories for her. I had to fight back the tears as we sorted through and packed the few we could fit in the station wagon. I was glad Mr. Reynolds was arranging the sale of the house and furniture, so that Sarah wouldn't have to stand in an empty house and watch strangers wander through her home, inspecting it and discussing the good and bad points of the home she had known since babyhood.

In the midst of the custody paper-work and the hearing, Bob and I got married. I took off one day to go home, with Sarah, for my wedding shower. The people in my church were captivated with Sarah and her story, but since they had always known me as a conservative, level-headed, cautious girl, they were shocked that I was marrying a person I had only known for about two months. One of my friends came out and asked why I seemed to be rushing things, and my mother was appalled when she heard me answer, "We have to get married right away because of our child."

Our wedding day arrived dark and stormy, but I didn't care. I was so happy that I couldn't hear the thunder or see the lightning. The ceremony was simple, but wonderful, with my ex-roommate from college as my only attendant and Bob's younger brother as his best man. Sarah was our flower girl. Paul and Janelle attended the wedding, and when they came through the reception line, I wholeheartedly hugged them both. Then I turned to Paul and said, "Thank you." He smiled, knowing what I meant.

After the wedding, Bob and I went on a honeymoon trip to Toronto, and although we had a wonderful, romantic time, we did visit government officials to finalize our gaining legal custody of Sarah. She stayed with my parents during the honeymoon, and I'm sure a good time was had by all.

Life has been exciting and blissful this year. Bob, Sarah, and I live in Randolph City in a 19th century, four-bedroom colonial house, and we're restoring it a little at a time. We haven't accomplished nearly as much as Sarah's parents had in the restoration of their house.

Bob is a considerate, thoughtful husband, most of the time, but even when we have our differences, the making up is fun. I did not even try to get a job in Randolph City because the psychiatrist felt it was important for Sarah to have someone to come home to after school.

We obtained Sarah's Canadian school records which confirmed the fact that she was an exceptionally bright little girl, well-mannered and hard working. She was put into the second grade, and since she had started taking French in Canada, I thought it would be worthwhile for her to continue, so I found a tutor who comes over once a week and teaches all three of us. We have lots of fun practicing French phrases together, but I have to admit that Sarah is doing better than either Bob or I.

We have also kept in contact with our police friends, Judy Baldwin, and Phil Jennings. Although Sarah doesn't have any blood-relatives, she has many surrogate grandparents, aunts, and uncles. Once when the police visited us, they told us they had found the kidnapper of little Jenny Summers, with the help of Bob's private investigator friend. They never did find the child's body because the demented man had dumped her into the deepest part of Lake Huron. Naturally the parents were sad, but the police said they were also relieved to know the search was over. I shuddered when I realized how close Sarah's story had come to that tragic end.

When we moved into our new home, Bob bought a beautiful Spinet piano to grace our living room, and to my delight I learned my new husband was an accomplished pianist. He is teaching Sarah to play, too. My job is to make sure she practices one half-hour every day.

Sarah is still a delightful child, not as quiet and solemn as she had been before. Naturally, there have been some times we had to be stern with her and even punish her, but those times have been few and far between. I always have the eerie feeling that Sarah's parents are looking over my shoulders, checking to see what kind of job I am doing. Once when Sarah wanted to swim on a day I felt was too cold, she used the ploy, "My real parents would have let me." It was hard not to give in to that kind of pressure, but I felt I had to go with my instincts. Actually, incidents like that are rare; all in all, we are getting along very well. I marvel at God's goodness to me, even when I was angry at Him for "taking Paul from me."

Today, I am in a happy, contemplative mood while waiting for Bob and Sarah to come back from grocery shopping. I didn't go with them because I didn't feel well this morning. In fact, I haven't felt well any morning for two weeks, but now I know why. A nurse from the hospital lab just called to tell me my pregnancy test turned out positive. I'm going to have a baby next April. I'm planning a special dinner tonight, but I don't think I'll tell Bob till Sarah goes to bed. I can't wait to see his face, but I already know he'll be happy. He told me when we moved into our house that there would be plenty of room for more children. I feel sure that Sarah will be happy, too, but we're going to have to make sure she doesn't feel like an outsider when we have our "own" baby.

Now I hear the familiar station wagon motor coming down the road. I don't know if I can wait to tell them the news. I'm sure they'll be able to detect the excitement in my voice. Oh well, I never was very good at hiding my feelings.